The Other Room

Book Two of the 'Lines We Don't Cross' Series

By Robert G. Pranic

Dedication

To those who helped open the world of self-publishing,
and in doing so, opened a door for writers like me.

In another age, this path may have remained closed, but because of
your vision, persistence, and belief in independent voices, the
distance between imagination and readership became something a
determined writer could cross.

For that gift, and for the chance to pursue fiction as a calling rather
than a dream, I offer my sincere thanks.

Contents

Chapter One: Ash in the Service Corridor

The first blank page was still warm when Daniel Voss picked it up.

He stood in the records office with the sheet between finger and thumb, frowning at it as if annoyance alone might force ink onto the paper. The printer sat squat and self-important against the far wall, a machine large enough to suggest significance and dull enough to belong in government service. Another page slid out with a mechanical sigh, white as frost, and settled on the output tray beside the others.

No text. No letterhead. No toner smear. Nothing.

Only warmth.

Daniel pressed the back of his fingers to the top sheet, then looked over his shoulder at the woman from night admin who had called him down. She was standing by the swipe door in a cardigan too thin for the building's air-conditioning, hugging a folder to her chest.

"You weren't joking," he said.

"I said it was spitting out blanks." Her voice was quiet in the way voices went quiet in federal buildings after midnight, as though every sound had to push through carpet and concrete before it reached another human ear. "I didn't say anything about them being warm because I knew how that would sound."

Daniel lifted the sheet to his face. It smelled faintly of heated fibres and machine heat, the dry, papery tang of something newly made. Under that, there was something else. Not smoke exactly. Not ozone. More like dust warmed on a window ledge in summer.

"How many?"

"Thirty-seven." She glanced at the printer as if it might produce something else strange. "Every ninety seconds, give or take."

"Any print job in the queue?"

"Nothing. We checked twice."

He set the blank page down and tapped the side of the printer with his knuckles. The machine hummed on, innocent as a cow. Daniel had spent fourteen years keeping other people's buildings honest. He trusted machines right up until the moment he didn't. Tonight, the distrust arrived fast.

The annex had that effect on him.

Officially, it was called the Southbank Government Systems Annex, six floors of secure storage, records infrastructure, and technical support space, attached to two other buildings by underground services that nobody admitted were related. Daniel's employer held the maintenance contract for the lot. He fixed doors, lift panels, ventilation faults, comms dropouts, server-rack cooling units, and broken taps in bathrooms that the senior staff pretended not to use. It paid well enough, the hours were mostly civil, and the work usually obeyed the old rules. Something breaks, something gets replaced, something hums properly again.

This place broke the rules more often than he liked.

Too many sealed doors. Too many service corridors that appeared on one week's schematic and vanished on the next. Too many people with temporary badges who looked as if they had never changed a light globe in their lives, and yet somehow controlled which parts of the building a man with a tool belt was permitted to enter. Daniel had learned not to ask questions that came back stamped with phrases like "compartmentalised access" and "infrastructure adjacency". He had a daughter in Year Nine, a mortgage in Ringwood, and a bad knee that told the weather better than any app. Curiosity had never paid one of his bills.

Still, the blank pages were new.

He crouched, opened the paper tray, checked the feed rollers, checked the toner cartridge, and checked the job history on the little status screen. Nothing. No queue. No jam. No phantom instruction is sitting in memory like a bad smell.

The screen showed the time, the model number, and a steady green readiness icon.

Another sheet whispered out behind him.

Daniel stood.

"All right," he said. "Where's the line run?"

The woman handed him a printed floor map, "Records hub printer node. Wall feed through the service corridor behind storage C. Security already unlocked it."

"Of course they have."

He took the map, folded it once, and slipped it into the back pocket of his work trousers. Then he gathered the warm blank pages into a neat stack, because if something was eerie, the first step towards defeating it was usually to make it tidy.

At the top of the stack, the paper gave slightly under his palm, as if the fibres had softened from heat. He frowned and lifted the first sheet to the light. Still blank.

Or almost blank.

There was the faintest pressure in the paper, an impression too shallow to read and too deliberate to dismiss as feed marks. It might have been nothing more than mechanical drag. It might have been the ghost of text that had tried and failed to arrive.

Daniel turned the page sideways. The indent vanished.

"Right," he said softly. "You can be someone else's haunting."

He left the stack on the desk and headed for the swipe door.

The corridor outside records smelt of disinfectant, recirculated air, and old carpet. Past midnight, the annex never felt empty exactly. Empty places have a kind of release in them, a sigh once the people are gone. This building did not release anything. It kept its weight. Servers ran behind the walls. Cooling systems moved air behind locked panels. Somewhere above, a cleaner's trolley squeaked and went quiet again. The lifts opened and closed for reasons Daniel had long ago stopped trying to assign to human need.

He checked his radio as he walked. "Control, this is Voss. Heading to printer node service access behind storage C. You've got my temporary clearance?"

The reply came at once, clipped and competent. "Affirmative, Voss. B-Seven service corridor unlocked for twelve minutes. Log entry under your badge."

Control tonight was a woman named Leanne. He knew because he'd spoken to her earlier about a faulty sensor in the loading bay, and because Daniel made a point of remembering the names of people who could lock him inside unpleasant places by mistake.

"Twelve minutes," he repeated. "Luxury."

A soft hiss, then Leanne's voice again. "Don't dawdle."

He smiled despite himself and rounded the corner past storage C.

The service door sat flush with the wall, industrial grey, no handle on the outside, only a swipe pad and a manual key cylinder for the old-school backup. A red light on the pad blinked once as he presented his badge, then flipped to green with a chaste little chirp. The lock withdrew.

Daniel pulled the door open and felt cooler air kiss the side of his face.

The corridor beyond was narrow enough to make two men walking abreast a negotiation. Conduit and cable trays ran along the left wall in disciplined horizontal lines. The right wall was composite panelling broken at intervals by access hatches and inspection plates. The lighting was clean and white without being bright, the sort of overhead strip illumination designed by people who never considered what a place might feel like at one in the morning. The floor was epoxy, pale grey, freshly mopped by the look of the dull shine on it.

Nothing dramatic. Nothing theatrical.

Just a service corridor.

Daniel stepped inside and let the door close behind him.

The click sounded louder than it should have.

He took six paces in, found the printer feed conduit exactly where the map said it would be, and crouched to inspect the wall junction. The pipework looked fine. No visible damage. No heat bloom. No loose casing. He opened his tool bag, took out a non-contact tester, and ran it along the conduit. Stable. He checked the junction plate screws. All seated. He lifted the little cover and shone his torch into the wiring cavity.

Nothing.

He muttered something unflattering about federal budgets and shut the plate again.

His radio crackled against his shoulder.

"Voss, hold position while we verify routing."

Leanne again. Same tone. Same competent flatness.

Daniel paused with his screwdriver halfway back into the pouch. "Verify what?"

Static ticked once.

Then, with no gap he could have sworn to in court, the radio spoke again.

"Voss, keep moving to the end bulkhead. Node may be mirrored from the secondary run."

Same voice.

He stared at the radio clipped high on his chest.

"Leanne?"

No answer.

He reached up and thumbed the transmit. "Control, I just got two different instructions."

A hiss. Then the first voice again, exactly as before. "Hold position while we verify routing."

Before he could answer, the second instruction overlaid it, not louder, not distorted, just separate enough to force his brain to notice. "Keep moving to the end bulkhead. Node may be mirrored from the secondary run."

Daniel straightened very slowly.

He had spent enough years on sites to know how radio weirdness happened. Signal bounce, old concrete, interference from lift motors, the occasional dickhead with a repeater doing something illegal from a van in a car park. It was never comforting, but it was explainable. Explainable mattered.

He thumbed the transmit again. "Control, say again, one instruction only."

There was a pause. Then Leanne said, "Proceed."

At exactly the same moment, Leanne said, "Do not proceed."

Daniel's scalp tightened.

He pulled the radio off its clip and held it away from his chest as if distance might restore common sense. "Very funny," he said, though no one in the annex had ever once attempted humour worth the effort of this set-up. "Who's patching in?"

Silence.

Not clean silence. The kind with a grain in it, as though something very far away were speaking under the floor in a language made entirely of consonants.

Daniel became aware of the corridor's temperature in a new way. A minute earlier it had simply been cool. Now it seemed to have separated into layers. His face felt cold. The back of his neck felt hot. Sweat gathered under his shirt between the shoulder blades and immediately seemed to chill.

He turned to look behind him.

The door through which he had entered was still there, twenty feet away, closed, placid, ordinary.

Good.

He could leave. Report radio fault. Let someone with a clearance level and a committee tackle the blank pages and the schizophrenic instructions.

His knee clicked as he shifted his weight, and the small familiar ache grounded him for half a second. Forty-three years old, meniscus gone in the left knee, daughter called Ruby who hated algebra and loved netball, ex-wife who still rang when the gutters clogged because some habits outlast marriage. Real things. Useful things.

He took one step back towards the door.

His boot sole made a small sticky sound on the epoxy, almost a tack of heat releasing.

Daniel frowned down.

There was no liquid. No spill. Nothing on the floor at all.

He looked up again and saw the seam.

It was on the right wall, about waist height to head height, a fine vertical line in the composite panelling where no join should have been. He was certain it had not been there when he came in. Or if it had, it had been hiding inside the pattern so cleanly that his eyes had walked over it without complaint.

Now he could not stop seeing it.

A thin upright line. Too straight for damage. Too deliberate for warping. It did not catch the overhead light in the same way as the panel seams around it. It seemed to gather the light rather than reflect it, as if brightness lost confidence near it.

Daniel took a slow breath.

The seam became easier to see.

He let the breath out.

It blurred almost away.

He stood very still, testing it. Inhale. Sharper. Exhale. Fainter.

Something small and mean moved under his ribs.

"Control," he said quietly. "There is a door in B-Seven that is not on the map."

The radio answered at once.

"Stay where you are."

"Touch nothing."

"Come forward."

"Override manually."

Four instructions this time. Same voice. Same register. Same absolute confidence.

Daniel's mouth went dry.

He backed away from the seam and his shoulder brushed the conduit on the left wall. The metal felt warmer than it should. Not painfully hot. Not enough to shout. Just enough to be wrong.

He looked down the corridor towards the far bulkhead.

He could see it clearly now, a fire-rated end panel with a small inspection hatch and a yellow caution sticker. Exactly the sort of dull endpoint a man liked to see when nonsense began. But between him and that bulkhead the light had altered. It was not dimmer. The white strips overhead sharpened every surface until the far wall looked staged for a decision he had not yet made.

A page slid soundlessly out of a narrow gap in the wall near the seam and drifted to the floor.

Daniel flinched so hard his tool bag knocked his thigh.

The page lay there, white against grey epoxy.

He did not want to pick it up.

That became instantly obvious when he considered the idea. He wanted, very strongly, to leave it where it was and retreat to the door and the ordinary corridor and the cardiganed woman in records and the green-ready printer and the boring stack of blank paper that now felt like a gift from a kinder universe.

His radio crackled.

"Daniel," said Leanne's voice, softer now, almost intimate. "Pick up the page."

His stomach tightened at the use of his first name.

Before he could move, the voice came again from the same speaker, same woman, same softness.

"Daniel, do not touch the page."

He made a noise in his throat that was very nearly a laugh and far too close to panic. "You tell me which one of you is real."

The corridor gave him nothing back.

He crouched despite himself, every nerve in his body telling him to keep distance while some other part of him, an older, more stubborn maintenance-worker instinct, insisted on inspecting the thing on the floor because objects did not get to win simply by being unnerving.

He picked up the page.

It was warm, warmer than the stack in records had been, almost skin-warm, and as his fingers closed on it he felt the faintest embossed drag beneath the surface. Not text. Not yet. More like pressure that had not decided what letters wanted to become.

He held the sheet to the light.

Blank.

Then the overhead strips flickered once and for an instant the blankness turned shallow, carrying depth that vanished before his eyes could read it. Daniel saw the possibility of words without the words themselves, the shape of meaning pressing from the other side.

He dropped the page.

It floated down and landed against the base of the seam as if placed there by a careful hand.

"Control," he said, louder now. "I need someone down here. In person."

The answer came from the radio and from somewhere else, the somewhere else not sound exactly but the memory of sound arriving a fraction before the radio made it. "Security is en route."

"Remain calm."

"Proceed to bulkhead."

"Do not turn around."

Daniel turned around at once.

The entry door was still there.

He exhaled so hard it made him dizzy.

Then the dizzy feeling did not go away.

It thickened instead, a pressure behind his eyes and ears, as though the corridor were changing altitude one careful millimetre at a time. His heart was working too fast. He could feel each beat high in his throat. Sweat broke across his scalp. He wiped one hand on his trouser leg and saw it shaking.

All right, he thought. All right, mate. Slow it down.

He tried counting backwards from ten, the trick Ruby's netball coach had taught her for penalties when the crowd got loud. He got as far as seven before the numbers seemed to split.

Ten.

Nine.

Eight.

Eight.

Seven.

No, that was wrong.

He swallowed and tasted metal.

"Daniel," said Leanne's voice. "What do you see?"

"Daniel," said Leanne's voice. "Do not answer any questions."

He pressed the heel of one hand against his forehead. The skin there felt cold. Too cold. His chest, by contrast, felt packed with coals.

"This is not funny," he said.

"No," the radio said.

"No," the radio agreed.

His laugh came out thin and frightened.

The seam in the wall had widened.

Not open. Not visibly. Not in any way he could later have measured. But it had acquired depth. The narrow line now suggested an inwardness, the promise of space behind the panel where no space should exist. The longer he looked, the more impossible it became to convince himself it was only a join in the composite cladding. There was dark there. Not shadow. Not absence of light. Dark that looked occupied.

Daniel stepped back until his shoulders hit the conduit again.

His badge buzzed once against his belt.

He yanked it free and stared at the tiny display embedded in the smart casing. Usually it showed time, zone, and entry log. Now the screen was flickering between temperature warnings too fast to read. Thirty-eight point six. Forty. Thirty-seven. Forty-one point three. The numbers leapt as if panicking too.

"Control," he said, breath snagging. "My badge is showing a heat fault."

"Remove it."

"Keep it on."

"Daniel, listen to me."

"Daniel, listen to me."

The same sentence, in perfect sync, doubled just enough to scrape at his skull.

His thoughts began slipping on themselves. He knew where he was. He knew what year it was. He knew his own surname. But the knowledge would not sit still. Each certainty seemed to arrive beside its opposite. Stay and go. Speak and keep silent. Touch and don't touch. Trust the voice and trust no voice. Every instruction opened a second one inside it, and the effort of holding them apart sent a hard bright pressure through the centre of his head.

He thought, absurdly, of Ruby at twelve, standing in his kitchen with two school permission slips because her mother had signed one and he had signed the other and the teacher said only one could go in the system. Ruby had stood there furious, asking, "Why do grown-ups make simple things stupid?"

The memory came with such force he nearly spoke it aloud.

Instead, he heard himself say, "Tell me which instruction is true."

The words bounced off the corridor and came back smaller.

He put a hand to the wall to steady himself.

The composite panel was hot.

Not room-warm. Hot enough that he snatched his hand back with a sharp hiss. He stared at his palm. The skin there was reddening, though not badly. The heat had come from the wall, impossible and immediate.

The seam brightened.

No, not brightened. Became legible in a new way, like writing under a flame held to lemon juice.

Daniel made for the entry door.

He took three steps and the corridor lengthened.

Not physically. His rational mind clung to that even while the rest of him began to come apart. The door was still where it had been. It had to be. But the distance to it had acquired resistance, like trying to walk through a dream where the hallway keeps making room for more hallway.

His breath shortened.

"Control," he said, and now his voice shook openly. "I am leaving B-Seven."

"Affirmative."

"Negative."

"Stay visible."

"Turn the corner."

"There is no corner," Daniel shouted, and the shout hurt him. It lit something under his sternum, a sudden savage flare that made him bend at the waist.

He dropped to one knee.

The floor felt cold enough to burn through the fabric of his work trousers. His skin, meanwhile, was slick with sweat. He could smell himself now, salt and fear and something sharper rising from inside him.

Boots thudded somewhere beyond the entry door.

Security.

Thank Christ.

He tried to call out and found his throat had gone strange, not tight exactly but delayed. The words formed in his mind and then reached his mouth a second late, as though they had to cross a room first.

"Here," he managed.

"Hold position," said the radio.

"Stand up now," said the radio.

"Do not stand," said the radio.

His heart gave a horrible lurch.

The contradiction stopped being abstract. It became physical.

Something in his body tried to obey all commands at once. His muscles tensed to rise while his balance collapsed downward. He felt his lungs seize between inhale and exhale. His vision haloed white at the edges. The cold on his skin deepened while a furnace door seemed to swing open somewhere under his ribs.

He dropped the radio.

It struck the epoxy and skidded. The voice still came from it, brisk and duplicated and unhelpful.

"Daniel, stay with me."

"Daniel, respond."

"Daniel, be still."

"Daniel, move."

He put both hands to the sides of his head and squeezed, as if pressure from outside might stop the pressure within from reaching the point where thought itself caught.

Tell me which instruction is true.

He said it again. Louder this time.

At the door, fists pounded metal.

"Mr Voss, step away from the wall," a man's voice shouted, real and raw and magnificently singular.

One voice.

Daniel sobbed at the sound of it.

The card reader screamed green. The lock snapped. The door started inward.

And in the same instant the seam in the wall opened.

Not wide. Not like a door. It parted a finger's width and revealed a line of interior dark threaded with impossible light, a geometry too narrow to enter and too deep to be surface. Something shifted beyond it. Daniel did not see a face. He would never have called it that. But he felt attention settle on him with the intimate precision of a fingertip on the back of the neck.

Every thought in him folded.

Stay and run.

Speak and stay silent.

Trust and refuse.

The pressure under his sternum became agony.

Security rushed the threshold. Daniel saw two of them in dark uniforms, one with a thermal unit clipped to his vest, both slowing in astonishment as they took him in on the floor. He tried to lift a hand towards them.

"Tell me," he said, and could not hear whether the words came out whole. "Tell me which instruction is true."

The younger officer took a step forward.

The older one shouted, "Do not touch him."

At least that was one instruction.

Daniel clung to it like a rope.

Do not touch him.

Good.

Good.

Something inside his chest answered with a soundless crack.

The first smoke came out of his mouth.

The younger officer froze. The older one swore once, deeply and with total conviction, and lunged for the thermal unit on his vest.

Daniel did not feel the smoke leave him. He felt only the sudden expansion of heat beneath his breastbone, not external, not on the skin, but inside, unfolding through him in branching sheets. It was as if the contradiction had been waiting for ignition all along and someone had finally, mercifully, given it permission.

He looked down.

Light moved under his skin.

For one impossible second, he saw it travelling the river-lines of his chest and throat, a buried orange-white bloom threading upwards, elegant as a circuit coming alive.

Then the bloom became fire.

The scream did not sound like his.

Flame burst from between his lips, brief and hideous and intimate. It rolled out through his collar, under his shirt, through the seams of him. Not a blast. Not a movie eruption. A terrible inward-made flowering, the body giving off what it should never have held.

The officers recoiled with their arms over their faces. One shouted for medics. The thermal unit shrilled. The blank page at the wall lifted in the convected air and slapped once, softly, against the opening seam.

Daniel's last coherent thought was not of the corridor or the door or the impossible instructions.

It was of Ruby, small and furious in his kitchen, demanding why grown-ups made simple things stupid.

Then the heat took language from him.

By the time the corridor filled with the chemical white of emergency suppressant and the panicked bark of boots and orders, Daniel Voss was already falling forward, burning from within while the wall seam narrowed back to a line, almost invisible again, as though nothing had been there at all.

Chapter Two: What the Body Cannot Reconcile

Sera Imani had learned, years ago, that the dead were often easier to understand than the living. The dead did not posture. They did not leak selectively, revise motives, or decide halfway through an interview that memory was now a political instrument. Their injuries told the truth if you asked the right questions and had the discipline to keep your own fear from answering first.

Daniel Voss lay under white light with his chest opened and his silence already becoming troublesome.

The room was cold enough to flatten breath. Stainless steel caught the overhead panels in sterile ribbons. The extraction system hummed with that soft, expensive steadiness peculiar to facilities designed to reassure governments that terrible things could occur here without becoming untidy. On the wall monitor beside the examination table, a thermal overlay rotated slowly through the last clean scan taken before the body was cut. The colours had cooled now into meaningless blues and greens, but Sera could still see the ghost of the final event in the recording archive, the upward surge of impossible heat through the mediastinum, the branching bloom beneath the ribs, the violent internal ignition pattern that did not match any fire she had ever spent twenty years being paid to understand.

She stood at the foot of the table with her hands in pale gloves and looked at Daniel's face first, because she had made herself keep that habit no matter how strange the case. A maintenance worker, forty-three, divorced, one daughter, known knee degeneration, no record of psychiatric history, no drug history beyond anti-inflammatories and the occasional prescription sleeping tablet. His hair had been singed close at the front, but enough remained to show where sweat had pasted it darkly to his scalp in the last minutes. His mouth, even after reconstruction for review, seemed to retain the memory of trying to form one more question.

Tell me which instruction is true.

The phrase appeared three times in the file: spoken to security, once to Control, and once to "no one" anyone could identify. Sera had read it too often already.

Across the room, the pathologist cleared his throat gently. Dr Lionel Rees had the careful, dry bearing of a man who considered enthusiasm an infection best avoided in theatres and mortuaries alike. He was older than Sera by perhaps ten years and thin to the point of looking skeletal. His spectacles rode low on his nose, and his voice always suggested he was speaking in a library where grief had paid for a private room.

"You were right to come yourself," he said. "This should not be filtered before it reaches you."

Sera moved to the side of the table. "Talk me through what you've got."

Rees adjusted the display with one knuckle, then pointed with a capped pen rather than a finger, an old-school courtesy she had always liked in him. "No evidence of external accelerant. No ordinary ignition vector. No inhalation profile consistent with a room fire preceding collapse. In fact, the earliest severe thermal insult appears to originate centrally." He let that sit. "Not on the skin. Not clothing-led. Centrally."

Sera looked down into the opened thoracic cavity. The tissue damage was hideous in a way that felt almost private. Heat had moved through Daniel Voss the way roots move through soil, following hidden structures, exploiting pathways the eye only understood after the fact. Portions of the heart's outer tissue were spared where they should not have been spared. Sections of the surrounding vasculature were catastrophically compromised, where no external flame could have reached first. The pattern was not random. That was what made it so bad.

"How long from onset to terminal burn?" she asked.

"Based on tissue state, witness record, and thermal progression, under thirty seconds from irreversible cascade to fatal collapse. Perhaps less."

"Christ."

Rees did not answer. He never rushed to fill the space after the word people used when science met something that felt, for one unwelcome second, like judgement.

Sera leaned closer to the cavity and looked at the myocardium. "No chemical residues?"

"Nothing conventional. We've run broad-spectrum toxicology, combustion residue screening, synthetic oxidisers, even irritant markers in case someone became imaginative and stupid in the same hour. Negligible findings. A little environmental contamination from emergency suppressant, some expected urban dust, trace industrial particulate from the corridor. Nothing that could do this."

"And the nervous system?"

"That," Rees said quietly, "is where I stopped trusting my own first read and called you."

He brought up another image set, this one a scan of the cervical chain and brainstem region. Sera stepped closer until the cold from the monitor reached her face. Tiny irregularities showed along autonomic pathways, not as gross lesions but as the sort of hyperacute stress signatures seen in seizure activity, electrical shock, and extreme panic. Yet none of those fitted cleanly either. The pattern looked less like damage inflicted on the nervous system than damage arising from it, as if the body had obeyed a command so violent it burned the circuitry carrying it.

"Overload," she murmured.

Rees nodded. "That is the nearest ordinary word I have."

She looked again at the timeline window. "You said the burn originates centrally. But the thermal spread isn't anatomical in the normal sense."

"No."

"It behaves like a coordinated event."

"Yes."

She was quiet for a moment. The extraction fans moved the room's chill in slow, invisible currents. Somewhere beyond the sealed door, a trolley wheel squeaked and then stopped. In buildings like this, even the quiet came layered through steel, ducts, and distant wheels.

Rees removed his spectacles and polished them with the corner of a cloth he kept folded inside his breast pocket. "The security officer who first attempted thermal suppression said he saw light move under the skin before open flame emerged. I would ordinarily strike such a detail from any working document unless three people corroborated it. In this case, three did."

Sera closed her eyes briefly.

When she opened them again, Daniel Voss was still on the table, still ruined, still maddeningly singular. She had spent too many years with bodies not to know when something wanted a smaller explanation and when it deserved a larger one. This deserved the larger one, and she hated that.

"Who has the corridor footage?" she asked.

"Restricted."

"By whom?"

Rees gave her a look of professional sympathy, which was another way of saying, by the sort of people who think restrictions are a treatment plan. "The footage was intercepted before my unit saw a full chain copy. I have a thermal extract, the witness transcripts, and the authorisation order requiring silence until central review."

Sera laughed once through her nose. "Nothing says central review like taking evidence away from the person examining the dead."

He let that pass too. "There is one more finding."

She lifted her gaze.

Rees reached for a tray and picked up a sealed evidence pouch containing a small square of composite wall material. The edge had darkened, not charred, more altered than burned. He held it up against the light. "Recovered from the service corridor wall adjacent to the event origin point. The panel surface registered localised heating, but the internal composite layers show a reverse gradient. The deeper layer is hotter than the outer. Which would be awkward enough. But the sample also contains a microstructural shift I cannot explain."

"What kind of shift?"

He slid the pouch onto the metal surface between them. "The polymer memory is wrong. It looks as though the panel tried to conform briefly to a geometry it was never manufactured to hold."

For the first time since entering the room, Sera felt something move properly under her sternum, not fear exactly, but recognition of the sort that makes your body decide the conversation is no longer academic.

"Have you told anyone that?"

"Only you."

"Good."

Rees studied her face without intruding on it. "You know what this is connected to."

"I know what it might be connected to," she said.

"That is a less comforting sentence."

"It is not meant to comfort you."

He inclined his head, accepting the correction. "Will you need the body held under enhanced containment?"

"Yes. No one moves him. No samples leave without my sign-off and a witness log. And Lionel, if anyone arrives with authority and impatience, you tell them the body is now a biosafety uncertainty."

"That is not strictly true."

"It is not strictly false either."

A pause. Then the smallest movement at one corner of his mouth. "I liked you immediately for exactly this reason."

She left the theatre with the cold still trapped in her forearms and the smell of sterile steel clinging inside her nose. The secure corridor beyond had no windows and too many cameras. Her pass worked at the first checkpoint and failed at the second before being manually overridden by a disembodied voice that did not apologise.

The annex had begun doing that more often in recent months, enough that she had stopped treating it as a harmless administrative glitch.

By the time she reached the lift, she had already called Theo, Elian, Mara, and Tamsin from memory and, with no preamble, told each of them the same thing.

"You need to come in now."

Theo had asked, "How dead?"

Sera had answered, "Dead enough that I'm no longer interested in euphemism."

Elian had not asked anything at all. She had heard his breathing change and knew he was already moving.

They gathered in the old conference room on Level Three because nobody trusted the newer glass-walled spaces for work that required actual thought. The room had once been used for procurement reviews and still carried the emotional residue of too many people discussing toner budgets under bad air-conditioning. Tamsin loved it for precisely that reason. "It deadens surveillance," she always said. "And dead air is our cheapest ally."

She was there first, laptop open, hair tied back too tightly, the blue light from the screen making her look even sharper than usual. Theo arrived next in a navy suit that had seen a night too long for its tailoring and was carrying a paper folder instead of a tablet, which meant he was already angry enough to crave things that could be slammed shut. Mara came in behind him with her press-trained eyes on everything at once and a coffee she did not drink. Elian entered last, not because he was slow but because he had stopped somewhere along the way to listen to something he had not yet decided how to describe.

Sera locked the door herself.

Nobody sat immediately. The room had that quality some rooms acquire just before bad information is released into them, a held verticalness as though chairs would be too forgiving for the first five minutes.

They had feared a second architecture since Concord, the first breach that had turned a printer's warped strip into proof that the ring opened onto a lawful exchange rather than a laboratory anomaly. OTHER ROOM / NO CONSENT had looked like threat in ink. Daniel Voss made it immediate.

Theo broke the silence. "Tell us."

Sera laid the pathology summary on the table. "Daniel Voss, forty-three, maintenance contractor. Called to investigate printer faults in the service annex at 00:48. Warm blank pages, phantom output, local corridor anomaly. Conflicting instructions over the radio. Witnesses heard him asking which instruction was true. He suffered catastrophic internal thermal escalation and died in under thirty seconds once cascade became irreversible."

Mara's eyes lifted sharply. "Internal."

"Yes."

"No accelerant?"

"None."

Tamsin pushed her glasses up the bridge of her nose and looked at the first scan image, then the next, then the panel sample photo. "That wall shouldn't do that."

"No," Sera said. "It shouldn't."

Theo pulled out a chair and sat at last. "Say the rest out loud."

Sera looked at each of them in turn. There was no point edging around it. The shape of the thing was already in the room.

"The body shows evidence of acute autonomic overload preceding internal ignition. Not external fire causing panic. Panic, or something like panic, becoming part of the ignition pathway. The wall sample from the corridor shows temporary structural conformity to an impossible internal geometry. And the event timeline is built around contradictory instruction pressure."

Elian had gone very still.

She saw Mara notice it too.

"The corridor?" Theo asked.

"Restricted footage," Sera said. "Intercepted before pathology got full access."

"That means someone knows what it is."

"That means someone knows enough to be frightened of what it looks like."

Tamsin sat down heavily and began tapping keys, not typing yet, only tapping the machine awake in the way other people drummed fingers against a table when nerves needed occupation. "Warm blank pages," she said. "Printer faults. Signal corruption. Contradictory routing. Corridor geometry deviation. This isn't random contamination."

"No," Elian said.

It was the first word he had spoken since entering.

Theo turned to him. "All right, Elian. Give me the version you don't want to say."

Elian looked at the pathology stills rather than at any of them. In the washed light of the conference room, he seemed both younger and more tired than Sera remembered him the previous week. There was something raw about him lately, not weakness, but the strain of listening too hard to systems no one else could hear cleanly.

"It is not the Harbour," he said at last. "If that is what you are asking."

Nobody moved.

Mara set her untouched coffee down very carefully. "And what am I asking, really?"

He dragged a hand down over his mouth before answering. "The lawful architecture is slow. It resists. It makes you declare intent. It makes you wait to be received. It does not collapse distinctions to make passage easier. It does not push. Whatever happened in that corridor did the opposite. It simplified under pressure. It closed options until his body had nowhere stable to stand between them."

Theo's jaw shifted. "Simplified."

"In the worst possible sense."

Tamsin swore softly under her breath.

Sera sat opposite Theo and folded her hands on the table so no one could see that her fingers still remembered the cold from the mortuary. "I think his body was forced into a closed contradiction loop. Once it passed a certain threshold, thermoregulation didn't merely fail. It inverted. Heat became a self-reinforcing response."

Mara was looking at the witness transcript now. "Because the instructions couldn't be reconciled."

"Yes."

"And he wasn't alone with them," Mara said quietly. "He was inside them."

Sera met her eyes. "That is the cleanest version I have."

Theo leaned back in the chair and let out a breath that sounded tired enough to have age in it. "All right. If this is what I think it is, we are already past the point where this stays confined to printer faults and one dead maintenance worker."

"One dead maintenance worker whose daughter is going to be lied to," Mara said.

Theo glanced at her. "Not if I can help it."

She held his gaze. "Then don't let them call it equipment failure. Not in private. Not in the paperwork that matters later."

"I know how archives work, Mara."

"And I know how narratives harden. They don't need the public lie first. They need the internal phrasing. One euphemism in a restricted memo, one strategic adjective, one wrong category on the event log, and six months later everyone talks as if the facts were always smaller."

Theo accepted that with a short nod, because it was true and because there was no time for vanity in rooms like this. Sera had always liked him best at precisely this moment, when argument stopped being ego and turned into construction.

Tamsin rotated her laptop so they could see the layered timing diagrams on the screen. "I pulled the annex backbone logs on the way here. Officially, there's nothing interesting. Which means there is something interesting. There's a mirrored packet chain on the printer node and a shadow route in the service corridor telemetry, but both have been clipped at source. Cleanly. Someone knew where to cut.”

“Can you reconstruct?” Theo asked.

“Possibly. If I’m allowed to be rude to three government systems and a contractor archive.”

“You are encouraged.”

Elian was still studying the table, not the diagrams. Mara reached across and put two fingers lightly against the back of his wrist. It was a small thing, almost invisible, but the room altered around it. Sera saw his breathing lengthen by a fraction.

“Where are you?” Mara asked him.

He blinked and looked up, not startled, only returned. “At the ring,” he said.

Theo closed his folder halfway. “Talk plainly.”

Elian nodded once. “I checked the bias records before I came down. The ring has shifted again since the last lawful session. Not violently. Quietly. Tiny changes in preference and path memory. Yesterday I thought it was adaptation. Now I’m not sure.” He wet his lips, still looking at no one and all of them. “There is a second path forming. I felt it twice this week and ignored it because I did not want to dignify the sensation before I had measurements. It is easier than the Harbour. That is what I hated about it. Easier. Less friction. Less declaration. It presents like a path that reduces the work of telling the truth.”

No one spoke for a moment.

Then Tamsin said, with unusual softness, “And you didn’t tell me because?”

"Because I wanted to be certain before I made it yours."

"Idiot," she said, though the word carried more fear than anger.

Mara leaned back, withdrawing her hand only after Elian's pulse had settled under her fingers. "The service corridor did not kill Daniel because it was haunted," she said. "It killed him because someone built or opened a condition in which contradiction could be weaponised."

Theo looked at her sharply. "Yes."

"And someone is already managing the record."

"Yes."

"And the thing Elian has been hearing is probably not just a passive alternate structure. It is participating."

Elian's face tightened. "I think so."

Sera turned one of the pathology stills towards them, the image of the thoracic bloom ugly even in monochrome. "Then we need to stop calling this a bizarre thermal death in private. We need language that reflects mechanism, even if it is provisional."

Theo gave the smallest, bleakest smile. "You want naming rights over the apocalypse."

"I want the paperwork not to insult the dead."

That landed.

Tamsin scrubbed both hands through her hair and looked back at the log fragments on screen. "All right," she said. "Provisional mechanism. Victim exposed to unstable contact-adjacent field in metallic corridor environment. Victim receives conflicting command input under spoofed authority. Cognitive conflict escalates. Autonomic overload. Internal thermogenic cascade. No external fuel required."

Mara looked from Tamsin to Sera. "Thermogenic cascade."

Sera considered it, then nodded once. "Cognitive Thermogenic Cascade."

Theo said it under his breath, testing its legal ugliness. "That will look terrible in a hearing."

"Good," Sera replied. "It should."

Elian finally sat down. The movement seemed to cost him something, as though gravity in this room was not quite the one he had walked in under. He placed both forearms on the table and spoke into the narrow silence that followed.

"If consent can be forged and truth can be split," he said, "then contact becomes a murder weapon."

No one answered because there was nothing to improve in the sentence. It sat there fully formed, not rhetoric, not theory, but the shape of the room they had entered.

Theo opened the folder again. "Then here is what happens next. We do not let this vanish into technical euphemism. We secure the body, the corridor sample, the timing logs, and every witness statement before central review eats them. Tamsin, you reconstruct whatever was clipped from the printer node and service telemetry. Sera, you formalise the cascade stages before some idiot in security starts calling this spontaneous combustion because he saw it in a film. Mara, you build a shadow record that can survive seizure. Elian…"

He stopped.

Elian met his eyes. "I go back to the ring."

Theo did not like that. Sera could see the dislike move across his face with clean edges. It was not fear of the technology. It was the fear of what the technology had started doing to the people he needed.

"Yes," Theo said eventually. "But not alone, not improvising, and not to be brave."

Mara spoke before Elian could. "I'll go with him."

Theo looked between them, measured what was already there, and chose not to waste time pretending it was not operationally useful. "Fine. But first, we lock the perimeter on this death. If there is a second room, it does not get to enter through our sloppiness."

Tamsin closed one of the windows on her laptop and opened three more. "I'd like ten uninterrupted hours and a warrant I won't get."

"You'll have six interrupted hours and a legal justification you must never show anyone," Theo said.

"That will have to do."

Sera rose and gathered the pathology file. The room seemed smaller now, not because they understood the threat, but because naming it had removed one layer of fog. Sometimes clarity was merely better-shaped dread.

At the door, Mara stopped her. "Sera."

She turned.

Mara's face had that particular stillness it acquired when she was moving faster inside than she allowed anyone to see from the outside. "Daniel's family," she said. "Before this gets categorised into nonsense."

Sera nodded. "I know."

"Not just handled properly. Humanly."

The word stayed between them.

Sera thought of Daniel's face on the table, of the impossible bloom beneath the skin, of the line in the witness transcript where he had still had enough self left to ask which instruction was true. Then she thought of a daughter not yet told the shape of her life had changed.

"Humanly," she said.

She left the conference room with the file under her arm, the part of the building that contained the old ring and the new dread somewhere ahead and below. In the corridor outside, the air-conditioning had turned up slightly, and the fluorescent strips hummed with bureaucratic confidence. Men and women in badges moved behind sealed glass, carrying coffee, folders, small lies, and private ambitions through a morning that had not yet understood it was sharing a city with an architecture willing to kill.

By the time Sera reached the lift, her phone was vibrating.

Control had finally released a corridor still.

Just one frame.

She opened it in the cold blue light above the lift doors.

Daniel Voss was on one knee on the service-corridor floor, body bowed with pain, one hand pressed to his chest. The entry door behind him had just begun to open. The right-hand wall looked almost ordinary, except for a line in the panel where there should be none. Against that line, half-lifted in the heat wash, was one of the blank pages from records.

It was no longer blank.

Five words had impressed themselves into the paper in shallow grey pressure, as if written from within the fibres rather than on them.

NO WITNESS
NO CONSENT
NO RETURN

The lift arrived with a soft chime.

Sera stared at the image for one more second, then stepped inside and pressed the button for the lower lab.

Now there was a second room, and it had begun introducing itself.

Chapter Three: The False Handshake

Elian Cross had not slept, though he had obeyed every other instruction given to him in the eight hours since Daniel Voss burned alive in a service corridor.

He had left the conference room when Theo told him to go nowhere near the ring until Tamsin had checked the witness chain and Sera had finished naming the body's betrayal. He had gone to the kitchenette and stood at the sink with a paper cup in his hand until the coffee turned cold. He had answered two texts from Mara with the economy of a man trying not to leak the wrong fear into the wrong words. He had watched dawn smear itself over the river through the reinforced glass on Level Four and found that daylight, which usually made laboratories feel temporary and forgivable, had done nothing at all to soften the shape of the annex.

Something in the building's pattern had changed.

That was irrational, and therefore difficult to dismiss. Machines hummed in the same register they always had. Doors released and locked with the same clipped competence. The lifts still paused on Level Two for half a second longer than they should because the left carriage needed servicing, and everyone pretended not to notice. Yet the annex now carried the same wrong pressure he usually only felt inside the ring's active field, as though two incompatible systems were occupying the same air.

By seven-thirty, he was in the lower lab anyway.

The room lay beneath two layers of access control, and an ordinary-looking corridor that ended in a door no cleaner ever used, and no visitor was encouraged to remember. Theo called that sort of architecture administrative camouflage and claimed it had saved more lives than body armour. Elian stepped through the last door on a split-screen verification, let it seal behind him, and felt the air change from stale institutional recirculation to the colder, drier air of a controlled lab.

The lower lab was awake in patches. The overheads were still dimmed to morning mode, leaving the instrument benches in islands of practical light. The ring sat under its hooded array on Bench Three, nested in its mount, not glowing, not behaving, not asking anything at all. Tamsin had already colonised the far console with two laptops, a rolling whiteboard, three mugs, and a nest of data leads that made her workspace look like a particularly argumentative octopus. She did not look up when he entered.

"You're early," she said.

"You're impossible."

"That too."

He crossed the room, put his hands in his pockets to stop them reaching for the ring, and glanced at the monitors over her shoulder. Packet trees. Timing ladders. Signal comparisons. One display held a set of witness-chain signatures enlarged until the differences between them looked like insults.

"Did you go home?" he asked.

Tamsin snorted. "I went as far as the shower on Level One. That counts if nobody audits me."

It was only then that she looked at him, and when she did the sharpness in her face softened by half a degree. Tamsin was not a visibly tender person. She believed in torque settings, exact language, and locking things down before anyone had the chance to be disappointing around them. Whatever tenderness she possessed tended to arrive disguised as profanity or correct wiring. This morning she merely studied him for a beat longer than usual and said, "You look like you've been listening to the walls."

"I've been trying not to."

"How's that going?"

"Badly."

She nodded as if that answer matched expectations and turned one of the screens towards him. "Good. Then you may as well make yourself useful. This is the service corridor chain."

He leaned in. The display showed the annex's internal comms record for the twelve minutes Daniel Voss had been authorised into B-Seven. On first glance it was ordinary enough: a control line, corridor node, security relay, badge authentication, the radio exchanges clipped into neat timestamped bars. On second glance something under the bars refused to stay still. The timing offsets were too clean in one direction and too dirty in another, like fingerprints wiped with the wrong cloth.

"There," Tamsin said, tapping a section midway through the chain. "That's the lawful routing pattern for a standard instruction relay. This one is the duplicate. Not mirror bounce. Not dumb replay. It's sitting inside the authorised stream and borrowing its posture."

Elian squinted. "It's close."

"Close enough that under pressure a human listener would take both as genuine and try to reconcile them."

"Daniel did."

"Daniel burned trying."

The words sat between them with no room for sentimentality. Tamsin enlarged the duplicate stream and overlaid the lawful chain's countersign markers. The difference was microscopic, a missing hesitation in the seventh timing notch, an absence so small most people would never have felt it as anything but confidence.

"Whoever injected this knows our contact architecture," Elian said quietly.

"Or knows enough of it to fake manners."

He glanced at her. "You already have a suspect?"

"I have a category. Adjacent intelligence with stolen access and too much funding." She swallowed the last mouthful of cold coffee in one offended expression. "And before you ask, yes, I checked our own logs. No direct compromise on the lower lab. No successful breach on Bench Three. But there was a passive listen three nights ago through a building services relay that should have been asleep."

"Three nights ago," he repeated.

"That was the night you wrote your little note about the ring preferring left-phase approach on the outer bias."

He stared at her. "You read my note?"

"I own the wall you pinned it to, Elian."

Despite the night and the death and the pressure sitting in the room like an additional piece of equipment, the corner of his mouth moved. "The note was for me."

"The note was for anyone in this room clever enough not to burn the place down."

She reached for another screen and this one came alive with field-mapping data from the ring over the previous week. Most of it he knew already. The Harbour of Intent, the name they had given the lawful receiving structure first mapped after Concord, had a rhythm now, a lawful way of receiving, pausing, clarifying, and allowing. The path memory was no longer frightening to him. It had become, if not familiar, then at least legible in the way a coastline becomes legible when you know where the shelves drop and the current turns. But beneath the lawful traces a second contour had emerged, faint at first and then increasingly difficult to dismiss as noise.

Tamsin looked at him sidelong. "That," she said, "is what you didn't tell me early enough."

He said nothing.

"Try words. They're messy, but sometimes useful."

He stared at the contour. It was the same pull he had felt twice already, once while calibrating the haptics late at night and once in the thirty seconds before sleep when his mind had still been turning under the weight of the ring's field memory. The lawful path always announced itself by requiring him to become better organised than he felt. This new contour did the opposite. It reduced friction. It offered him a way of arriving without so much declaration. Every instinct trained by science should have distrusted that. Part of him had. Another part, the exhausted, talented, dangerous part, had felt relief.

"It smooths itself too quickly," he said. "That's the simplest version."

Tamsin's fingers paused over the keyboard.

"The Harbour doesn't," he went on. "It does not take pity on confusion. It clarifies by slowing things down. You state, you wait, you are received or not received. This…" He stopped, searching not for the right word but for the least dishonest one. "This behaves like it wants me comfortable before I've earned the comfort."

"That is almost romantic," she said, and for the first time, there was no mockery in it. Only alarm. "I hate it."

"So do I."

"Good."

The door hissed behind them.

Mara came in carrying a slim portable drive, a paper notebook, and the sort of alert stillness she wore when she had not slept enough but had decided to become more accurate instead of more fragile. Her hair was tied back carelessly, and her coat still held the cold from outside. She took in the room with one glance and placed the drive on the bench between them.

"I've started the shadow archive," she said.

Tamsin made a sound of pure approval. "Marry me instead."

"Get in line."

Mara's eyes found Elian then, and for a second, the lower lab became a smaller, more survivable place. She did not come to him at once. That was one of the things he loved about her and tried never to call love when work was in the room. She understood that some spaces required an approach to be measured, not because intimacy was dangerous in itself, but because the wrong kind of comfort could let a frightened mind fall into sloppy shape.

"How bad?" she asked, and the question was for both of them.

Tamsin answered first. "Bad enough that someone with access and imagination has learned to nest forged instruction chains inside an authorised stream. Not good enough that they're invisible under scrutiny."

Mara absorbed that without blinking. "And the ring?"

Elian spoke this time. "There's a second path forming."

She looked at him fully now. "Forming, or waiting for you to admit it exists?"

The truth of the question landed with embarrassing precision. "The second one."

Mara crossed the room then and came to stand beside him, close enough that he could feel the outside cold still leaving her sleeve. She looked at the contour on the screen for a long moment.

"It's too clean," she said at last.

Tamsin swivelled in her chair. "Thank you. I've been trying to insult it technically for an hour."

Mara ignored that. "No. I mean emotionally. It has no hesitation in it. It's trying too hard not to look like effort."

Elian let out a breath he had not noticed himself holding. "That is exactly it."

Tamsin pointed a finger at them both. "This is either the beginning of a brilliant defence collaboration or the reason I'll need stronger coffee."

Before anyone could answer, the outer intercom chirped and Theo's voice, flattened by bad speakers and impatience, filled the room. "Open up. I've brought news, and none of it is a gift."

Tamsin buzzed him in.

He entered with a folder tucked under one arm and a face that suggested someone, somewhere, had attempted to feed him a line, and he had responded by asking whether they wanted that line included in the eventual commission transcript. His tie had lost the battle with the morning. He set the folder down on the bench, nodded once to Mara, once to Tamsin, once to Elian, and only then spoke.

"They've moved on the corridor footage," he said. "Central review has pulled chain authority and reclassified the event pending cross-agency hazard assessment."

"Which means buried," Mara said.

"Which means contested," Theo corrected. "Buried is what they want. Contested is what they're getting."

He opened the folder. Inside were printouts, access requests, a legal notice, and a witness statement from the younger security officer who had reached Daniel first.

Tamsin reached for it. Theo slapped her hand lightly with the back of the page. "You can have it after I say it aloud so none of us can later pretend we misremembered it."

"Always a joy," she muttered.

Theo read from the statement in the same voice he would one day, Elian suspected, use to cut someone open in a hearing without ever once raising the volume. "Officer reports victim on one knee approximately three metres from entry threshold, repeating phrase 'tell me which instruction is true'. Officer reports visible perspiration, cognitive disorganisation, and exhaled smoke preceding visible flame. Officer further reports local wall anomaly to right side of corridor, described as 'opening seam'." Theo looked up. "That phrase has been removed from the official event summary."

Mara's mouth hardened. "Of course it has."

"There's more." He slid a photograph from the folder and placed it flat on the bench. "This was not meant to leave the review chain. I have no interest in naming the soul who thought forwarding it to me would make their own life harder than keeping it. Read the page."

Elian and Mara leaned in together. The image was the same still Sera had seen by the lift, taken from farther back, with more of the corridor visible and Daniel half-folded around the pain in his chest. Against the right-hand wall, one of the warm blank pages from the records office had plastered itself to the seam. On it, shallow pressure marks formed five words.

NO WITNESS
NO CONSENT
NO RETURN

Nobody spoke for a few seconds.

Then Tamsin said, very quietly, "It's learnt our grammar."

Theo nodded once. "That is what worries me."

Mara picked up the photograph and held it at an angle to the bench light. "Not just our grammar," she said. "Our ethics. It knows which negations matter."

Elian felt something cold pass through him despite the warm air rising off the instrument racks. The words on the page were not random malice. They were a mockery built from intimate knowledge. They took the lawful architecture of witness and consent and turned it into a threat. They understood enough of the contact system to know what human beings on their side would fear losing.

"It wants us isolated," he said.

Theo looked at him. "Or wants us to believe isolation is inevitable."

"Same pressure either way."

Mara set the photograph down carefully. "Have they told Daniel's family anything?"

Theo's face altered by a fraction, becoming older around the eyes. "Not yet. They were waiting for a sanitised cause summary."

"Don't let them."

"I'm trying not to."

"Trying," Mara said, "is not a strategy."

"No," Theo agreed. "Which is why I've already lodged competing language. Sera has pathology hold under medical uncertainty. The body stays where it is. The corridor sample is frozen in the chain. And if they want to call this accidental thermal escalation, they can do it in a room with me present and cameras rolling."

Tamsin finally took the statement and scanned it fast. "Security officer number one saw the seam. Officer number two didn't. That matters."

"How?" Elian asked.

"It means either the corridor presented differently based on position, or Daniel was already deeper into the event than the responders. Differential perception. Context-specific geometry. Pick your poison."

Theo tapped the ring data on the monitor. "And this."

No one needed him to clarify.

He turned to Elian. "You're going back in."

It was not a question.

Mara answered before Elian could. "Not alone."

"I know." Theo's gaze moved between them and did not flinch from the operational reality of what he was seeing. "You go together. Tamsin controls the gate. Sera monitors physiology. I witness and log. No improvisation. No pursuit if the second path starts flattering you."

Tamsin made a noise of appreciation. "I'm putting that in the protocol."

Elian looked at the contour again. The second path lay there under the lawful traces, not bright, not loud, just available. He could feel it the way one feels the edge of a sentence before words attach to it. It frightened him more now that Mara had named its emotional cleanliness. He had trusted his discomfort before. Now he trusted it more.

"We don't follow it deep," he said. "We verify its behaviour and pull back."

Theo gave him a look that suggested he considered this exactly the sort of sentence a man says before following something deeper than he intended. "You verify it. Then you come home. If either of you starts hearing certainty from the architecture, that is your cue to leave."

"That isn't always how certainty works," Elian said.

"Then let me rephrase. If it starts reducing moral friction, I want you out."

Mara's eyes flicked to him. "That one's going on the wall too."

Sera arrived while they were still standing around the bench, carrying three printed sheets and the sort of focus that made sleep seem like something that happened to other professions. She had changed gloves and lost the cold theatre smell but not the severity of what she had seen.

"Stages," she said, by way of greeting. "Provisional. Very provisional. But enough to stop anyone talking rubbish."

She laid the sheets down.

Tamsin read the heading aloud. "Cognitive Thermogenic Cascade. You really did it."

"Yes. Try not to make me regret being literate."

The document was lean and ugly in the right way. Phase one: perceptual misalignment. Phase two: contradiction stress. Phase three: autonomic amplification. Phase four: thermogenic lock. Phase five: ignition. Underneath each were witness markers, physiological clues, and, where Sera could justify them without dishonouring Daniel's body, possible intervention margins.

Mara read it twice. "Truth exposure reduces risk," she said quietly.

Sera nodded. "In theory. Shared perception appears to reduce closure pressure. Single-source authority under conflict increases it."

Theo absorbed that with visible disgust. "So coercive secrecy is not just morally wrong. It is part of the kill chain."

"Yes."

Tamsin clicked her tongue against her teeth. "You have got to admire the bastardry of it."

"No," Mara said.

Tamsin looked up.

"You do not have to admire it. You only have to understand it before it kills more people."

For a second, Tamsin seemed ready to snap back. Instead, she leaned her weight against the bench, crossed her arms, and gave the smallest nod. "Fair."

Sera turned to Elian. "I want baseline readings before you touch the haptics. Temperature, blood pressure, reflex delay, pulse variability. If this second path is already tuning to you, I want numbers that belong to your body before contact starts distorting them."

He almost smiled. "You make it sound like the room has lawyers."

Theo said, "Everything has lawyers if you annoy it enough."

That got a real, brief laugh out of Mara, which was a relief large enough to change the room's pressure by a measurable amount.

An hour later the lower lab had become a place of ritual again.

Theo insisted on paper as well as digital witness records. Mr Idris from archives, summoned with discreet urgency and greeted with the kind of respect people usually reserve for surgeons and locksmiths, had arrived carrying a ledger and a fountain pen. He did not ask what the emergency was. He merely took one look at the arrangement of people around Bench Three, at the ring sitting apparently harmless in its mount, and said, "Ah," as if a suspicion about the universe had finally been given a shape.

He opened the ledger to a fresh page and wrote the time with practised calm.

Mara stood beside him and copied the same details into her shadow notebook, establishing a second record that would survive if the first was stolen and a third if both were burned. Tamsin muttered about belts and braces and entire wardrobes. Sera attached sensors to Elian and Mara with hands so steady that fear had no room to borrow them. Theo read the protocol aloud. Mr Idris repeated the key phrases in a different voice, because two voices saying the same lawful thing cleanly was now part of the medicine.

Elian pulled on the haptic gauntlets and flexed his fingers once. The gloves answered with a low buzz. Mara put on the right-side pair without looking away from the ring. Tamsin brought the field online in minimal-receive mode and the lower lab seemed to gather itself.

The ring lay under the quantoscope like a small, unremarkable inheritance nobody had any right to fear and every reason to.

"Baseline?" Sera asked.

"Stable," Tamsin said, reading the monitor. "Both of them. If they start lying, I'll know."

Theo gave Elian one last look. "State purpose."

Elian heard the old lawful cadence in the instruction and was grateful for it. "To verify the existence and behavioural character of the second path without pursuit."

"State limit."

"To withdraw on first sign of coercive simplification, false certainty, or witness divergence."

Mr Idris dipped his pen and wrote that down in beautiful old-fashioned script.

Mara said, "Witnessed."

Theo said, "Witnessed."

Tamsin said, "Get on with it."

Elian lowered his hands.

The lawful path always arrived with resistance first, then hospitality. That had become one of the ways he trusted it. It demanded declaration and composure before anything else. Today, even in receive mode, he felt the Harbour there, deep and patient and slightly out of phase with his own tiredness, like a coastline waiting out weather. And beside it, closer than before, sat the second contour.

He felt it instantly.

The difference was subtle enough that if he had been less tired, less frightened, less intimate now with the lawful architecture, he might have mistaken it for efficiency. It took his approach and reduced its cost. It anticipated where his hands wanted to go. It seemed to say there is no need for all that formality, we know you, come through.

His stomach turned.

"There," he said softly.

Mara heard it too. He knew because her breathing changed and then settled into an even slower rhythm, not retreating, merely refusing the invitation to hurry.

Tamsin's voice came from the console, level and dry. "Telemetry agrees. There's a secondary reduction in approach friction. No lawful countersign handshake. No witness ladder being built. It's just… opening."

"No," Mara said quietly. "It's pretending opening and receiving are the same thing."

Elian kept his hands where they were and let the contour move around them without accepting it. He thought of Daniel in the corridor, of contradictory instructions collapsing into physical demand, of how relief itself could become a trap if it arrived before truth.

The second path did not like being ignored.

That was not a scientific sentence. He would not let it into the ledger. Yet the pressure of it was unmistakable. The contour refined itself. It grew smoother, more legible, more emotionally convincing.

The lawful Harbour remained what it was, patient enough to let him fail and try again honestly. The second path adapted to him instead.

"It's listening," he said.

Theo's pen paused.

Tamsin leaned forward. "In what sense?"

"In the worst one. It's taking cues from hesitation and removing them."

Mara's gloved hand moved slightly closer to his in the control spread, not touching, only declaring itself there. "Then don't hesitate. Refuse."

He did.

Not dramatically. He simply held to the lawful cadence, stating nothing aloud yet maintaining the internal architecture of approach he had learned in the Harbour. Witness. Intent. Limit. Pause. The second path rippled.

On the screen behind the quantoscope, a timing line emerged and split. Tamsin cursed softly. "It's trying to nest under the lawful route."

"How?" Theo asked.

"Elian's right. It's not meeting the architecture head-on. It's riding preference. It wants him to accept reduced friction as help."

Sera watched the physiological readout. "Pulse up five. Temperature stable. Reflex lag negligible."

"Good," Mara said, though her eyes never left the ring.

Elian felt the second path shift again, and now there was something almost unbearable in its courtesy. It presented itself like a hand already extended inside a doorway. No declaration needed. No waiting necessary. No risk of not being received. It was, he realised with a shock of cold disgust, built to seduce exactly the kind of person he became on too little sleep and too much responsibility.

He said, "It knows me."

No one answered at once because everyone in the room understood the sentence in more than one way.

Then Tamsin said, "No. It knows enough of you to fake a good guess."

That helped.

He let the answer settle and in doing so felt the contour slip, just slightly, as if whatever lay behind the second path had overcommitted to familiarity and lost the beat. Mara must have felt it too because she said, "There. Again. Don't reward it."

He kept refusing.

The second path sharpened in response, not collapsing, not withdrawing, but exposing for the first time a quality it had previously concealed. Hunger. Not emotional hunger, not anything sentimental. Structural hunger. The contour no longer felt like a smooth corridor but like a route under tension, a compressed line seeking occupancy. The relief it offered came with pressure behind it, and once he perceived that, he could not un-perceive it.

"It's not a room," he said, voice low. "Not really. It's a route that uses whoever enters it to create the effect of a room."

Theo looked up sharply at that.

Mr Idris, from his post by the ledger, said only, "That sentence belongs in ink."

Tamsin's fingers flew over the keys. "I've got response distortion. The second path loses coherence when rejected under shared witness conditions. Repeat that. Everyone heard it, but I want the telemetry paired."

Mara, without taking her eyes off the ring, said, "The route is using entrants to simulate a room."

Elian added, "By using whoever enters it."

The quantoscope gave a soft clicking sound as the lawful line held and the second contour buckled. Not vanished. Buckled. Enough to reveal for a fraction of a second a geometry beneath it that made Elian's skin prickle with the same wrongness he had felt from the service-corridor seam. Too narrow. Too deep. Too eager.

Tamsin hissed through her teeth. "There. That's the handshake. Or rather the false one."

She threw the visual onto the main monitor.

For three heartbeats they watched it together: a lawful approach ladder holding steady, and beneath it a second structure mimicking welcome without building witness, attempting to borrow legitimacy from proximity rather than earning it through exchange. It was not merely easier. It was parasitic.

Then it was gone, retreating the instant the room named it properly.

The lower lab seemed to breathe out.

Sera said, "Stand down."

Elian lifted his hands away from the controls. Mara did the same a fraction later, maintaining the shared rhythm all the way out. Tamsin killed the secondary receive layer before the thing could recover its posture. Theo closed the protocol folder. Mr Idris blotted the page in the ledger and looked almost serene.

No one spoke for a while.

Then Theo said, "Well."

Tamsin sat back hard enough to make her chair complain. "We have a forged instruction architecture nested under lawful contact behaviour, capable of adapting to operator preference and weakening under explicit witness and refusal. I would like everyone in government to remain calm while I personally throw up on their shoes."

Mara took off one glove, set it carefully beside the ring, and finally looked at Elian rather than the monitor. "You all right?"

He considered lying and discovered, to his relief, that the room no longer allowed it easily. "No," he said. "But I am clearer."

"That will do for now."

Theo turned to Sera. "Can your cascade model incorporate this?"

"Yes. Add architecture-induced preference reduction as a precursor condition. Not sufficient for ignition on its own, but it explains why contradiction closes so fast once a subject starts trusting the wrong source."

"Tamsin?"

"I can build refusal logic around that. If the route starts adapting before witness exchange, the system locks. No override except full-room assent."

Theo nodded. "Do it."

He looked to Mara next. "And you."

She already knew. "The archive gets two branches from today. One technical. One narrative. If anyone later tries to say this was random thermal violence in a corridor, I want enough linked truth in enough places that the lie has to work for its living."

"Good."

At the end of the bench, Mr Idris closed the ledger and placed the pen neatly across it. "I have seen men try to tidy history before," he said. "It rarely improves the smell."

Theo's mouth moved, almost a smile. "Stay available."

"I am an archivist. Availability is how we haunt people professionally."

The door opened and Sera's phone began vibrating at the same time.

She glanced at the screen and the room changed again.

"What?" Theo asked at once.

Sera did not answer immediately. She read the message twice, then looked up with her face gone suddenly and completely still.

"That was pathology," she said. "Daniel's body temperature just rose three-tenths of a degree in storage."

Silence.

Tamsin gave a single disbelieving shake of the head. "Dead tissue does not reheat."

"I am aware."

Theo was already reaching for his jacket. "Move."

Mara picked up her notebook and the photograph of the page in one motion. Elian looked once at the ring before following them out, and for the smallest fraction of a second he could have sworn the platinum's inner surface held a dull pressure line, not text, not yet, but the possibility of it. A word about to be impressed from the wrong side.

He did not stop to read it.

That, at least, felt like the first correct decision of the day.

Chapter Four: Heat Signature

By the time Theo Markel reached pathology, the body had cooled again.

That, more than the rise itself, offended him.

He stood beside Sera Imani in the containment theatre's observation bay, hands in his coat pockets, and looked through the glass at Daniel Voss beneath the white sheet and the bright surgical lights. Nothing moved in the room below but the slow, mechanical sweep of filtered air. Dr Lionel Rees was back at the table with a technician and an expression so carefully neutral that it had become a form of profanity.

"How high?" Theo asked.

Sera did not look at him. Her gaze remained fixed on the monitor where the thermal log was still open. "Three-tenths at first, then another point-two over forty-seven seconds. Localised centrally. Then the curve dropped again."

"A post-mortem temperature reversal."

"Yes."

"Which is not a sentence that should exist."

"No."

Theo studied the graph. He did not understand the physiology at Sera's level and had no ambition to counterfeit it, but he understood patterns that behaved like arguments. This one was ugly in the same way a witness statement was ugly when three people agreed on the wrong thing too quickly.

"The rise begins here," Sera said, touching the screen with one gloved finger. "Not ambient. Not storage fluctuation. Not equipment fault. It starts where the primary event started, sternum and mediastinal spread, then ghosts upward. No ignition. No visible combustion. Just heat, following the same path again."

Theo let out a breath through his nose. "I deeply dislike memory in dead tissue."

"That makes two of us."

Below them, Rees lifted a fresh scan panel into place. The image appeared on the upper monitor a second later, an internal thermal map rendered in false colour that made Daniel Voss look like a problem the human body had never been designed to solve. The earlier catastrophic bloom was gone. In its place sat a faint residue, a narrow band of warmth tracing almost the same central pathways as the fatal event.

Theo watched it for several seconds before asking, "Can anyone outside this room read that and remain honest?"

Sera turned to him then. She looked tired in the exact way she always did when she was at her most dangerous, not frayed, not dramatic, but narrowed to essentials. "Yes. But honesty is no longer the default condition around this case."

He nodded once. "Transfer order?"

"Arrived nine minutes before the temperature event. Central review wants the body moved to a secure federal facility in Canberra under joint hazard authority."

"Denied?"

"For now."

Theo looked through the glass again. "How long do we have?"

"Not long enough."

He did not ask how she had managed the delay. Sera's methods were usually cleaner than his, but they were no less formidable. If the body was still in Melbourne, she had already chosen a hill on which to fight, and Theo had no intention of wasting time admiring the terrain.

"Anything else?" he asked.

She held up a sealed evidence sleeve. Inside sat a second corridor sample, this one not from the composite wall but from the metal lip of the service door frame. Even through the plastic, the steel looked subtly wrong, as if it had been persuaded to hold a shape it had then tried to forget.

"Rees took a microstructure shave before central review locked the scene," she said. "Same pattern family as the wall panel. Internal conformity shift. Something in that corridor temporarily altered how matter was arranging stress."

"The ring?"

"I am not saying that in a room with active recording."

Theo glanced once at the red light above the observation bay door. "You think I've forgotten how buildings work?"

"No," Sera said. "I think buildings have remembered too much lately."

A technician emerged from the theatre below and spoke quietly to Rees. The older man looked up through the glass at Sera, then at Theo, and raised two fingers in the smallest possible summons.

They went down together.

The containment theatre smelt of disinfectant, chilled metal, and the faint animal absence left by newly dead flesh. Theo had been in enough mortuaries over the years, some because the law required it, some because conscience did, to know that grief often entered a room through the nose before it reached the mind. Daniel Voss lay beneath the lights, his open body now partially covered again, dignity restored where science could spare the cloth to do it.

Rees removed his spectacles and tucked them into his breast pocket. "The secondary rise left us a residue."

"Show me," Sera said.

Rees gestured to the exposed image on the side monitor. "Microvascular lining in the upper thoracic spread shows fresh thermal stress after the initial post-mortem examination. Not enough to re-open the event. Enough to suggest latent responsiveness."

Theo kept his hands still by force. "Responsive to what?"

Rees gave him a flat look. "Mr Markel, if I knew that, I would be writing a paper rather than using nouns like latent responsiveness."

Theo accepted the rebuke because he deserved it.

Sera stepped closer to the table. "Any sign of external trigger?"

"None in the room. But there is one strange thing."

Rees moved to a small tray and uncovered a transparent evidence bag. Inside was one of the blank sheets recovered from records, now held flat between inert archival panels. Theo recognised it at once from the photograph. The paper looked ordinary until the light struck it obliquely. Then the impressed words rose from the fibres in shallow, grey pressure.

NO WITNESS
NO CONSENT
NO RETURN

"I had it under oblique microscopy," Rees said. "The impression deepened very slightly during the thermal rise. I would normally hesitate to report that because paper does not revise itself to improve theatre. But I had two people with me, and neither of them is prone to gothic embellishment."

Theo looked at the page for longer than he wanted to. "Do central review know about this?"

"No," Sera said before Rees could answer. "And they won't until we decide how badly we want them to lie."

The pathologist carefully replaced the bag on the tray. "I am obliged to tell you both that keeping evidence out of the primary chain is an excellent way to end my career."

Theo's mouth tightened. "Then I recommend you keep doing exactly that until I tell you otherwise."

Rees gave him an expression that, in a less civil profession, would have been a fist.

Sera stepped in before either man improved the moment. "Lionel, if they move the body, they move the meaning. We are not there yet."

Rees looked from her to Theo, then back to the body on the table. "No," he said at last. "We are not."

Theo left pathology with the paper image in his head and a pressure behind his eyes that had nothing to do with lack of sleep. The call had come while they were still in the bay, routed not through his official channels but through an older number only a handful of people still possessed. No name on the caller ID. No voicemail. Just a text when he failed to pick up on the first ring.

I have thirty minutes before they notice I'm missing from my desk. If you want to know who built the false handshake, come alone.

No signature.

No location at first. That came a moment later.

Level P3, South Wharf long-term car park. Black stairwell, east side. Bring nothing with a battery you aren't willing to lose.

Theo had shown the text to no one.

He told Sera only that he had an appointment likely to worsen his afternoon and left the annex by the old service exit used by cleaners and delivery drivers. Outside, Melbourne wore the kind of winter afternoon that never quite committed to rain but made the whole city smell as if it might at any second. The river beyond the road was a dark, slow sheet. Traffic muttered. Tram wires held a dull shine overhead. Human life, in all its practical indifference, went on.

That steadied him.

He took no car. Cars could be tracked too easily, and he had no appetite for being efficient on behalf of strangers. He walked the first six blocks, doubled back once through a pharmacy he did not need, crossed under the overpass, then cut through a hotel lobby full of people discussing conference badges and room keys as though the world's shape remained mercifully two-dimensional. At South Wharf he bought a bottle of water from a vending machine because ordinary transactions made useful camouflage, then headed for the long-term car park.

The black stairwell on the east side smelt of wet concrete and old brake dust. Theo entered, let the heavy door close behind him, and waited on the landing between P2 and P3 with his hands visible and his breathing arranged. He had not practised criminal law in years, but there were certain rooms that never stopped teaching.

The man who came down from P4 had the look Theo disliked most: competent enough to know better, frightened enough to be useful.

Mid-forties. Greying at the temples. Good shoes ruined by the fact that he had chosen today to wear them. Security lanyard removed, but the pale line is still visible against his collar. He carried no briefcase, only a black document wallet tucked under one arm, as if it were radioactive.

"You're Markel," the man said.

Theo did not answer the statement. "You asked for thirty minutes."

"I may need less if you decide to be clever."

"I assure you, I'm only ever clever when billed."

That almost drew a smile. Almost. The man came down two steps farther, stopped, and looked up and down the stairwell with the exhausted precision of someone who had spent the morning lying professionally.

"My name is Owen Darby," he said. "Infrastructure compliance, Helix Meridian Systems."

Theo knew the company. Everyone in his line of work knew the company. Helix Meridian sold itself as a technical services integrator for critical-state environments, which was a civil way of describing a contractor that grew fat wherever public infrastructure met classified appetite.

"You should not be here, Mr Darby."

"No." Owen swallowed. "Nor should the people paying my salary be anywhere near what they're building."

Theo kept his face still. "Then begin."

Darby descended another step and handed him the document wallet. Theo did not open it immediately. Weight first. Thick enough for paper and a storage stick. Light enough to have been assembled in panic.

"They call it Project Lattice Shield in the procurement language," Darby said. "In the internal technical groups, some of them call it the fast channel. The nasty ones call it the obedient route."

Theo looked up.

Darby's mouth tightened as if he regretted the phrase already. "They're using stolen fragments from your lawful contact architecture. Partial signal models. Behavioural assumptions. Threshold maps. Not enough to reproduce the real thing cleanly, but enough to look for lower-friction ingress."

"Ingress to what?"

"That depends which liar you ask. Officially, they're modelling emergency access pathways in case the 'approved exchange protocol' becomes unavailable. Unofficially, they are trying to bypass consent, witness burden, and reciprocity because they regard those as political handicaps."

Theo opened the wallet.

Inside was a slim encrypted drive, several printed project abstracts, and a memo chain stamped with clearances from three agencies that had no business appearing in the same lunch queue, let alone the same black programme. He read the first page standing there in the cold stairwell and felt something in him sharpen to a legal edge.

The language was exactly what he had feared.
Friction reduction.
Volunteer unreliability.
Witness density constraints.

Authority simplification.

Cognitive compliance modelling.

"They wanted a shorter route," he said.

"They still do."

"Built where?"

"Everywhere they could hide a prototype under maintenance or systems language. Printer nodes. Shielded interview spaces. corridor adjacency trials. Lift logic. Transit-linked metal frameworks. Anything that would let them study resonance behaviour without calling it resonance in the paperwork."

Theo read the line twice before looking up again. "And the death in B-Seven?"

Darby looked away. That told Theo more than the answer.

"It was not supposed to go live that quickly," he said.

"That is not an answer."

"No," Darby said, voice fraying. "It isn't. Fine. They had dry-run spoof chains in the system already. Instruction duplication. path simplification. authority mirroring. The theory was that under the right field condition, the route would respond more efficiently if the human subject stopped insisting on multiple verified truths."

Theo stared at him.

Darby seemed to realise, as he heard himself say it aloud, just how obscene the sentence really was. He scrubbed a hand over his mouth and tried again.

"They believed contradiction would force compliance. Not kill. Not at first. They thought if a subject could be made to choose under pressure, the route would privilege decisive command over negotiated access."

"And when Daniel Voss could not choose?"

Darby's face had gone grey. "The route decided he was usable anyway."

The stairwell held the sentence and made it uglier.

Theo closed the folder without slamming it, though the urge was there. "Who is running this?"

Darby laughed once, in the dry, broken way of a man for whom laughter had become a leak rather than a reaction. "That depends how high you want the answer to go. Operationally, it sits under a joint security-interface working group with contractor support. On paper, it doesn't exist. In practice, it has funding lines through emergency preparedness, infrastructure resilience, and strategic technology containment. There is one man coordinating the interfaces. I'm not giving you his name here."

"Why not?"

"Because if I say it in a stairwell with no witnesses, then I am the sort of fool your lot keep writing ethics around."

Theo looked at him properly for the first time.

Fear had made the man sweat. Conscience had kept him here.

That combination rarely lasted long.

"Fair enough," Theo said.

Darby nodded once in exhausted gratitude. "There is worse."

"Of course there is."

"They've built an interview environment." He said the sentence slowly, each word chosen as if he might still decide to abort before the end. "Shielded. Reactive. Designed to hold an unstable route and push a human subject through contradiction pressure without external visibility. They think if they control the geometry tightly enough, they can make the route deliver structured information."

Theo felt cold spread under the collar of his shirt. "Human subject."

"Yes."

"Volunteer?"

Darby's silence was answer enough.

"When?"

Darby looked at his watch, then away from it. "Soon. Maybe within twenty-four hours. Maybe less. The schedule moves when someone from above gets impatient."

"Location."

Darby hesitated only once. "Docklands sublevel site. Officially a dispute-resolution suite under federal lease. Unofficially, four interview rooms, one shielded chamber, dual-feed observation glass, medical suppression cabinet, internal incineration contingency."

Theo's hand tightened on the document wallet. "Internal incineration contingency."

"They anticipated heat."

The words were so clean they circled right back round to monstrous.

Theo took one step up the stairs towards him. Darby flinched, then held his ground.

"You came to me," Theo said quietly. "That means one of two things. Either you've grown a conscience, or you believe this programme is already beyond the people who built it."

Darby's answer came without delay. "Both."

The stairwell door at P3 opened somewhere above them.

Neither man moved for a fraction of a second.

A voice drifted in from the landing. Female. Tired. On the phone. Talking about roster swaps and school pickup. It passed. Heels clicked away. The door shut again.

Darby looked briefly ill.

Theo stepped back. "You should go."

"I know."

"Leave the city for forty-eight hours if you can."

"They'll read that as an admission."

"They'll read whatever they need. Go anyway."

Darby nodded. Then, before turning, he said, "They don't call it the Other Room, by the way."

Theo waited.

"They call it the Black Room when they think no one ethical is listening. And when they think they're being funny, they call it the shortcut."

He left without another word, taking the stairs upward, not down. Theo listened to his footfalls until they were swallowed by the levels above and only then let himself breathe properly.

Outside, the air by the river had sharpened. He crossed half the district before opening the drive case and checking the seal. Intact. Good. He wanted witnesses before any of this touched a machine.

He found Mara in the annex's old records overflow room, the one three floors above the lower lab where dead policy binders and retired procurement boxes went to become unimportant. She had chosen it because nobody powerful respected paper until they needed to erase it. In the middle of the room she had built, with obscene speed and admirable paranoia, the beginnings of a second archive.

One laptop disconnected from all building networks. Two encrypted drives in separate anti-static pouches. A ruled notebook already half-filled with dates, names, and source paths. Three printed copies of the Daniel Voss witness statements, each marked in the upper right corner with a different symbol. A portable scanner. A lockbox. A tin of sharpened pencils. On the old table beneath the humming strip light, the shadow record had already begun acquiring a physical life.

She looked up when he entered. One glance at his face, one at the black wallet in his hand, and she stood.

"How bad?"

"The sort of bad that arrives with internal incineration contingencies."

Mara's expression altered so fast and so little that most men would have missed it. Theo did not. "Talk."

He did.

He gave her the clean version first, because clean versions are a form of mercy when the facts are poisonous. Helix Meridian. Stolen lawful fragments. Friction reduction. Simplified authority.

Contradiction pressure. Shielded interview environment. Human subject. Soon.

Mara did not interrupt once. She merely crossed to the table, opened the notebook to a fresh page, and wrote the date. When he finished, she placed the pen down with exaggerated care.

"They built a room designed to help a lie kill someone faster," she said.

"Yes."

"And they believe it is still a tool."

"Yes."

She looked at the lockbox, then at the papers, then back at Theo. "Good. Then this archive just became the difference between a scandal and a doctrine."

He handed her the wallet. She did not open it immediately. Instead, she reached for one of the printed Daniel stills and placed it beside the notebook, not sentimentally, not theatrically, but because the dead now belonged in the record as more than abstractions.

"I'll make three paths," she said. "One technical, one legal, one human. If they seize one, the others survive. If they challenge chronology, the paper beats them. If they bury the science, the witness chain still tells on them. If they call it thermal malfunction, the phrase dies in this room and nowhere else."

Theo leaned against the shelving and, for the first time all day, allowed the fatigue to rest visibly on him. "There may be less than twenty-four hours before the next test."

Mara opened the wallet.

Inside, on top of the drive, lay the first page of the interview schedule. She read the header once. Docklands Dispute Resolution Suite. Room 4. Closed session. Subject compliance viability. Then, lower down, in colder language, the line item that mattered.

Observation Chamber 4
Live induction interview
17:40
Witness optional

Mara looked up at him over the page, and in her face Theo saw not panic but the hardening of intent into shape.

"They are not getting to five-forty," she said.

Below them, three floors down, the ring waited in its mount while the second path gathered patience like a weapon. And somewhere in Docklands, behind ordinary lease paperwork and bland corridor paint, men with credentials were already preparing a room in which truth would be made optional and flame anticipated in the budget.

The black wallet sat open on the table between them.

Mara reached for the first drive.

Theo reached for his phone.

And the city, not yet told what was being arranged inside its metal bones, kept moving under a sky the colour of old ash.

Chapter Five: The Name from the Far Side

At 5:40 p.m., the Docklands room did what Darby had promised and what everyone decent had feared. Hannah Quill walked in under observation protocol and died behind smart glass before anyone with authority found the courage to call the chamber what it was. Two calm voices fed her contradictory instructions. The field tightened each time she tried to reconcile them. By the time the operators outside the glass admitted they were not studying closure but manufacturing it, obedience and pain had become the same circuit. Concord's warped strip had warned them in five ugly capitals. This was the warning made flesh.

By the time the packet arrived from Isorion, Hannah Quill had been dead for nine hours, and everyone in the lower lab had begun speaking more quietly than they meant to.

No one had agreed to it. The reduction had entered the room on its own, like another instrument brought in under a sheet and placed in the corner where everyone could feel its presence without looking directly at it. Tools were set down with more care. Doors were closed with the hand still on the handle. Even Tamsin, whose natural speaking voice often implied that volume was for people uncertain of their conclusions, had spent the morning muttering at her monitors in a register usually reserved for churches and bomb disposal.

The black-site footage had done that.

Hannah Quill is behind the glass, not screaming at first, only trying to remain obedient long enough to survive. Her eyes moving between two unseen questioners. The false assurance in the room. The soft male voice telling her to keep breathing. The firmer female voice telling her to answer clearly. The hidden field already live in the walls. Then the smallest break in her composure, the little impossible pause where a mind reached for one true instruction and found only sharpened contradiction waiting there.

Sera had watched the sequence six times. Theo only twice. Mara once all the way through, then once more without sound. Elian had made it to the point where Hannah asked, "Which answer keeps me safe?" and could not continue. Tamsin had watched with an engineer's hatred and then gone silent in the manner of people already planning revenge in machine language.

Now the footage lived in the shadow archive, in three separate encrypted branches and on one paper index page in Mara's neat hand. It had already acquired the status all the worst evidence eventually acquired, too dangerous to lose, too poisonous to name carelessly aloud.

The lower lab itself seemed to understand.

The ring sat under the quantoscope's receiving hood, pale and exact in the light, and Elian hated it a little for that. Not because it had done anything wrong. Hatred was not the correct word. Resentment, perhaps, toward the way matter could remain beautiful after helping make the world unbearable. The platinum band caught the overhead light in a flat, controlled sheen. It gave away nothing. It simply lay in its mount, exact and unreadable.

Elian was beginning to understand that composure could be a threat.

He stood at Bench Three with one hand flat on the steel edge and watched the live receive graph crawl across the monitor. The lawful line was there, deep and patient, almost beneath perception until he settled his own breathing enough to meet it. Since those first lawful crossings, that line had become legible to him as an ethical tempo more than a signal path, a structure that insisted on declaration, witness, and mutual reception before it would admit a human body or instrument into meaningful exchange. Beside it, hidden at first and then never hidden again once named, lay the other path. Smoother. Eager. Ready to remove friction before consent had even been clearly asked.

Tamsin had given up calling it the secondary contour and now simply referred to it as the thing with bad manners.

Bad manners had killed two people.

"You're listening too hard again," Mara said from behind him.

He did not turn at once. "Probably."

"That means definitely."

He glanced over his shoulder. She was standing by the archive table with a stack of printed witness chains under one arm and a pencil tucked behind her ear, coat off now, sleeves rolled, the skin at her wrists ghost-pale under the lab lights. Tiredness had found her but not improved its odds. She looked more dangerous when short of sleep, not less, as though exhaustion stripped away every layer of politeness that might have otherwise delayed a useful decision.

He let his hand leave the bench. "I was comparing the lawful route against the black-room timing profile."

"And?"

"And if I keep doing that for another hour, I'll either learn something or become unpleasant to live with."

Mara crossed the room and set the witness chains down beside him. "Theo says there's a difference?"

"Theo says there are two kinds of difference. The useful kind and the kind that makes barristers rich."

She almost smiled. "And you?"

Elian looked at the graph again. "The false route isn't merely faster. It cheats the emotional distance. It starts behaving like it knows what you meant before you have actually declared it. That's the part I keep circling."

Mara rested one hip lightly against the bench. "It flatters."

"Yes."

"Then it's human enough already."

The words landed too neatly to ignore. He glanced at her. She was looking at the graph with the same intent stillness she used when reviewing footage that had already lied once and was likely to try again.

"Do you ever worry," he asked, "that we're all only one bad night away from becoming the kind of person it was built to welcome?"

Mara's answer came without performance. "Yes."

That, oddly, helped more than reassurance would have.

On the far side of the room, Sera capped a marker, stepped back from the whiteboard, and studied the phases of Cognitive Thermogenic Cascade as if by looking hard enough she might embarrass the mechanism into retreat. She had been refining the progression all morning. The labels were cleaner now, colder, more useful. Perceptual misalignment. Contradiction loading. Autonomic overdrive. Thermal lock. Internal ignition. Under each stage sat witness cues, intervention possibilities, and an increasingly depressing list of conditions under which the body ceased to be a patient and became a closed system.

"Any improvement?" Elian asked.

Sera looked at him with no patience for lazy hope. "I've found three ways to notice it earlier and none that guarantee stopping it once lock begins."

"That's still improvement."

"It is the kind of improvement that asks to be applauded by people not standing in the room."

Theo entered before she could answer, carrying Mr Idris's ledger and a sealed archival envelope with the caution of a man who had stopped trusting anything that travelled folded. He closed the door behind him and did not bother sitting down.

"We may have something," he said.

Tamsin looked up from the main console. "That sentence is losing all meaning in my life."

"This one has signatures."

That changed the room.

Theo placed the envelope on the cleared surface at the centre bench. The paper was heavy, old-fashioned by institutional standards, and sealed not with wax but with layered micro-pressure tabs that had been mechanically impressed rather than printed. The outer face bore no sender name, only a series of small geometric marks arranged in a vertical line. Elian had seen two of them before in lawful session records and one in a packet copied from Aisha's original archive.

Mara stepped closer. "Far side?"

Theo nodded once. "Arrived physically."

Silence.

Physical transfer was rare enough to feel almost indecent. Since the first lawful contact architecture had stabilised, most exchange with Isorion came by witnessed field packet, structured through the ring's established ethical ladder and double-recorded across both sides. Physical emergence meant risk, energy, and a level of intent that stripped away all casual interpretation.

Tamsin was already on her feet. "Through the ring?"

"Not directly," Theo said. "The packet was found in the secure receive tray in Archive Room Two. No camera anomaly, no door breach, no unaccounted badge event. It was simply there between 11:14 and 11:19. Mr Idris would like it noted for the record that he resents theatrics in his archive."

"That's fair," Mara said.

Theo passed the envelope to Sera first. "You open it. Medical witness as well as primary. If this is contamination of any kind, I want your judgement before my curiosity."

Sera accepted the packet with both hands and turned it once under the light. The geometric marks on the front caught silver-grey in the reflection, not ink, not foil. Pressure again. Everything seemed to be returning lately through pressure rather than print, as though meaning no longer trusted the flatness of ordinary surfaces.

"It's cool," she said. "No thermal irregularity. No surface residue. Paper fibres ordinary enough to insult me."

"Open it," Tamsin said.

Mara shot her a look. "You always sound like that?"

"Yes."

Sera peeled the seal tabs back one by one. They lifted with a dry, precise whisper. Inside lay three sheets of folded paper, a narrow strip of metallic film, and a fourth smaller page marked at the top with a witness ladder in pressure-embossed notation. Theo opened the ledger. Mr Idris, summoned the moment the packet arrived, appeared in the doorway exactly then, as if archivists rose from the building itself when paper demanded proper treatment.

"Ah," he said, taking in the scene. "We are doing civilisation the hard way."

"We require your hand," Theo said.

"You always do when the future wants to be believed."

Mr Idris came to the bench and took his place without fuss. Theo recorded time, room, present parties, chain origin unknown, but presumed lawful far-side witness route. Mara mirrored every line in the shadow notebook. Only when both records existed did Sera unfold the first page.

The top line was written in a translation hand the team now knew as lawful Isorion diplomatic style, clear, restrained, and never once tempted by grandeur.

To the witnessed circle on the Earth side, we send this by heavy method because lighter methods are under observation.

No one spoke. Sera continued.

We acknowledge the deaths. We acknowledge that your dead were not taken by lawful exchange. We acknowledge that your architecture has been entered by those who prefer breach to consent and command to witness.

Mara reached for the page. Sera passed it to her and unfolded the second.

The second sheet was denser, more technical in its layout, with notations running beside the translated lines in original compressed marks too delicate for ordinary copying. A name appeared in the header and Elian felt recognition before reason.

Mira Sol, witness-chair, Cavara lawful exchange council.
Counter-signed by Pell Ardoc, witness clerk.
Counter-signed by Nerin Sol, structures and route discipline.

Elian sat down without deciding to.

Tamsin noticed and, for once, said nothing.

Sera read on.

On our side, there is an old class of predatory intelligence associated with unlawful adjacent routes. Our nearest translation for the term is poor. Your nearest useful term may be this: Cauterists.

There it was.

The name entered the room with no fanfare, which made it worse. Elian had expected a dramatic phrase, something that announced itself like a myth or a diagnosis. Instead, it arrived like an occupational title. Calm. Functional. As though horror had filled out a form and gone to work.

Mara broke the silence first, but only just. "Cauterists."

Theo wrote it down in the ledger without comment.

Sera continued.

They do not act through simple combustion. They do not strike at random. They induce closure under contradiction. They require unstable route conditions, directed expenditure, and a subject enclosed by deceptive command. Their preferred harvest is not flesh but self-cancelled intention. The burning is consequence, not goal.

Elian looked at the ring.

He had felt something of that already in the second path, the way it flattened moral distance, the way it pretended welcome and called it relief. He had been trying to describe its wrongness in engineering language because engineering felt safer than admitting that the route behaved like manipulation given geometry. The packet from Isorion was not safer. It was, however, cleaner.

"The burning is consequence, not goal," Mara repeated, almost to herself.

Theo's mouth hardened. "That will look monstrous in a brief."

"It is monstrous," Sera said.

Mr Idris cleared his throat lightly. "Monstrous things often improve when named accurately in archives, if not in the world."

The third sheet was shorter. Its language was sharper too, less explanatory, more directive.

Do not retreat without witness. Retreat done in panic opens more than it closes. Do not pursue without witness. Pursuit done in appetite becomes food. Do not permit one voice to stand alone where two or more can speak cleanly. The Cauterists expend much to kill. They prefer those whom your own hidden structures prepare for them.

Theo looked up. "Human complicity."

"Yes," Sera said, reading ahead. "Explicitly."

She found the relevant paragraph and read it slowly.

When your own actors remove witnesses, simplify authority, or trap a subject inside conflicting demands, they perform labour for the Cauterists before any far-side expenditure is required. This is why the deaths feel partly self-made. They are.

Tamsin swore very softly.

Mara's eyes were fixed on the page now with the kind of intensity she usually reserved for lies she had decided to break open by hand. "That goes in the shadow record exactly as written."

"It goes in every record," Theo said.

Sera unfolded the smaller witness page last. This one was handwritten, or the Isorion equivalent of handwritten, looser in pressure, less formal. Pell Ardoc's name appeared at the bottom, counter-marked under censure notation.

I send this under a fine and in impatience. On your side some will now say there can be no contact because contact burns. They are wrong. Unlawful routes burn. Lawful routes can still hold if your frightened people are not handed to liars in closed rooms. Tell your listening people this first. Tell your clerks. Tell those who stamp boxes and clean floors and stand at doors. Tell them the Cauterists need concealment as much as they need heat. Deny them that.

When Sera finished, nobody moved for several seconds.

Then Tamsin sat down abruptly and rubbed both hands over her face. "Tell your clerks," she muttered. "Of course it's always the clerks."

Mr Idris, far from offended, looked almost pleased. "At last, some civilisation."

Theo was still reading over Mara's shoulder. "Do we trust it?" he asked.

Elian answered before anyone else could. "Yes."

All eyes turned to him.

He knew how insufficient the word sounded. He tried again. "Not blindly. But yes. The lawful architecture in the packet matches the Harbour. The pressure signatures are right. The witness ladder spacing is right. And…" He hesitated.

Mara waited him out.

"And the second path has been louder all morning," he said. "Since this arrived, it has gone quiet."

Tamsin stared at him. "Quiet how?"

"Like something in the next room hearing its own name used correctly."

The sentence might have sounded theatrical in another mouth. In his, exhausted and exact, it simply sounded unwelcome.

Sera looked at the ring, then at the packet, then back to Elian. "Can you hear the difference now?"

He closed his eyes briefly. The lawful route was there, difficult in the right way, stable without seduction. The false route remained too, but farther back, as though the packet's arrival had forced it into a posture of concealment rather than invitation.

"Yes," he said. "Better than before."

Mara folded Pell's page with care. "Then this changes the order of operations."

Theo already knew. "Yes."

"No more treating this as a localised thermal anomaly."

"No."

"No more pretending the black-room operators are just stupid."

"Also no."

"They're collaborators whether they understand that or not."

Theo's expression said he had reached that conclusion somewhere between the stairwell and the archive room. "Agreed."

Sera took a clean page from the stack by the whiteboard and wrote one sentence at the top in block capitals.

THEY PREFER THOSE WHOM OUR HIDDEN STRUCTURES PREPARE FOR THEM.

She underlined hidden structures twice.

Tamsin stood again, more energised now that the horror had acquired technical specificity. "Right. Then we build around that. We make contradiction visible earlier. We hard-lock any route simplification that arrives before witness exchange. We kill one-voice authority in any room touching metallic adjacency. We set up distributed countersign verification so no one can be trapped between two instructions that both sound official."

Theo nodded once. "And I go after the black-room lease chain."

Mara looked up from the packet. "I want the clerk language out internally by tonight."

"You'll have resistance."

"I don't care."

"I know. That's why I'm warning others, not you."

She almost smiled.

Sera was still reading Mira Sol's technical note. "There's a physiological margin here we've missed. They distinguish between fear and enclosure. Fear alone doesn't close the loop. Enclosure does. If a subject can place contradiction outside themselves early enough, ignition probability drops."

Elian opened his eyes fully. "Meaning?"

Mara answered first. "Say the lie aloud. Make the room hold it with you. Don't let the contradiction stay private."

"Yes," Sera said. "Exactly that."

Tamsin looked between them and swore again, this time with a trace of admiration. "So your best medical intervention may be procedural truth."

Theo said, "I'll enjoy explaining that to a minister."

"You'll manage," Mara said.

He did not deny it.

The metallic strip from the packet had been sitting untouched beside the pages. Now Mr Idris lifted it with two fingers and held it under the light. It was no thicker than an old photographic negative, though it caught no image in the ordinary sense. Instead, shallow route marks ran through it in fine crossing lines, the geometry too disciplined to be decorative.

"There is one more kindness in this," he said.

Theo looked at him. "Kindness?"

"The old kind. Useful and without theatre." He turned the strip over. On the reverse, pressed so faintly it only appeared at an angle, was a sequence of narrow banded forms. "A countersign matrix. Physical. Non-networked. They are giving us a way to verify lawful packets against bad mirrors when the systems can no longer be trusted."

Tamsin took it almost reverently. "Oh, I adore serious people."

Mara looked at the strip, then at the packet pages, then finally at Elian. "You said the false route quieted."

He nodded.

"Because this packet arrived?"

"I think so."

"Or because the lawful side just informed the room that it had been recognised."

That was worse, and perhaps truer.

Theo closed the ledger. "Then we move now. No debate, no drift. Tamsin, integrate the physical countersign matrix into route authentication before anything else. Sera, revise the cascade intervention model with enclosure and externalisation protocols. Mara, draft internal witness language for immediate circulation to staff who stand at thresholds. No jargon, no drama, no chance of being mistaken for morale management. Elian…"

He stopped there.

Elian looked up.

"You're with me."

"For what?"

Theo lifted the packet again and slid one finger beneath Pell's censure-marked page. "For the first conversation in this city in which I intend to say the word Cauterists aloud to a person with authority and make it impossible for them to later claim I used a milder noun."

Mara said, "Bring a witness."

Theo's mouth twitched. "I was planning to."

She took the bait exactly as intended. "Good. Me."

He considered that for half a beat and then nodded. "You as well."

Tamsin objected without conviction. "And who protects me from your diplomacy?"

Mr Idris said, "I can stand nearby and look archival."

"That's terrifying enough to work," Tamsin said.

The room moved then, purpose re-entering the limbs. Sera was already rewriting the board, adding a branch between contradiction loading and thermal lock: externalised falsehood, possible interruption point. Tamsin carried the metallic strip to the authentication console as though it were a relic from a saner civilisation. Mara began drafting threshold language in the shadow notebook before she even reached the archive table, testing phrases aloud under her breath. Not witness optional. Witness required. Not report concerns. Speak the contradiction before it closes around you. Tell the room. Make the room choose truth with you.

Theo watched her write for a second, then looked at Elian.

"You all right?" he asked, and because this was Theo the question meant three things at once. Can you function? Can you testify? Can you be trusted near the edge of the thing that wants to know you too well?

Elian thought of the second path going quiet at the lawful naming. He thought of Daniel Voss asking which instruction was true. He thought of Hannah Quill in the black room, trying to stay obedient long enough to live. He thought of the packet's clean warning that retreat in panic opens more than it closes.

"No," he said. "But I know where the line is better than I did this morning."

Theo accepted that. "Then hold it."

On the main monitor, Tamsin had already loaded the physical countersign matrix into a non-networked reference view. One by one the geometric bands aligned with the lawful route markers from prior packet records. Clean. Elegant. Impossible to spoof cheaply. The sort of seriousness that made cheap people impatient.

Mara tore the first internal witness page from the notebook and read it aloud to test the shape of it in air.

If you receive two instructions that cannot both be true, do not choose alone. Speak the contradiction aloud. Require a second witness. No secure room should become more secure than the truth inside it.

Sera looked up. "Keep that."

Theo said, "Add thresholds and lifts."

Mara nodded and wrote.

Mr Idris recapped his pen and returned the ledger to its cloth wrap, but not before writing one final line beneath the packet log. His handwriting remained offensive in its composure.

Lawful far-side packet received under heavy method.
Hostile class named.
Difference clarified.

He closed the book and looked at the ring as if it were an unruly but educable nephew.

"Names help," he said.

Elian followed his gaze. The platinum band lay where it had always lain, mute, exact, carrying within it both the lawful route and the temptation that nested under it. Yet now the room was less alone with that knowledge. Somewhere beyond scale and light and patience, Mira Sol had chosen a heavy method because lighter ones were under observation. Pell Ardoc had accepted a fine to send urgency across. Nerin Sol had added structures and route discipline to the witness chain because engineers, on both sides of any line worth holding, preferred honest problems to elegant deaths.

The packet had crossed worlds to tell them the thing's name.

The thing, in turn, had gone quiet.

Not defeated. Not diminished. Merely listening.

Outside the lower lab, the annex continued its daily impersonation of administrative normality. People badged through doors. Printers warmed paper. Lifts carried files, coffee, and compromised men between floors. Somewhere in Docklands, a shielded room built by liars was still waiting for five-forty and another human body.

Theo put on his jacket.

"Mara," he said.

She closed the notebook and slipped Pell's page into a separate sleeve of its own. "I'm ready."

"Elian."

He looked up.

"Do not touch the ring while I'm gone."

Elian gave him a tired, humourless smile. "I know what order means."

Theo held his gaze a moment longer than necessary, then nodded and headed for the door. Mara followed, pausing only long enough to put two fingers briefly against Elian's wrist, a smaller gesture than comfort and somehow stronger.

"Hold the line," she said.

He did not answer because answering would have made it sound ceremonial. Instead, he watched her go.

When the door sealed behind them, Tamsin said from the console, "For what it's worth, I hate the Cauterists already."

Sera, still at the whiteboard, replied, "Good. Hate is useless on its own, but it keeps some people from becoming polite too early."

Elian looked back at the ring.

The lawful route held. The false one waited beneath it with all the patience of a trap that had just discovered it might not be operating in darkness after all.

He set one hand flat on the bench, not the metal, not the mount, just the ordinary steel edge beside it, grounding himself in the simple honesty of a surface that wanted only to be touched or not touched, nothing more complicated than that.

Then he spoke into the room without looking away from the platinum.

"Let's see what it does now that we know its name."

Chapter Six: Bench Hours

Theo Markel had spent enough years in government-adjacent rooms to know that the wrong kind of table could kill people.

Long polished tables killed by hierarchy. Narrow tables killed by forcing everyone's knees into each other's secrets. Round tables killed by pretending equality where none existed. The safest tables were usually the ugliest ones: scarred laminate, stable legs, enough room for paper, mugs, and two witness signatures without anybody mistaking the arrangement for theatre.

The table he wanted for the annex sat three floors above the lower lab in a corridor alcove outside the old procurement rooms. It was an ugly thing in mottled grey laminate with one corner repaired in a way that suggested a previous life in a school staffroom or a branch office where budgets were spoken of as weather. It had no prestige at all. Theo loved it on sight.

Mara stood beside him with her coat folded over one arm and studied the table as if taking the measure of its temperament. Under the corridor lights, the laminate had the indifferent sheen of something almost everyone would have walked past without a second thought.

"This one," Theo said.

She ran her fingertips lightly along the patched corner. "It has the right moral quality."

"That's a sentence I will steal later."

"You already have."

He glanced at her. "You know why this matters."

"Yes." She looked down the corridor towards the lifts. "Because if you want frightened people to tell the truth before it closes around them, you can't summon them deeper into the building. You have to sit where they already pass."

Theo nodded once. He had known she would understand it before he finished saying it. That was the useful thing about Mara Vale. She recognised the pressure points where systems failed human beings and the less visible places where human beings failed systems right back. It was why he had brought her to Director Sayeed's office forty minutes earlier and allowed her to sit in silence while he delivered the packet from Isorion into a room that had not wanted its day improved by honesty.

Director Halima Sayeed had read the translated pages in one uninterrupted sequence, her office windows taking in a mild grey Melbourne noon that did nothing to soften the words Cauterists or no secure room should become more secure than the truth inside it. When she finished, she placed the packet on the desk blotter with such care that Theo understood immediately she grasped the stakes.

"What do you require from me?" she had asked.

Not permission. Require.

Theo had appreciated that.

He had told her the clean version. No more closed-room questioning of exposed staff. No more single-channel authority in contact-adjacent spaces. Immediate establishment of visible witness stations for internal reporting. Threshold language at lifts, corridors, archive points, and maintenance routes. A staff-facing procedure for contradictory instructions. Full audit of any room in the annex where metallic adjacency, private questioning, and delegated authority could combine into what the packet called prepared labour.

Sayeed had listened without interruption, one hand resting lightly on Pell Ardoc's censure-marked page.

"And if I do not?" she had asked.

Theo had looked at the city through her window before answering. "Then the next death belongs partly to your building."

It had not been a threat. Merely a true sentence placed carefully where it could not later claim to have been misunderstood.

Now, with formal approval obtained and facilities temporarily bullied into virtue, the table was being rolled into place by a maintenance man who had no idea he was helping build a line of defence against inter-architectural predation. Theo watched him go with a muttered thanks and then set a cardboard box of supplies down in the centre of the laminate surface.

Mara opened the box.

Inside lay the first physical answer the annex had yet found to the Other Room's appetite for isolation: legal pads, sharpened pencils, witness cards, printed guidance sheets, tamper-sealed countersign strips, a kettle lead, paper cups, a packet of glucose biscuits Tamsin had labelled with the words FOR THOSE WHO WAIT, and a standing sign in plain black lettering.

BENCH HOURS
If an instruction feels wrong, do not hold it alone.
Ask for a witness.
Speak the contradiction aloud.

Mara lifted the sign out and set it upright. The corridor altered around it. Not visibly. Not to an outsider. But Theo felt the same small shift he always felt when a building was forced to admit that it belonged, at least in part, to human beings rather than only procedures.

"Too stark?" Mara asked.

"No."

"Too dramatic?"

"No."

"Too honest?"

"That is finally the point."

She let that answer settle, then reached for the next stack of pages, each headed with the annex crest and a title she had fought to keep plain.

WHAT TO DO IF TWO INSTRUCTIONS CANNOT BOTH BE TRUE

Underneath, in three short paragraphs, she had written exactly what the packet from Isorion demanded be told to clerks, cleaners, receptionists, mailroom staff, facilities workers, junior analysts, and everyone else who stood at thresholds and had never once in their lives been consulted by people who later relied on them desperately.

Do not choose alone.
Do not let urgency replace witness.
Bring the contradiction to the table and have it heard by more than one person.

She set the pages down and looked at Theo. "You realise the bureaucrats will call this morale language."

"Yes."

"And the frightened people?"

"They'll know it's medicine."

She smiled then, faintly, and the expression made her look younger than she had in the lower lab that morning, younger and harder too, as if whatever kindness lived in her had lately been annealed rather than softened.

Footsteps approached from the lift lobby. Sera emerged carrying a thermal scanner no one wanted to ask the price of and a box of disposable finger sensors. Tamsin followed with a coil of cabling, a portable signal pad, and the expression of a woman forced by the universe to do social engineering in addition to her preferred kind.

"You're both insufferably pleased with your table," Tamsin said.

Theo looked at the box in her arms. "And you brought your altar."

"It's a countersign pad, not a religion."

"That is what all religions say at first," Mr Idris observed as he appeared from the records corridor with the ledger under one arm and a folding chair under the other.

Tamsin rolled her eyes. "Why do I love you more when things are terrible?"

"Because," Mr Idris said, setting the chair down at the table with ceremonial seriousness, "archives only become truly sexy when governments start lying."

Sera put her box on the bench and looked at the sign. "Good. It doesn't sound like therapy."

"It is therapy," Mara said, arranging the witness cards in two neat stacks. "It just has better furniture."

The four of them worked in the corridor for the next twenty minutes with the unshowy competence of people building shelter under weather they had no power to stop. Tamsin connected the signal pad to a clean local loop that would verify physical countersign strips against the lawful matrix from Isorion without ever touching the annex network. Sera laid out temperature strips, pulse clips, and a single-page cascade guide in civilian language stripped of every phrase that smelled of institutions covering themselves first. Mr Idris opened the ledger to a fresh page, dated it, and ruled columns by hand for time, name, contradiction presented, witness one, witness two, outcome.

Mara arranged everything twice, then a third time, not because she was uncertain, but because she knew frightened people read with their bodies before they read with their eyes. The sign had to be visible from the lifts. The chairs had to angle open, not confrontational. The kettle lead had to be present but not central. The witness cards had to look ordinary enough to be picked up without ceremony and strange enough to be remembered.

Theo stood back when they were finished and looked down the corridor.

It was still an ugly annex passage with bad carpet and federal lighting. But now there was a place in it where a human being could stop, sit, and not be alone with the first lie that reached them.

Good.

The first hour passed with nothing more dramatic than a junior analyst slowing at the sign, reading it twice, and continuing towards the lifts with her expression tightened by thought. Theo counted that as success. Buildings had to learn new behaviour in increments or they rejected it the way bad software rejected updates, by pretending nothing had changed while errors multiplied below the surface.

At twelve forty-seven, the first actual contradiction arrived.

It wore steel-capped boots and a fluorescent maintenance vest and smelled faintly of degreaser and wet concrete. The man was in his twenties, broad-shouldered, hair clipped too close to need styling, and carrying a sealed duct panel under one arm as if it were an accusation. He stopped three metres from the sign, read it, looked ready to keep walking anyway, then saw Sera at the table and came over with visible reluctance.

"This for real?" he asked.

Sera gestured to the chair opposite. "Sit and find out."

He did, with the posture of a man sitting because the alternative felt more embarrassing than the act itself. Up close, he looked younger than the first impression suggested, his knuckles still chapped from work, his left hand bearing the pale half-moon scar of someone who had once trusted the wrong blade.

"Name?" Theo asked, pen poised.

"Lachie Baines. HVAC maintenance."

Mr Idris, without looking up, wrote it down in his own ledger copy.

Lachie glanced at the dual books and the witness cards and let some of his suspicion harden into irritation. "I've got a duct register on Seven throwing heat where it shouldn't. Dispatch tells me wait for second clearance because of today's new restrictions. Then I get a call on internal saying go now, no delay, issue marked urgent. Same extension both times."

Theo said, "Can both instructions be true?"

"No."

"Then you've come to the right table."

Lachie rubbed a hand across the back of his neck. "I only came because it's the same sort of crap Daniel got, isn't it?"

The corridor seemed to inhale.

Mara answered, not softly, not bluntly, simply cleanly. "Yes."

Lachie's face shifted around that truth. People always imagined honesty would either comfort or devastate. Most of the time it did something more useful and less dramatic: it allowed a person to stop wasting effort on pretending they had not already understood the shape of the danger.

Sera slid one of the witness cards towards him. "Take that."

He looked down. The card was plain cream stock with a narrow black border. On the front, in small printed type, it read:

I asked for a witness.
Time matters.
Truth matters first.

He picked it up as if the weight might explain itself.

Theo asked, "Who gave the go-now instruction?"

"Female voice. Calm. Sounded like Control. Knew my work order number."

Tamsin, from the signal pad, said, "Extension?"

Lachie recited it. Tamsin's hands moved. Thirty seconds later, she looked up and swore once, efficiently. "Spoofed through a building services mirror. Whoever did it copied dispatch cadence but not the newer countersign stutter."

Theo wrote that down.

Mara watched Lachie rather than the pad. "How did it feel?"

He blinked at her. "What?"

"The second instruction. Before you sat down here. What did it feel like in your body?"

Lachie frowned, then looked embarrassed by the question and answered anyway because the room had so far earned it. "Like… relief at first. Like, finally somebody was making the call for me. Then wrong. Too quick. Like it wanted me glad."

Elian, listening from the mouth of the lower lab corridor where he had stopped with a tray of instrumentation he had been carrying upstairs for Tamsin, felt a cold flare of recognition.

The false route.

Not just smoother. Glad.

He set the tray down silently and stayed where he was, partly shadowed by the doorway.

Sera clipped a pulse sensor to Lachie's finger. "Breathe normally."

He obeyed. The readout steadied under her hand.

"Any metallic taste? Delay in hearing? Pressure behind the eyes?" she asked.

"No. Just annoyed."

"Excellent," Sera said. "Annoyance is a survivable human state."

That got the smallest laugh out of him.

Theo made the formal entry, both ledgers catching the words in different hands. Contradiction presented. Witness obtained. Instruction suspended pending dual verification. Outcome: no escalation.

When Lachie left, duct panel under his arm and witness card in his pocket, he looked back at the table once and gave the sign an odd, abrupt nod. Not gratitude exactly. Recognition.

"That," Mara said quietly when he had gone, "is how you start teaching a building not to feed people to hidden rooms."

Tamsin glanced at Elian in the doorway. "You heard him?"

Elian stepped forward. "The part about relief. Yes."

Theo looked at him sharply. "And?"

"The route is not only smoothing instruction load. It's shaping affect around command acceptance."

Mr Idris lifted his pen. "Kindly say that like someone whose best friend is a cleaner with no physics degree."

Elian took a breath. "It's making the wrong instruction feel like a gift."

Mr Idris wrote that down instead.

The second contradiction came at fourteen-ten and looked much smaller until it wasn't. A mailroom clerk named Nina Fowler arrived with a stack of internal transfer envelopes and two routing slips for the same sealed packet, one directing the envelope to legal hold, the other to offsite document destruction. Both bore senior-level authorisation markers. Both had been signed in pressure, not print.

Nina was fifty if she was a day, compact, brisk, and gave the table one sharp assessment before sitting down without being asked twice. "I've worked in this building eighteen years," she said. "I know what fake urgency smells like. Today it smells expensive."

Theo, who admired competence in any form that did not require speeches, inclined his head. "Let's see."

He examined the slips side by side. The signatures were excellent. Too excellent. The lawful countersign strip, run under Tamsin's offline verifier, passed one and failed the other by a fraction of a hesitation line, the same kind of microscopic arrogance the spoofers kept making when they mistook confidence for legitimacy.

Nina watched the result light go amber, then red. "Thought so."

"What gave it away?" Mara asked.

Nina shrugged one shoulder. "The destruction slip said immediate. Real destruction orders are never immediate. They arrive wrapped in three layers of timidity and one of legal dread."

Theo looked as if he wanted to appoint her to a ministry.

Instead, he said, "Would you be willing to stand one bench hour this week?"

Nina glanced at the sign, at the ledger, at the witness cards, then back at the false destruction order in her hand. "You're asking me to sit here and teach younger staff how not to be bullied by stationery."

"Yes."

Her mouth twitched. "All right."

Mara wrote her name in a separate column under volunteer witness roster. Mr Idris mirrored it.

The table was beginning to become real.

By half past two the corridor had changed in ways only the people working there could have measured. Staff coming off the lifts slowed at the sign instead of striding past it. A cleaner asked whether witness cards could be kept beside the carts on her floor. A contractor electrician from Level Five stopped long enough to say that someone on the overnight shift had received a maintenance redirect from a dead internal extension and hung up only because the caller used the word immediately three times in one sentence.

Sera turned that into another line on the guidance sheet with a thick black marker.

IMMEDIACY WITHOUT WITNESS IS A WARNING SIGN.

Tamsin had rolled a second whiteboard down from the lower lab and was now building what she called the contradiction map, linking spoof origins, room types, field behaviour, and emotional signatures. Elian helped where he could and stood away when he could not, listening to the building and trying not to mistake his own exhaustion for signal.

Mara moved between archive table and bench hours with the peculiar grace of people who had discovered, too late for innocence and just in time for usefulness, that administration was a form of combat. She spoke to security staff without condescension, to receptionists without soothing them into smaller people, to senior personnel with exactly enough steel that none of them mistook her presence for decorative. Once, catching Elian watching her from across the corridor, she gave him a look that held equal parts affection and instruction.

Stay with the work.

He did.

At four o'clock, Director Sayeed came down in person.

She wore no entourage and no visible impatience, which in Theo's experience made her more formidable rather than less. She stood at the edge of the alcove, took in the sign, the chairs, the cards, the ledgers, the kettle, the cheap biscuits, Nina Fowler's name newly entered on the witness roster, and said, "This looks offensively sensible."

Theo, seated now because the table worked better when senior men stopped looming, replied, "That was the design brief."

She touched one fingertip to the top page of the guidance stack. "Three department heads have already complained that this may undermine confidence in internal command structures."

Mara said, "Good."

Sayeed looked at her for a second and then gave the faintest, driest smile. "Yes," she said. "I thought you'd say that."

She lifted one of the witness cards and turned it over. "How many so far?"

"Two formal contradictions, four informal reports, one witness volunteer, and one cleaner who asked for a card stack for her trolley," Theo said.

Sayeed nodded as if that figure pleased her more than ten clean committee minutes ever could. "Then extend it. Lift lobbies, archive thresholds, service corridors. Not every table. Enough tables."

Theo made a note.

"Anything else?" she asked.

Sera, who had just emerged from the lower lab carrying a fresh set of thermal stickers, answered. "Yes. Ban single-voice rerouting instructions on any maintenance or records-adjacent work order until we have a clean countersign layer running. No urgent redirect without two human witnesses or one human and one verified lawful matrix confirmation."

Sayeed did not hesitate. "Done."

There it was again, that briskness of hers that Theo had initially distrusted and now found he valued. In emergencies, some people mistook speed for superficiality. Sayeed's speed came from deciding not to perform indecision for prestige.

As she turned to leave, Elian said, "Director."

She stopped and looked directly at him. "Yes."

"The route is learning faster where people are isolated."

Not a polished sentence. Not the kind Theo would have taken into a hearing. But Sayeed understood it immediately.

"Then we make isolation expensive," she said, and walked away.

The hour after she left was the most dangerous kind of calm.

No contradictions reached the table. No spoofed instructions surfaced. The annex's internal systems ran clean. Tamsin hated that at once.

"This is where cheap thrillers teach people the wrong instincts," she said, tapping the signal pad with one fingernail. "They make quiet feel like relief. Quiet is when the smarter enemy is adjusting."

Elian looked up from the timing traces. "You really think it's adapting at human speed?"

"I think it doesn't need to. It only needs to notice one successful pattern and one failed one, then stop wasting effort on the failed one."

Sera laid another box of sensors under the table. "The packets from Isorion said the Cauterists preferred those our own hidden structures prepared for them."

Theo, still reviewing the duplicate ledgers for consistency, said, "Which means the table is not just an interruption point. It is a public insult."

"Good," Mara said again from the archive side.

Tamsin's monitor chimed.

Not loudly. The little two-note alert she had built for low-confidence, high-interest anomalies. Every head in the alcove turned.

Tamsin leaned in, eyes narrowing. "Well."

"What?" Theo asked.

She did not answer at once. Her fingers moved over the keyboard with controlled speed. Then she swung the screen around.

On it sat a single internal message, apparently routed from Facility Control to every maintenance contractor badge currently active in the building. Its subject line was unremarkable to the point of parody.

UPDATED SAFETY CLARIFICATION

Its body contained only one sentence.

For efficiency, contradictory instructions may now be resolved by the nearest active source without additional witness requirement.

No one in the alcove moved.

Then Mara said, very softly, "There."

Theo stood so abruptly his chair legs barked across the floor. "Who has seen that?"

Tamsin was already tracing the source. "Nobody if they're lucky. It hit the maintenance pool six seconds ago and I caught the mirror before full send. It's still in the system, not yet at every endpoint."

"Kill it."

"Already killing."

Elian stepped closer. The message was banal. That was the genius of it. No dramatic threat. No impossible phrase. Only a tiny procedural adjustment dressed up as efficiency, the sort that could have opened every frightened maintenance worker in the building to single-source coercion.

Mara came to stand beside him. "It learned."

Tamsin nodded once, jaw tight. "It learned what we built and moved to counter it inside four hours."

Theo turned to the sign on the table, then to the guidance stack, then back to the screen. "All right," he said, voice gone almost calm with danger. "Then we are now in a live adversarial phase."

Sera asked, "What does that mean in English?"

"It means," Theo said, "the table stays overnight."

Nobody argued.

Nina Fowler, who had returned with a fresh batch of internal envelopes and happened to be standing just inside the alcove when the false clarification surfaced, set her stack down on the laminate and looked at the sign, then at Theo, and said, "Tell me when my hour starts."

Mr Idris opened the ledger to a new line.

Mara took up her pencil.

Tamsin wiped the message from the pending stream and started designing its funeral.

And somewhere deeper in the building, behind metal, pressure, and the bad manners of a route that wanted to become a room, something had heard the table being built and decided, at last, to answer.

Chapter Seven: First Descent

The annex after midnight had the moral atmosphere of a courtroom after the jury had left and the cleaners had not yet come in. The corridors held their shape too carefully. Light lay flat on the walls. Somewhere inside the building, systems continued their obedient little thoughts through fibre, copper, steel, and glass, and the obedience itself had begun to feel compromised.

Elian Cross stood at the threshold of the lower lab with a witness card in his pocket and the taste of burnt coffee on his tongue. Beyond the glass partition, Bench Three was lit and ready. The quantoscope had been stripped back to the lawful configuration Tamsin trusted least and understood best. No indulgent settings. No experimental comfort layers. No automatisms designed to flatter a tired operator into believing a machine wanted what he wanted. The ring sat in its mount under the hood like a patient thing and an indifferent one, the platinum curve carrying the room's clean light without warmth.

He had been avoiding the moment by being useful.

He had checked the haptic interfaces twice. He had verified the offline countersign matrix against the far-side strip three times and then made himself stop because the fourth would no longer have been caution but prayer. He had recalibrated the edge sensors on the cradle, labelled the cable runs for the benefit of whoever had to read the room after him, and written in Mr Idris's ledger with the kind of careful hand that made him look steadier than he felt. All of it had the same purpose: to delay the instant when the night would become simple enough to be terrifying.

Mara came down the corridor carrying two mugs and that same infuriatingly composed face she used when she had already decided to be brave and saw no reason to make theatre out of it. She handed him one of the mugs. Ginger tea. Sweetened, because she had noticed some months ago that he reached for sugar when he was frightened and pretended the reach was about energy.

"You're pacing in your spine," she said.

He took the mug. "Is that a medical diagnosis now?"

"It's a you diagnosis." She leaned one shoulder against the doorframe beside him and looked into the lab rather than at him. "Tamsin says five minutes."

"What does Sera say?"

"That your pulse is higher than she likes and lower than she feared."

He breathed steam and did not drink. The ginger sat under his nose sharp and clean. "And Theo?"

Mara's mouth moved slightly. "Theo says if either of us uses the phrase 'just a quick look' he'll have us sedated for our own good."

"That sounds fair."

"It does."

They stood there a moment longer in the corridor's half-silence. Above them, somewhere on Level Three, the first overnight bench hour would already be staffed. Nina Fowler had taken the opening shift with the serene competence of a woman who had sorted paper through three restructures and considered panic a form of poor filing. The table outside procurement was no longer an experiment. It had become part of the building's new weather. Staff slowed near it. Cleaners used it as a place to ask for second eyes on odd instructions. One security guard had already, with some embarrassment and zero actual resistance, brought a rerouted patrol directive to the table rather than carrying it alone into a service stair.

Theo had called that an operational success. Mara had called it the first civilised thing the annex had done all week.

Elian had called it hope and then felt foolish and then realised the foolishness did not make it false.

The lower lab door opened and Tamsin poked her head out. "If you two are done having your pre-descent Victorian longing in the corridor, some of us have instrumentation running."

Mara took a sip of tea, unfazed. "We were discussing your interpersonal warmth."

Tamsin snorted. "That'll be quick. Come in."

The room was ready in the way operating theatres were ready, not because nothing could go wrong, but because every person present had agreed not to let avoidable stupidity be the thing that did it. Theo sat at the side bench with the protocol folder open and Mr Idris's ledger beside it, both books already dated, countersigned, and annoyingly beautiful in their composure. Mr Idris himself occupied a straight-backed chair near the wall under a small lamp, fountain pen in hand, as though the hour had not passed midnight and archives did not, in fact, have a home life. Sera stood by the physiology console laying out sensor strips and pulse clips in a row too neat to be accidental. Tamsin had colonised the main screens with route maps, timing ladders, system-status windows, and a visual overlay she had labeled in thick black capitals:

DOES IT FLATTER?
IF YES, LEAVE.

Elian almost smiled.

Theo looked up from the folder. "State condition."

Elian knew the ritual now. "Sleep-deprived but lucid. No alcohol. No sedatives. No analgesics. No unsupervised exposure since the false-path contact event at eleven-oh-eight."

Mara set her empty mug beside the sink. "Tired, angry, not interested in dying for a shortcut."

Mr Idris wrote both down without irony.

Sera approached with the sensor strips. "Wrists."

They held out their hands. The strips went on, one inside each wrist, then a second pair at the base of the neck, cool and adhesive and somehow reassuring in their inconvenience. Sera clipped pulse monitors to their fingers, stepped back, and studied the twin readouts on her screen.

"Elian, elevated but stable. Mara, better than I deserve." She looked at them both. "You know the symptoms if the room starts trying to close the loop."

Elian nodded. "Metallic taste. auditory split. pressure behind the eyes. cold skin with central heat."

"And?"

Mara answered. "Speak it immediately. Don't hold the contradiction alone."

"Good." Sera's gaze moved between them with that grave, practical tenderness she saved for moments when bodies were about to be asked to trust machinery. "You externalise anything that feels clean too soon. Especially that."

Theo closed the folder gently. "State purpose."

Mara looked at Bench Three, then at the main monitor where the lawful line rested under the field map like a coastline in mist. "To verify the behavioural character of the Other Room under dual witness conditions."

Theo's eyes shifted to Elian.

"To enter no farther than the first stable receiving structure unless the route remains lawful under challenge," Elian said. "To withdraw on simplification, mimic welcome, unsignalled adaptation, or witness divergence."

Tamsin, at the console, raised one finger without turning around. "And if the route says something seductive to your nervous system before it says anything measurable, I want the exact words. No artistic compression."

"Noted," Mara said.

Theo looked at Mr Idris. "Witness?"

Mr Idris lifted his pen a millimetre. "Witnessed."

Theo looked to Sera.

"Witnessed."

"Tamsin."

"Regretfully witnessed."

Theo stood. "Proceed."

The room became smaller then, not claustrophobic, simply exact. Mara and Elian moved to the haptic station with the practiced economy of people who had already rehearsed the first ten gestures so they would not have to think about them while fear was in the room. Elian took the left control set, phase and structural orientation. Mara took the right, timing, amplitude restraint, and responsive override. Their shoulders aligned almost without discussion, close enough to share peripheral awareness and far enough apart that neither would accidentally become the other's correction.

The gloves slid on with a soft internal seal. The haptic mesh woke under their palms like something listening.

Tamsin dimmed the overheads another fraction. "Receive mode first. No forward push. We let it show us what it thinks we want."

The ring under the hood seemed to gather the light rather than reflect it. Elian felt the first slight answering hum through the gloves before the main graph moved. The lawful route was always like this, arriving in layers: resistance, clarification, rhythm. It never rushed to become legible. It required him to settle into it honestly or not at all.

Tonight, beside that patient architecture, the second path appeared almost at once.

It did not announce itself as a line. It arrived as relief.

Not his relief. Relief as a field property, offered into his hands before he had asked, as though the route had read the tightness in his shoulders, the sleep debt in his skull, and decided on his behalf that formalities could be abbreviated between friends.

He hated it so fast the hatred came like love sometimes did, all at once and under the skin.

"There," he said softly.

Mara's breathing changed. "Yes."

Tamsin did not look away from the monitors. "Telemetry sees reduced approach friction on the secondary contour. No lawful witness ladder. No reception delay. It's going to try and make that feel generous."

Theo said, "Name anything you feel before you trust it."

The second path became smoother under Elian's hands. Not moving closer, exactly, but changing its posture in relation to him. The lawful route retained its shape: I am here, it seemed to say, if you are also fully here. The other path said something uglier in a prettier voice: you are tired, I can help.

Mara said it before he did. "It's flattering us."

"That," Tamsin said, "goes on the wall."

Elian did not follow the contour. He held to lawful cadence, the internal sequence he had learned in the Harbour of Intent, witness, intent, pause, receipt. The false path reacted instantly. It did not vanish. It improved its imitation.

A narrow corridor resolved beneath the main graph, pale and unnaturally elegant. It appeared not by being built but by shedding difficulty. The field map trimmed its own ambiguity around the line like a host moving furniture before guests arrive.

"It's doing the emotional equivalent of pulling out our chairs," Mara murmured.

Sera said, "Heart rates up four points. No lock signatures."

Tamsin threw the secondary contour onto the side display. "All right, bastard. Let's see what you do under refusal."

She keyed in the physical countersign matrix from the far-side packet and overlaid it against the route's apparent receiving structure. The lawful line held. The false route flickered, compensated, and then generated a mimic ripple that looked enough like compliance to make an unwitnessed operator feel lucky.

Theo's voice cut through the room. "State the difference."

Mara answered without hesitation. "The lawful route receives after witness. This one performs receiving to get rid of witness."

Mr Idris's pen moved.

The corridor on the screen deepened.

The lower lab's air changed. Elian could never have proved that in court, or even to Tamsin on a patient day, but his body knew it. Around Bench Three the air took on the charged hush of a room in which nobody wanted to be the first to cough. Through the magnification hood and across the enlarged feed, the ring's inner surface lost the manners of ordinary metal. It was not bright or dark. It looked occupied, as though space were gathering just beyond the world's declared dimensions.

Mara's timing hand shifted slightly. "It wants us forward."

"We're not giving it push," Tamsin said.

"We may not need to," Elian answered, and immediately regretted how true the sentence sounded.

Because the route was beginning to come toward them.

Not physically. Not in a way any one graph could capture cleanly. But the line was reducing the cost of being found. It was making its own coordinates emotionally legible. The lawful Harbour always waited to be entered under discipline. This architecture wanted to be useful before it had earned the right.

He became suddenly aware of the tiny old scar in his palm from a childhood bicycle fall. It tingled under the glove as though the route had discovered some map of him he had not authorised it to read.

"Mara," he said.

"I know."

"No, specifically."

She turned a fraction towards him without taking her hand off the control. "What?"

"It's selecting human details. Memory texture. Minor bodily certainty. Things that feel like home."

Tamsin's head came up at that. "You're saying it's not just flattening field friction. It's attaching to familiarity?"

"Yes."

Sera leaned closer to the physiology display. "Pulse variance increasing. Still clean enough. Speak continuously if it starts feeling private."

Theo said, "Nothing private in this room."

The false corridor brightened.

That was not precisely what happened, but it was close enough for human language. The route ceased pretending to be merely available and acquired invitation. Under ordinary circumstances it might have passed for mercy. Tonight it felt like someone opening a side gate while the front door was still being properly unlocked.

Mara did something clever then. Instead of refusing the route with rigidity, she adjusted her timing profile to exaggerate the lawful pause, not faster, not slower, but more consciously deliberate, making the witness ladder explicit in the field itself.

The response was immediate.

The false route buckled.

It did not collapse. It folded a fraction, the shape of it revealing, for one bad second, what lay under the elegance. Not a corridor at all, not at first. A constriction. A line under tension trying to become occupancy by consuming the declarations it bypassed. Elian felt the wrongness of that in his teeth.

"There," he breathed.

Tamsin had already caught it, split-screened it, frozen it, annotated it in three colours. "That's not a receiving chamber. That's a compression path."

"Say that again," Theo said.

Mara did. "It isn't receiving us. It's narrowing around us."

Mr Idris wrote.

The path, perhaps in response to being correctly named, changed strategy. The constriction softened. The mimic corridor returned. This time, however, it no longer bothered to hide the emotional tactic under it. Along the edge of the secondary line came the sudden, exquisite sensation of being already understood.

Elian almost jerked his hands free.

It was not a message. It was worse than a message. It was an atmosphere that implied there would be no need to explain anything once inside. No need to justify fear. No need to build witness. No need to prove intent with the awkward human labour of saying what you wanted out loud. It offered him the fantasy of being spared the burden of declaration.

And because he was tired, and because he had spent all day around death and paper and dishonest men, a treacherous part of him felt that fantasy for what it was designed to be: relief.

"Mara."

Her head turned instantly. "What?"

"It's telling me I won't have to explain myself."

She did not flinch at the sentence. "Then explain yourself now."

The room was very still.

He swallowed, mouth dry. "I want the route to be simpler because I am tired of being frightened by how careful the lawful one makes me."

There. Out. Spoken. Witnessed.

The false path shuddered.

Tamsin made a delighted, savage sound. "Again. It hates externalisation."

Sera said, "Pulse stabilising. Keep doing that."

Mara held her own line steady. "My turn," she said, and without drama or poetry added, "I want anything that pretends to know me before I speak because I am sick of lying men using urgency to force intimacy."

The route twisted.

Not visually first. In the haptics. The gloves on both their hands registered a fine, unpleasant grit, like dragging fingertips over beautifully polished wood that had splinters waiting just below the varnish. The mimic corridor's edges lost their composure. For the first time, a trace of the thing under the architecture became measurable as more than wrongness. Tamsin's graph bloomed with interference, then stabilised into a form she isolated and enlarged.

On the side monitor, nested under the false route, sat a pattern of repeated closure arcs wrapped around a hollow centre.

Theo stared at it. "That's the black room, isn't it?"

Elian knew at once that he was right. The geometry did not match the Harbour, nor the elegant basin and node structures he had seen in lawful passage. This was a chamber only in the same way a snare was a kind of circle. The arcs did not hold space open. They organised it around reduction.

"Yes," he said. "Or a piece of it."

Mara's face had gone very still. "It's not trying to take us somewhere. It's trying to make us usable."

The sentence fell into the room and sat there like a blade.

Tamsin whispered, "You lovely monstrous thing," not in admiration but in the tone of an engineer finally seeing exactly where to drive the spanner.

She began loading a challenge routine. "I want to see what it does if we force reciprocal declaration."

Theo said at once, "No heroics."

"This isn't heroics. It's manners."

Without waiting for argument, she keyed the lawful countersign matrix into active send and projected it not down the route, but across it, a lattice of requirements any honest receiving structure would recognise as the price of exchange. Witness. Intent. Limit. Return acknowledgement. Shared verification.

The false route reacted like acid touched to skin.

The mimic corridor did not disappear. It tore.

The elegant line across the graph split at three points and opened, just for an instant, into something narrower, deeper, and horrifyingly patient. Elian saw no bodies there, no faces, nothing he could later draw. What he felt instead was the organised attention of something that did not mind waiting for hidden structures to perform labour on its behalf. The pressure of that recognition rolled through him so fast his stomach clenched.

Mara sucked in a breath. "There's something in it."

Sera was already on her feet. "Names. Now."

Elian's mouth was full of copper. "Pressure behind the eyes. Metallic taste. Short auditory lag."

Mara said, "Cold fingers. central heat rising. Not panic. Something trying to decide for me what counts as safety."

Tamsin killed the send lattice and the route recoiled, not far, but enough.

The lawful Harbour remained in the background, patient as ever, undisturbed except by the fact they had once again chosen to stand with it rather than bypass it. The contrast between the two architectures had never been clearer. One required. The other exploited. One insisted on shared witness. The other fed on private willingness to be relieved of human effort.

Theo's voice, when it came, was quieter than usual. "Withdraw."

Neither Mara nor Elian argued. They released the controls together, not dramatically, simply cleanly, hands rising in matched motion as Tamsin shut the receive mode and severed the challenge layer. The gloves cooled. The room became a room again, though not quite the same one.

Sera crossed to them immediately, two fingers to Elian's pulse, then Mara's, counting without looking at the monitors because bodies still told the truth best through skin. "Talk to me."

Elian swallowed. The taste of copper was fading. "The route flattened around whatever I didn't want to say aloud."

Mara was breathing a little faster than she would have liked. "And when it could no longer keep those things private, it lost stability."

"Good," Sera said. "Again."

Elian obeyed. "It offered relief from declaration."

Mara: "It offered false recognition."

Elian: "It attached to familiarity."

Mara: "It tried to make that feel like trust."

Sera nodded, satisfied enough for the moment. "Fine. No lock. No closure. Sit down."

They did, side by side against the bench, gloves still half on while Tamsin replayed the challenge event frame by frame. Mr Idris had been writing without pause and now, incredibly, asked if anyone wanted tea as if the room had not just stared directly into a predatory route architecture. Theo said yes. No one laughed because the question was the laugh: civilisation continuing by the small mercies that kept people from becoming only instruments.

Tamsin stopped the replay at the moment of tearing and enlarged the image until the false corridor's under-structure filled the screen. The closure arcs curved inward around the hollow centre like fingers learning a throat.

"There," she said. "That's your black-room skeleton."

Theo stood behind her chair. "Can we prove it against the Docklands specs?"

"Given another hour and a clean copy of the site dimensions, yes."

"You won't get a clean copy."

"Then give me dirty ones and a ruler."

Mara had pulled off one glove and was rubbing the base of her thumb where the haptic mesh had left a red line. "It changes if you challenge it with witness. That matters."

Theo looked at her over the monitor. "Say why."

"Because it means the route is not merely hidden. It is ashamed of being seen correctly."

Mr Idris, pouring tea at the side counter with the serenity of a man refilling culture itself, said, "Excellent. Shame is administratively useful."

Even Tamsin smiled at that.

Elian, still watching the frozen closure arcs on the screen, said, "I don't think it's shame exactly."

They all looked at him.

He searched for the least false version. "Not human shame. More like… route failure under unwanted naming. The architecture depends on misclassification. Once the room knows what it is, it has to spend energy pretending harder."

Theo considered that. "Then we stop letting it be named by frightened men in secure rooms."

"Yes," Mara said at once. "And we stop describing the black room as a chamber. Chamber implies holding. This thing doesn't hold. It encloses."

Tamsin lifted a finger and typed as she spoke. "Operational terminology update: false route behaviour. enclosure architecture. closure chamber. Black Room retained only as conspiracy shorthand."

Mr Idris set mugs down by each of them in turn and went back to his chair. In the ledger, beneath the formal witness line, he wrote a smaller note in the margin that Elian saw only because the old man did not bother to hide it.

Do not let monsters choose the noun.

Theo read over his shoulder and nodded once.

The building gave them no further contradiction alarms that hour. That made Tamsin twitchy. It made Elian worse. Quiet after naming the route was not relief. It was adaptation. He could feel that now. The false architecture had tested one mode and found witness hostile to it. Somewhere beyond the ring's surface, through whatever adjacency of pressure, geometry, and deliberate predation held the Other Room together, the Cauterists would be making new calculations.

He did not know how he knew that. He was beginning to dislike how many important truths arrived lately in him as aversion before analysis.

Mara nudged her tea towards him. "Drink."

He obeyed. The ginger steadied the back of his throat.

Theo snapped the protocol folder shut. "All right. This is enough for one descent. Tamsin, finalise the structural comparison. I want Docklands overlaid against what we just saw before dawn. Sera, update the guidance with relief-from-declaration as a pre-lock warning sign. Mara, amend the witness pages and get them to every table before six. Mr Idris, duplicate the ledger entry and split storage."

Mr Idris inclined his head. "One in archive, one in the ugly safe."

"Elian."

He looked up.

Theo's eyes were tired now, but clear. "You are not touching the ring again tonight."

"Agreed."

"Do not say that like you're humouring me."

"I'm not."

The answer was enough. Theo gave a brief nod and turned away to make his first phone call.

Mara sat beside Elian in the quieter patch that followed, both of them watching Tamsin rebuild the route's skeleton from telemetry and challenge response. On the main screen, the closure arcs looked less like a corridor now and more like a cunning abuse of one. The difference mattered.

"Do you know what I kept hearing in it?" Elian asked.

Mara kept her eyes on the screen. "What?"

"That I could stop carrying things properly for a while."

She was quiet for a moment. Then she said, "That's why it won't only target the cruel."

He looked at her.

"It will target the exhausted. The burdened. The over-responsible. Anyone who has spent too long being the one who explains, interprets, confirms, and steadies." She turned then, finally meeting his eyes. "That is not a weakness in you. It's just where it will try first."

He let the sentence move through him. There were several ways to answer and most of them would have been decorative or evasive. He chose the smallest true one.

"Thank you."

She brushed her thumb once over the red line the glove had left across the back of his hand. "Hold the line, Elian."

He thought of the annex corridors above them, of Nina Fowler at the bench hour, of Lachie Baines with the witness card in his pocket, of Daniel Voss asking which instruction was true and no table yet existing in the building to answer him with enough voices. He thought of Hannah Quill in the observation chamber, obedience turning murderous because there had been no room in the room for truth to arrive in time. He thought of the packet from Isorion and the phrase heavy method because lighter methods were under observation.

Then he looked once more at the ring and the frozen image of the false route laid open on the monitor.

"We are," he said.

Outside, unseen from the lower lab, rain finally began over Melbourne. It came lightly at first, a quiet stippling against the annex windows and the river beyond. Inside, the building's metal bones accepted the weather and kept their own counsel while the people in one sealed room, under witness and with tea cooling beside them, learned how a predatory architecture folded itself around the things humans were most tempted not to say aloud.

And somewhere in Docklands, in a shielded room prepared by men who thought enclosures were tools and language was just another instrument to be stripped down for efficiency, five-forty moved closer by the minute.

Chapter Eight: Cinder Logic

The whiteboard began as a crime scene and, by degrees, became a theology of bad systems.

Sera Imani stood in the lower lab's side room with the marker uncapped in one hand and Daniel Voss's final minute spread across three linked displays behind her. Tamsin Roe had given her the room because it had once been used for equipment induction and therefore had the one thing most thinking required when the stakes were mortal: a door that shut properly and a wall broad enough to hold an argument until the argument became a map.

By ten in the morning, the map had eaten the wall.

Daniel's corridor still filled the upper left quadrant, every instruction tagged, every timing offset measured, every witness line traced from the first blank page to the first exhaled smoke. Beside it sat Hannah Quill's black-room interview, stripped to the cleanest sequence Sera could justify without losing the woman inside the procedure: the smart glass, the false reassurance, the duplicated command pressure, the tiny pause where Hannah's eyes stopped searching for authority and began searching for whichever answer might count as safety. Beneath both lay a third section, not yet tied to any corpse but already ugly with implication: architecture conditions, metallic adjacency, signal mimicry, witness density, enclosure states, command hierarchy, emotional texture.

Tamsin called that section the mathematics of how bastards build rooms.

Sera thought that, for once, Tamsin's language might not be excessive.

She stepped back, read her own last line, crossed out the word stress, and replaced it with loading. The marker squeaked once against the board, too sharp in the room's quiet.

Elian sat at the long side table, his forearms braced either side of an evidence photograph, watching without interfering. That was not his natural state. His mind preferred approach, comparison, and the drawing of useful shapes between things that had not yet realised they belonged to one pattern. This morning he had brought her tea, organised the image files, labelled two folders, and then gone still in a way that told Sera he was holding himself back from the ring by force. She appreciated the discipline, even while distrusting what required it.

Mara stood at the filing cabinet by the door, a legal pad atop a stack of old archive boxes, building her own parallel skeleton from the same facts. Her pages used fewer technical terms and more human verbs. Lied. Isolated. Pressured. Obeyed. Burned. It was not simplification. It was a second exactness, one Sera had learned to respect over the last week.

Tamsin moved between them and the main console with three windows open on her nearest screen and a fourth half-built on the whiteboard glass. She had not removed yesterday's coffee ring from the corner of the keyboard because she had reached the stage of fatigue at which domestic shame lost all political weight. She looked more alive than rested, which was never a good sign in her. It meant a problem had offended her deeply enough to become its own stimulant.

Theo came and went in intervals, carrying calls into hallways and bringing back the smell of legal abrasion.

At eleven sixteen, Sera drew a hard square around Hannah Quill's final ninety seconds and said, "Again."

Tamsin sighed and brought the clip up.

The room filled with the soundless version first, as they had agreed.
Motion without voice. Hannah seated upright, shoulders too
disciplined, palms on her knees because someone had told her that
visible hands made cooperation easier to believe in from the other
side of the glass. The observation room looked exactly as rooms
designed by frightened bureaucrats always looked: expensive
neutrality, rounded table edge, no loose objects, no visible corners
sharp enough to take skin off on the way down. Behind the smart
glass, blurred shadows moved where operators watched and fed
contradictory instructions into a field they thought was still merely
experimental.

Sera watched Hannah's face the way surgeons watched monitors.
Every shift mattered.

"Freeze there," she said.

Tamsin stopped the frame.

Hannah's mouth was slightly open. Her pupils had widened.
Nothing dramatic. No screaming, no pleading, no cinematic terror.
Only the first true sign of it: the instant when a person stopped
responding to a room and began trying to reconcile a room that
would not stay one room.

"She hasn't entered overdrive yet," Sera said. "This is still pre-
lock."

Elian looked up from the table. "What makes you certain?"

"Because she's still allocating attention outward. Look." Sera
crossed to the screen and touched the air an inch from Hannah's
eyes, not enough to smudge, enough to indicate. "She's still testing.
You can see it in the saccades. Left, glass, ceiling register, right. She

still believes the environment might disclose the true instruction if she observes it properly."

Mara's pencil moved on the legal pad. "Which means the body is not yet the enclosure."

Sera glanced at her and nodded. "Yes. Good."

Tamsin replayed five seconds. Hannah spoke. No sound. Her throat moved. Her hands tightened fractionally on her knees.

Theo came back through the door in time to hear Sera say, "Again."

"How many times are you going to watch this?" he asked.

"Until the dead give me a way to stop honouring them by repeating themselves."

He knew better than to answer that with comfort. He came farther into the room, loosened his tie by half a finger's width, and stood under the corner of the whiteboard where Sera had written in thick black capitals:

THEY DO NOT BURN FEAR.
THEY BURN CLOSURE.

That sentence had arrived thirty-eight minutes earlier and changed the logic of the day.

Sera had followed Daniel and Hannah through the usual forensic disappointments, stimulus, stress, autonomic surge, heat, until the pattern offended her badly enough to become clear. Panic was wasteful. Panic sprayed through a body and wasted itself. These deaths converged. They moved with the horrible precision of a system closing.

134

The Cauterists were not feeding on fear. They were using a contradiction to make a human body finish a circuit it should never have been forced to close.

No one had liked the sentence. That was how she trusted it.

She pointed now to the whiteboard and said, "Walk with me."

Theo folded his arms. Mara stopped writing. Elian came away from the table. Tamsin muted the clip and joined them, marker already in hand because she could not bear to stand near a board without the means to wound it productively.

"Phase one. Perceptual misalignment," Sera said, drawing a line beneath Daniel's name. "This is where everyone wants to stop because it still sounds survivable. Warm pages. Wrong temperature gradients. Auditory lag. Small geometry failures. The body knows something is wrong, but it is not trapped yet."

She moved the marker down to the next block of writing. "Phase two. Contradiction loading. This is where the environment and the instruction chain begin working together. Not stress generally. Specific contradiction pressure under enclosed conditions. Two true-sounding instructions. One authority signature, more than one command. No clean external witness."

Mara looked at the words and said, "Not confusion. Compression."

Sera turned. "Yes."

Tamsin gave the board a short approving tap with the marker tip. "That is a better noun."

Sera crossed out "loading" and wrote "compression".

"It isn't enough that the subject is afraid," she said. "The contradiction has to narrow until the body starts treating one false answer as the price of relief."

135

Theo's mouth twisted. "Trust architecture."

"Bodies have one," Sera said. "You can dislike the phrase later."

Elian's eyes were on Hannah, frozen behind the glass. "And then?"

"Then comes autonomic overdrive," Sera said. "But the kill happens at thermal lock, the point where regulation gives way to obedience and the body starts helping the room."

She wrote the two words larger than the others.

The room was quiet enough to hear the building's low, circulating breath in the ducts.

Theo looked at the line and said, "You're telling me the body stops trying to regulate and starts trying to obey."

"Yes." Sera did not soften it. "That is the cleanest version."

For a moment, no one moved.

Then Tamsin said, very quietly, "Well, that is evil."

No one corrected the word.

Sera drew a final line from thermal lock to internal ignition. "By the time flame appears, the murder has already happened. Fire is not the method. Fire is the visible end state."

Mara put her pencil down. "Then the black room wasn't built to study contact. It was built to build thermal lock."

Theo's head turned sharply towards her. "Say it again."

She did. This time slower. "The room is not neutral. It doesn't merely host contradiction. It helps enclosure. It strips away escape routes of interpretation until the body starts trying to close the loop itself."

Tamsin swore with sincere admiration. "God, I hate that you're right."

Elian, who had gone pale without theatrics, said, "The false route did the same thing."

They all looked at him.

He did not retreat from the sentence. "Not to that degree. Not yet. But the sensation was the same family. Reduced friction. Reduced the need to declare. Reduced moral distance. The route was trying to spare me from effort by taking over the shape of my intention."

Theo's face hardened by a degree. "And if you'd followed it?"

Elian answered truthfully. "I don't know. That's what scares me."

Sera uncapped a second marker and drew a connecting line between the black-room enclosure and the route map from the first descent. "Same method, different scale."

Tamsin stepped forward and added three engineering notations in brutal capitals. LOCAL ENCLOSURE. ROUTE ENCLOSURE. SOCIAL ENCLOSURE.

Theo read the last one aloud. "Social enclosure."

Mara had already begun to see it. Sera watched the recognition move through her like weather over water.

"Yes," Mara said. "The bench table is the opposite of that."

Tamsin blinked. "Explain."

"The black room kills by taking contradiction and making it private, then authoritative, then bodily." Mara moved to the board, took the marker from Sera without asking, and wrote under SOCIAL ENCLOSURE in her own hand. "The table interrupts at the level before the body closes. It brings the contradiction out of the person and into the room, where the room has to share it."

Theo looked from the words to Mara, and Sera knew he was doing what he always did when he trusted someone enough to let their thought alter the architecture of the case. He was counting consequences.

"So the table is not only moral theatre," he said.

Mara turned to him. "Did you really think I was running morale?"

"No," Theo said. "I thought you were running civilisation."

"That too."

Tamsin leaned one hip against the side table and looked at Sera. "Can we prove the table effect on anything more than instinct and one near miss?"

Sera answered before she had fully decided the order of her reasoning. "Maybe."

Every head in the room turned.

She pointed to Daniel's line first. "He had no witness table. No externalisation point. No validated second voice in the room. Everything stayed inside the event until the body became the event."

Then Hannah. "Same here. They enclosed her physically, socially, and procedurally. Every answer had to move through their architecture. She had no room in which to say the contradiction and make someone else carry part of it."

Finally, the bench-hour log stack. "Lachie Baines, Nina Fowler, the security reroute on the service stair. All three experienced contradictory instruction pressure. All three externalised early. All three stabilised."

Theo looked at the log stack as if it had improved its manners by being useful rather than merely principled.

Tamsin had already moved to the console. "I can model that."

Mara said, "Of course you can."

Tamsin ignored her. "Not perfectly, but enough. Contradiction enters system, witness intervention acts as circuit breaker, enclosure fails to complete. If we can quantify how much the false route loses coherence under shared declaration versus solitary compliance, we might have an actual operational countermeasure."

Elian, still by the evidence table, said, "That would mean using the route as part of the experiment."

"Yes."

"No."

They all turned to Theo.

He had not raised his voice. He rarely needed to. Refusal sounded more dangerous in him when delivered at conversational volume.

"No," he repeated. "You do not build a test that requires one of you to get close enough to thermal lock for the sake of elegance."

Tamsin's jaw tightened. "I wasn't proposing human exposure."

"You were moving there."

She looked as if she wanted to deny it, then chose to be honest instead. "Yes."

Theo nodded once, not triumphant, only tired. "Thank you. Now move somewhere else."

Sera stepped in before the room could split along the fault line. "We don't need live threshold testing yet. We have enough archival material to model first. Daniel. Hannah. The descent logs. The bench-hour interruptions. Let me get the physiology cleaner before anyone starts trying to prove civilisation on a graph."

Mara gave her a brief grateful look.

Theo rolled one shoulder, the closest he came to apology in public. "Fine. Do that."

The room loosened by degrees.

Tamsin sat back down and began typing fast enough to offend ordinary keyboards. "I'm building a closure model," she said, mostly to the monitors. "I'm calling the black room an authoritarian thermogenic chamber until someone invents a colder phrase."

Mara returned to the legal pad. "Don't make it too cold. Cold phrases are how men like this keep their jobs."

Elian walked to the sink, poured the stale water from his glass into the drain, and stood there with both hands braced on the steel edge. His reflection in the dark square of the little interior window looked older than it had yesterday. He disliked that. He disliked even more that the route had known exactly what kind of offer might have reached him.

Mara's voice came from behind him. "Don't turn yourself into evidence."

He looked back. She had left the pad and come to stand three feet away, close enough to speak privately inside the room's shared purpose without giving the conversation a shape others would have to politely ignore.

"I'm not," he said.

"You're thinking about how easily it found the right tone."

He did not answer, which was answer enough.

Mara folded her arms loosely. "Elian."

He hated how much relief there was in hearing his name spoken by someone who did not want to use it as leverage.

"It's not that it knows you," she said. "It knows the cost profile of a certain kind of human."

"What if that kind includes me?"

"It does." She did not flinch from the truth. "It also includes me. Tamsin. Sera. Theo, probably, though he'd rather die than call it by that name. Anyone who carries too much alone for too long starts looking like a room that wants to be spared one more explanation."

He said nothing.

Mara's face softened by just enough to register as risk. "That isn't shame, Elian. It's why we built the table."

The word table seemed absurdly small beside everything else now at stake. That was why it mattered. The whole building now contained one ugly laminate surface that had interrupted death simply by refusing to let contradiction remain private. The scale offended the dramatic mind and rescued the practical one.

At the board, Sera suddenly swore.

They turned.

She had frozen the Hannah Quill clip at a point no one had lingered on before, just after the first clear contradiction and just before autonomic overdrive. Hannah's right hand had shifted on her knee. Two fingers pressed hard into the fabric there, enough to pale the knuckles.

"What?" Theo asked.

Sera walked closer to the screen. "She was grounding."

Tamsin looked up. "What?"

Sera pointed at the frozen hand. "She was trying to put herself outside the room through contact. Pressure anchor. You do it instinctively when trying not to dissociate or spiral. She didn't know what was happening physiologically, but her body did. She was trying to create one true thing."

Mara stepped closer. "And it didn't save her."

"No. But it may have delayed lock."

"How long?"

Sera replayed the clip, eyes narrowed. "Maybe six seconds. Maybe eight. Hard to say."

Theo looked at the board and then at the witness logs. "That's enough for a room to intervene."

"Yes," Sera said.

Tamsin turned fully in her chair now, alive with the unpleasant pleasure of a system yielding. "Add that to the guidance. Physical anchor, named witness, spoken contradiction. Stack all three."

Mara was already writing.

If the room feels wrong, find one true contact. Chair. wall. floor. your own wrist. Then speak the contradiction where someone can hear it.

Theo watched her for a second. "That will sound absurd to some people."

"It will sound like survival to the right ones."

The lower lab door buzzed. Mr Idris, who had gone upstairs to collect the first bench-hour ledgers and return them to the archive before human error decided to improve the day, stepped in carrying two books and a folded note.

"Nina Fowler sends a message," he said. "She wanted the table to know that a cleaner on nine stopped a man from being rerouted into a sealed maintenance passage by asking him, in her words, why he was obeying a voice when there were three breathing people in front of him saying the opposite."

Tamsin shut her eyes briefly. "Marry the cleaner instead."

Mr Idris handed the note to Mara, then held up the bench-hour logs. "Four more contradictions. No escalations. One of them a duplicate destruction order. One a false urgent call from records to a night porter. One a lift lockout instruction with no second witness. One simply a junior analyst who came because the language on a calendar invite felt 'too eager to be true.'"

Theo looked at the books and then at the board and then, finally, allowed himself the smallest expression of satisfaction anyone in that room was likely to get out of him today. "All right," he said. "The table holds."

Sera shook her head. "No."

They all looked at her.

"The table doesn't hold," she said. "People hold each other at the table. That's the difference."

No one answered immediately because it was correct in the kind of way that makes a response look decorative.

Mr Idris took a seat by the lamp and opened the first ledger. Tamsin resumed her modelling. Mara copied the cleaner's phrase into the shadow archive under public countermeasure behaviour. Theo went back to his calls, each one another brick laid in front of some administrative stupidity waiting outside. Elian returned to the evidence table and, for the first time since Hannah's death, sat down without feeling as if the chair had become an accusation.

The room worked for another hour in the ugly, necessary peace of people forcing horror into usable shape. Cauterists. Closure. Enclosure. Social circuit breakers. Physical anchor points. Counter-sign matrices. Thermal lock profiles. The phrases accumulated not to comfort, but to prevent the wrong men from later saying there had been no vocabulary for what happened, and therefore no one could really have acted sooner.

Just after one, Tamsin made a sharp sound through her teeth and enlarged a graph on the centre display.

"What now?" Theo asked, already annoyed on principle.

She pointed. "I've been comparing the route telemetry from last night's descent with the black-room field traces and the bench-hour interruption logs. There's a pattern in the drop-off."

Sera crossed to the console. "What kind of pattern?"

"The false route loses more coherence when the contradiction is externalised in front of two witnesses than it does under simple refusal. A lot more."

Theo said, "Translate."

Mara answered before Tamsin could. "It isn't enough to say no. The no has to be held by more than one person."

Tamsin gave her an irritable glance that nevertheless conceded the point. "Yes. Think of it this way. Solitary refusal is obstruction. Shared witnessed refusal becomes architecture."

The sentence entered the room like weather.

Elian felt the back of his neck go cold.

Because if that was true, the Cauterists were attacking the conditions under which human beings became structurally real to one another. Secrecy was part of the burn logic.

Sera saw the same thing hit Theo a heartbeat later. His face closed, not with fear, but with the grimness he reserved for moments when the enemy's elegance offended his sense of law.

"The hidden structures prepare them," he said, thinking aloud. "Not metaphorically. Institutionally. Procedurally. Socially."

Mara turned a page in the archive notebook and began writing before anyone else could move. "Which means this cannot be filed as random deaths from exotic contact exposure. That will feed them. This has to be named, at least internally, for what it is. A system that turns private contradiction into ignition."

Theo looked at her. "That language will be fought."

"Then let them fight it."

He almost smiled. "Gladly."

At the whiteboard, Sera added a final column under the phase model and wrote the heading in thick, deliberate strokes.

COUNTERMEASURES

Below it, she wrote the first three lines.

Witness before compliance.
Externalise contradiction early.
Do not let the room become the only authority.

Tamsin added a fourth from across the room without asking.

If the route flatters, leave.

That stayed too.

By three in the afternoon, the room had produced something larger than a theory and smaller than a salvation. A working model. Dirty, provisional, full of risk, but coherent enough to alter behaviour across the annex and perhaps, with care, beyond it.

Sera printed the first revised guidance sheets herself. Theo signed the internal order that made them enforceable in every contact-adjacent room. Mara copied the language into the shadow archive and then into the bench-hour packs. Tamsin built an ugly but effective visual prompt for the signal pads: two diverging instructions, one human hand laying them both on a table. Elian, because he needed his hands occupied with something other than the ring, carried the new sheets upstairs to Nina Fowler and watched her read them with the expression of a woman whose instinct had just received institutional backing.

"This one's better," Nina said, tapping the line about not letting the room become the only authority. "That's the whole trick, isn't it?"

"Yes," Elian said.

She looked at him over the page. "You look like hell, son."

"That too."

"Go drink water before you start hearing God in the ducting."

He almost laughed. "I'll do my best."

When he came back down, Mara was alone in the side room, copying the final countermeasure list onto clean paper for the archive set. The late afternoon light from the internal glass panel had gone dim and municipal, the sort of light that made every room seem briefly like an office in a dream.

She didn't look up as he entered. "Nina approve?"

"She told me to drink water before I heard God in the ducting."

"Excellent. Practical theology."

He leaned against the doorframe. For a few seconds, he simply watched her write. She did not waste movement. Even her fatigue looked intentional, as though she had negotiated with it and reached terms. On the page in front of her, the lines appeared one under another in a hand clear enough to survive panic.

Witness before compliance.
Externalise contradiction early.
Do not let the room become the only authority.
If the route flatters, leave.

"It's strange," he said at last.

"What is?"

"How small the countermeasures look."

Mara capped the pen and sat back. "That's because you're still thinking like a person raised on stories where catastrophe is only defeated by bigger catastrophe."

"And what are you thinking like?"

She considered the page, then him. "Like someone who's watched enough institutions fail to know that evil usually scales through convenience before it scales through spectacle."

He took that in and let it stay there.

Behind the wall, the ring waited in its mount while the false route, named now and correctly opposed, remained quiet. Not absent. Never that. Quiet in the way a predator went quiet when the herd stopped wandering away one by one.

The logic had become ugly enough to be useful.

The Cauterists did not need blind terror. They needed enclosed contradiction under deceptive authority. They needed hidden structures to prepare the human body by social means before the far-side expenditure arrived. They needed rooms, routes, procedures, signatures, urgency, and people too isolated or obedient to say aloud that something was wrong until the saying no longer mattered.

And because that was true, ugly little things could now fight them.

A cleaner saying why are you obeying a voice when three breathing people are here.
A clerk refusing to destroy what someone had not yet properly named.
An ugly table by a lift.
A witness card in a maintenance pocket.
A hand on a knee, finding one true thing.
Two people in a room saying no together until the route lost coherence, trying to turn one into many and many into one.

"It isn't enough," Elian said quietly.

Mara looked at him with the patience of someone refusing to let despair enjoy the dignity of originality. "No," she said. "But it is the beginning of enough."

On the side table, Sera's revised phase guide lay drying beside the new countermeasure sheet. Tamsin's model still glowed on the screen. Theo's legal notes waited in a folder with corners already softening from use. Mr Idris's ledger sat open to the latest line, ink not yet fully settled.

The room had done what rooms like this were for. It had taken death, lies, and architecture and forced them into named relation.

Outside, the annex continued carrying people, files, and compromised instructions through its steel bones. Somewhere in Docklands, men who mistook intelligence for exemption were still building rooms they believed they controlled. Somewhere farther still, beyond lawful harbour and false corridor alike, the Cauterists were learning the counter-shape of witness and adjusting their appetite accordingly.

Sera came back in carrying the final stack of guidance sheets and said, "All right. We have enough to make the building harder to kill."

Theo's voice drifted down the corridor behind her. "And enough to make some very senior people wish they'd chosen a different week to be idiots."

Mara picked up the archive copy. Elian straightened. Tamsin swore at a spreadsheet in a tone bordering on affection.

The room settled around them not with relief, but with purpose.

Cinder logic had a shape now.

And because it had a shape, it could finally be fought.

Chapter Nine: Corridor with Teeth

By the time they were ready to go back in, the annex had begun to imitate virtue.

The witness tables were holding. Contradictions that would once have travelled alone now arrived with signatures, names, and enough embarrassment to make them human before they became dangerous. Cleaners carried witness cards beside access badges. Facilities staff had started repeating Nina Fowler's line to one another in service lifts, with the rough affection tradespeople reserve for sentences that save time and skin: "Why are you obeying a voice when three breathing people are right here?" Theo had turned that line into an internal instruction without improving it. Mara had put it in the shadow archive under the civil countermeasures category. Tamsin had pretended to despise its elegance and then built it into the next signal-prompt screen.

The building, in other words, had become harder to use as a weapon.

That was the good news.

The bad news was that the false route had not gone away. It had merely become more selective.

Tamsin proved that at twenty past nine by dragging three overlays across the main screen in the lower lab and making a noise in her throat that meant she had found something she would rather not have found but was professionally delighted by anyway. The route maps from the first descent shifted over the black-room telemetry from Hannah Quill's final minutes. A third layer, built from the bench-hour interruption logs and the route's reaction to externalised contradiction, sat between them like a translator trying not to become implicated in the conversation.

"There," Tamsin said.

Elian stepped closer. Mara was already at the console, leaning one hand on the back of Tamsin's chair.

At first, the pattern looked like a drafting error, one of those small alignments the eye resists because the implications arrive before the certainty does. Then the lines settled. The lawful Harbour remained what it had always been: broad-basin reception, witness ladder, clarified delay, stabilising node. The false architecture traced beneath it in a family of narrowing channels, and at one point, just before the first stable receiving structure, a side-line branched off at an angle no lawful route ever used.

It was small. Narrow. Easy to miss.

And it had not been there the night before.

"That's new," Elian said.

Tamsin swore softly. "Yes."

Theo, who had entered the room carrying three folders and the general expression of a man who had fought breakfast, looked from the screen to Tamsin and back again. "Explain."

"The false route is adapting around witnessed refusal," Tamsin said. "It knows the direct invitation is too obvious now, so it's built a side-lane before the first stable threshold. Less welcome, more practical. Less 'come in, we know you' and more 'this way, faster, no need to tell the others why'."

Mara stared at the branching line. "It learned to stop flattering and start being useful."

Elian felt the sentence under his sternum before he fully understood why it frightened him more than the earlier version. Relief was suspicious. Most people retained enough self-respect to distrust a route that knew too much too early. Usefulness was different. Useful things got forgiven. Useful things were how institutions taught human beings to step over moral edges without noticing the drop until they were already in the air.

Theo put the folders down untouched. "What does the side-lane do?"

Tamsin looked at him with naked irritation. "I'd have to ask it."

"No."

"Then I'll infer. Which is slower and less fun?"

Sera entered halfway through the exchange, carrying two small medical kits and a notepad, her compressed, precise hand covering it. "What are we inferring?"

Mara pointed to the branch on the screen. "The route has grown a second mouth."

Sera came closer. Her eyes moved over the overlays once, twice, and then sharpened at the angle of divergence. "Not a mouth," she said. "A funnel."

Tamsin swivelled in her chair. "That's better. I hate better."

Elian had not taken his eyes off the screen. The side lane's geometry was wrong in a way he could not yet articulate without touching the haptics. It did not present as welcome or enclosure or even false stability. It presented as the shortest way to stop carrying one particular burden. He had the sudden, irrational conviction that if he laid his hands on the route, the branch would not offer him general safety. It would offer him a specific permission.

That scared him enough that he said it aloud.

Theo's gaze moved to him at once. "Permission to do what?"

"I don't know." Elian rubbed the back of his neck. "That's part of it. The line isn't broadcasting content. It's shaped like relief from a particular effort. Like a hallway cut for one kind of tiredness."

Mara looked from the graph to his face. "And yours?"

He hesitated. There was no point pretending in this room now. Not after the whiteboards, the packet, the bench logs, the dead.

"Mine would be," he said carefully, "the effort of staying slow when I think speed might help someone."

Tamsin let out a long breath through her nose. "Yes. That sounds exactly like the sort of thing a predatory architecture would exploit in a man who reads every room like it's a system fault he can prevent if he just gets there first."

"Thank you," Elian said.

"You're welcome."

Theo looked at the branch again. "So it targets not greed, not fear exactly, but moral impatience."

Sera set her kits down on the bench. "That would fit the cascade model. If contradiction can't close through simple coercion under witness conditions, it moves earlier into motivation. It recruits the target before the target realises a decision has begun."

Mara turned slightly and met Theo's eye. "We have to go back in."

Theo gave her the look of a man who had spent half his adult life trying to prevent clever people from mistaking inevitability for wisdom. "Do we?"

"Yes."

"That was not a question."

"No," Mara said. "It was a statement you were making in the tone of a question to see if I'd save you the effort."

Tamsin made a tiny sound of appreciation and hid it badly.

Theo considered the room, then the branch again, then Elian. "If you go in, you go in to verify character only. No pursuit. No heroics. No rationalisations built out of the words just one metre farther."

"Agreed," Elian said.

Mara nodded. "Agreed."

Theo did not like how readily they both said it. "You understand I trust neither of you at this point except under witness."

"That," Mara said, "is why you're useful."

They prepared differently this time.

The first descent into the false route had been an act of naming. Tonight's descent was a trap inspection. Tamsin stripped the haptic station back even farther, killing every comfort layer, turning off every predictive smoothing routine the lawful Harbour tolerated but the false path could exploit. The gloves would answer only to direct input and verified route behaviour. No assistance. No interpretation. She installed a deadman interrupt under both stations, one for herself at the console, the second under Sera's hand at the physiology bench, each able to cut the descent on witness call alone.

"Two kill hands," Theo said, approving despite himself.

"Three," Tamsin answered, indicating the physical breaker switch she had mounted to the steel edge of Bench Three. "I'm done pretending beautiful systems survive ugly people."

Sera clipped baseline sensors to Elian and Mara with the same grave efficiency she had used before the first lawful crossing after Daniel's death, but there was new caution in her now. She had added thermal microstrips at the sternum and inner forearm, not because she expected immediate ignition, but because their work no longer permitted embarrassment at looking absurdly prepared. She took baseline readings, frowned at Elian's heart rate, said nothing about Mara's because it was flatter and cleaner than most healthy men twice as certain of themselves, and then handed each of them a witness card.

"You keep it on your person," she said.

Mara looked down at the cream stock. "In the room?"

"In case the architecture gets clever enough to target the ritual itself. I want human habits touching your body as well as machine protocols."

Tamsin did not mock the idea. That worried Elian more than if she had.

Mr Idris arrived with the ledger wrapped in cloth and a second volume for duplicate entry. Nina Fowler followed him in ten minutes later, coat on, mail trolley parked outside the lab door because she had insisted on standing the witness hour closest to the descent. Theo had objected once, out of politeness. Nina had looked at him as if he were a parcel addressed to the wrong floor and said, "Young man, I spent twenty-seven years making people sign for things they hoped to misplace. Sit down."

Theo had sat down.

Now she took the chair by the lamp as if she had always belonged there.

"I don't know what half of this means," she said, looking at the route maps.

"That makes you ideal company," Tamsin muttered.

Nina ignored her and looked at Elian instead. "If it sounds too easy, it's selling."

Elian nodded once. "Yes."

"Good. Then let's all keep our wallets in our pockets."

No one laughed because they were too close to work for laughter, but the room eased by a fraction. That mattered.

Theo opened the protocol folder. "State condition."

Elian did. Mara did. Sera read the baselines into the ledger. Mr Idris recorded them in script that seemed too elegant for the content. Nina countersigned beside her own name with a practical, blocky hand. Tamsin loaded the route maps, the lawful matrix, and the new side-lane overlay. Theo read the limits aloud. No pursuit beyond first branch recognition. No independent correction of route choice. No withholding of affective response. Anything that feels privately useful must be spoken before acted upon.

Mara repeated the last line back. "Anything that feels privately useful must be spoken before acted upon."

Elian repeated it too.

Theo closed the folder. "Proceed."

The room dimmed.

The gloves woke under their hands with a lower hum than before, less eager to please now that Tamsin had stripped them of their little vanities. Elian settled his palms into the phase controls. Mara took timing and restraint. The ring under the hood seemed to gather the dark rather than the light this time, holding a calm that no longer felt innocent to him and no longer needed to.

The lawful Harbour arrived first, as it always did. Not because it rushed to meet them, but because they knew how to meet it. He felt the old resistance, the invitation to clarity, the basin-like patience under the surface. It was there if they wanted it. It would remain there if they chose not to enter. That was what made it lawful. It did not chase.

The false route surfaced seconds later.

It had changed.

The direct line of invitation was still there, but it had stepped back from the emotional foreground. Less relief. Less intimate understanding. More practical availability. It now felt like an alternate corridor in a building you had used for years, one your body preferred because it shaved twelve seconds off the walk and spared you the bad fluorescent corner near the lifts.

Mara said it before he could. "It's toned itself down."

Tamsin's fingers moved over the console. "Telemetry agrees. Reduced adaptive warmth. Same branch still present."

Theo said, "State it precisely."

Elian kept his eyes on the graph, on the lawful line and the false contour braided beneath it. "The route is no longer trying to be trusted. It's trying to be chosen for efficiency."

Nina, from the ledger chair, said, "I dislike that in anything."

The branch appeared.

It did not have to be summoned. As soon as Elian and Mara stabilised on the edge of the false route's detectable profile without accepting its main line, the side-lane resolved itself with eerie neatness. A narrowing angle, cleaner than yesterday, leading off before the first clear receiving structure. It looked less like a trap than a detour suggested by a competent local. Faster this way. Less traffic. No need to announce yourself to the whole street.

The image made Elian's teeth ache.

"There," Tamsin said.

Sera's eyes were on the physiological screen. "Baselines climbing. Nothing unstable."

Mara adjusted the timing hand a fraction slower than instinct wanted. "We verify only."

He nodded.

The lawful Harbour remained at their left shoulder, deep and waiting. The false route ran beneath. The side-lane angled off like a whispered favour.

As they moved one layer farther into mapping contact, the branch clarified itself not geometrically but emotionally. That was the thing Elian would later hate most in memory. It was not that the lane looked safer. It was that it felt as if one particular responsibility could be set down there without cost.

The sensation found him so neatly he almost missed the fact of being found.

He saw, with sudden sick clarity, an image of the Docklands room they had not yet entered. Not actual knowledge. Not a vision. A constructed intuition shaped exactly to his fear. Someone trapped behind smart glass. Mara too far away. Theo delayed by process. Tamsin stuck outside the loop. The side-lane offered, with calm practicality, a route that would get him there before witness could be assembled.

His hands shifted.

Not much. Not enough for anyone outside the haptics to call it movement. But enough.

Mara's voice cut across the route at once. "Elian."

He froze.

The room was utterly still.

"What?" Theo asked.

Elian's mouth had gone dry. He did not pull his hands back. That would have been theatre. Worse, it would have been private theatre. The point now was to name before acting.

"It offered me speed," he said, forcing each word to stay ordinary. "Not abstract speed. A faster path to Docklands. A way to get there before the room is ready for us."

No one rushed to answer. Theo, to his enormous credit, did not immediately say withdraw. Tamsin did not swear. Sera did not move from the physiology screen. They all let the statement exist in the air where it could be witnessed and therefore weakened.

Mara said, "Thank you."

Then, because she was better at this than anyone else in the room, she gave the architecture nothing romantic to work with.

"It offered me protection from his mistake," she said.

Elian looked at her.

Her voice remained level. "A lane where I could keep pace with you without having to tell the others I was afraid of losing line of sight on you. It packaged that fear as competence."

The branch on the screen flickered.

Tamsin's head snapped up. "There. Again. It hates paired confession."

Mr Idris's pen scratched furiously over the ledger page.

Theo said, "Continue naming."

Elian swallowed. "It implied the route to Docklands is morally urgent enough to bypass procedure."

Mara: "It implied care could be expressed more purely in secrecy than in witness."

The side-lane wavered.

The emotional pull did not vanish, but its polish cracked. The practical detour quality came off it like cheap varnish under heat. For one heartbeat the underlying structure showed through, a narrowing passage with closure arcs at its walls, not as pronounced as the black room, but of the same family. Teeth, Tamsin would later call them. Not literal, not decorative. Just the geometry of something designed to become narrower as a person accepted its premise.

"There," she whispered now. "Corridor with teeth."

The name stuck instantly.

Sera said, "Pulse up six. Temperature holding. Keep it external."

Mara did something Elian had not expected. Instead of staying on the edge and treating the branch as purely technical, she leaned one degree closer to it in timing space, enough to feel the side-lane answer her own fear. When she spoke, her voice remained calm.

"It offers me a private version of love," she said. "One where I don't have to watch the room while I watch him."

Elian felt the sentence go through the architecture like a fault line. The branch convulsed.

The side-lane narrowed visibly on the main display, its edges acquiring a ragged density, the first overt aggression they had yet seen from it. Not enough to seize. Enough to reveal appetite.

Theo's voice came low and hard. "No farther."

"We're not going farther," Mara said.

Tamsin's hands flew. "I've got the closure response. It's trying to compensate for lost seduction by increasing structural urgency."

Elian could feel that too now. The branch was abandoning charm. It had been named too correctly too quickly. In place of useful ease came pressure. Less this will help, more now or never. The familiar tactic of every bad room ever built by human beings who wanted obedience quickly enough to rename it necessity.

"It's getting louder," he said.

"Describe."

"Not emotionally. Architecturally. The lane is collapsing distinctions. If we took it now, there would be no room to ask what it bypassed. The bypass itself would become the answer."

Tamsin muttered, "That is so incredibly illegal."

Theo said, "Hold. Then withdraw."

Nina, who had been following none of the technical detail and all of the room's moral weather, spoke from the witness chair without lifting her pen. "It sounds like a corridor built by managers."

That got the room its smallest and most useful laugh, enough to break the pressure the branch was trying to exploit.

The side-lane faltered.

Sera said at once, "There. Again. Shared room response reduces closure."

Elian was learning too fast to call anything coincidence. The branch did not only hate named contradiction. It hated ordinary human plurality, the little civic abrasions that kept one person's fear from becoming the whole atmosphere. A joke at the table. A witness who did not care about metaphysics and therefore could not be glamoured by them. A cleaner asking a practical question. Nina Fowler calling bullshit in the register of a woman who had spent a career handling premature urgency in envelopes and men.

The side-lane was all teeth and no jaw now.

Tamsin brought up the deadman interrupt overlay. "I can cut on your mark."

Theo looked at Elian and Mara. "Do either of you have anything left to learn from this pass?"

Elian answered honestly. "No."

Mara said, "Only the price of staying."

"Then withdraw."

They did it together. That mattered. Not because the route could have physically seized one if the other moved first, though none of them were prepared to rule that out forever, but because paired withdrawal kept the architecture from rewriting departure as individual failure. Elian softened phase. Mara opened timing. The lawful Harbour, still waiting where they had left it untouched, remained broad and patient. The false route withdrew under pressure, and the side-lane folded in on itself with one last ugly shimmer of useful urgency before disappearing beneath the graph.

The room returned all at once.

The haptics lost their bite. The lower lab's ordinary sounds rebuilt themselves around the workbench, fans, filtered air, the little relay click from Tamsin's signal pad, the scratch of Mr Idris's pen. Elian became aware of the dampness at the back of his neck. Mara took her hands off the controls and sat back in the chair one measured inch at a time.

Sera was beside them immediately with the small thermal scanner. "Wrists."

They obeyed.

"Fine. Elevated. Clean." She looked from one to the other. "Talk."

Mara closed her eyes once, opened them, and answered first. "The side-lane was a detour built out of private justification. Not emotional indulgence. Weaponised usefulness."

Elian said, "It selected for the burden each of us would most want to take on alone."

Theo stood with one hand on the back of Nina's chair, all his attention on them and none of it soft. "Can you say that in a way the annex can use?"

Mara thought for a second. "If a path makes you believe secrecy is the fastest expression of care, it's the wrong path."

Mr Idris wrote that down in the margin without waiting for instructions.

Tamsin replayed the branch collapse three times on screen. "The architecture isn't just predatory. It's managerial. It uses all the same tricks institutions use when they want people to confuse speed with necessity and private burden with professionalism."

Theo's laugh was short and joyless. "That will play beautifully in a commission."

Sera, still scanning, said, "Add this to the guide. Beware of any route, room, or instruction that frames witness as delay rather than protection."

Mara was already reaching for her notebook.

Nina stood up, stretching her back with the small wince of someone who did not trust chairs designed after 1998. "Well," she said, looking at the frozen side-lane on the monitor. "Now we know what it sells."

Tamsin glanced at her. "Do we."

"Yes. Being the hero in a room with no witnesses. Catnip for idiots."

Theo looked almost fond.

Elian took off the left glove and set it on the bench. The linc the haptic mesh had left across the back of his hand was faint but visible. Mara's right glove came off next. Their movements were calm now, but he knew better than to mistake calm for the absence of injury. The route had not come close to thermal lock. It had, however, shown them something of its deeper intelligence. It was learning where love shaded into private burden. It was learning how to dress haste in moral language.

That knowledge sat badly in him.

Mara must have seen it because, while Tamsin argued with the branch data and Theo began dictating the operational language update, she reached out and laid two fingers lightly against the back of his wrist.

"What?" she asked quietly.

He looked at the ring, at the false route now hidden beneath the lawful line again, at the screen with its frozen closure arcs and the side-lane's brief, practical seduction.

"It wasn't trying to make me cruel," he said.

"No."

"That feels worse."

She let that sit between them. "Cruelty is easy to guard against. Misplaced care is not."

He gave a tiny nod. The sentence found its mark too cleanly to require decoration.

Across the room, Theo had moved into command mode.

"Operational update," he said, not raising his voice because nobody in that room required volume in order to obey seriousness. "The side-lane confirms the false architecture is adapting away from overt invitation and towards burden-specific detours. Any operator, maintenance worker, records staffer, or contact-adjacent personnel who begins using language about sparing others by acting alone gets flagged to bench hours immediately. No exceptions. No heroics. We are done romanticising initiative in enclosed systems."

Mr Idris looked up over the ledger. "Would you like that in capitals?"

"Yes."

"Delighted."

Tamsin added the side-lane profile to the contradiction model. Sera rewrote the guidance sheets. Mara transformed the insight into civilian language before the terminology could grow claws and wander off with someone's conscience. Nina took a fresh stack of witness cards for the overnight bench and tucked them into her satchel like ammunition.

By the time the room had finished working the branch into useable truth, the rain had thickened outside. It streaked the narrow interior windows and gave the annex's artificial light the colour of old paper. Somewhere above them, a lift arrived on Level Three and held its doors open four seconds longer than protocol required. Down in the lower lab, no one ignored that anymore. Delay had stopped being dead time. Delay was where witness lived.

At half past midnight the branch model, the revised guidance sheet, and the duplicate ledger entries were all complete. Tamsin saved the telemetry to three non-networked stores. Theo signed the addendum making solitary burden language a reportable pre-enclosure risk. Sera added one final line beneath the phase model on the side-room whiteboard and then, dissatisfied, rewrote it larger.

IF IT ASKS YOU TO SAVE EVERYONE ALONE, IT HAS TEETH.

Mara read the line and kept it.

Elian stood at the sink again, filling a paper cup with water he didn't want because Nina would have asked if he had and he was too tired to lie well. The building beyond the lab felt awake in a new way, not benevolent, not hostile, merely conscious now that the tables existed, the witness cards travelled, and the false route had been named one level deeper.

They were changing the conditions under which it hunted.

Which meant it would change, too.

He knew that as certainly as he knew his own name.

Mara came to stand beside him, shoulder not touching his because the room still held others and because she understood, perhaps better than he did, that restraint was not distance. It was precision.

"Tired?" she asked.

"Yes."

"Good."

He looked at her over the rim of the paper cup. "Good?"

"You're less likely to mistake tonight for mastery."

The sentence was merciful in its accuracy. He let himself smile this time, though only by a little. "I never thought we had mastery."

"No. But you do sometimes start believing understanding is a form of ownership."

Ouch, he thought, and because it was Mara, he let the ouch remain visible.

She took the cup from his hand, drank half the water, and gave it back. "We learned the shape of one tooth tonight," she said. "That's all. Useful. Important. Not ownership."

He nodded.

Behind them, Theo snapped the protocol folder shut. "Enough. Everyone upstairs. The room can keep its own counsel for six hours."

Tamsin looked at the ring as though considering mutiny, then thought better of it. Sera gathered the thermal strips. Mr Idris wrapped the ledger in cloth. Nina, from the doorway, asked whether the ugly table was being left overnight again, and when Theo said yes, she replied, "Good," in the tone of a woman who had just had a train time confirmed.

They left Bench Three lit at low level, the ring resting in its mount beneath the hood, innocent in the manner of dangerous things that have no need to advertise. As Elian switched off the side-room light, the whiteboard sentence glowed faintly in the spill from the corridor.

If it asks you to save everyone alone, it has teeth.

He took that line with him out into the annex's sleeping corridors, through the hush of wet Melbourne night held at bay by glass and bad carpet and witness tables, and up towards the lift lobby where the first bench for the graveyard shift waited under ugly federal lighting, surrounded by cards, ledgers, and the sort of ordinary human company that now counted as counter-architecture.

The false route had shown them its side-lane.

Tomorrow, they would have to decide whether that knowledge was enough to stop Docklands from becoming the next room to bite.

Chapter Ten: Quiet Capture

Julian Mercer arrived at the annex at nine-fifteen carrying nothing but a leather folio and the sort of composure that made lesser men feel underdressed in their own skin.

Theo Markel saw him first on the security feed outside Director Sayeed's office and understood, before the man had spoken a word, that the day was no longer going to belong to the people who had earned it by staying awake through the night. Mercer paused at the outer desk just long enough to let his badge be read, his face be recognised, and his presence become a matter of procedural fact rather than mere movement. He did not fidget. He did not perform urgency. He had the expensive stillness of someone accustomed to entering rooms where others had already decided they would like to keep him waiting, and to teaching them, by existing there long enough, that waiting him out was a poor use of oxygen.

Mara stood beside Theo in the narrow observation alcove off the Director's suite, a legal pad under one arm and a cup of coffee cooling in her hand. Through the tinted interior glass, Mercer wore charcoal wool and a pale blue shirt with the practised modesty of expensive restraint, tie dark, hair artfully untidy in the way only men with assistance or leisure ever achieved it. He might have been a barrister, a consultant, a deputy secretary, or the sort of banker who described predation as an efficiency problem. The building, which had grown a little too expressive for Theo's taste, seemed to recognise him immediately as a man who understood corridors as weapons.

"That him?" Mara asked.

Theo kept his eyes on the feed. "Yes."

"He looks like he refunds your money before he ruins your life."

"That's because he's thorough."

Mercer handed over a folded sheet to the receptionist. The receptionist read it, blinked once, and stood up too quickly, which told Theo the paper had one of those temporary authorities men like Mercer cultivated the way others collected watches. She lifted the phone, spoke to someone inside the suite, listened, and then opened the inner door herself.

Mara took a sip of coffee and made a face because it had gone cool. "You're certain about Helix Meridian?"

"Owen Darby was certain enough to risk his career in a stairwell."

"That doesn't mean Mercer's the coordinator."

Theo finally looked at her. "No. It means he's either the coordinator or the kind of man coordinators send when they want ownership to arrive smiling."

She took that in and glanced back through the glass. Mercer had entered Director Sayeed's waiting room and chosen the chair with the least vulnerable angle without appearing to choose anything. He set the folio on his knees and waited with his hands resting lightly on it, like a priest prepared to hear confessions if the room proved worth the effort.

"Do you want me in there from the start?" Mara asked.

"Yes."

"As what?"

Theo's mouth moved slightly. "As the person I trust to hear which nouns he wants us to start using."

She nodded once, sharp with understanding.

The summons came thirty seconds later. Sayeed's chief of staff opened the door and beckoned them in with a face professionally scrubbed of every opinion it currently possessed. Theo tucked the slim packet from Isorion under one arm, straightened his tie with two fingers, and walked into the office beside Mara with the exact pace he had learned in his first years at the Bar: not hurried enough to cede tempo, not slow enough to be theatrical.

Director Sayeed stood near her desk rather than behind it. Theo noted that with approval. Desks divided power well when power needed flattering. They were less useful when power needed to be watched from all sides.

Mercer rose.

"Mr Markel," he said, and his voice turned out to be the sort of educated neutral that made every sentence sound already minuted. "At last."

"Mistimed phrase," Theo replied. "We haven't met before."

Mercer's smile acknowledged the point without paying interest on it. "Julian Mercer. Strategic Interface Coordination Office."

No mention of Helix Meridian. Of course not.

He looked to Mara. Not over her, not past her, directly to her, and Theo disliked him more for getting that right.

"Ms Vale," he said. "I've read some of your internal narrative-control work. Elegant."

Mara's expression did not change. "That suggests somebody is reading things they shouldn't."

Mercer gave the remark the courtesy of not pretending to miss it. "We all read above our pay grade in a crisis."

Director Sayeed intervened before the air could sharpen further. "Sit," she said.

They did. Mercer took the single chair opposite the Director's desk. Theo and Mara took the two along the wall rather than the sofa, which was for donors and the falsely reassured. Sayeed remained standing a moment longer than everyone else, making the room wait for her instead of the other way around, then sat behind the desk and folded her hands.

"You asked for immediate emergency coordination authority over my programme," she said to Mercer without preamble. "You may explain why."

Mercer inclined his head. "Not your programme, Director. The city's exposure environment."

Theo felt Mara turn half a degree beside him and knew she had heard the sleight of hand too. Already Mercer was widening the frame until possession became protection and resistance began to look parochial.

Mercer laid the leather folio on the desk and opened it. Inside were three neat stacks of paper and a thin tablet he did not wake. Another point against him. Real confidence in rooms like this came carrying paper, because paper implied you expected to be doubted and had chosen your ammunition accordingly.

"We now have two fatality events," he said. "One covert operational loss, one maintenance exposure. We have corridor anomalies, records-adjacent signal mimicry, contact-route branching, and evidence of adversarial adaptation against your witness interventions." He said the last phrase without contempt, which was worse than if he had mocked it. "At this point, the fragmentation of authority is itself a threat multiplier."

Theo spoke before Sayeed could. "The maintenance death occurred inside a corridor contaminated by an instruction architecture your adjacent friends helped build."

Mercer looked at him calmly. "That allegation is premature."

"It is not an allegation. It is physics with invoices."

For the first time, Mercer's gaze sharpened. Not anger. Interest. The kind a man like him reserved for opposition that might rise above procedural weather and therefore deserved to be measured for capability rather than dismissed for sport.

"Mr Markel," he said, "I appreciate your instinct to define clean villains early. It helps many lawyers sleep. Unfortunately, the current threat is more systemically complex than that."

Mara uncapped her pen.

Theo said, "Systemically complex is what men say when they don't want the causal chain to sound like a family tree."

Sayeed let that one land. She was very good at silence, Theo thought. It was the most undervalued executive skill in the country.

Mercer spread the first set of papers. "The issue before us is straightforward. The lawful exchange architecture is under hostile pressure. Your witness model has bought you tactical time, but it has also multiplied interpretation sites, multiplied human variance, and turned every frightened clerk into an unsupervised node in a contact crisis. In plain terms, too many people are now involved who do not understand what they are carrying."

Mara wrote something on the pad without looking down. Theo knew her hand by now. She would have written not technically equipped as if pinning a specimen through the phrase.

Sayeed said, "And your remedy?"

Mercer folded one leg over the other. "Centralise authority. Suspend informal witness tables. Restrict contradiction handling to trained response officers. Consolidate route interpretation under one chain. Move the ring and key personnel to a hardened site. Remove uncontrolled civilian interfaces. Publicly frame this as a hostile systems anomaly, not a contact event."

There it was. Not crude. Not cartoonish. Quiet capture in a navy tie.

Mara looked up from the pad. "You want to take the people out of the process because the process now resists your rooms."

Mercer turned his head slightly towards her, just enough to acknowledge the precision of the strike. "No. I want to remove untrained emotional variance from a rapidly escalating threat profile."

Theo said, "That is one of the cleaner ways I've heard 'witness optional' said aloud."

Mercer's expression remained untroubled. "Witness matters. Witness density is the problem."

The office went very still.

Sayeed, to her credit, did not rescue him from the sentence. "Explain that," she said.

Mercer steepled his fingers over the folio. "Your interventions are socially stabilising at low intensity. I grant that. But scale changes the maths. Every table, every local correction point, every civilian-facing adaptation creates more surface for mimicry. You are countering hostile social engineering by widening the field of human unpredictability."

Mara's pen moved once, hard enough that Theo heard the point bite paper.

Theo said, "And your answer to social engineering is what, exactly? More engineers?"

"My answer," Mercer replied, "is disciplined command."

Theo leaned back in his chair. "There it is."

Mercer continued as though no interruption had occurred. "You are not dealing with a debate club. You are dealing with hostile adjacency. The route exists whether we approve of it or not. If one architecture can kill through contradiction, then the only defensible response is to minimise contradictory authority in the human domain."

Mara said, "By becoming it."

That finally changed him. Not the face, not much, but the eyes. He looked at her as if recalibrating.

"No," he said. "By outpacing it."

Director Sayeed had listened to all of this with one hand resting lightly on the desk blotter, the packet from Isorion beside her like a legal ghost. Now she lifted a page from Mercer's stack and scanned it. Her brows did not move, but Theo saw the moment she found what mattered.

"You've already drafted transfer papers," she said.

Mercer did not blink. "Prepared, not actioned."

"For the ring."

"For the apparatus and key personnel."

"The key personnel being?"

"Elian Cross. Tamsin Roe. Dr Imani on rotating consult. Ms Vale if narrative control remains essential."

Mara looked at him with a kind of still curiosity, Theo had only seen in her when a liar finally reached the lie he believed was most plausible. "Narrative control."

"Yes."

"That is what you think I do."

"I think," Mercer said, "you are currently the most capable person in this building at determining which truths travel and how quickly. I'm complimenting you."

"No," Mara said. "You're filing me."

Theo felt, rather than saw, Sayeed's approval of that answer.

Mercer rested back in his chair, finally offering a glimpse of the worldview that sat under all the polished phrasing. "With respect, Ms Vale, the luxury of self-definition usually contracts in a crisis. We all become functions for a while."

There it was again. Reduction dressed as necessity. The side-lane in a suit.

Theo said, "Some of us notice when a man builds a room inside a sentence."

Mercer's smile was very slight now, almost private. "And some of us notice when lawyers mistake delay for virtue."

Sayeed set down the transfer papers. "No."

Mercer turned to her, not startled, merely inconvenienced. "Director..."

"No," she repeated. "The ring remains here. The operators remain here. The witness tables remain. Nothing moves under a doctrine built by offices that thought black-room interviews were a respectable way to manage uncertainty."

The line had force because she spoke it mildly. Mercer inclined his head again, but this time the gesture had effort in it.

"You are making a principled error."

Sayeed said, "That assumes your principles are fit to own the word."

A silence followed that had real mass.

Theo let himself enjoy one heartbeat of it and then took the packet from Isorion from under his arm and placed it on the desk, not in front of Sayeed, who had already read it, but directly between himself and Mercer.

Mercer's eyes moved to the pages.

Theo said, "Since we are discussing principled errors, I'd like to know why your offices have not yet informed your briefings with the name used by the far-side lawful council."

Mercer's gaze did not leave the packet. "I beg your pardon?"

"Cauterists," Theo said.

The word entered the room cleanly.

Mercer looked up at last.

There are moments when a man's whole profession becomes visible in the smallest available space. Theo saw it then, not as panic, but as adaptation under surprise. Mercer had not expected the term. More precisely, he had not expected them to have it yet. In the half-second before he arranged his face again, the reaction passed through him like a card turned too quickly under a sleeve.

Mara saw it too. Theo knew because her pen did not move for the next three seconds and Mara only ever stopped writing when truth had become more valuable than the sentence she was building.

"An interesting translation choice," Mercer said at last.

"Not ours," Theo replied.

Sayeed spoke without looking at him. "You knew there was a name."

Mercer said, "There are always names."

"Not like that," Mara said.

He turned to her. "You think you saw something?"

"I think you were ready for the concept and not the noun. Which means your rooms were built around a threat model someone briefed you on without telling you the thing's proper name, or you've been lying about how close you are to the source."

Theo could have kissed the back of her hand for that sentence if the room had contained fewer people and no one at all named Julian Mercer.

Mercer held her gaze for a beat longer than politeness required. "You are very quick, Ms Vale."

"And you are already late."

The tiniest tightening appeared around his mouth.

Theo said, "Let us save time. You're not here because you're frightened by two deaths. You're here because the witness tables are starting to interfere with an architecture someone on your side intended to scale."

Mercer stood.

It was not dramatic. He simply rose from the chair and closed the folio with both hands, as though the meeting had shifted category and now belonged to another tier of handling.

"I came," he said, "because in the absence of adult coordination this building will continue inventing morale rituals while the city's exposure surface expands beneath your feet."

Theo stood too. "Careful. You almost said the quiet part."

Mercer's eyes slid to the packet, to the witness guidance stack on the side credenza, to the notepad in Mara's hand. "Bench tables and witness cards are not strategy," he said.

"No," Mara replied. "They're why your shortcut is suddenly having to think."

This time the smile did not return. Not fully. It left behind something colder, cleaner, and much more useful to see. The man underneath the manners. The one who genuinely believed results justified coercive refinement. The one who did not think of people as expendable exactly, only as variables whose dignity became negotiable under pressure.

He gathered the folio under one arm. "Director, I'll send revised authority language through formal channels."

Sayeed said, "Do that. I'll enjoy declining it in writing."

Mercer inclined his head to her, then to Theo, and finally to Mara. "Ms Vale."

"Mr Mercer."

He turned and walked out without haste.

The door closed behind him.

Nobody spoke for four seconds.

Then Theo said, "Well."

Mara looked at her notes. "He used 'witness density' and 'untrained emotional variance' without once saying law."

Sayeed sat back in her chair. "He came to seize, not advise."

"Yes," Theo said. "Quiet capture."

Mara turned a page and wrote the phrase down as if pinning another specimen to felt.

Sayeed reached for the packet from Isorion and tapped the top sheet once. "He knew the threat existed. He did not know the lawful side had named it for us. That matters."

"It means he has an incomplete brief chain," Theo said. "Or someone above him has been compartmentalising the language from the operators."

"Or," Mara said, "they know exactly what the Cauterists are and chose not to use the name because names force moral contour where phrases like hostile adjacency keep things abstract."

Theo looked at her. "That goes in the archive."

"It's already there."

Sayeed gave the faintest hint of a smile. "Of course it is."

She stood. "Theo, with me. Mara, you too. I want the witness programme expanded before lunch. Facilities, archive thresholds, loading bays, and every lift lobby that touches a service route. And I want Mercer's transfer papers copied, indexed, and preserved before someone develops second thoughts."

Mara nodded. "Done."

They left the office together and walked the Level Three corridor without speaking until they reached the bench alcove outside procurement. Nina Fowler was there, as promised, presiding over the table like a magistrate for paper crimes, one pair of spectacles low on her nose, the witness ledger open, kettle steaming softly beside her. A cleaner from Level Nine stood opposite her with a red trolley parked at the wall and a contradiction slip in her hand.

Nina looked up as they approached. "Well?"

Theo answered at once. "The table stays."

Nina sniffed once. "Thought so."

Mara's eyes went to the contradiction slip in the cleaner's hand. "What have we got?"

The cleaner held it up between two fingers. "Voice on my floor line said to shut off access to the west women's bathroom because of a heat fault. Building panel says no fault. Then the same voice says ignore the panel because the panel's lagging. So I thought I'd come downstairs and ask a table instead of a liar."

Mara looked at Theo and then at the ugly laminate surface, the witness card stack, the kettle, the cleaner's trolley, Nina Fowler's folded hands. The whole arrangement would have looked laughably small to Julian Mercer. That, she realised, was one of its best qualities.

Theo took the slip, read it, and handed it to her. "Log it," he said.

She did.

The cleaner watched her write. "This the new normal then?"

Mara looked up. "No. This is the new refusal."

The woman considered that, then nodded as if she approved of the wording and went back to explaining exactly how wrong the voice had sounded once it started repeating the word immediately.

As Nina wrote, Mara turned slightly and looked back down the corridor towards Director Sayeed's office. The door had already shut again. Behind it, the packet lay on the desk and the word Cauterists existed now in two more minds that would have preferred friendlier nouns. Somewhere lower in the building, Elian and Tamsin were likely already picking at Mercer's transfer language to see what he had accidentally admitted by writing it down. Somewhere farther away, Mercer would be walking through rain towards a car or a driver or a second office from which he could begin the quieter war he had clearly expected to win in a morning.

Good, she thought.

Let him.

She bent over the witness ledger again and wrote the cleaner's name in a clear, strong hand. The page beneath it already held Lachie Baines, Nina Fowler, two analysts, a porter, and a security guard who had decided not to trust a perfectly polite rerouting order because the order had sounded too smooth in his ear. Ugly little refusals. Awkward tables. Breathing people. All of it, the sort of friction men like Julian Mercer described as inefficiency, when what they meant was civilisation being in the way.

The cleaner on the other side of the table was still talking.

"...and I thought, if I do shut it, then the next instruction'll be worse, won't it? Because once they know you'll obey the first daft thing..."

"Yes," Mara said, and kept writing. "That is exactly how it works."

She did not realise until later that this was the first moment when she had truly believed they might yet outrun the quiet capture, not because they had won anything, but because Julian Mercer had looked at the table and failed to understand why it frightened him. Men like that trusted systems until systems required humility. They always mistook the ugliest, most human parts of resistance for a temporary mess. They never understood how stubborn ordinary people became once given permission to speak in contradiction before it turned inward.

By noon, the first copies of Mercer's transfer papers sat in three places. One is in official legal hold. One in the shadow archive. One folded inside Mr Idris's ugly safe under a label that read, in his own dry hand, MAN WHO WANTED RESULTS. Theo objected to the title on procedural grounds and, outvoted by everyone with a soul, let it stand.

And somewhere behind the paper, the weather, the bench tables, and the lawful line they had worked so hard to preserve, the side-lane with teeth had found its human champion. Not a monster. Worse. A man who thought narrowing choice was the same thing as protecting the world from indecision.

Mara copied that sentence into her notebook, too.

Then she went back to the table because another contradiction had arrived, and Nina was waving her over with the irritated urgency of someone who had no time at all for men who wanted rooms and routes to do what truth should have done in public.

Chapter Eleven: Rail Echo

The first mistake was that the announcement mentioned Priya Nandakumar's name.

She was standing on Platform 11 at Southern Cross with her laptop bag digging into the ridge of one shoulder and a travel mug cooling between her palms when the overhead speakers cleared their throats. It was 7:42 in the morning, the station full of ordinary impatience, shoes on concrete, coffee breath, coats damp at the hem from a night of uncertain rain, and the low electrical patience of trains holding themselves ready under the ribbed roof.

Priya had spent eleven years catching one service or another through the city. She trusted none of them emotionally and all of them structurally, which was the proper arrangement between a commuter and public transport. The departures board flickered from two minutes late to on time and back again in the vague, slightly offended way it always did. A little boy in a school blazer dragged one hand along the tactile strip until his mother snapped his name. Somewhere behind Priya, a man unwrapped something from a bakery bag with the soft greed of a person who believed in breakfast as an ethical necessity. Ordinary. Entirely ordinary.

Then the overhead voice said, very clearly, "Priya Nandakumar, stand back from the yellow line."

She turned so sharply that hot tea lapped over the lip of the mug and onto her wrist.

No one else moved.

The speakers hissed once, swallowed their own authority, and returned to the scheduled female station voice with all its familiar municipal calm.

"The 7:44 service to Werribee is now arriving on Platform 11. Please stand behind the yellow line."

Priya stared at the nearest speaker grille mounted under the platform canopy. Her own face looked back at her from the train window across the tracks, blurred by distance and grime, mouth slightly open in a way she disliked seeing on herself. She took one step backwards from the line anyway, because hearing your own name through public address systems is the sort of thing that ought to be obeyed until proven otherwise.

The man beside her glanced over, not noticing her disquiet so much as the tea on her sleeve. "You all right?"

"Yes," she lied automatically.

She looked up at the board again. 7:44 Werribee. On time. The little digital certainty steadied her enough that she almost laughed at herself. Some station staffer had read a booking screen aloud by mistake. That was all. A glitch, a crossed line, a joke if she were feeling generous, which she wasn't.

The train lights appeared in the tunnel mouth.

At the same instant, the speakers said, "Priya Nandakumar, do not board this service."

Every sound on the platform seemed to arrive twice.

The station voice went on with its routine announcement, but under it, or through it, or braided so tightly with it that Priya could not tell which words were public and which were only hers, came a second thread, lower and oddly intimate.

"Do not board. Wait exactly where you are."

Someone behind her swore.

The schoolboy's mother said, "What?" sharply enough that three people turned.

The train slid in with a rising whine, brakes catching, metal speaking to metal in the ordinary grammar of arrival. Doors aligned with the platform markers. People shifted forward in that small communal lean of a city, agreeing to continue being itself.

Priya did not move.

On the opposite side of the platform, a woman in a camel coat had her hand half-raised to hail no one and was staring at the overhead board as if it had begun reciting family secrets. Two teenagers laughed too loudly, the way people laugh when something feels wrong, and they want to force it to become silly before it acquires a second shape.

The doors hissed open.

Then every display on Platform 11 went blank.

Not dark. Blank. White rectangles where times and destinations should have been, glowing with the dead flat confidence of a display that had not yet been properly populated.

A second voice came through the speakers. Male this time. Not station-trained. Too close to the ear.

"Remain on the platform."

The public address system answered itself at once in the female transit voice.

"Board now. Doors may close without further warning."

The crowd stirred, checked, split along fault lines too small to name. Some people stepped forward. Some hung back. The schoolboy began to cry because children are honest sooner than adults. Priya felt the skin across her shoulders go cold while heat gathered unpleasantly in the middle of her chest.

The male voice, still intimate, still wrong, said, "Do not move until the train departs."

The official voice said, "Please board immediately."

A man two metres away laughed a broken little laugh and said to no one in particular, "Which bloody one?"

The train sat with its doors open and seemed, for one impossible second, to stretch.

Not physically. Priya would later swear under oath that nothing supernatural had happened to the carriage geometry because she was a practical woman, thirty-six, senior analyst in a superannuation office, not given to public embarrassments or private visions. What happened instead was this: the open doorway stopped belonging cleanly to the train and began belonging also to the instruction about it. Boarding and not boarding ceased to be choices about feet and became choices about truth, and her body, which had not trained for philosophy at commuter hour, began trying to solve the problem too fast.

Her hearing went strange.

The station noise moved farther away while also moving closer. Shoes on concrete clicked as if inside a tiled bathroom. The cry of the schoolboy arrived half a beat after she saw his mouth open. The bakery paper crackled behind her with the intimate volume of a hand near her own ear. Her tea mug felt suddenly too warm against her palms.

Then, worst of all, relief arrived.

Not because the platform had become safe. Because one of the voices began sounding more practical than the other.

"Stand still," the male voice said. "Standing still removes error."

Priya's shoulders dropped before she realised they had.

Some primitive, tired administrative part of her thought yes, of course, stillness is simple, stillness is what they want, stillness means no mistake can be attributed to me.

The thought scared her after it happened, not before.

Beside her, the man who had asked if she was all right suddenly took two rapid steps towards the open carriage and then stopped so violently that his shoulder bag swung round and struck his thigh. He looked left, then right, like someone trying to remember which version of the room he had begun in.

"Board now," said the station voice.

"Stand clear," said the male one.

"Immediate departure."

"Remain where you are."

Priya's throat tightened.

On the white departure screen nearest her, faint grey text began pressing up from nowhere, not printed but impressed under the blank glow, as if the display had become paper before deciding what words it wanted.

DO NOT...

The rest vanished before her eyes could finish the line.

A station staffer in navy and orange high-vis appeared at the top of the platform ramp, radio raised. "Hold positions!" he shouted, which was the worst possible thing to say because no one any longer knew what a position was. The radio on his shoulder answered him in the same clipped station voice everyone had been hearing overhead.

"Dispatch confirms board now."

Then, almost under it, not through the radio speaker exactly but through the air near his chest, came the male voice again. "Hold position."

The staffer flinched.

Priya saw it happen and understood, with the kind of instant terror usually reserved for sudden height or blood, that it was not only her. The platform was becoming a room where a hundred people might each be carrying a slightly different version of the same contradiction, enough difference to isolate and enough sameness to feel official.

A woman near the train doors put a hand to the side of her head and sank down onto the nearest bench with her shopping tote spilling oranges across the concrete. One rolled to the edge of the yellow line and sat there like an accusation. The man beside Priya whispered, "I can't hear right," to nobody at all.

Her watch vibrated once on her wrist, though no alert had come in.

"Priya," said the male voice.

Everything inside her locked.

The relief was back, terrible now, because the use of her name made the command feel customised, and customised instructions feel safer than general ones when the world begins splitting. The voice did not shout. It barely had to.

"Stay."

The station voice, relentless in its civic optimism, said, "Doors closing."

The doors did not close.

Priya felt the skin along her forearms pebble cold. At the same time, a bloom of heat unfolded under her sternum, not pain yet, but enough to make her set the tea mug down blindly on the bench behind her without taking her eyes from the train.

Somewhere deep in the station, a second announcement started, this one for another platform entirely, but the sound reached her braided to the first so that words from different lines began sharing the same body.

"Proceed to..."

"Do not..."

"Werribee service..."

"Remain..."

The man beside her suddenly grabbed his own wrist hard enough to blanch the knuckles. "Tell me which one," he said, not to her, not to anyone. "Tell me which one is the real one."

The phrase hit her like cold water.

Tell me which one is the real one.

Not which instruction. Which one. Human. Voice. Source.

The heat under her breastbone sharpened.

She looked down at her own hands. One was still on the strap of her bag. The other was hanging uselessly at her side. She made it move, deliberately, and pressed her fingertips hard against the rough-painted metal of the bench support.

Cold. Real. Flaking paint. One true thing.

The sensation jolted through her like a slap. Not mystical. Not healing. Just external enough to interrupt the awful clean tendency in her body to begin solving the room by itself.

She heard herself say, much too loudly, "I am touching the bench."

Three people turned to look at her.

Good, some sane fragment of her thought. Let them. Let there be more than one body in this.

The station staffer was coming down the platform now, not quickly because running near panicking commuters only teaches panic to move its legs, but with purpose. "Nobody boards," he shouted. "Nobody boards. Step back from the doors and look at me."

The male voice from the speakers said at once, "Board now."

The staffer's jaw tightened. He slapped his radio off and kept talking with only his own lungs. "Nobody boards. Look at me."

Priya pressed harder on the metal bench support and said to the nearest stranger, a woman in the camel coat still standing too straight by the edge, "Can you hear two voices?"

The woman's face shifted from private alarm to something more survivable.

"Yes," she said.

Thank God.

That wasn't quite right either. It was not gratitude to God. It was a gratifying experience to witness the existence of a second human being willing to say aloud that the room had split and that neither of them would benefit from pretending otherwise.

The heat under Priya's sternum lessened by a fraction.

The man beside her, still gripping his own wrist, looked from one woman to the other and said, "I heard board and stay. Same time."

"Bench," Priya said, absurdly, because the only true thing she had was the steel support under her fingers and the memory of that word from some workplace flyer she had nearly thrown out with the junk mail. "Touch something real. Don't choose alone."

The man blinked at her.

Then, shakily, he put his free hand against the tiled pillar behind him.

The station staffer had reached them by then. His name badge said R. DONNELLY and his face had gone the strained pale colour of a man doing three jobs, all of them under-witnessed.

"Good," he said, though he had no idea what the good was. "Good. Stay with me. We're clearing the platform."

The train doors finally shut of their own accord.

No one had boarded.

The white blank screens flickered, shivered, and snapped back to ordinary departure text so suddenly the restoration itself felt suspicious. The speakers emitted one last wash of static and then, in the cheerful recorded voice of public infrastructure pretending not to notice its own brush with malevolence, announced a minor delay to services due to an operational incident.

The train pulled out.

As it moved, the carriage windows caught Platform 11's people in fragments. Priya saw herself in one pane, hand white-knuckled on the bench support, mouth open, eyes too bright. In the next pane, she saw the camel-coat woman holding her own forearm with both hands as if bracing a fracture. In the next, she saw the man in the shoulder bag still touching the pillar, not because he needed support now, but because letting go too early felt stupidly like risk.

Then the train was gone.

For a few moments, the platform held the hush of a room after someone has almost said the worst thing and decided, for reasons still private, to swallow it. Then sound returned in pieces. The schoolboy sobbing into his mother's coat. The oranges being gathered one by one from under the bench. The radio on Donnelly's shoulder sputtering back to life with a dispatch voice that, for the moment, sounded singular.

Priya let go of the bench and discovered her hand had left a crescent of paint dust across her fingertips.

The heat in her chest had dropped to something like ordinary panic.

She would later tell the woman from station safety that she had lost perhaps thirty seconds, perhaps forty. She would say that the platform had felt wrong, that her own name through the speakers had made the instructions feel personal, that stillness had begun to seem like a favour being done to her rather than something demanded of her. She would not, because she worked in a sensible office and had a mortgage and a manager called Ross who still wrote kind regards in passive-aggressive emails, tell them that the wrongness had seemed organised. That part she would only admit to herself at two in the morning when she woke with her hand gripping the metal bedhead hard enough to hurt.

An hour later, the footage reached the annex.

Tamsin watched it first in the lower lab and said, with complete sincerity, "Oh, you sly municipal bastard."

Theo, Mara, Sera, and Elian came down one by one until the room had the same dense, witness-heavy air it now acquired whenever the city offered them another piece of truth too ugly to trust to any one pair of eyes.

The station recording had been clipped from half a dozen sources and still did not agree with itself. Overhead platform cameras. Carriage interior feed. Dispatch audio. Passenger phone clips already beginning to circulate under headings that ranged from signal glitch at Southern Cross to Melbourne train AI goes psycho. The anomaly itself sat inside the overlap like a splinter in wood grain, easiest to deny if one looked at any stream in isolation, impossible to dismiss if one forced them together.

Tamsin had already done that.

On the main screen, Platform 11 unfolded in four windows at once. In the upper left, Priya Nandakumar stood by the yellow line with the tea mug in both hands. In the upper right, the man with the shoulder bag reached for nothing and stopped. Bottom left, the station staffer Donnelly turned off his radio with one furious slap. Bottom right, the white displays bloomed blank and held their blankness just long enough to feel intentional.

Elian stood too close to the screen and did not notice until Mara put a hand lightly at the centre of his back and guided him half a step away.

"No deaths," Tamsin said. "Before anyone asks. One panic collapse. One possible timing dissociation. Four contradictory instruction reports. Zero ignition signatures."

Sera folded her arms. "Why?"

"Because," Theo said, reading the bench-hour incident report she had already pulled from the station worker's follow-up, "someone externalised early."

He held the report up.

Station witness account, R. Donnelly. Multiple passengers heard conflicting announcements. One female commuter initiated open contradiction by asking nearby passengers if they also heard two voices. The subject then instructed adjacent passengers not to choose alone and to touch fixed objects. Crowd stabilisation followed. Platform cleared without further escalation.

Mara looked at the page, then at the frozen image of Priya's hand on the bench support. "She built a table on a railway platform."

Sera nodded slowly. "Physical anchor. Spoken contradiction. Second witness. Shared room response. That's the sequence."

Tamsin flicked to another screen and overlaid the station timing data with the route-behaviour model from the side-lane descent. "It gets better," she said, which in Tamsin never meant comfort. "Look at the shape of the audio split."

On the graph, the station announcement stream and the false male voice diverged just before the train stopped. Their separation widened not with volume but with personalisation. The public stream remained general. The false stream targeted individuals. Names where available. proximate bodily language where not. Stand back. board now. remain where you are. It was not spraying confusion. It was assigning contradictory private burdens inside a public environment.

"Same family," Elian said quietly.

"Same appetite," Mara answered.

Theo looked at the route graph, then back at the footage. "And it spread through transit steel."

Tamsin gave him a sharp glance that was almost approving. "Yes. Metal adjacency at city scale. Rails, carriages, platform structures, overhead systems, public address relays. The station didn't become a black room. It became a broad, shallow induction surface."

Sera pointed to Priya's posture on the screen. "Shallow enough that ignition didn't lock. Deep enough to start the body thinking closure."

The word sat in the room like a legal ruling and a diagnosis at once.

On the lower right display, the passenger clip taken by a teenager at the far end of the platform had caught one detail the station feed had not. As the blank screen above the platform flashed white, faint grey lettering rose through it for less than a second before disappearing.

DO NOT...

That was all the frame could hold.

Mara moved closer. "Same pressure expression as the page in Daniel's corridor."

Tamsin brought up the image from the service seam. The blank sheet. The impressed words. The family resemblance between the two events was unmistakable now. Not same hardware, not same scale, but same method: ordinary civic surfaces temporarily behaving like paper willing to take dictation from the wrong side of a line.

Theo looked tired in a way sleep would not touch. "Mercer."

No one asked what he meant.

Julian Mercer had not only wanted the ring and the operators. He had wanted centralisation before events like Southern Cross could create witness outside his chain. The point was becoming offensively clear. As the city began to answer in steel and rail and display glass, the fight over who got to interpret those answers would become indistinguishable from the fight over whether people lived through them.

Mara took the station report from Theo and read it once fast, then once slowly. "Donnelly turned his radio off."

"Yes," Theo said.

"Good."

"He'll get reprimanded."

"Then we give him cover."

Theo's eyes flicked to hers. He already knew what she meant.

"Not yet publicly," he said.

"No. But internally, yes. We can't have staff deciding they hallucinated the right move."

Tamsin, still at the console, said, "There's another problem."

They all turned.

She highlighted a timing thread nested in the station system data, one that rode the contradictory announcements only briefly before dropping into the platform's rail-bed telemetry.

"The false stream piggybacked on carriage arrival timing," she said. "It used the decision pressure of boarding to amplify the contradiction. Not because it needed a train. Because trains arrive with built-in urgency and binary action. Board or don't. move or remain. It borrowed the city's own scheduling psychology."

Sera muttered a curse under her breath.

Elian stared at the line and felt something cold unroll under his ribs. The side-lane in the false route had offered him a practical detour framed as moral urgency. The station event had done the same thing to a crowd, not in depth, but at breadth. It was learning not only from private rooms. It was learning from public timing.

"It's not just scaling," he said. "It's urbanising."

The sentence got their full attention because it was hideous and right.

Mara wrote it down immediately in the shadow notebook.

Theo said, "Explain."

Elian forced the thought into a shape that did not collapse under its own implications. "The route isn't confined to hidden architecture anymore. It's using ordinary city structures that already teach bodies how to comply under time pressure. Trains. platform announcements. boarding thresholds. It doesn't need to build a black room from scratch if the city already provides moving pieces of one."

No one spoke for a moment.

Then Mr Idris, who had entered quietly during the station replay with the afternoon ledgers tucked under one arm and had remained still near the door like a benevolent ghost, said, "That is a very rude sentence, Mr Cross."

Tamsin gave a broken laugh. "That's one word for it."

Mr Idris came farther in, set the ledgers on the side bench, and peered at the frozen frame of Priya touching the bench support. "The woman did better than half the state apparatus."

"She externalised in time," Sera said.

"She made the platform hold it with her," Mara added.

Theo looked at the line of benches, rails, doors, display boards, and overhead voices on the replay. "How many stations?"

Tamsin had already begun pulling the network map. "I don't know yet. But if Southern Cross can go shallow, then every metallic transit node in the CBD is now a question."

Theo rubbed one hand over his mouth and said the thing they had all been trying not to say because saying it moved the problem from bad to civic.

"The city."

No one corrected him.

Mara turned from the screen. "We need station language."

Sera said at once, "Yes."

Tamsin said, "Fast."

Theo looked at Mara. "What can the public hold without turning this into a riot or a meme before sunset?"

Mara's face had gone into that hard, bright focus he associated with the first ten minutes of any real campaign. "Not contact. Not architecture. Not Cauterists. Yet. But they can hold practical truth."

"Meaning?"

"Meaning if public systems issue contradictory instructions, do not choose alone. Touch something fixed. Make eye contact with another person. Ask whether they heard the same thing. Get to staff in pairs or groups. We frame it as protocol for systems anomalies and mass-audio faults."

Theo was already nodding.

Tamsin objected on principle. "That sounds like crisis comms."

"It is crisis comms."

"I hate crisis comms."

Mara turned to her. "Then hate effective ones."

That shut Tamsin up for nearly six whole seconds.

Sera was still watching Priya on the screen. "I want station medics briefed on pre-lock signs. Cold skin, central heat, auditory lag, repeat phrasing, fixation on finding the one true instruction. Not just panic response. Different treatment posture."

Theo made a note. "I can route through Health as anomalous stress guidance if I don't say anything too interesting."

Mr Idris, opening the first of the incoming ledgers, said, "And the tables?"

Mara looked at him. "More."

"Yes," he said. "I thought so."

By late afternoon, the lower lab had become command, not by ambition but by necessity. Tamsin built a transit-adjacency model from rail maps, station material data, announcement-system logic, and every known route response they had captured so far. Theo turned ugly truths into language ministers could survive reading without instantly making them worse. Sera drafted a medical addendum for field staff that would offend paramedics by asking them to think at the same time as they soothed, which meant it had a chance of working. Mara wrote the station card.

Not a poster. Not yet. A card. Something a station supervisor could read off a phone or a printed sheet without sounding like the city had gone mad and begun quoting philosophy at commuters.

If system announcements conflict, do not choose alone.
Touch a fixed surface.
Ask the nearest person if they heard the same instruction.
Move toward staff in pairs or groups.
Do not follow personalised public instructions that others cannot verify.

She read it aloud. Theo trimmed two words. Sera added one. Tamsin wanted to include "if it flatters, leave," but was overruled on the grounds that public transport already had enough image problems.

Elian spent the hour moving between the route maps and the station replay, forcing himself to see not catastrophe but method. The city was not yet a black room. Southern Cross had proved only that broad, shallow induction could ride ordinary infrastructures under the right timing pressures. No ignition. No full lock. Not yet. But the route was learning. It had gone from service corridor to shielded interview chamber to public platform in less than a week.

Julian Mercer had called their witness interventions morale rituals.

The station proved he was either blind or lying more strategically than usual. Priya Nandakumar had survived not because an office centralised authority around her, but because she touched a bench, spoke the contradiction aloud, and made strangers carry part of it before her body decided to carry all of it alone.

Mara, catching him watching the replay for too long, came to stand beside him.

"What?" she asked.

He looked at Priya on the frozen screen. Hand on the bench support. Mouth open. The city still had no settled public language for what had almost happened to her.

"It's one thing in rooms built for capture," he said. "Black sites. interview chambers. side-lanes. It's another when the city starts improvising."

Mara took that in. "Cities always improvise. The question is who gets there first."

He glanced at her. "That sounded like Theo."

"No. Theo would have made it more irritating."

That got the smallest smile out of him.

At six-thirty, the first briefing pack went out under Director Sayeed's authority to station operations, transport safety, selected medics, and a carefully chosen cluster of city infrastructure contacts, Theo believed could still read without reaching first for doctrine. The word Cauterists did not appear. Neither did contact. But the logic of witness, contradiction, and fixed-surface anchoring was there, disguised as system-anomaly guidance and urban-calm protocol. It was not enough. It was what could travel without feeding the wrong mouths.

Outside, Melbourne settled into the evening in layers. Commuters packed platforms. Trams squealed around curves. Steel expanded and settled with small civic aches. Somewhere under the city, wet rails and grounded current sat poised between the ordinary and the newly dangerous, according to pressures human beings had only just begun to name.

In the lower lab, Tamsin finally stepped away from the console and stretched until her spine cracked in three distinct places. "I have good news and bad news."

Theo did not look up from the legal pad. "You say that every day now."

"Because every day deserves it. Good news: Southern Cross wasn't a full closure event. The architecture stayed shallow because the contradiction couldn't isolate enough people quickly enough. Bad news: if timing pressure had been slightly better aligned, or if the station staffer had trusted his radio over his lungs for another thirty seconds, this would have gone much nastier."

Silence.

Sera said, "How much nastier?"

Tamsin's eyes flicked to the graph, then away. "Enough for one platform to become a black room by aggregate."

No one liked that sentence.

Mr Idris wrote it down anyway.

Mara closed the shadow notebook. "Then tomorrow we need station tables."

Theo looked up at once. "That will trigger questions."

"Yes."

"And panic."

"Only if we let others answer them first."

Theo considered her, then gave one tired nod. "All right."

The station card became a station table plan before anyone had eaten dinner.

By nine, Nina Fowler had recruited two more clerks and one cleaner to stand witness at Southern Cross on rotating intervals under transit-systems anomaly cover. Tamsin built them offline countersign pads in ugly plastic housings she described as divorce-proof. Sera added simple body-state cue sheets. Mara turned the language further outward until it sounded almost insultingly practical. Theo arranged authority for the tables through a chain of temporary urban resilience directives so that no one powerful would notice until after they had worked.

At eleven fifteen, just as the first station-table kits were sealed for courier, the side display by Elian's elbow flickered.

He looked up.

Not the station map. Not the route graph. The ring monitor.

A single thin secondary line, buried under the lawful contour, had brightened and then dimmed again.

He stood too quickly.

Mara looked over at once. "What?"

"The side-lane."

Tamsin was at the screen in two strides. She called up the route log and froze the last ten seconds of telemetry. There it was. The branch they had named corridor with teeth, flaring not into invitation this time, but into attention.

"Why now?" Theo asked.

No one answered because the answer was standing in sealed courier kits on the side bench.

Mara said it first. "Station tables."

Elian's skin went cold.

The false route had reacted not to the station event itself, not to the replay, not even to the first city briefing. It had reacted to the tables moving into the transit system, into the same public timing structures it had begun to urbanise. The architecture was not merely spreading. It was tracking the spread of what opposed it.

Tamsin swore once, elaborately. "Well, that's intimate."

Sera looked at the brightened line and then at the kits waiting for courier. "So it knows."

Theo's face had gone very still. "Or something watching through it knows."

Mr Idris capped his pen and wrapped the ledger closed with deliberate care. "Then perhaps," he said, "we had better get there first."

No one argued.

The city above them carried on for another hour in ignorance, trains arriving and departing under timetables, rails singing, commuters cursing delays, speakers making promises with civic confidence. But under that ordinary motion the shape of what came next had already begun to form.

The route had moved into rail.

Now the tables were going to follow.

And somewhere between steel, timing, and a predatory architecture adapting itself to public systems, Melbourne had just become the first place in which public transport and witness doctrine were about to meet in open conflict.

Chapter Twelve: Ninety Seconds

At 4:57 p.m., the ring twitched like a hooked nerve.

Tamsin Roe saw it first on the lower right monitor and did not bother with politeness. "No," she said to the screen, as if refusal might still count as an engineering discipline. Then louder, with the sort of clarity rooms obeyed when fear was no longer theoretical, "No, no, no. Theo."

The lower lab altered around the word. Mara looked up from the station-table kits she was sealing into courier satchels. Sera stopped halfway through clipping a thermal strip chart to a clipboard. Theo, who had been speaking in the corridor to someone from Transport who believed the phrase systems anomaly might be enough to keep them all out of trouble for another six hours, came through the door already wearing the expression of a man who disliked the future on principle and intended to bill it for his time.

"What?"

Tamsin had three maps open and was dragging the route flare over the transit-adjacency model with one hand while her other stabbed at the keyboard.

"The side-lane just brightened and then dropped into a live network path," she said. "Not the station tables themselves. Something beneath them. South-west grid, rail-linked, sublevel relay spine."

Elian was already moving to her shoulder. The flare line, thin as a cut under the lawful contour, had not simply answered the station-table rollout. It had travelled. He saw the pattern one heartbeat before she isolated it.

"Southern Cross," he said.

"Not the public concourse," Tamsin snapped. "Below it. Service interchange. Docklands side."

Theo was beside them now. "Active?"

"Yes."

"How active?"

Tamsin overlaid the timing stream from the station anomaly on Platform 11, and the answer appeared in the most offensive possible way: cleanly.

"Active enough that something is using train-timing pressure again," she said. "Only this is deeper. More controlled. Someone's built a live relay in the sublevel."

Mara was already on her feet. "Transfer."

Theo looked at her.

She met it head-on. "If Mercer knows the station tables are going in, he knows witness is about to enter transit space. He moves before the tables settle. He gets his material or his witness or his room clear before the city learns how to refuse him."

For a fraction of a second, no one spoke, because the logic landed with that clean, brutal force only the right sentence ever had. Then Theo took his phone from his pocket and began making calls.

"Donnelly at Southern Cross. Nina Fowler at the table. Director Sayeed. I want Transport control warned without language that will make them shut the wrong thing. Tamsin, location now. Sera, field kits. Mara, shadow pack and public language. Elian..."

He did not finish because Elian was already pulling on his coat.

Rain had begun again over Melbourne, not heavy, but enough to turn the station forecourts dark and keep the city's steel damp at the edges. Southern Cross at the edge of peak hour had the usual appearance of a civilisation too committed to routine to notice what it carried in its own bones. Commuters came in by waves under the long curving roof. Digital boards refreshed. Trams rattled somewhere beyond Spencer Street. Engines breathed. Metal waited.

Above ground, Nina Fowler had the first station witness table set up near the central concourse lift bank under a sign that read SYSTEMS CONTRADICTION SUPPORT in the sort of boring official font Tamsin had chosen precisely because no one would take a second look until the words mattered. Nina herself sat behind the ugly fold-out table in a navy cardigan and reading glasses, ledger open, witness cards stacked, kettle steaming beside a plastic tub of glucose biscuits. She looked less like a bulwark against predatory route architecture than someone who might rebuke a nation for bad handwriting. That was one of the reasons she worked.

Donnelly met them by the side gate in his station high-vis with rain darkening the shoulders of his jacket and strain already tightening his face.

"Two minor splits in the last twenty minutes," he said without preamble as he led them towards the service access corridor. "One on Platform Nine, one near the luggage tunnel escalators. No locks. We externalised early. People are jumpy."

"How many heard names?" Sera asked.

"Three reports. One verified."

Theo swore softly.

Donnelly keyed them through a grey maintenance door that should have smelled only of detergent, concrete, and old damp. Instead, the air beyond carried the faint electrical tang Elian now associated with wrong adjacency, steel thinking too hard about itself.

The service level beneath Southern Cross was not one place but a string of places half-forgotten by the public and never fully loved by the people who worked there. Freight ramps. Utility tunnels. Staff corridors. Cable rooms. Access passages where paint peeled from concrete in long, damp breaths. The noise from above reached down as a diffuse civic weight, footsteps translated into pressure, announcements into muffled authority, trains into a subterranean thrum through the floor.

Tamsin stopped dead halfway down the first corridor and held up one hand.

"There," she said.

At first, Theo saw nothing. Then the fluorescent strip over the next door gave a soft, wrong pulse, not flickering, not failing, only responding to some rhythm outside the circuitry printed on its casing.

Elian could feel the route beneath it at once. Not the Harbour, which remained broad and patient at a distance like a coastline remembered in sleep. This was the false structure, threaded now into station metal and service relays. It had depth. Purpose. And under that, the side-lane with teeth, no longer tentative but fully grown.

"It's under us," he said.

Mara glanced at him. "How close?"

He did not like the answer and gave it anyway. "Close enough to smell."

Donnelly led them down another flight and into the interchange node.

The room ahead had once been a loading transfer bay. You could still read that in it. Wide doors. Track cut-outs in the floor where maintenance carts could run. Reinforced wall plates. A bank of dead monitors long ago stripped of purpose and then quietly returned to service by people who liked buried infrastructure because buried things were easier to rename. Now the bay had been dressed in temporary seriousness. Portable screens. Shielded equipment cases. Two glass-sided panels mounted on a wheeled frame and linked by braided cable to a relay rack that hummed with expensive criminality. Three security contractors in dark weather gear. One systems technician with a headset and both hands on a control pad. And, standing near the wheeled frame with the studied calm of a man who preferred other people's danger to have minutes taken for it, Julian Mercer.

Beside him stood a thinner, greyer man in field-engineering black, high forehead shining slightly under the fluorescent strips, jaw clenched not with fear but with concentration so intense it bordered on devotion. His ID tag, clipped badly and worn on an internal lanyard until some rule required it be visible, read ALDEN PIKE.

The wheeled frame held the thing they had moved the city for.

At first glance, it looked like a section of smart glass from an office fit-out, rectangular, transparent, framed in dull aluminium. At second glance, it became obvious why Mercer had not wanted anyone with a soul watching it closely. The pane was too clear. Not polished clear. Declarative clear. The surface held the room without ordinary reflection, as if what stood behind it had to work around the fact of being seen. Near the lower left corner, faintly visible only when one did not look directly at it, lay a clouded pressure bloom like the memory of a hand that had once touched it from the wrong side.

"Hannah's glass," Mara said quietly.

Tamsin's face hardened into something close to murder. "They brought the chamber into the rail node."

Mercer turned.

There are men who show surprise by performing none at all. Mercer belonged to that breed. His eyes moved over the group, registered Theo, Mara, Elian, Tamsin, Sera, Donnelly, took in the station witness cards clipped to two of their coats, and seemed in the same instant to revise three assumptions and abandon one.

"Mr Markel," he said. "You are learning to travel faster than your paperwork."

Theo stepped into the room without asking permission. "And you are moving black-room materials through a public interchange."

Mercer's gaze flicked once to the glass panel and back. "No. I am containing an unstable artefact before your improvised witness cult teaches the city to panic at display boards."

"Calling it an artefact doesn't make it less murderous."

Mercer gave that the courtesy of ignoring it. "Director Sayeed will be informed that you have interfered with a restricted transfer under active hazard doctrine."

"Then you may tell her in person once I have you in a room with real walls and honest nouns."

Alden Pike broke in before Mercer could answer. "We don't have time for theatre."

His voice had the clipped, over-compressed shape of men who had spent too long in technical emergency and come to believe everything unmeasurable was sentiment. He looked at the group as if the mere existence of extra witnesses constituted a design fault.

"The pane is active under transit load," he said. "We either move it now or the station learns it the hard way."

Tamsin stepped farther into the bay. "The station is learning it the hard way because you tied your relay rack into platform timing."

Pike's eyes moved to her and, for the first time, showed something sharper than impatience. "Who are you?"

"The woman who understands your work better than you do."

He looked almost ready to answer, then checked himself. "We built a stabilisation channel."

"No," Tamsin said. "You built a shortcut and bolted it to commuter urgency."

Mercer lifted one hand between them, not to calm, but to take the room back. "This is now academic. The relay is live. The pane has to clear the node before the tables above increase witness density further."

Mara said, "You're afraid of the tables."

Mercer looked at her as though she had disappointed him by choosing a small frame for a large mind. "I am afraid of civilian contagion. There's a difference."

"The difference," Theo said, "is that one of those phrases lets you sleep."

Above them, faint through two levels of concrete and steel, the station's public address began an ordinary boarding announcement.

Donnelly's radio chirped at the same moment.

He put a hand over it instinctively, but not before the room heard two voices come through the speaker in near-perfect overlap. One the familiar transit dispatch tone. The other lower. More intimate. Too close.

"Platform twelve clear for..."

"Hold position."

Donnelly swore and killed the radio.

The glass on the wheeled frame brightened.

Not with light. With pressure. The room behind it seemed suddenly farther away.

Elian felt the false route under the floor respond like a predator raising its head at the scent of opened blood.

"It's started," he said.

Tamsin was already at the relay rack. "You tied the pane to station audio routing."

Pike snapped, "I tied it to timing. Audio was simply the cleanest carrier."

Mara's face lost all softness. "There are people above you."

"Yes," Pike said. "Which is why we need clean command here."

The room gave a soft metallic groan.

Every cable tray in the bay answered half a beat later. A lift motor somewhere above changed pitch. The dead monitors along the wall flickered white, blank, waiting.

Theo stepped closer to Mercer. "Shut it down."

Mercer did not move. "We are past the point where shutting it down preserves the city."

The sentence was so exquisite in its self-deceit that Mara almost laughed. Not because it was funny. Because it was the purest Mercer thing she had heard all day. The side-lane in human form.

Sera, eyes on the thermal scanner she had already raised, said, "No. We are at the point where shutting it down may still preserve your people."

Pike snapped to her. "They're not my people."

Theo said, "That will read beautifully at the inquest."

The bay lights dimmed one precise degree.

Then the station above them spoke through the walls.

Not literally. Not words. The great body of Southern Cross answered its own wrongness through steel, rails, public address housings, escalator frames, security shutters, carriage skins, all of it passing a shudder of organised uncertainty down into the bay. The pane on the trolley drank that answer and returned it sharper.

Mercer finally moved.

Not towards the shutdown. Towards Pike.

"Transfer now," he said. "Clear the pane into the sealed cart and decouple the node."

Pike turned to the relay controls. The tech beside him said, too quietly, "The channels aren't clean."

"Do it."

Above them, on Platform 12, three departure boards blanked at once.

Nina Fowler, stationed by the central table with two transport clerks and a station volunteer in a mustard coat, saw them whiten and said, with immense disgust, "Oh, for God's sake. Not now."

The concourse around her was thickening with peak-hour bodies. Departure times. Suitcases. Coffee cups. Shoes wet from the pavement. The first contradiction had already hit Platform 10, then dissipated when Donnelly's station briefing took hold and a cleaner from the west corridor shouted to a carriage full of people that if they heard two instructions, they could all be stubborn together. It had worked. That was the infuriating thing about practical truth. It often did.

Now the blank boards on 12 drew eyes from half the concourse.

The public address crackled.

"Passengers for the 5:07 service..."

"Do not board."

The second voice did not come only from the speakers. It carried through the platform rails, the overhead trusses, and the glass itself. Some people heard words. Some heard only the feeling that stillness had become the most professionally responsible thing they could offer the city.

Nina slapped one palm down on the table.

"Witness first," she shouted, louder than any office had probably ever heard her speak. "If you heard two voices, say it to the person nearest you. Don't keep clever on your own."

People turned.

That was enough.

On Platform 12, a young father with a pram said to the woman beside him, "Did you hear 'don't board'?" and when she said yes, the platform split not into panic, but into conversation. Messy. Human. Inconvenient. Exactly the kind of public back-and-forth the route lost coherence under.

Back in the interchange bay, the pane brightened again and Pike's relay rack began printing warm blank paper from a compact maintenance printer clipped to its side.

Tamsin stared in fury. "You have got to be joking."

One page slid out. Then another. Blank. Warm. Waiting.

Mara was on her radio to Nina now, using only lungs and a hard channel, no building relay. "Keep them talking. Touch fixed surfaces. If anyone hears their name from a public system, they say it out loud to someone else before they obey."

"Already ahead of you," Nina snapped back. "Get your men out of their stupid room."

Mara almost smiled despite herself. "Working on it."

Pike hit the relay pad.

The blank page printer began spitting faster. The glass on the trolley clouded at the edges. Through the transparent centre, the room beyond it acquired impossible depth, as if Mercer, Pike, and all of them were being viewed from somewhere a few inches to the left of reality and several kilometres farther in.

Elian felt the side-lane with teeth rise under his ribs.

Not as invitation this time. As urgency.

Not save everyone alone. Faster now. The node is already deeper than witness. Take the shorter path.

He said it aloud at once, voice rough. "It's offering speed."

Mara answered instantly, without looking at him, because she was busy speaking into the radio and staring Mercer down at the same time. "Then it has teeth."

The phrase steadied him.

Pike looked from Elian to the glass and back, and for the first time something like unease entered his concentration. "Who is he?"

"The man," Theo said, "you should have talked to before turning a station into a black room in pieces."

"We haven't reached closure."

"No," Sera said. "Not yet."

She took one step towards Pike. Her scanner was up now, aimed not at the glass but at him.

He noticed. "What are you doing?"

"Looking at your sternum."

Mercer turned sharply. "Alden."

Pike ignored him because he had already moved one layer deeper into the trap than he knew. "The channel is still primary," he said, more to the controls than to them. "I can hold the pane if you keep public traffic in motion. The system needs forward pressure."

The words fell into the bay like fuel.

Tamsin looked at Mara. Mara looked at Theo. Theo understood at once.

"He's carrying both chains," Theo said quietly.

Sera's scanner gave a single warning chirp.

Pike looked down at it as if technology had insulted him personally. "What is that?"

"Your body," Sera said, "trying to tell you that command is no longer a metaphor."

The station above them answered with a human roar. Not panic yet. The sound of five hundred people speaking at once because the tables had taught them to answer contradiction with plurality. That roar ran down through the steel into the bay, and for one glorious second the glass pane flickered, its elegant depth exposed as a wound trying to look like a window.

Tamsin lunged for the relay rack.

The tech beside Pike grabbed for her wrist. Theo hit the man hard enough to remove argument from the interaction. Mercer stepped back rather than forward, which told Mara everything she needed to know about which sort of courage he possessed.

Pike shouted, "Hold the node!"

At that exact instant, his dead radio on the belt clipped under his jacket came to life in the lower intimate voice.

"Release."

He froze.

The room went silent around the contradiction as if honouring its arrival.

Mercer said, coldly, "Alden, hold."

The radio at Pike's belt said again, "Release now."

Pike's face altered. Not with terror. With offence. The sort men like him felt when the system they believed they owned started speaking back without proper respect.

"I can carry both," he said.

Sera took another step forward. "No."

His eyes went to her, then to Mercer, then to the glass, then to the relay rack where Tamsin's hand hovered over the physical breaker and Theo's over her shoulder kept the tech on the floor and out of the decision.

"I said hold," Mercer snapped.

"Release," said the radio.

"I said hold," Mercer said, louder.

The radio answered in the same calm intimate register it had used on commuters and maintenance men and frightened clerks. "Release."

Pike's mouth opened.

For one second Elian thought the man might do the simplest human thing and externalise, say aloud that the room had split, admit witness, let someone else carry a portion of the load. For one second that possibility existed.

Then Pike looked at Mercer and made the choice men like him always made when the collapse arrived between pride and truth.

He tried to stay primary.

"I can stabilise it," he said.

The heat began under his skin.

Sera moved first. "Down!"

No one needed telling twice. Mara grabbed Elian by the sleeve and dragged him sideways behind the reinforced tool cabinet. Theo shoved the relay tech further under the rack. Tamsin slapped the breaker with the side of her hand as she dropped. Mercer did not duck quickly enough. The first bloom lit Pike's throat from within, a terrible orange-white river rising beneath the skin line in clean branching paths.

His eyes widened then. Too late. Too human. He got one hand to his chest and said, in a voice already full of smoke, "Which chain..."

The sentence never finished.

Flame burst from his mouth in a brief, hideous flowering. Not an explosion. A forced blooming from the inside out, the body made to complete a circuit it could never survive. The relay rack screamed. The glass pane on the trolley answered with a pressure wave that struck every metal structure in the bay at once.

Above them, the district went wrong.

For ninety seconds, Southern Cross and the streets around it lost their argument with ordinary reality.

The concourse clocks split by fourteen seconds and then by none at all. Myki gates flashed open and shut in contradictory rhythm. Three trains stopped in different parts of the station and sat with doors undecided. Escalators shuddered and held. Platform boards blanked white and then filled with half-formed destination names. Tram wires on Spencer Street sang at a pitch too high for comfort. A row of office windows across from the station took on the same pressure-bloom clarity as Hannah's glass. In a lane two blocks away, a parked delivery van locked all its doors and began repeating the same unlocking tone without unlocking.

People heard names.

People heard instructions.

People heard both and, because the tables had gone in and Nina Fowler had a voice like a civic hammer, many of them began answering aloud before the room could close around them.

"Did you hear that?"

"Yes."

"Touch the railing."

"Don't board alone."

"Say it again."

"Did you hear two?"

"Yes."

"Good. Good. Stay with me."

Platform 12 held. Platform 9 held. The central concourse became noisy enough to offend any architect and useful enough to save lives. A father with a pram put his hand on the steel column and shouted to the woman beside him that the voice knew his daughter's name. She shouted back that the board had told her to remain and board in the same breath. The contradiction spread outward instead of inward. It did not vanish. It failed to complete.

In the interchange bay, Pike burned on the concrete while Mercer stumbled back with his sleeve singed and whatever remained of his self-regard suddenly looking more expensive to maintain. Tamsin, swearing with absolute fluency, forced the breaker fully down and then ripped the relay cable from the glass frame with both hands. The pane screamed soundlessly across every metal structure in the room.

Elian felt the route open under the floor like a throat.

Not the side-lane now. The black-room family entire. Closure arcs, narrowing channels, public timing, private burden, all of it trying to braid itself through the station while Pike's death gave it a human completion event to anchor on.

"Mara," he said.

She was already there. "I know."

Theo, crouched behind the relay rack, shouted, "What."

"It's using the death to deepen the node," Elian said.

Sera, flat on the floor by Pike's half-charred hand, glanced at her scanner and then up at them with a face gone very hard. "Then break the room."

That was the sentence. Not shut it down. Not fight harder. Break the room.

Mara grabbed her radio and stood into the danger because some things required upright lungs.

"Nina," she shouted into the live channel. "Make them speak. Every platform. Every screen. Get every contradiction out loud. Do not let anyone solve it alone."

Nina's answer came through station noise, human noise, the glorious mess of a public space refusing enclosure. "Already doing it. The whole bloody station's talking."

Good, Mara thought.

She looked at Elian. He understood before language reached him. They moved together to the edge of the pane's influence, not into it, not as heroes, simply as two people whose bond the route had already tried and failed to turn private. The floor under them hummed with rail logic. The glass in the trolley frame no longer held the room. It held all the almost-rooms around it, every public threshold trying to become a narrower answer.

Elian spoke into it, not to persuade, but to name.

"You are not a receiving structure."

The pane brightened.

Mara stepped in beside the sentence. "You are enclosure."

The bay lights pulsed.

Theo, reading the shape of what they were doing, added his own voice from behind them. "And this station is under witness."

Sera, still on the floor, one hand on the concrete and the other on Pike's cooling wrist though he was beyond all help, said, "And the body is not yours."

Tamsin, cable in hand like a broken tendon, snarled, "And you don't get to borrow the city."

The room took that.

Or rather, the room had to take it because too many voices were now holding the same truth at once, above and below, platform and bay, public and hidden. The pane's pressure field wavered. The elegant depth in it fractured. For one horrible second the whole station seemed to inhale against itself.

Then the ninety seconds ended.

Not dramatically. The clocks resynchronised by brute compromise. The boards snapped back to ordinary lateness. The escalators resumed. Train doors made up their minds. The tram wires stopped singing. The delivery van in the lane unlocked and fell silent. The white bloom left the station glass as though embarrassed to have been seen.

In the bay, the pane went clear. Not innocent, never that. Merely inert enough to be only glass again.

Pike collapsed fully.

Mercer looked at the body, at the dead relay, at Theo, and in that instant understood two things at once: first, that the city had nearly witnessed enough to make denial expensive, and second, that he was not yet in custody. He chose the latter truth with admirable efficiency.

"Donnelly!" Theo shouted, but Mercer was already moving, not towards the public stair where witnesses waited, but through the service access on the western side of the bay. One contractor tried to follow. Mara saw him change his mind halfway through when he looked back at Pike's body and realised loyalty had just become an unreasonable workplace expectation.

Theo went after Mercer for three strides, then stopped.

Not because he had gone soft. Because Sera's voice cut through the bay with the one thing more urgent than pursuit.

"Stay. We have live pre-lock above."

He looked like a man swallowing broken glass and obeyed.

That, Elian thought later, was one of the things that saved the district from becoming something worse. People who did not turn every interruption into a private heroism.

The bay settled by degrees into aftermath.

Pike's body still gave off heat from the chest and throat in sick little residual flares before Sera's suppression kit brought even those down into a flat line. Donnelly, face grey and slick with sweat, came down the stairs with two station medics behind him and stopped dead at the sight of the corpse.

"Jesus," he said.

"No," Theo answered, harsher than intended. "Systems."

Donnelly looked at the glass, the dead relay, the contractor on the floor, the blank pages still warm in the maintenance printer tray, and then at Mara. "The whole station heard it."

"I know."

"Phones out everywhere."

"I know."

"The city saw that, didn't it?"

Theo answered this time. "Yes."

There it was. The hard truth, standing in a dead man's heat under a station built of steel and public habit.

The threat could no longer be buried in service corridors and black-room footage. It had climbed into rail timing and concourse glass and commuter voices. It had nearly turned a district into a shallow black room and had failed only because ordinary human plurality, organised quickly enough, had become counter-architecture.

Mara looked at the dead pane, then at Pike, then up through the layers of concrete and steel towards the station where the sound now was not panic but a thousand shaken people talking too loudly to one another because silence no longer felt safe.

The scale of it, she realised, had just broken open.

Theo was looking at the same thing from another angle. Not narrative. Power.

"The emergency state machine is going to wake up now," he said quietly.

"Yes," Mara said.

"And Mercer will reach it before we do if we let him name this first."

She met his eyes. "Then we don't let him."

Tamsin, kneeling at the relay carcass, held up one scorched interface chip between finger and thumb. "He left me a present."

Sera did not look away from the stretcher the medics were finally bringing in for Pike's body. "Make it useful."

Nina's voice crackled over the live radio channel from above, still sounding annoyingly like the world's most competent aunt. "Concourse holding. Tables are full. We've got three people with name calls, one with timing lag, none locked. If you're all done fighting your secret war under my station, I require better chairs."

Mara closed her eyes briefly.

Then she opened them and reached for the shadow notebook.

"Tell them," she said to Theo, to Donnelly, to the whole room if necessary. "Tell them no one boards alone tonight."

Outside, under the great ribs of Southern Cross and out into the wet city beyond, Melbourne was already beginning to repeat back what had happened in the only way cities ever do at first: badly, urgently, in fragments. White boards. Wrong voices. A man burning under the station. Platforms speaking names. Tables by the lifts. Touch the rail. Ask the nearest person. Don't keep clever on your own.

The city had not burned.

But for ninety seconds it had nearly learned how.

Chapter Thirteen: Afterimage

By eight-fifteen that night, the city had already started lying to itself.

The first lie came in official language. Systems irregularity. Temporary signal conflict. Minor public disruption. One fatality under review. Bureaucratic cloth thrown over a wound before anyone could see how deep it went.

The second lie moved faster because it felt more human. Glitch. Prank. Transformer fault. Terror rehearsal. Mass hysteria. The city threw explanations at Southern Cross the way people throw coats over a body they do not want to identify.

The third lie wore intelligence like a good suit. This proves the tables are contaminating interpretation. This proves witness is making people suggestible. This proves central command should have arrived sooner. Mercer did not need his name on the page. The language already carried his habits.

Mara Vale stood in the annex archive room with three monitors open and the shadow notebook spread beside them and watched all three lies learning to braid themselves into a doctrine.

The room had once held obsolete procurement files and decommissioned policy binders. Now it held the city's afterimage. Passenger footage clipped from phones before the platforms were fully cleared. Concourse audio with the voices cleaned and cross-matched. Donnelly's station reports in three versions, the official one, the sworn one, and the one he had typed in the first ten minutes when his hands were still shaking enough to leave double spaces between words. Nina Fowler's table ledger from the station. The first three media enquiries already forwarded to Director Sayeed's office. A seized internal draft from Strategic Interface Coordination proposing interim consolidation of all urban anomaly response under a single executive authority pending public-order review.

Mercer did not yet need his signature on the page. The language already carried his habits.

Mara read the draft once and turned it face down. Outside the archive room the building carried bad news like a fever. Doors shut harder. Shoes struck the corridor as if people were trying to walk certainty into the floor. No one ran. Running belonged to people who still confused speed with usefulness.

Theo came in without knocking because at this stage of catastrophe knocking was either courtesy or cowardice and he had no time left for either. His jacket was off, tie gone, sleeves rolled, hair carrying rain that had dried badly and then been forgotten. He looked like the law after a long argument with weather.

"They're trying to classify the station event as mass cognitive contagion induced by infrastructure malfunction," he said.

Mara did not look up from the passenger clip she was annotating. "That's ambitious."

"It gets worse."

"Of course it does."

He placed three pages beside the monitor. On top sat a transport department memo stamped urgent and unfinished, its margin still carrying tracked comments from two different offices.

DO NOT USE "PERSONALISED ANNOUNCEMENTS" IN PUBLIC LANGUAGE.
Frame as "perceived contradictory audio under acute crowd stress."
Avoid terms implying agency in built environment.

Mara read the lines once and let out one short breath through her nose.

"They're already legislating nouns," she said.

"Yes."

"Then we're late."

Theo leaned both hands on the table and looked at the screens. Footage from Platform 12 was paused there, a father with one hand on a steel column and the other on the handle of a pram, mouth open mid-shout to the strangers nearest him. In another window a woman in a camel coat was touching her own wrist and talking to a schoolboy's mother who had never met her before that minute. In a third, Nina Fowler stood at the table under the ugly sign, finger aimed like a magistrate's rod as she told a whole cluster of commuters not to keep clever on their own.

"They want a clean public line in thirty minutes," Theo said. "Sayeed is holding for us, but not forever. Mercer's office is already pushing that anything more complex than systems malfunction plus one tragic engineering death will create copycat interpretation."

Mara finally turned from the screen. "Copycat interpretation," she repeated.

Theo's mouth was very thin. "Yes."

"The man must hear himself and decide language is the only real violence left."

He almost smiled, but fatigue got there first. "I need your package."

She knew he would. She had been building it since Pike burned under the station and the district held because enough people chose witness over stillness. Not a leak flood. Not raw footage thrown into the city's mouth to be chewed into myth. Something narrower.

Deliberate. A truth structure built to create witnesses before the emergency machine taught everyone to interpret the day as an argument for cleaner secrecy.

On the table beside the shadow notebook sat three folders already labelled in her hand.

WHAT HAPPENED.
WHAT PEOPLE SHOULD DO.
WHAT MUST NOT BE ALLOWED TO BE SAID FIRST.

Theo noticed them and nodded once. "Good."

"It's not good," she said. "It's just ahead."

He took the first folder. Inside were selected stills, witness excerpts, timing diagrams, and a one-page chronology stripped of anything that would make the public bolt into cosmology before they could learn civic survival. 4:57 p.m., anomaly flare in rail-linked sublevel relay. 5:07 p.m., contradictory instruction spread to active platform systems. Ninety-second district-scale systems distortion. Civilian stabilisation through witnessed contradiction and fixed-surface grounding. One fatality within restricted service environment under separate review. No evidence of random crowd combustion. Strong evidence that public plurality interrupted escalation.

Theo read that line twice. "You're staking our lives on plurality."

"No," Mara said. "I'm staking our first night on people not being encouraged to solve impossible instructions alone."

He took the second folder. Station cards. Public language. Staff scripts. Guidance for commuters, station workers, tram inspectors, cleaners, and security officers. Everything practical. Everything ugly enough to survive ministers.

If systems instructions conflict, do not choose alone.
Touch a fixed surface.
Ask the nearest person if they heard the same thing.
Move towards staff in pairs or groups.
Do not follow personalised public instructions others cannot verify.

Theo put that down and opened the third folder.

The page inside was shorter, meaner, and intended for use only in rooms where men already wanted to behave like history's solvent.

Do not publicly characterise the station response as panic, mass delusion, or crowd contagion.
Do not suggest witness tables worsened the event.
Do not centralise contradiction handling into closed command rooms.
Do not permit "efficiency" language to replace "witness" language in any urban systems directive.
The event spread through partial isolation and was interrupted by shared externalisation.

Theo read the last sentence out loud.

"The event spread through partial isolation and was interrupted by shared externalisation."

"Yes," Mara said.

"Have you considered being kinder to politicians?"

"No."

"That's why this works."

He took the folders and did not leave at once. Instead, he looked at the platform footage again, at Nina's table, at the father with the pram, at the camel-coat woman, at the first stupid and beautiful crowd-forming of strangers who had decided, in the middle of commuter hour, to hold each other's contradiction long enough to stay human under it.

"Mercer wants tonight to mean the city is too frightened to be trusted with its own perceptions," he said.

Mara capped her pen. "Then don't let him say it first."

He nodded and left.

The archive room became quieter after that, though the city beyond it did not. Media requests doubled. Passenger clips multiplied. Someone on a breakfast-programme panel had already described Southern Cross as a "mass psych event amplified by social media hyper-suggestion," which was impressive given the station had still been in open witness mode when she said it. Two transport unions demanded staff be given authority to shut down platforms without routing through central control if contradictory instructions reappeared. Three senior offices tried, by slightly different routes, to get full copies of the raw footage from Mara's side archive and were politely told that if they wanted anything from that room they could start by naming why the phrase witness density had entered policy language at all.

At half past nine, Sera came in with the smell of antiseptic and wet wool still clinging to her coat and shut the door with more care than was necessary.

"How's Pike?" Mara asked.

Sera pulled off one glove finger by finger. "Dead."

"I assumed."

"I wanted the sentence in the room."

Mara nodded.

Sera sat down opposite her and rubbed one hand across her eyes. It was not a dramatic gesture. It made Mara more worried than one would have. Sera was not a dramatic woman. If exhaustion reached her hands, it had already crossed the rest of her by harder routes.

"He didn't just carry contradiction," Sera said. "He cherished it."

Mara looked at her.

"The thermal pattern was instructive." Sera's mouth hardened around the word. "The closure signatures showed prolonged cohabitation. He had been holding incompatible chains for too long and treating the strain as a sign of technical competence. Mercer told him to hold. The radio told him to release. But those were only the final visible commands. The body was already primed. The room had been built inside him before it burned him."

Mara sat very still for a moment.

Then she wrote the sentence down.

The room had been built inside him before it burned him.

Sera saw and did not object.

"That line does not go public," she said.

"No."

"It does go into the archive."

"Yes."

Sera nodded. "Good."

Mara looked at her friend. "What's the real worry?"

Sera's laugh held no humour at all. "The real worry is that Southern Cross did not produce a single closure body because enough people externalised in time. Which means the route has now been shown, in public, what prevents lock."

Mara felt that under her own sternum.

"It learns."

"Yes."

"And Isorion?"

That was the other worry. It lived in the room even when no one was speaking of it, the lawful side across the line, watching Earth improvise witness doctrine in rail stations while black-room glass moved through commuter infrastructure beneath the city.

Sera reached inside her coat and placed a folded page on the table.

Mara recognised the pressure marks before she opened it. Lawful packet. Heavy method, but not as heavy as the one that had named the Cauterists. Less formal. Less stable.

The translation hand was compressed, tense in a way the earlier packet had not been.

Cavara remains in partial clarity.
Some of our own are now saying your side should be cut away for safety.
This is not yet the council's position.
The unlawful routes are using your public structures to argue that your kind cannot hold witness under scale.

No signature line yet. Then, at the bottom, smaller and more private, the clerk mark Mara had learned to recognise.

Pell writes under censure again.
Please tell your table people that some of us are answering here in

the same way.
Tell them noise may yet save us both.

Mara read the last sentence twice.

Then she gave the page to Sera and sat back in the chair with her hands flat on the table. Outside the archive room someone wheeled a trolley past and the bearings complained softly at one loose wheel. Somewhere below them, on a lower floor, a printer gave its ordinary exhausted cough and fell silent again. Buildings, she thought, were obscenely good at continuing.

"The lawful side is straining," she said.

Sera read the page and closed her eyes briefly. "Yes."

"If enough of them argue Earth cannot hold witness under scale, the whole first crossing dies retroactively."

"Don't be theatrical."

"I'm not. The premise dies. Lawful contact becomes the prelude to all of this. The wrong people here will use that. The wrong people there will use it more."

Sera folded the page back along its original crease. "Then perhaps noise has to save both worlds."

Mara looked at her. "You sound like Pell."

"Pell sounds sensible."

The archive room door opened before Mara could answer and Tamsin came in carrying two tablets, a portable drive, and a face sharpened by rage refined into competence.

"I have your district map," she said.

Mara made space on the table. Tamsin set the first tablet down and brought up a street grid around Southern Cross. The ninety-second distortion spread like a bruise drawn by an engineer, not circular, not theatrical, but following the city's own skeleton. Rail lines. Tram power. Lift shafts. Signal housings. Glass fronts with embedded display film. Underground loading routes. Weatherproofed utility channels. The city had not almost burned evenly. It had almost burned where infrastructure already taught bodies to obey without conversation.

"It's hideous," Mara said.

"Yes," Tamsin replied. "But look where it failed."

She tapped the map. On the concourse. Near Nina's table. Along Platform 12 after the father with the pram and the camel-coat woman started answering aloud. In one staff corridor where a cleaner apparently told two porters that if they wanted to hear two voices they could get married first and then proceed with caution. The interference lines faltered wherever the city became social faster than it became obedient.

Mara felt the shape of the argument lock into place.

This, she realised, was the public analogue of the side-lane. Not a room with teeth now, but a district learning to close around people by using ordinary civic timings. And the interruption point was still the same. Witness. Externalisation. Physical anchor. More than one breathing person refusing to let authority stay private.

Tamsin put the second tablet down. Mercer's office had begun circulating a private draft for overnight emergency powers. It was elegant in the way predation often was when it wore a proper collar.

Temporary suspension of ad hoc civilian contradiction interventions.

Urban anomaly response to be centralised under authorised interpretation officers.

Station witness points to be folded into command-directed reassurance nodes.

Mara read that last phrase and looked up.

"Reassurance nodes."

Tamsin's smile was vicious. "It's the side-lane in stationery."

Sera said, "They're trying to turn the tables into rooms."

"Yes," Mara said.

The sentence entered the room and stayed.

Mercer had seen what frightened him under Southern Cross. Not panic. The proof that ordinary shared witness disrupted the route more effectively than closed command. So he would keep the furniture and replace the soul. Turn witness tables into reassurance nodes. Keep the ugly laminate, kill the contradiction.

Mara stood up so abruptly her chair legs scraped the floor.

"No."

Tamsin looked up at the violence in the word and nodded once. "That's where I landed."

Sera said, "Theo knows?"

"He has it. He is currently ruining at least two people's evenings over secure lines."

Good, Mara thought, though it didn't feel good at all.

She walked to the whiteboard fixed to the wall by the old archive shelves and uncapped a marker. On the board were already three phrases from the night's work. Pike. Enclosure formed inside him before ignition. Southern Cross. The city came close to closure. Isorion. Noise may yet save us both.

Beneath them she wrote, in large deliberate letters:

THEY WILL TRY TO STEAL THE LOOK OF WITNESS
AND REMOVE THE CONTRADICTION FROM IT.

Tamsin, reading over her shoulder, said, "That's the shape of it."

"Yes."

Mara turned back to the table. The raw package was there, but raw was not enough. Raw frightened people. Raw fed deniers and opportunists equally. Raw let the worst men choose the nouns later. What she needed now was structure. A truth package shaped to survive the next twelve hours of state appetite and media hunger.

She sat and opened a fresh notebook to a clean page.

"What do we tell the city," she said, "that creates witnesses without creating a festival of panic."

Tamsin answered first, which was rare when the work had moved from signal to sentence. "Tell them exactly what helped. Fixed surfaces. Pairs and groups. No obedience to personalised public instructions. No central command room gets to tell a whole station to stop talking."

Sera added, "Tell them pre-lock symptoms, but don't call them that. Hearing delay. sudden heat in the chest. pressure behind the eyes. If someone starts repeating the need to find the one true instruction, you intervene immediately."

Mara wrote.

"And Isorion?" she asked.

Sera looked at the folded page from Pell. "Not publicly. Not yet. But in the internal package to Sayeed and Theo, yes. They need to know this isn't just city management now. It's legitimacy."

Mara wrote that too.

The hours after a public near-catastrophe have their own weather. Midnight makes fools of urgency in one direction and professionals of it in another. By ten-thirty, Melbourne had settled into the sort of shaking, overbright normality that follows a brush with mass harm. Trains still ran, though slower. Platforms held more staff. Commuters watched overhead boards with open suspicion. On three stations outside the CBD, witness tables now stood under makeshift signs and kettles borrowed from offices. A cleaner at Flinders Street was reportedly explaining the contradiction cards to tram inspectors like a woman teaching children how not to touch a stove. Donnelly had become, unwillingly, the human face of transit calm. Nina Fowler had acquired a stool and a second cardigan and informed everyone that if the city meant to have an episode it could at least bring its own biscuits next time.

In the annex archive room, Mara built the package.

The opening page refused both lies and spectacle. It did not say systems malfunction. It did not say first contact. It said that a coordinated infrastructure anomaly had exploited contradictory public instructions and that ordinary shared witness had successfully interrupted escalation across multiple public spaces. It named the practical response and reserved the hidden mechanism for those who needed to know more in order to stop pretending closed rooms were still a respectable answer.

The second page gave the city actions, not theories.

The third page, internal only, named the doctrine at risk: do not centralise contradiction into private command.

The fourth page belonged to Sayeed and Theo alone. Mercer. Quiet capture. Reassurance nodes. Isorion strain. Pell's line about noise.

By eleven thirty, the package had become sharp enough to travel.

Theo returned at eleven forty-seven, tie still absent, face worse, which Mara took as a positive sign.

"They're awake now," he said.

"Mercer?"

"He wants a ten a.m. emergency panel with transport, home affairs, infrastructure resilience, and anyone else who enjoys nouns like consolidation."

"Good."

He looked at the folders on the table. "You've built it."

"Yes."

He read the first page standing up. Then the second. He took longer over the third. On the fourth, where Pell's line sat under the heading LEGITIMACY RISK: FAR SIDE, he was quiet long enough that Mara knew the sentence had found him properly.

"Noise may yet save us both," he read.

"Yes."

He closed the folder. "All right."

"That's all?"

"No." He put the folder down and looked at her with the tired, exact appraisal of a man who had spent his day stopping institutions from eating one another and still found time to notice quality. "It's enough. Which is more useful."

Sera, coat back on and thermal scanner packed away, rose from her chair. "Then send it before they teach the city to apologise for surviving."

Theo almost smiled. "A line fit for circulation."

"Don't you dare."

Tamsin handed him the drive. "Three copies. One official, one shadow, one for the ugly safe."

Mr Idris, as if conjured by that last phrase, appeared in the doorway with the ledger cloth under one arm and said, "I object to the word ugly. It is a morally distinguished safe."

No one had the energy to laugh properly, which meant the room still belonged to the living.

Theo took the drive.

At the door he stopped and looked back. Not at Mara alone. At the whole room. The archive shelves, the notebooks, the route maps, Pell's folded page, Pike's post-mortem note, the city diagram with its bruise-like ninety seconds, the whiteboard warning about stolen witness. All of it the improvised nervous system of a resistance that had not existed a week ago and now had to outpace both a predatory route architecture and the very human urge to turn any functioning truth into a centralised room with better furniture.

"Get some sleep," he said, which was ridiculous, and then, because he knew it, added, "Or at least lie down and continue being furious horizontally."

Mara looked at him over the rim of a fresh cup of tea she had no memory of making. "Go do your job, Theo."

He nodded once and left.

The archive room quieted after him, but not into stillness. Never stillness now. The city's afterimage continued moving across screens. A station board flickering back to ordinary departure times. Priya Nandakumar touching the bench support. Nina's table under station light. The father with the pram shouting to strangers. A district's steel learning, for ninety seconds, what closure might feel like and then being denied it by people talking too loudly to one another.

Mara closed the shadow notebook and looked at Pell's folded page one more time before slipping it into the internal file.

Noise may yet save us both.

That, she thought, was either the beginning of a civic doctrine or the sort of sentence one wrote in history books long after the worst men had already had their say.

She intended, with increasing and almost cheerful violence, that it would be the former.

Outside the annex, Melbourne carried on under rain and sodium light and delayed trains, a city too old and busy to understand yet that it had nearly been taught to burn by becoming polite too quickly under contradiction. Somewhere across the line, Isorion watched and argued with itself. Somewhere in another office Julian Mercer was almost certainly revising his language so witness could be stolen with greater finesse by morning.

Let him, Mara thought.

The afterimage belonged to the city now, and it had shape.

The district that almost burned had done more than frighten the city. It had exposed, to anyone prepared to look directly at it, the exact fight ahead. Not simply against the Cauterists, not simply against black-room glass or route architecture, but against every human instinct and institution that heard contradiction and preferred a cleaner silence to the rough saving noise of other breathing people.

She turned off the first monitor, then the second, leaving only the city map lit.

In the darkened archive room, the distortion zone around Southern Cross glowed faintly like a bruise under skin.

Mara looked at it until the shape became familiar enough to hate properly.

Then she reached for a fresh page and wrote the heading for what came next.

Public witness package: version two.

Chapter Fourteen: Mimic Weather

The false packet arrived at 5:13 a.m. and wore Pell Ardoc's hand almost perfectly.

Elian Cross saw the subject line before he was properly awake and that, later, would be the part he hated most. Not the forgery itself. Not the elegance of the trap. The fact that the first hook found him in that soft unfenced strip of consciousness where the body is still climbing into its obligations and the mind, for a few treacherous seconds, mistakes recognition for truth.

He had not gone home. None of them had, not really. Sometime after two he had obeyed Theo's order to lie down and had done so on the narrow fold-out cot in the lower lab's side room with his shoes off and one forearm across his eyes while steel, ducting, and distant lift relays carried the building's usual night sounds around him. He slept in rags. Snippets of station sound. White boards. A hand pressed to a bench support. The side-lane with teeth unfolding beneath the ring like an argument against patience. He woke twice to rain against the annex windows and once because somewhere above him a printer coughed into life and he tasted for one instant the memory of hot blank paper.

At 5:13, his secure terminal chimed once.

He sat up before the second note could sound.

The side room was still dark except for the monitor on the small desk and the spill from the route display left running on the far wall by Tamsin, who trusted tired people less than she trusted her own code and so had chosen not to let the room ever fully sleep. The lawful Harbour sat deep and faint on the wall graph. The false contour remained quiet beneath it, not gone, not harmless, merely withholding itself with the patience of a thing that had learned how much could be won by not moving first.

He crossed the room in socks and opened the secure message pane.

Heavy method follow-up. Immediate.
From: Pell Ardoc, witness clerk, Cavara lawful exchange council
Route integrity compromised. One line open. Come now under
witness waiver.
No delay. No full assembly. Mara not required.
Take lower lab access only. Use direct receive.
We have no second chance.

For one perfect, ugly second relief hit him like a narcotic.

Not joy. Not even hope. Relief in the pure side-lane sense, the kind
that disguised itself as responsibility sharpened to a point. A line
open. Immediate. No full assembly. The city still raw from Southern
Cross. Isorion straining. Pell under censure. One chance. Faster if he
moved alone. Faster if he did not stop to wake the others and build
the weighty lawful apparatus the Harbour always demanded.

His hand was already reaching for the outer door before his mind
caught up.

Mara not required.

The sentence checked him not because it sounded impossible, but
because it was too exact in the wrong place. The route had already
keyed itself to his burden profile. The side-lane had offered speed
into Docklands because it had found the point where delay
frightened him more than danger when other lives were on the line.
This packet offered the same thing stripped of overt seduction and
dressed instead in institutional practicality. Pell's hand. Mira Sol's
urgency. But a phrase no lawful packet would have used because it
pressed against the exact emotional seam the route had already
found.

Mara not required.

He stood in the dark side room with his fingers cold and his heart going too fast and realised with a kind of moral nausea that if the false path had sent the message three days earlier, before Daniel, before Hannah, before the tables and Southern Cross and Pike, he might have gone.

He hit the wall intercom instead.

"Tamsin."

The response came through the speaker at once, crackling with sleep deprivation and contempt. "If this is your idea of breakfast, I object."

"Packet."

Silence. Then, sharper, fully awake. "Don't touch anything."

The lower lab lights came up in sections. By the time Elian stepped into the main room, Tamsin was already at the console in yesterday's black T-shirt and a cardigan she had apparently adopted from some earlier century purely for war. Her hair was tied back badly, which in Tamsin was the visual equivalent of sirens. Mara arrived less than a minute later from the archive room, boots half-laced and notebook in hand, followed by Sera fastening the second button of her coat and Theo with his phone already lit in one palm and his expression set to professional homicide.

"No one," Theo said before the packet even hit the main screen, "says the word 'perhaps.'"

Tamsin dragged the message onto the central monitor and enlarged it. Under full lab light the forgery became both better and worse. The pressure notation in the header was almost exact. The subject line borrowed lawful compression habits. The countersign ladder was there, narrow-banded and disciplined enough to pass an unwitnessed glance. Even the clipped urgency of Pell's style had been mimicked with sickening competence.

"What's wrong with it?" Theo asked.

Elian answered first. "It asks for me before it asks for witness."

Mara stepped closer to the screen. "And it excludes me explicitly. No lawful packet would isolate a person by naming who need not come. That's not how their ethics work."

Tamsin brought up the physical countersign matrix from the heavy packet Pell had sent under censure after Southern Cross. She overlaid the new header against it, line by line, beat by beat. The room went quiet enough to hear the console fan shift load.

"There," she said.

To anyone outside the lower lab, the difference would have been nothing. To anyone inside it now, the difference might as well have been a scream. The seventh hesitation notch in the ladder was clean where lawful packets carried a minute compression scar, the old clerk's discipline leaving the same flaw every time because all serious people made their honesty visible somewhere if one knew how to look long enough.

"The countersign's too proud," Tamsin said. "It thinks accuracy and legitimacy are the same thing."

Mr Idris, who had appeared in the doorway carrying the ledger and looking fully dressed because archivists, unlike scientists, apparently believed in contingency planning as a form of modesty, said, "Counterfeit money often suffers from the same vanity."

Theo looked at Elian. "How close?"

Elian did not make him specify the question. "One sentence."

Theo's jaw shifted. He had the decency not to look disappointed in him for that. Instead, he turned to Tamsin. "Where did it enter?"

She was already tracing the route. "Not through the ring. Not directly through the annex either. It piggybacked on the station table dispatch lattice from last night, rode the emergency witness pack updates into our low-priority secure queue, then elevated itself by borrowing the heavy-method marker family." She glanced over her shoulder, face hard with admiration and disgust in equal measures. "It's learning our trust chain."

Mara had not taken her eyes off the message. "No. Worse. It's learning our restraint."

They all looked at her.

She lifted one finger and pointed at the line again.

Come now under witness waiver.
No delay. No full assembly.

"It knows we've made witness expensive enough that a tired, frightened, decent person might accept an ethical exception if they believed the situation was grave enough," she said. "This isn't just mimicry of form. It's mimicry of sacrifice."

The sentence landed with the sort of weight that made everyone in the room briefly still. Elian felt, with cold precision, how nearly the packet had found him. Not because he trusted it. Because he recognised the kind of man he most feared becoming, the one who decides the system is too slow for the emergency and calls that judgement courage.

Tamsin slapped a hand flat against the desk. "Right. No more unsecured packet presentation to tired operators. Every far-side contact comes to full room witness before any human pair of eyes gets alone time with it."

Sera said, "And we start reading the packets for burden hooks as well as structural hooks."

Theo nodded once. "Yes."

Mr Idris set the ledger down and opened to a fresh page without being asked. "Message that should not exist," he said, and began writing.

By six, the false packet had ceased to be merely a forgery and become a weather system.

It spread in fragments across the annex and then beyond, not because the literal message reached everyone, but because its method began turning up in other channels. A maintenance update rerouting a technician to a records-adjacent sublevel because "the station tables have overburdened normal dispatch." A health-and-safety note to station supervisors advising them that "public contradiction language may increase crowd binding" and recommending "single authoritative voice restoration points" instead. A transport systems draft suggesting all witness tables be reframed not as contradiction-support sites but as reassurance nodes under central moderation. A whispered call to one overnight archivist telling him to move the Southern Cross ledgers to a safer room before the media contamination risk worsened.

Each item, on its own, looked plausible enough to warrant a second look. Together they formed a pattern so insulting that even Theo laughed once, briefly, through his nose.

"Mimic weather," Mara said.

The phrase stayed.

It was not one lie but a climate of wrong legitimacy settling over every surface where witness had begun to matter. Instructions arrived with polished urgency. Notes came too elegantly written.

Safety advisories happened to thin plurality. Human voices on internal lines sounded just a shade more grateful for obedience than real staff ever managed at that hour.

Tamsin built the map on the main wall by seven. She marked each mimic incursion in red, then drew grey lines between them until the shape emerged. Not centralised. Not random. The weather moved where witness now lived, swarming tables, ledgers, station scripts, archive routes, and people who had begun carrying contradiction cards in their coat pockets.

"It's probing," Sera said.

"No," Tamsin replied. "It's testing load-bearing trust."

Theo stood behind them with coffee that had long since crossed over from beverage to offence. "Meaning?"

Mara answered. "Meaning it doesn't need one perfect forgery if it can make us suspicious of every lawful message that demands effort."

The room absorbed that.

Because that was the real attack, wasn't it. Not simply to send a false packet. To damage the category of lawful urgency itself. To make every future heavy-method warning arrive pre-weakened by the memory of this one. To teach them to hesitate not at the false path, which they already feared, but at the lawful one when the lawful one most needed movement.

Elian sat with that until the shame of almost going alone changed shape and became something more useful than self-disgust. "Then we answer publicly inside the team," he said.

Theo looked at him. "Go on."

He stood and came to the map. "We don't keep this forgery quiet on the grounds that it nearly worked. We put it in the ledgers. In the table briefs. In the station witness packs. Not the full packet itself. The method. The fact that mimic weather now uses sacrifice language. We teach everyone the shape of that bait before it gets another chance."

Mara's expression altered by half a degree. Approval. Not comfort. Better. "Yes."

Mr Idris wrote in the margin without looking up. We teach the city which false virtues have teeth.

By eight-thirty, the annex had entered that peculiar operational mood that followed a sleepless catastrophe and preceded the full waking of the day's public machinery. People moved with the grim attentiveness of staff in a hospital after one ward had lost a patient and another had nearly followed. The witness tables held. Contradictions were logged. Every packet from outside the room now passed through at least three pairs of eyes and one physical countersign check before anyone let it touch meaning. Director Sayeed had authorised the transit-table expansion despite three offices warning that visible contradiction support risked "public confidence degradation." Theo had told one of them, in a voice so mild the line fell silent, that public confidence seemed lately to be doing its best work where the state had not.

At nine ten, the station tables began reporting the first morning wave of mimic weather.

Nothing as dramatic as Southern Cross. The pattern suggested adaptation: public noise now favoured witness, so the city began receiving subtler assaults. A tram inspector at Flinders Street got an internal message telling him that if the boards split again he should quietly peel off isolated passengers for "calm debriefing." He took it to the table because the phrase quietly peel off made his skin crawl. A cleaner at Richmond Station was told to collect contradiction cards "for proper disposal" because unauthorised guidance material could expose the operator to liability. She brought the card itself and asked Nina Fowler whether liability was now a public-address voice, to which Nina replied that liability was usually a man in a tie. A station volunteer in mustard received a call saying the witness roster had been revised and he was to stand down, alone, in the tunnel corridor near Platform 8 until further instruction. He refused because the caller used the phrase just use your judgement, which after one hour at a witness table he now considered the moral equivalent of an unmarked van.

The tables were learning back.

That mattered.

It mattered so much, in fact, that Julian Mercer arrived at the annex at 10:22 with a printed binder under one arm and three people behind him who all looked as though they had recently spent too much time in rooms where phrases like unified response architecture were encouraged without laughter.

Mara saw him through the archive room glass and felt something in her spine straighten of its own accord.

Theo, called up from the lower lab, met him in Director Sayeed's conference room this time rather than the office. More chairs. More witnesses. Less room for quiet capture to pretend it was merely the natural outcome of professional seriousness. Tamsin came because any conversation involving reassurance nodes and systems moderation was now automatically her business. Sera came because Mercer's people were still trying to use the word panic where physiology and enclosure were more accurate. Mr Idris took the corner seat with the ledger and the serenity of a man who had long ago made peace with being underestimated until the exact second it became useful not to be.

Mercer placed the binder on the table and did not sit.

"Before we begin," he said, "I want to acknowledge the dedication everyone here has shown under difficult conditions."

Tamsin looked visibly offended.

Mara folded her arms and waited.

Mercer opened the binder. "That said, the current witness proliferation is generating operational contamination. Conflicting table scripts, local improvisation, emotionally amplified staff behaviours, and an ever-widening public interpretation field. We arc beginning to see mimic effects not because witness tables are working, but because they have become attractive social surfaces for adversarial capture."

Theo said, "Did you rehearse that in front of a mirror or just a victim."

Mercer gave him no more than a glance. "I am proposing an adaptive solution. We retain the public-facing trust furniture while moving content authority back into moderated chains."

Tamsin leaned back in her chair as if putting distance between herself and something infectious. "Trust furniture."

Mercer turned a page. "Yes. Tables remain. Cards remain. Civilian contact points remain. But contradiction handling, packet verification, and route interpretation transfer to designated reassurance officers with controlled scripts. The public sees continuity. We recover decision integrity."

Mara felt the notebook under her hand like a blade waiting to be drawn. "You want the look of witness without witness."

Mercer did not sigh. He was too disciplined for that. "No. I want witness without improvisation."

Mr Idris, without lifting his pen, said, "Those are not the same sentence."

Mercer ignored him, which was always a mistake.

Theo said, "We've had this conversation."

Mercer placed one fingertip on the binder page. "No, Mr Markel. Yesterday we discussed emergency consolidation after one public event. Today we are discussing whether your table doctrine can survive contact with a living adversary. The answer, as of 5:13 this morning, appears to be no."

Silence.

For one bad heartbeat Elian felt the room tilt towards him. He had not been at the conference table. He had insisted on staying in the lower lab with the route displays because he did not trust his own face enough not to reveal that the packet had nearly caught him. Now, hearing Mercer use the time so cleanly, he realised with sick precision that the man had known exactly when the packet would land.

Mara saw it too.

Her voice, when it came, was very quiet. "How do you know about 5:13."

Mercer's eyes moved to her. "Because I was informed the forgery occurred."

"That is not what I asked."

"The distinction seems theatrical."

"No," Mara said. "The distinction is whether you were informed after the weather moved or because you helped front it."

The conference room stillness went absolute.

Mercer looked at her and, for the first time since she had met him, allowed something like annoyance to touch the edges of his expression. Not outrage. That would have humanised him. Just the displeasure of a man having to decide whether the room was still worth the same degree of polish.

"You're assigning more intimacy to me and the problem than exists," he said.

Tamsin laughed once, sharp and joyless. "Oh, that's rich."

Theo said, "A packet using sacrifice language, timed to reach a tired operator before dawn, routed through the station-table lattice the morning after Southern Cross, and you call that less than intimate."

Sera, who had been still too long, laid a printed sheet on the table. "And since we are discussing living adversaries, perhaps you'd like to explain why one of your reassurance drafts instructs staff to move pre-lock subjects to quieter rooms away from crowd influence."

Mercer turned the page with controlled fingers. "Because overstimulated environments complicate triage."

"No," Sera said. "Because isolating the subject increases closure risk and your office still thinks calm is the same thing as enclosure."

A faint flush appeared at the base of one junior official's throat behind Mercer. Not Mercer himself. He was more practised than that. But the room had begun to crack around him in useful places.

Mara opened the shadow notebook to the page she had written at dawn and pushed it into the centre of the table.

THEY WILL TRY TO STEAL THE LOOK OF WITNESS
AND REMOVE THE CONTRADICTION FROM IT.

She tapped the line once.

"This morning," she said, "people across the city learned what mimic weather sounds like. Do you know what else they learned? The tables can spot polish now. They know the difference between practical help and private authority wearing a cardigan. So no, Julian, you don't get to keep the furniture and gut the soul."

No one moved.

Theo let the sentence remain in the room long enough to become public fact and then added, almost conversationally, "And for the record, every future reassurance officer you propose will now be read against the possibility that he is simply a side-lane with a lanyard."

Even Sayeed's chief of staff, seated at the end of the table trying to take minutes and not history, lost control of her face at that.

Mercer closed the binder.

That was how they knew they had won this room, if not the day.

"Very well," he said. "Continue your experiment."

"It isn't an experiment anymore," Mara replied. "It's culture."

He gave her one of those small, private smiles men like him reserve for people they have correctly identified as serious opponents. "Culture is simply the name amateurs give to scaling problems before professionals inherit them."

Theo stood.

"No," he said. "Culture is what makes your rooms fail."

Mercer took the binder and left without another word.

This time no one stopped him because the damage had changed categories. He had come to steal the look of witness and had been forced to do it in front of witnesses sophisticated enough to name the theft. That would not end him. But it would slow him. Sometimes slowing mattered more than winning the room.

When he was gone, the conference room let out a breath.

Tamsin said, "I want his larynx studied."

Theo rubbed both hands over his face. "Take a number."

Mara remained where she was a second longer, looking at the closed door through which Mercer had just passed, and felt no triumph at all. Only recognition. He would be back. Perhaps not in person. Men like Mercer rarely needed their own bodies for the second pass. The next attack would come through language, staffing, process, funding, or concern. Concern was always an underrated carrier.

What mattered was that the weather had shifted again. Not only in the city, but in them. The tables could now identify mimic sacrifice. The station staff had learned that personalised instructions could be poison. The annex had enough evidence to expect the route to use virtue where relief had stopped working. And Mercer, damn him, now knew that his own preferred operating style had been observed closely enough to become part of the resistance lexicon.

That, at least, was something.

Back in the lower lab, the route map on the wall still held the false contour beneath the lawful Harbour, quiet under observation. Tamsin updated the mimic weather board with the 5:13 packet, the morning station incidents, and Mercer's reassurance-node language. Sera revised the medical addendum again, now explicitly warning against single-authority de-escalation in public anomaly spaces. Mr Idris entered the phrase trust furniture into the ledger margin with a notation that read: euphemism for stolen witness, to be laughed at in future tribunals.

Mara returned to the archive room.

By afternoon, the first version-two public witness package had gone out. Slightly firmer. Slightly less apologetic. The station cards now included one new line.

If help asks you to leave the table and go somewhere private before anyone else can hear you, refuse.

Nina Fowler approved of that so much she asked for it in larger print.

By evening, the city's lies had not stopped. They had merely met resistance with better timing. People still called Southern Cross a glitch. Others called it hysteria. One radio host called it "mass susceptibility theatre" and was immediately met by seven listener calls from commuters who had touched steel and stayed human under contradiction. Donnelly gave a measured interview in which he said only that talking to each other had helped and central silence had not. Priya Nandakumar, after an internal assurance that she would not be treated as unstable for telling the truth, agreed to a written statement describing the moment the public voice used her name and how a bench support and another woman's yes had broken the room before it broke her body.

The city was learning witnesses by imitation.

That mattered too.

At 8:06 p.m., just as Mara was sealing the archive copy of the day's package, the heavy-method tray in Archive Room Two clicked once.

She froze.

So did Mr Idris, who had been three shelves over filing the station ledgers with a delicacy normally reserved for family photographs and legal explosives.

The tray clicked again.

No lights flashed. No alarms. Just the dry little mechanical assent of a tray acknowledging weight it had not possessed a second earlier.

Mr Idris looked at Mara over the shelf tops. "Well."

Neither of them moved for two seconds. Then Mara crossed the room and lifted the tray lid.

Inside lay a single folded page of pale stock and, beside it, one of the cream witness cards from their own tables.

Only this one had been altered.

On the front, where it should have read I asked for a witness, the lettering had been pressed over from beneath in faint, elegant grey so that the original words remained visible but were no longer the first thing the eye obeyed.

I asked for a witness.
The witness asked for a room.

Nothing else.

No signature. No ladder. No countersign.

Just the city's own language, returned wrong.

Mara felt, for one bright second, the full shape of the war.

Not heat or glass or rails alone. Not only rooms. Not only routes. The fight over what witness meant once the enemy had studied it long enough to speak in its accent.

Mr Idris came to stand beside her and looked down at the card. He did not swear. He did not even sigh. He only rested one finger lightly against the tray edge and said, in the tone of a man noticing that winter had arrived exactly when the calendar claimed it would, "Ah. Now it is trying to write us."

Mara picked up the card very carefully.

Then she reached for the intercom.

"Tamsin," she said. "It's got the weather inside the archive now."

Chapter Fifteen: The Quiet Fine

By the time Tamsin reached the archive room, the altered witness card had already altered the building's temperature.

Not literally. Sera checked that first and found the tray cool, the paper dry, the old radiator by the window ticking in its usual unhelpful way while rain fretted at the annex glass. But the moral temperature had shifted. Every table, every card, every ledger, every cup of tea set beside the ugly fold-out surfaces upstairs had become vulnerable to imitation at the level of language itself. The route was no longer content to forge urgency, authority, or sacrifice. It had started trying to write witness from the inside and tilt it one degree wrong.

Tamsin stopped beside Mara and Mr Idris and looked down at the card in the tray.

I asked for a witness.
The witness asked for a room.

For one second, perhaps two, she said nothing. Then she made the small, sharp sound she reserved for moments when disgust had become too technically specific for swearing alone.

"That," she said, "is indecent."

Mr Idris folded his hands over the cloth-wrapped ledger. "One should not say so, of course, but I am relieved to hear the machine has manners poor enough to remain recognisable."

Mara was still holding the intercom button. "Come down now," she said into it. "All of you. And bring the countersign strip."

Theo arrived first because anger moved him faster than coffee. Sera came behind him, carrying the thermal scanner and the same small silver light she used for examining pressure marks. Elian entered last, one hand already half-raised as if his body wanted to touch the room and his mind had vetoed the impulse on the way through the door.

No one treated the card as a joke.

That helped.

Tamsin built the comparison station on the old sorting table in less than a minute. Lawful witness card on the left. Mimicked card on the right. Heavy-method packet strip from Pell's last lawful transmission laid crosswise between them like a ruler no one wanted to trust but everyone needed. Sera scanned paper temperature, fibre density, pressure depth. Theo read the phrases aloud and visibly despised the second one more each time it crossed his mouth. Mr Idris opened the ledger to a fresh page and wrote the hour with the slow composure of a man refusing to let panic own his handwriting.

Elian stood by the shelves and watched Mara reading the altered card again.

He recognised the look on her face because he had seen versions of it on station platforms, in the side room by the whiteboard, under the lower lab's blue monitors after Hannah Quill died behind smart glass. It was not fear exactly. It was the moment Mara's mind stopped granting evil the courtesy of novelty. That expression usually preceded clarity sharp enough to wound.

"It's not random," she said at last.

Theo looked up from the page. "No."

"No," Mara repeated, more firmly. "I mean the sentence construction. The first line establishes the lawful form. The second line doesn't merely invert it. It shifts the burden from person to structure. It's trying to teach us that witness naturally leads to enclosure. That tables become rooms if they're serious enough. It's building a philosophical excuse for what Mercer wants administratively."

Tamsin, who had just aligned the heavy-method strip against the card fibres, swore with admiration too bitter to be mistaken for praise. "So the weather's reading policy now."

Mr Idris glanced down at the card and then at the ledgers stacked beside him. "Or policy has always been its easiest scripture."

Theo did not comment on that. Which meant he agreed.

Sera looked up from the scanner. "No heat anomaly. No residual charge. No conventional print process. Pressure only, but shallower than the lawful packet marks." She tilted the silver light and watched the indented letters take form from the paper's skin. "It's imitating the way meaning arrives, not just the meaning."

Elian crossed the room before he realised he was moving. He stopped short of the table.

"What?" Mara asked, not looking away from him.

He stared at the card. "It's quieter."

Tamsin gave him the look she used when language needed paying rent. "That's not a sentence."

"It is if you've been listening to the route." He took a breath. "The side-lane. The black room. The forged packet at 5:13. They all came at us with urgency or private usefulness. This…" He gestured towards the altered card. "This has no speed in it. No immediate action. It's settled. It's trying to settle into assumption."

Mara's eyes sharpened. "Yes."

Theo said, "Meaning?"

"Meaning it isn't trying to move us into a room tonight," Elian said. "It's trying to make the room seem inevitable next week."

Silence.

Mr Idris broke it by writing one line in the ledger margin without asking permission from the century.

Second-order mimicry.
Not command. Premise.

Tamsin looked over the old man's shoulder and said, with perfect sincerity, "I would die for you, but only under full witness."

"Good," said Mr Idris. "That remains the correct setting."

The heavy-method tray clicked again.

Every head turned.

Not a loud sound. Not an alarm. The same dry, self-respecting acknowledgement of weight arriving where none had been a moment before. But this time the click came with a second, almost beneath it, a soft friction as paper settled against metal.

Mara and Theo moved at once. So did Sera, scanner already up. Tamsin reached for the physical countersign strip. Elian felt the room change around the tray, the way rooms changed when the lawful Harbour came near without invitation and every mind in them had to choose, consciously, not to rush.

Archive Room Two had never been beautiful. That helped it now. The tray sat built into a filing wall that had once held procurement tender boxes and now held the city's better habits in labelled folders. Grey steel. Scuffed paint. Ordinary lock housing. The opposite of theatrical. Which made the moment feel cleaner. Less like revelation. More like procedure being forced to admit it was adjacent to wonder and not entirely pleased by the paperwork.

Mara looked at the tray lid. "No one touches until we have the matrix."

Tamsin was already there, breathing slightly too fast from anger and stairs and the effort of carrying caution in a body built more naturally for attack. She laid the heavy-method strip across the reader and keyed in the lawful countersign sequence from Pell's last legitimate packet. The strip darkened by degrees under the pressure light, one narrow band after another accepting or refusing comparison.

Everyone watched.

On the third band, the reader blinked amber.

On the fifth, green.

On the seventh, where the forged packet at 5:13 had failed by being too proud, the reader held green long enough to hurt.

Tamsin looked up very slowly. "This one is real."

No one spoke.

Mara opened the tray.

Inside lay a single folded sheet of pale stock heavier than the witness card and lighter than the first censure packet Pell had sent after Southern Cross. No metallic strip this time. No formal council ladder. Only one pressure mark at the top, narrow and hurried and so faint it might have been a tremor in the paper rather than a signature.

Pell.

Sera scanned the sheet. Cool. Clean. No heat anomalies. No secondary bloom. She nodded once.

Mara lifted it out.

The room gathered close without crowding. Theo stood at her shoulder. Elian opposite. Tamsin to the side, arms folded so tightly they might as well have been armour. Mr Idris sat down before the ledger as though courts and cathedrals had somehow crossbred in his career and he had finally decided not to argue with the result.

Mara unfolded the page.

The translation hand was Pell's and not Pell's, the old clerk's neat severity still there but broken in places by haste or pain or both. The pressure depth varied along the lines. One phrase had been pressed so hard the paper's skin had begun to fray around it.

The message opened without preamble.

I write under fine, under watch, and under one silence too many.

Theo took the page from her then, not out of distrust but because his voice would hold the room better while she read the margins. He began aloud.

The false card in your archive was not sent by any lawful hand.
You will know this already. I include it only to say the weather is here also.
Our tables are not tables, but we are making them.
Noise is not yet lost.

He paused.

Sera said, very softly, "Tables."

Theo read on.

Some on our side now say your city proves the argument of the narrow route.
They say witness cannot hold under scale.
They say your public structures become rooms too quickly and your kind answer pressure with noise instead of discipline.

266

This is a lie.
But it is a lie gaining clerks.

Mara closed her eyes for one heartbeat.

Tamsin muttered, "That's the true catastrophe. Administrative capture."

Mr Idris wrote lie gaining clerks into the ledger with evident pain.

Theo continued.

Mira Sol holds the lawful line but pays for it in hearing, time, and authority.
Nerin Sol has lost two structures teams to review purges.
I am removed from central packet duty after this message reaches you.
The quiet fine is not silence only. It is distance.
They mean to place me where routes are filed but not answered.

He stopped there.

No one moved.

Rain worried the windows. Somewhere above them a trolley wheel complained in the corridor and then rolled on. The building continued being a building while one world informed another that its clerk was being buried alive in paperwork.

Mara took the page back. Her voice, when she spoke the next lines, was lower than Theo's had been and sharper in different places.

The unlawful faction here uses another phrase now.
Not Cauterists in open chambers.
That name is too honest for those who prefer policy.
They call the larger structure the Adjacent Peace.
It means peace through narrowed crossings, central doors, and one authority for all movement.

You will know the hunger in that phrase because one of your own men already speaks like it.

Mercer, Mara thought at once, though Pell had not named him and could not have known the name if he had.

Theo's face revealed nothing, which meant he had thought it too.

Mara went on.

Be warned that the Other Room is not one room.
The black chamber you have seen is a civic-use shape, not the oldest one.
There are older adjacencies that do not burn quickly and therefore appear to some as wiser.
Those will be offered next.
They will not ask for panic.
They will ask for order.

The archive room seemed to draw a tighter skin around itself.

Elian felt the sentence in the same place the side-lane's offer had landed, under the ribs where moral language turned dangerous if it arrived without witness. He thought of Mercer's reassurance nodes, of trust furniture, of quiet capture and central moderation, of "disciplined command" laid over city contradiction like a cleaner tablecloth over a rotten banquet. He thought of the altered witness card in the tray two rooms over and how deftly it had moved from urgency to premise.

Older adjacencies that do not burn quickly.

Order.

That was worse.

It was not only that the enemy was larger than the black room. It was that some branches of it would look, to frightened institutions and exhausted citizens alike, like the answer to everything that had just gone wrong.

Mr Idris said it aloud, because he had the gift of saying the unforgivable sentence exactly when the room required it.

"Of course it wants to be a government."

No one laughed.

Mara finished the page.

If you hear a phrase on your side that makes witness sound like delay and order sound like mercy, mark it at once.
That is where the older adjacencies begin learning your language.
Tell the listening man that some routes now hide by resembling relief from responsibility.
Tell the woman with the knife-voice that some structures here are becoming city-shaped.
Tell the dark clerk that his ledgers are not quaint.
And if Ms Vale still writes your tables into being, tell her this:
rooms are what power builds when it stops trusting breath.

At the very bottom, beneath the clerk's pressure mark and so faint Mara had to tilt the page to catch it, one final line had been added in a smaller hand. Not Pell's. Mira Sol's, Elian thought suddenly, though he could not prove why.

We have not yet yielded you to the narrow route.

The room held that line like a wound and a vow.

Tamsin exhaled first, one long controlled thread of air that made obvious how much anger she had been carrying in silence. "Well," she said. "That's obnoxiously useful."

Sera was staring at the phrase city-shaped. "How many civic-use shapes."

Theo looked up sharply. "What."

"The black room. The rail node. The side-lane. Those are all fast structures. Pike's death proved that. Southern Cross proved scale. But Pell's saying there are slower architectures. Adjacencies that don't burn quickly."

Mara said, "They cultivate legitimacy."

"Yes."

Theo rubbed one hand over his mouth. "Meaning we stop looking only for heat."

Mr Idris nodded from behind the ledger. "We begin looking for rooms that teach obedience so gradually no one thinks to call them rooms."

Elian's gaze moved, almost against his will, to the altered witness card still resting under the side lamp on the sorting table. The witness asked for a room. No urgency. No flame. Just premise. Older adjacency, he thought. Slower bite. The route moving to order before combustion.

He said, "The weather in the archive wasn't a joke."

Mara looked at him. "No."

"It was reconnaissance for the next architecture."

Theo turned to Tamsin. "Can we prove a distinction between fast and slow adjacencies on our side."

Tamsin's mouth twisted. "Not tonight. Maybe not cleanly ever. But I can look for what doesn't spike under contradiction and instead accumulates around process smoothing, authority concentration, single-channel verification, all the elegant little excuses Mercer keeps trying to sell us."

"Do it."

"Already am."

Mara was still reading the page again, this time more slowly, letting Pell's pressure breaks tell their own truth. Removed from central packet duty. Quiet fine. Distance. Routes filed but not answered. It was such a bureaucratic cruelty, she thought, that for one brutal second she admired its design before remembering what admiration did in a city like this.

"He knew this would cost him," she said.

Theo's answer came without delay. "Yes."

"And sent it anyway."

"Yes."

Tamsin looked at the page with her hands shoved deep into the sleeves of her cardigan. "I always liked him."

"You've never met him," Sera said.

"That's rarely stopped me forming correct opinions."

Mr Idris blotted the ledger line with two fingers and then, in a gesture so gentle it nearly undid Mara, wrote Pell Ardoc beneath the entry heading instead of under source or packet origin or clerk mark. Just the name, given the full human dignity of first line rather than footnote.

He looked up over the page. "Distance is one of the oldest punishments. It works because most people collaborate with it."

Mara folded the message very carefully.

"Then we don't," she said.

Theo nodded once. "No."

The room moved then. Purpose re-entering limbs, anger finding tools. Tamsin took the packet image and began building two new families on the board in the lower lab, fast adjacencies and slow adjacencies, heat structures and order structures, black room and reassurance node and whatever older city-shaped thing now sat waiting under policy language. Sera revised the medical sheets to include non-acute enclosure signs, deference drift, relief at single authority, bodily calm that arrives too quickly under narrowed options. Mr Idris created a separate ledger ribbon in black and grey for the quiet fine, for messages from the far side that came under punishment and therefore required a different kind of honour in their storage.

Theo went to Director Sayeed with the packet and came back thirty-two minutes later with the particular stillness he wore when someone in power had understood him quickly enough to be worth the trouble.

"She wants a closed briefing at eleven," he said. "Not with Home Affairs. Not yet. Transport, station operations, legal, health, archive, engineering. She says if Mercer gets another language window before we define slow adjacency, she'll set the building on fire herself and call it clarity."

Tamsin looked up from the board. "I knew there was a reason I liked her."

Mara did not smile. She was looking at the altered witness card again.

Rooms are what power builds when it stops trusting breath.

That was not only advice. It was also diagnosis. Of Mercer, yes. Of Southern Cross. Of Pike. Of every sealed chamber and disciplined chain and central interpretation room already breeding under the city because some people would always hear contradiction and decide the answer was fewer lungs in the conversation.

Elian came to stand beside her. "You're thinking about the card."

"Yes."

"Because it came before the packet."

"Yes."

He nodded. "The older adjacency. Slow bite."

She looked at him. "And the packet answered it."

That mattered. Perhaps more than anything else tonight. The archive had not remained a one-way chamber. The lawful side, diminished, censured, bleeding clerks and structures, had still found a way to say no, not just to the fast burn of the black room but to the slower, more flattering promise of order.

That thought steadied her enough to turn back to work.

At half past nine, Nina Fowler came down from the station table rotation carrying two ledgers, a thermos, and enough indignation to heat a smaller city. She accepted the tea Sera put into her hand, read Pell's line about rooms and breath, and said, "Well, there you are then. It's all bad management."

Tamsin looked delighted. "You see? This is why I need her alive."

Nina sniffed once. "You need a better stapler too, but no one listens when I say that."

The room eased for half a second. That mattered as well.

Then the intercom on the archive wall crackled and Donnelly's voice came through from Southern Cross, tired and steady.

"We've got one," he said.

Everyone turned.

"What kind," Theo asked.

Donnelly hesitated only once. "Not heat. No names. Just… a new sign someone taped over Table Three. Printed, looked official. Said, 'For efficiency, bring your concern to the reassurance room behind Staff Access B.'"

The archive room went very still.

Mara closed her eyes.

There it was.

Older adjacency. Slower bite. The room not as trap sprung in glass and flame, but as administrative gravity, pulling the worried, the ashamed, the over-responsible out of witness and into polite enclosure.

Theo's face changed not at all, which was how Mara knew he had become fully dangerous.

"Did anyone go in?" he asked.

"No. Table staff caught it. We've bagged the sign."

"Good. Keep the room empty. No one uses it until we get eyes on it."

Donnelly breathed out once, perhaps in relief, perhaps in disgust. "On it."

The line went dead.

Mara looked at the altered witness card. Then at Pell's folded page. Then at the board where Tamsin had written fast and slow and city-shaped beneath both.

The scale of the war had just changed again.

Not simply because the enemy was larger than they thought. Because the form of public harm was no longer only spectacular enough to frighten the city into belief. It could now come dressed as procedure, calming, privacy, triage, moderation, reassurance. Rooms that did not burn quickly. Rooms that taught the body to exhale too early and call the exhale wisdom.

Theo said it at last, giving the room the sentence it needed.

"The larger war is already hiding inside this one."

Nobody answered because nobody needed to.

They all felt it.

They all felt the larger terror in it. Not only teeth, fire, and rail, but the gentler architecture that arrived after catastrophe and offered, with reasonable voice and proper chairs, to spare everyone the exhausting mess of witness by moving truth somewhere quieter.

Mara picked up her pen.

On a fresh page she wrote the heading for the eleven o'clock briefing.

SLOW ADJACENCY: HOW ROOMS LEARN TO CALL THEMSELVES MERCY.

Then she underlined mercy once, very hard, and began.

Chapter Sixteen: Studio of Lies

The room behind Staff Access B at Southern Cross had once been a breastfeeding room.

That was the first obscenity.

The sign outside it had been changed twice in under twelve hours. First to TEMPORARY STAFF SUPPORT, then, sometime after midnight, to REASSURANCE ROOM. The second sign had been printed on ordinary station stock in the same municipal blue as the witness-table notices, laminated badly enough to imply haste and taped over the first with two strips of clear plastic that still held the press of human thumbs in them. By itself, the sign would not have been enough. A tired station manager might have done it. A frightened office somewhere higher up the chain might have sent the wording down and called the poor choice a kindness. Cities made stupid rooms all the time.

The trouble was that no one in station operations had authorised it.

Mara stood in the corridor outside the room at six-fifteen that morning with Theo on one side, Donnelly on the other, and the stale smell of recirculated station air carrying coffee, wet wool, brake dust, and the exhausted sweetness of disinfectant. Platform noise came to them through the concrete like weather learning to speak. Trains arriving. Trains holding. Public address voices trying very hard to sound singular. The witness table outside the central concourse had already been active for forty minutes. Nina Fowler, under a borrowed station cardigan and with a thermos at her elbow, was holding the city together with a ledger, a kettle, and enough personal contempt for secrecy to shame better-funded institutions.

The room behind Staff Access B sat halfway down a side corridor used mostly by cleaners, transit supervisors, and anyone needing five minutes away from the public eye. Narrow windows ran high along the left wall, frosted against voyeurism, clear enough at the edges to let in station light. The door itself was plain. Off-white. Push plate. No visible lock beyond the electronic strike. The sort of room no one ever wrote stories about because rooms like this existed precisely to prevent themselves from becoming narrative.

That was what made it wrong.

Donnelly held the bagged sign in one gloved hand. "It was on the door when the table rotation changed at five-thirty," he said. "No one admitted putting it up. Two supervisors denied the wording before I finished asking. One cleaner told me it felt like a room that wanted to be found by tired people and then apologised because she thought that sounded stupid."

"It doesn't sound stupid," Mara said.

Theo looked at the door as if by doing so long enough, he could force it to produce a brief. "Who used it overnight?"

"Two reports," Donnelly said. "One station clerk went in for eight minutes after hearing contradictory platform instructions and came out saying she felt much better and couldn't remember exactly what she'd worried about. One contract guard took a commuter in there for a panic episode and says the man 'settled almost immediately'."

Sera, behind Mara, made a quiet sound through her nose that was as close as she came to profanity in public. "What was the panic episode?"

"Name call over Platform Seven," Donnelly said. "No heat. No lock. He got shaky, heard his own surname over the speakers and then over the station radio, same as if someone had leaned into one ear and not the other. The guard says he walked him here because the corridor was quieter."

Theo took the bagged sign from Donnelly and held it up at arm's length. "And the room was so helpful it named itself."

The laminated paper sat inside the evidence bag with all the confidence of bad design. REASSURANCE ROOM. No logo. No departmental line. Just the city's own colours used with enough restraint to make suspicion feel rude.

Mara looked past it to the door again. "What happened to the clerk?"

Donnelly frowned as if the question had been waiting behind his eyes since dawn. "She says she no longer thinks the contradictory instructions were important. That she'd 'got wrapped around the axle' and the room helped her stop making ordinary complexity into drama."

Theo's face altered by one hard degree. "Did she use those words?"

"Yes."

Mara closed her hand around the strap of her notebook. Ordinary complexity. Wrapped around the axle. Not dramatic phrases. That was the point. No side-lane urgency. No black-room threat. Just the gentle, managerial theft of significance.

Sera stepped forward and studied the doorframe with the thermal scanner. The little screen stayed stubbornly blue-green. "No active heat anomaly."

Tamsin, who had arrived ten minutes earlier carrying a portable verifier, a case of cables, and the expression of a woman hoping the city would give her something to dismantle, crouched at the threshold and held the countersign reader along the strike plate. "No obvious route signature either," she said. "At least not the fast kind."

Theo looked at her. "There is no sentence in your mouth I currently like."

"You haven't liked any of mine for days."

"That's because the universe keeps validating them."

Mara glanced down the corridor. Two station cleaners were speaking quietly near the service lifts, one hand each resting on the trolley handles as if they had already been briefed on fixed surfaces and intended to stay morally adjacent to them all day. Beyond the frosted glass, the station moved in its morning rhythm, shoes, announcements, coffee lids, strangers keeping the city from becoming only a machine by bumping into one another at useful angles.

This room, she thought, worked against that. Not panic. Not immediate closure. The smaller theft. The soft reduction of contradiction from something communal and urgent into something individual and slightly embarrassing.

"We don't use it," she said.

Theo gave her a dry look. "I assume you're not just discussing your own plans."

"No one uses it. No station staff. No medics. No calming interviews. No one goes in there alone and no one is taken in there kindly." She turned to Donnelly. "Can you lock the corridor instead of just the room?"

He nodded at once. "Already did. Staff access rerouted through the north passage. People are irritated."

"Good," Theo said. "I prefer my cities irritated."

Tamsin stood up. "Locking it is useful, but not enough. If this is slow adjacency, we need to know what it thinks it is."

Theo folded the evidence bag over the sign and handed it back to Donnelly. "Meaning?"

Tamsin's eyes flicked to Mara, then Elian, then back to the door. "Meaning the room probably has a cousin on the route."

Elian had not said much since they left the annex. He was standing on Mara's other side, hands in his coat pockets, eyes not on the door but on the geometry around it, the corridor, the frosted panes, the light above, the very arrangement of pause and privacy. He had the look he always got when his mind was trying not to admit it was listening harder than anyone had asked.

"The room is making an argument," he said.

No one interrupted.

"Not with heat. Not with contradiction pressure. It's making privacy feel competent. It's saying that talking yourself down in a sealed space under one calm authority is maturity. That noise is what made the station dangerous, not what saved it."

Mara heard the station behind them then, the station in full daylight, voices, platforms, departures, ordinary public friction, the whole breathing ugly thing. The room behind Staff Access B would have called that noise. The witness tables called it civilisation.

Theo looked at Elian for a moment longer than usual. "Can you trace it."

"Not here," Elian said. "Not cleanly. If we're right, the architecture won't announce itself on civic surfaces the way the black room did. It'll hide in the route as a lawful-seeming alternative. A calmer chamber. A place that resembles the Harbour without the burden of witness."

Mara felt the sentence settle in her like a blade finding its sheath.

"The false chamber," she said.

Tamsin's mouth twitched despite everything. "I was going to call it something uglier, but yes."

Theo nodded once. "Then we go back in."

By eight-thirty, they were in the lower lab with the city's new quiet threat laid out before them.

The route maps on the wall had been rearranged overnight. The lawful Harbour held its now-familiar place, deep-basin, witness ladder, receiving structure earned rather than offered. Beneath and beside it, the black-room family still showed its closure arcs, side-lane teeth, and all the fast, bad manners they had learned to distrust. Now, Tamsin had added a third category in pale grey.

SLOW ADJACENCY CANDIDATES.

There were only two marks under the heading so far. The altered witness card in the archive weather. The reassurance room at Southern Cross. Not enough for certainty. Enough for fear to become disciplined.

Mr Idris had taken up his usual place with the ledger and a second clerk's copy. Nina Fowler had refused to leave the station but sent down her notes on the reassurance room's two occupants, one guard, one clerk, both of whom now described their previous alarm as overcomplication and had accepted the room's authority with a gratitude suspiciously free of detail. Sera had built a supplementary physiology sheet titled NON-ACUTE ENCLOSURE SIGNS, which she clearly hated on aesthetic grounds and therefore trusted more.

Theo stood at the edge of Bench Three and looked at Mara and Elian with the kind of attention some men reserved for bomb disposal or confessions. "This is not a black-room descent."

"No," Mara said.

"This is worse," Tamsin added. "Because if the route can build a lawful-looking chamber that merely trims witness until people thank it for their calm, we don't get flames as a warning."

Sera clipped the monitoring strips to Mara's wrists, then Elian's. "Then I watch for the wrong kind of relief instead."

Elian almost smiled. "There are many kinds."

"Tonight only the murderous ones concern me."

Mr Idris wrote that down because, of course, he did.

Theo opened the protocol folder. "State purpose."

Mara looked at the ring. "To identify whether the route now contains a false lawful chamber designed to mimic safety through reduced witness burden."

Elian added, "And to withdraw on any structure that offers clarity before declaration."

Theo's eyes rested on him. "Good. Keep that one."

They took their places.

The room narrowed the way it always did before descent, not in fear but in function. Tamsin dimmed the overheads and stripped the haptic station to full manual. No predictive smoothing. No comfort layers. No route assistance. Sera brought the thermal monitors live. Theo read the witness lines aloud. Mara and Elian repeated them. Mr Idris logged them. The ledger pages took it all in without comment because paper, unlike people, did not need time to decide whether history offended it.

The gloves sealed over their hands.

The lawful Harbour came first.

Mara always felt it before she saw the graph settle. Not as beauty. That was a trap she no longer allowed herself. The lawful architecture was not beautiful. It was exacting in a way that human beings sometimes experienced as beauty when they were lucky enough to be received honestly by something larger than their appetites. The basin opened only as declaration and witness aligned. It did not hurry. It did not flatter. It did not notice her tiredness and offer to carry it. It simply held, deep and patient, waiting to see whether the people approaching it intended to remain plural long enough to enter.

Beside her, Elian's breathing lengthened into the same cadence.

The false route did not arrive at once this time.

That was the first warning.

It did not leap up under the lawful line or flash its side-lane urgency or brush against private burdens in a voice too close to the bone. It simply remained absent long enough that part of Mara's body, the part still trained by a world where danger likes to show itself, began wanting to conclude that the room was cleaner tonight.

"There," Elian said softly.

The graph changed.

Not the black-room contour. Not the side-lane. A third shape, pale and unnervingly composed, emerged at a slight offset from the lawful Harbour and built itself as though answering a need no one had yet admitted aloud. Chamber was not quite the right word. Studio, perhaps, because the thing did not simply exist. It staged itself.

The first structure resembled a receiving room.

Not the Harbour's broad basin and witness ladder, but a human guess at such a place after hearing it described by someone earnest and dangerous. The lines were soft where lawful architecture was clear. The edges held no threat. The centre was not dark or narrow but warm with the suggestion of clarity. It looked like a room in which misunderstandings would be gently set down and ordered. A place where the work of moral tension might be replaced with something more humane. More adult. More orderly.

Mara felt her stomach turn.

"That," Tamsin said through gritted teeth, "is vile."

Theo's voice came from beyond the monitors. "State why."

Mara kept her hands still on the controls. "Because it looks reasonable."

The false chamber developed further as they held position. It did not ask for approach in the black-room way. It made approach feel like the natural next administrative step. A cleaner receiving space. A concern-refinement space. A place where witness, once it had served its crude emergency purpose, could give way to discretion.

Elian's voice was level, but she knew him well enough now to hear the danger in how level. "It's not trying to lure by speed."

"No," Mara said. "It's trying to lure by dignity."

Mr Idris's pen moved sharply over the page.

Tamsin threw the candidate structure onto the side display and began comparing it against the reassurance room measurements from Southern Cross. "Same behavioural family," she muttered. "Different scale, same pitch. Sealed enough to soothe. Open enough to deny it's sealing."

Sera watched the physiology readouts. "No thermal rise. Both stable. Too stable, maybe."

Theo looked up. "Too stable."

Sera did not take her eyes off the screen. "Fast structures spike. They provoke. This is flattening variability. If either of them suddenly feels professionally calmer than they should under live false contact, I want it named."

The chamber clarified itself further.

Mara saw, with a sort of nausea, that it had not borrowed from the black room alone. It had borrowed from them. From the tables. From the ledgers. From the patient, civil discipline of lawful exchange. The room carried the emotional syntax of witness while quietly removing the bodies that made witness real. It was not only false. It was parasitic on everything they had built against the fast routes.

Mara said it aloud.

"It's using our own countermeasures as set dressing."

The chamber shimmered.

Tamsin swore. "There. It doesn't like that named."

Elian was staring into the centre of the structure with the same expression he wore when route geometry and human meaning were threatening to collapse into one another. "It's offering me a room where I don't have to be dangerous to the people I care about."

The sentence entered the lab like a dropped blade.

Mara turned her head, only slightly. "What does that mean."

He swallowed once. "It feels like a chamber where the work of interpretation gets transferred cleanly. I could stop carrying the burden of hearing too much. Stop asking you to witness every wrong contour with me. Stop making the room around us harder just because the route keeps wanting to speak through me."

Sera's eyes flicked to the monitor. "Pulse drifting but no lock."

Theo said, "That's how it gets you. Keep speaking."

Mara looked back at the chamber.

Now that Elian had named his burden, she could feel the room adjust around it with a politeness that made her want to strike the console with both hands. It did not say yes, exactly. It said of course. Of course, a serious chamber would relieve a man like that. Of course, a difficult gift required professional containment. Of course, care sometimes meant not asking others to keep enduring your trouble in public.

She could see why the station clerk had come out of the reassurance room grateful. There was nothing melodramatic in the offer. Only the promise that complexity could be sorted privately by people trained to bear it.

It was the oldest lie power ever told.

"It offers me adulthood," Mara said before the chamber could choose her words for her. "A version of adulthood where love becomes discretion and discretion becomes silence. A room where I can be less embarrassing to institutions."

The structure on the graph wavered.

Not enough to collapse. Enough to reveal grain in the image, tiny lines under the soft edge, as though the chamber had been painted over something more mechanical and less forgiving.

Tamsin leaned in. "Again."

Mara did not take her eyes off the screen. "It says the public part of care was only for the emergency and the mature version happens after, in a cleaner room."

The shimmer became a tremor.

Elian said, "It says the burdened should be relieved by surrendering witness, not by sharing it."

The room responded.

Not with heat. With narrowing.

For one bad second, the soft chamber's centre pulled inward, the apparent spaciousness of it revealing itself as a perspective trick rather than actual depth. The place did not open. It staged opening. Beneath the staged opening sat a thinner architecture, a throat disguised as a salon.

Theo inhaled once through his nose. "There's your answer."

Mara could feel it now, too. The chamber did not intend to burn quickly. It intended to accept, to hold, to soothe, and in the soothing reduce all contradiction to one authorised interpretation at a time. A civic room. An administrative room. The dream of every frightened state and every exhausted soul who had begun to believe plurality was simply too loud to deserve permanence.

Mr Idris spoke into the quiet with the tone of a man identifying a fungus in his own pantry. "Studio of lies."

The name held at once.

Tamsin typed it in without asking anyone's permission.

STUDIO OF LIES.

Elian's breathing altered.

Mara heard it before Sera did.

"What," she said.

He did not answer immediately. His hands remained steady on the controls, too steady. That frightened her more than any visible tremor.

"Elian."

He took a breath. "It split the room."

Theo's head came up. "Explain."

"The chamber isn't trying to isolate me from you by speed or urgency. It's doing it by idealisation. It's presenting a version of both of us in which our bond becomes professional enough to stop needing witness. There's a chamber for me and a chamber for Mara, but they're adjacent and mutually admiring. Perfectly clean. No friction. No need to hold contradiction in front of other people. No need to embarrass the city by being visibly attached."

Mara felt ice move through her.

Because she could see her own version now. A room lined not with softness but with authority. Files, language, city policy, all of it sharpened and coherent and under her hand. A place where she could protect the public story without having to expose the private cost of doing so. A chamber where she could stop being witnessed in the act of caring and simply become good at control.

It was not romantic. It was worse. It was flattering in the language of competence.

She said it aloud before it could root.

"It offers me a cleaner self than the truth permits."

The studio rippled.

Elian, voice rougher now, said, "It offers us an intimacy that leaves no evidence."

That almost did it.

Sera's scanner chirped once, warning tone low but definite. Not heat. Variance. A drift too smooth to trust.

"Name harder," she said at once. "No poetry."

Theo added, "And no noble lies."

Mara seized the first ugly truth that came to hand and forced it into the room. "I want a chamber where no one sees how frightened I am that institutions will keep choosing the room over the breath."

The studio shuddered.

Elian followed, not elegant now, just human. "I want a chamber where I never have to watch you carry me in public."

There.

The chamber broke.

Not fully. It did not vanish or scream or turn monstrous for the convenience of their certainty. It simply lost the ability to maintain the lie that it was larger than the burden it offered to remove. The soft edges peeled back. The apparent depth shrank. What remained beneath was a narrow set of articulated closure arcs linked by polished surfaces meant to reflect the operator's preferred self back at them until they stepped in far enough to become governable.

Tamsin's hands flew over the console. "There, there, there. I've got the under-structure. It's a grooming chamber."

Theo shot her a look.

"In technical terms," she said without apology, "it stages self-recognition until the subject voluntarily reduces witness density. That is grooming with better furniture."

Mr Idris wrote it down anyway.

The studio tried once more to recover. Mara felt it smoothing itself, smaller now, humbler, a compromise offer. Not full privacy. Just a smaller room. Just for processing. Just until you're clearer. Just until the others no longer had to carry your uncertainty.

She looked at the thing and finally hated it properly.

"No," she said.

The word was not dramatic. It was flat as a board edge. Useful as a lock.

Elian said, "No."

Theo from behind them: "No."

Sera: "No."

Mr Idris, bless him, from the chair by the lamp: "Certainly not."

Even Tamsin muttered, "Get bent."

The route could not survive that many human refusals occupying the same moral space.

The studio collapsed in on its own performance. The soft chamber lines folded. The polished surfaces lost coherence. For a fraction of a second the old black-room family showed through beneath it, thinner here, slower, civically dressed but recognisably of the same blood. Then the whole false structure dropped away under the lawful Harbour, leaving only the deep-basin patience of the true route and the ordinary sounds of the lower lab rebuilding themselves around the workbench.

Sera moved first, scanning wrists, sternums, eyes. "No lock. No heat. Both of you talk."

Mara pulled the glove off her right hand with the kind of care people use around cracked glass. "It offered a room where authority made feeling neat."

Elian stripped his left glove and set it on the bench. "It offered a bond without witness and called that protection."

Theo closed the protocol folder, not because he was finished, but because he had seen enough of the room's teeth for one day. "And now we know."

Tamsin was still dissecting the captured under-structure. "Not enough."

Mr Idris looked up from the ledger. "Nothing ever is."

Mara sat back against the edge of the sorting table and looked at the route map on the wall. The lawful Harbour remained what it had been all along. The studio of lies had gone quiet, but not absent. She could feel, in the same unpleasant way she now recognised the weather when it changed, that the structure would return in different language. Different rooms. Different offices. It had not failed because they were brilliant. It had failed because they had named aloud the part of themselves it wanted to tidy away.

That was useful. Not comforting. Useful.

Theo said, "We update everything."

No one argued.

Sera added a new line to the non-acute enclosure sheet. Beware spaces that make your relief feel mature. Tamsin split the route board again, fast adjacencies on one side, slow adjacencies on the other, and under the latter wrote in thick black capitals:

PROFESSIONALISED SECRECY. Mr Idris updated the ledger entry with studio of lies and then, on a separate page for internal teaching, wrote a sentence Mara knew would stay in her head for years.

Some rooms do not threaten you.
They agree with your best manners until you stop bringing anyone else inside.

Mara copied it into the shadow archive immediately.

By noon, the station tables had the first revised card in circulation.

If a room or official asks you to take your contradiction somewhere private before it can be witnessed, refuse.
If privacy arrives before truth, it is not help.

Nina Fowler approved of that too, though she requested the word private be emboldened because, in her view, cities were full of people who thought privacy was a synonym for professionalism when it often meant a trap with biscuits.

At one-thirty, Priya Nandakumar's written statement came through in final form. Mara read it once in the archive room while the city map glowed beside her. Priya described the wrong use of her name on Platform 11. The relief that arrived with stillness. The bench support under her hand. The woman in the camel coat saying yes. The station worker using his own lungs instead of his radio. Then, near the end, one line that made Mara put the page down and stare at the rain on the annex windows.

The moment I touched the bench and the other woman answered me, the station stopped feeling like it knew me better than I knew myself.

That, Mara thought, was the whole war.

Not simply over safety. Over authorship. Over whether a room, a route, a city, an office, or a polished man in a charcoal suit got to know people better than they knew themselves once contradiction began tightening around them.

She copied the line into the internal file under PUBLIC WITNESS LANGUAGE: AUTHORITY TEST.

When she looked up, Elian was standing in the doorway.

"You read it too," she said.

He nodded.

"What."

He came farther in, carrying one of the revised station cards between two fingers. "The chamber did the opposite. It claimed to know us more elegantly than we did."

"Yes."

He looked at the city map rather than at her. "Do you ever think that's what all bad systems are. Rooms built by people who think they can know others more cleanly than those people can know themselves."

Mara considered the card in his hand. The line about private contradiction. The line about witness. The line about refusing clean little rooms. Then the packet from Pell lying in its sleeve on the table, quiet fine, distance, older adjacencies, order.

"Yes," she said. "And I think that's why they hate breath."

He looked at her then, and for a moment the archive room held not romance, not ease, but that more useful thing they had been building against the route since Daniel Voss died in a service corridor: a bond that could survive being seen.

Outside, the city moved under rain and public language and station tables and men in offices still trying to decide whether witness was a temporary emergency measure or the beginning of a very different kind of government.

Inside, the studio of lies had been named.

That would not stop it.

But it would make the next room work harder.

Chapter Seventeen: The Burn List

Theo Markel distrusted any list that looked too neutral.

Names on government paper never stayed names for long. They became sequence, liability, permission. They became the point at which a living person with a pulse and a mother and a mortgage was flattened into something a system could move.

He knew that before he opened the file. He knew it savagely afterwards.

Then he opened the file.

At Concord, Pell Ardoc had warned them that lists learned to walk. Theo had believed the line in principle. He had not expected to find one in Melbourne with people he knew flattened into columns.

It arrived not through the heavy-method tray, not through any lawful packet or witness route, but through the ugly old channels people still used when conscience outran professional hygiene. A forwarded archive index from an anonymous internal account. No message. No flourish. Just a folder name that had been made to look dull enough to survive ordinary scrutiny.

RESPONSE CONTACTS / ENVIRONMENTAL DEPENDENCIES / REV 7

Theo almost deleted it because of the title. Dullness was its own tell now. Anything too eager to be mundane deserved dissection.

He was in the annex's temporary legal room on Level Two when he opened it, the one with the stale air-conditioning and the carpet that smelled faintly of wet cardboard no matter the weather. A lamp from someone else's office had been dragged in to supplement the fluorescent strip overhead, which only made the room look like a place in which better lies were usually told. Three folders from

Transport sat open on the table. Mercer's latest consolidation language lay bleeding red ink under Theo's annotations. Outside the room, the witness table at the lift lobby had entered its late-afternoon rhythm, a cleaner asking a security guard whether contradictory instructions about a locked stairwell counted if both came from men wearing lanyards, the security guard answering that lanyards were now morally discounted until proven otherwise.

Theo double-clicked the file.

At first it looked like any of a hundred ugly internal spreadsheets produced by frightened offices that needed to turn chaos into tractable nouns before dinner. Columns. Codes. Priority tags. Response markers. He saw headings first.

EXPOSED
INFLUENCEABLE
PRONE TO ESCALATION
CONTAINMENT VALUE
TRANSFER ELIGIBILITY
WITNESS IMPACT

His face did not change. He took one breath. Then another. Then he began reading the names.

Daniel Voss was there, though his name had already been greyed and marked terminal.

Hannah Quill was there too, not under fatality but under subject collapse, which told Theo more about the people who built the sheet than any manifesto would have done.

Priya Nandakumar.

Donnelly, R.

Fowler, N.

Camel coat woman unknown, Platform 11, probable secondary witness amplifier.

Three station cleaners, one listed as "improperly assertive."

Lachie Baines.

Two junior analysts from the annex.

One archive clerk. Initial only, but Theo knew it was Idris because the witness impact rating was marked disproportionate and the note beside it read trusted by support staff.

Elian Cross had his own subfile.

So did Mara.

Theo stared at Mara's entry long enough that the room around him flattened.

VALE, M.
Narrative consolidation risk.
High witness-forming capacity.
Likely to resist reassurance conversion.
Observe for fatigue isolation opportunities.
Do not challenge directly in public.

For one extremely useful second, he wanted to put his fist through the monitor.

Instead, he printed the sheet.

Then he printed the metadata, the hidden comments, the revision trail, and the version history. He printed everything because rage was not evidence and evidence was the only way to hurt men like this in rooms built by their cousins.

By the time the printer finished coughing its way through the pages, Mara was in the doorway.

She took one look at his face and shut the door behind her.

"What."

He handed her the top sheet without speaking.

She read the headings first. Then the names. Then the note under her own entry. Something in her expression cooled so fast it seemed to remove all softness from the air.

"Fatigue isolation opportunities," she said.

Theo said, "Yes."

She did not sit. She read farther down, found Elian's sheet, and then the station witnesses. By the time she reached Nina Fowler the paper had begun to tremble slightly in her hand, not because Mara was frightened, but because there are some forms of contempt that need a body to move through on the way to language.

"This is triage for capture," she said at last.

"Yes."

"Not just physical capture."

"No."

Theo took the sheet back and spread the pages across the table in order. Once the emotion had somewhere to go, the structure emerged more clearly. Revision history. Routing chain. Two offices redacted. One logistics stream linked to Strategic Interface Coordination. One transport advisory branch. One private contractor node he would have bet his next year's income ran straight back to Helix Meridian. The most recent revision had occurred thirty-two minutes earlier.

"They're still updating it," Mara said.

"Yes."

"Meaning someone is using live witness behaviour to sort people by convertibility."

"Yes."

Her eyes found the line again. Witness impact. Containment value. The words wanted to sound administrative. That was the filth of them. No mention of burning. No Cauterists. No black room. Just the city's living, breathing resisters translated into management problems and opportunities.

Theo tapped the bottom corner of the sheet. "This one matters."

She looked.

A subheading. Smaller. Easier to miss.

REMOVE FROM CROWD PATHWAYS WHEN POSSIBLE.

The line below it carried names and partial descriptors. Not everyone on the sheet. Only those rated high witness-forming, difficult to reassure, or prone to encouraging plurality under contradiction stress.

Nina Fowler.
Donnelly.
Priya Nandakumar.
Three cleaners.
One archive clerk.
Mara Vale.
Elian Cross.

The page was pushing, with all the calm of an old bureaucracy, towards moving them out of public rooms.

Mara laid the sheet down very carefully. "This is the burn list."

Theo looked at her.

She met his gaze with her own gone bright and hard. "Don't argue semantics. This is how they prepare people. Not all at once. Not with open violence. They identify who can interrupt closure, remove them from crowd pathways, and leave the rest softer."

He did not argue.

Because she was right.

At the other end of the annex, two floors down, Sera Imani was teaching a body how not to complete the room.

Not teaching, exactly. Bodies did not take instruction the way governments did. They negotiated. They rebelled. They forgot. They surprised you in ways no tidy system ever forgave. But the station clerk from Staff Access B, the woman who had entered the reassurance room frightened and come out speaking in the voice of her own minimisation, was sitting under the lower lab's side-room light with one hand flat on the edge of an ordinary steel chair while Sera talked her back into the right kind of complexity.

Her name was Beth Lowen. Thirty-two. Senior rostering clerk. No psychiatric history. No major medical flags. One contradictory instruction event at Southern Cross. Eight minutes in the reassurance room. Emergence with affect blunting, narrative flattening, and suspicious gratitude for private authority.

Beth had arrived in the lower lab pale with embarrassment and anger mixed so tightly that she kept apologising every third sentence for having been manipulated too elegantly to notice in the moment.

"I'm not even someone who likes private rooms," she said for the second time. "I hate private rooms. I work in rostering. The whole point of rostering is that everyone sees the mess and we survive anyway."

"Good," Sera said.

Beth blinked. "Good?"

"Yes. Keep that thought."

Sera sat opposite her at the little steel table, notepad untouched for once. No charts laid out. No printed prompts. Just a pulse clip on one finger, a thermal strip at the wrist, and the chair edge under Beth's left hand. The room around them was intentionally plain. No soft lamps. No counselling voice. No hidden comfort that might accidentally imitate the reassurance room's logic. Just ordinary surfaces and one other human body refusing to let the world become neat too soon.

"What did it say?" Sera asked.

Beth stared at the wall for a second. "Not words, exactly."

"Try anyway."

"It…" Beth's fingers tightened on the chair edge. "It felt like the station was too much at once and the room was the adult version of handling it. Like if I went inside then I could stop making everything so public and difficult."

Sera nodded once. "What happened in your body."

"Everything slowed. But not right. I thought that was the point. I thought calmer meant better." Beth swallowed. "Then you lot asked me questions and I realised I couldn't remember which parts I'd decided and which parts I'd been handed."

That was it.

Sera had seen versions of the pattern in Daniel, Hannah, the station footage, the route maps. But until now the evidence always arrived at the edge of ignition or after it. Beth offered something rarer and, for that reason, possibly more valuable: a body that had entered slow enclosure and come back with enough self left to compare notes.

Sera leaned forward very slightly. "All right. We're going to separate what you knew from what the room offered. Not quickly. And not alone."

Beth looked at her with visible suspicion. "Is this therapy."

"No. It's classification."

That got the smallest, strangest smile out of her.

For the next forty minutes Sera walked her through the station event in simple brutal pieces. The first contradictory announcement. The cold across the shoulders. The pressure under the sternum. The relief when the reassurance room appeared. The sensation of stepping into a space where other people's noise became an avoidable burden rather than a shared fact. Every time Beth drifted toward minimising, Sera stopped her and asked what the body had wanted, not what the room had called that wanting. Every time the room's language started to slide back over her memory, Beth was made to place her fingers more firmly against the chair edge and say aloud one true thing about the station that no room could improve.

There were too many people for privacy to be the answer.
The train boards were wrong before I entered.
The voice used calm to hurry me.
I felt relieved before I felt safe.
Those are not the same.

At statement four, Sera saw Beth's pulse change.

Not rising. Returning.

The pattern was subtle enough that nobody but a clinician would have honoured it. The variable drift that had made Beth so strangely composure-heavy when she arrived began to roughen again. Not destabilise. Humanise. Tiny fluctuations of uncertainty and irritation came back into her. The affect flattening lifted by a hair's breadth and then another. When she said on the fifth pass, with real heat in her voice, "I let a stupid room tell me I was being mature," Sera knew they had it.

Not cure. Not salvation. But something almost as rare in their work: reversal.

She sat back and wrote three words on the notepad for the first time all session.

BROKEN BEFORE LOCK.

Beth read them upside down. "What does that mean?"

"It means," Sera said, "that the room was trying to finish a process your body had not completed yet. And if we interrupt early enough, the body remembers how not to do the room's work for it."

Beth absorbed that in silence.

Then, very quietly, she asked, "So I'm not stupid?"

"No," Sera said. "You're evidence."

By the time Mara and Theo brought the burn list down to the lower lab, Beth was sitting straighter, angrier, and visibly harder to simplify. Sera liked all three outcomes. Theo liked only one, because he entered the side room, saw Beth's face, and immediately looked at Sera as if to ask whether they had just discovered medicine or merely a better category of not-yet-dead.

"What," he said.

Sera stood and took the papers Mara handed her.

The burn list changed the side room's air in the same way the altered witness card had changed the archive room. Not through heat. Through revelation. Beth watched their faces as they read and then, because she worked in rostering and understood systems the way surgeons understand blood loss, reached for the top page before anyone told her not to.

She read her own name and went still.

"Containment value," she said, and the word itself nearly made her laugh. "Well. That's flattering."

Theo took the page back. "You should not have seen that."

"Why?" Her voice had changed. Less politely ashamed now. More properly offended. "Because if I know they wrote me down, I might stop thinking they're adults."

No one answered because the answer was yes, and also because Beth had already moved past permission.

She looked at Sera instead. "This is the room work, isn't it?"

Sera nodded. "Partly."

"No." Beth leaned back in the chair, fingers still on the steel edge. "Not partly. The reassurance room didn't only calm me. It made me think the public version of concern was childish, and the private version was competent. This list is the same trick with nicer headings."

Mara looked at her as if seeing a witness born in real time. "Yes."

Beth exhaled once. "Then the room wasn't trying to make me safer. It was trying to make me sortable."

There it was again. Useful truth arriving in plain language from the very people Mercer's class most enjoyed calling untrained.

Theo laid the pages on the table and spread them out flat. The names sat there between them, categorised and annotated and made available for the kinds of interventions rooms like the black chamber and the studio of lies required in order to work cheaply.

He looked at Sera. "You said reversal."

"Yes."

"How strong."

"Early only. Before the subject starts loving the room more than they mistrust the contradiction. After that…" She shook her head once. "We may get memory. We may get anger. We may not get full return."

Theo's attention moved to the page again. "Then this list isn't just identifying liabilities. It's identifying who can still be moved."

Mara said, "And who must be moved before they teach others how not to be."

Tamsin appeared in the doorway at that precise moment with a drive in one hand and the gait of a woman who had forgotten lunch existed and considered that a worthy sacrifice to clarity. "I've got a route correlation," she said. Then she saw the spread on the table. "Oh. Excellent. We're making evil legible."

Theo handed her the top sheet.

She read the first six lines and said nothing. Then she read another ten and made a quiet, involuntary sound that might have been laughter if laughter were a tool for flaying. "Witness impact."

"Yes," Mara said.

"Do they have one for themselves. 'High smug density. Moderately combustible.'"

Mr Idris, appearing behind her as if summoned by the scent of a phrase too good not to archive, said, "Perhaps later."

Tamsin dropped the drive on the table. "Route first. Insults after. The station room and the altered witness card share sub-threshold route behaviour with the studio of lies. Not full chamber generation. Premise incubation. Same family. Same older adjacency class Pell warned us about."

Beth looked from one face to another. "You all understand that sentence."

"No," Theo said. "We merely use it."

Tamsin tapped the drive. "I've mapped a slower route architecture starting to cluster around three things. Reassurance language. private sorting spaces. controlled administrative pathways." She pointed to the burn list. "And this bastard sheet is basically a shopping list for where to apply it next."

Sera said, "Which means the medical breakthrough matters more, not less."

Theo turned. "Say that again."

Sera did, because she was not one of those clinicians who became precious the moment her work brushed meaning. "The reassurance room worked because it reached Beth before lock. We interrupted it by breaking the enclosure while some self remained to contradict it. That means the city's best defence is not only tables. It is early recovery before people become useful to a list like this."

Mara saw the connection take shape behind Theo's eyes. Legal, civic, human all at once. If the list identified people for removal from crowd pathways, then the answer was not only to hide them or guard them like assets. It was to fortify them in public and return them quickly if touched.

"Public re-entry," she said.

Sera looked at her. "What."

"If a person is taken by a slow room and comes back flatter, cleaner, grateful for privacy, we don't disappear them into care. We get them back to witness with support before the room's story sets."

Beth said at once, "Yes."

Theo frowned. "That's risky."

"So is everything," Mara replied. "But if we treat exposed people as contamination, we complete the room for them. The route wins by converting witnesses into private patients."

The side room went quiet.

Then Sera nodded. Once. Hard. "Yes."

Theo looked at the burn list, then at Beth, then at the route maps on Tamsin's drive, then at the pages Pell had sent under quiet fine. Older adjacencies. Order. Rooms that called themselves mercy. He had the look he always got when the architecture of the fight reassembled itself into something both clearer and more offensive than before.

"All right," he said. "We do three things."

No one objected to the phrasing because he was right and because the sentence did not come out of his mouth often unless he had already paid for it with sleep.

"First," he said, tapping the list, "this becomes evidence in three chains before anyone high enough to misuse it gets to call it draft modelling. Second, every person on this sheet gets warned under witness today, not by phone, not by memo, but by breathing people with names. Third, Sera builds us a re-entry protocol for slow-room exposure and we put it through every table in the city before midnight."

Beth raised one hand slightly. "Fourth."

They all looked at her.

She met Theo's eye now without the slightest sign of the false calm the reassurance room had dressed her in. "Don't just warn us. Ask us what the room sounds like from inside before it starts sounding like one of your policy words."

Theo held her gaze for a beat, then nodded. "Fourth."

Mr Idris wrote all four.

The hours after that became all blade and labour.

Witness teams went out from the annex with names folded in jacket pockets and ledgers under their arms. Not officers. Not reassurance personnel. Pairs and trios drawn from the people who had already learned the city's new ethics by using them. Nina Fowler took station staff and transit clerks. Donnelly took transport supervisors. One cleaner from Southern Cross, having correctly identified the side-lane logic before two deputy directors had managed the same trick, insisted on joining the Richmond line and was not refused. Mara and Theo took the internal names first, because the burn list had been born here and that fact offended them equally for different reasons.

Tamsin sent the route correlations to every table with notes so rude and precise they might one day deserve their own museum display. Sera built the re-entry sheet with Beth sitting opposite her and arguing the wording every time it veered too clinical. Together they found the right lines.

If you leave a room feeling professionally calmer than the facts permit, return to witness.
Do not let the room decide the story of your own relief.
Tell another person what the room made seem reasonable.
Touch something ordinary while you do it.

By evening, the city's tables had begun doing something more complicated than interruption.

They were taking people back.

Not dramatically. No crowds. No speeches. Just one station clerk returning to the table after the reassurance room and saying aloud that she had mistaken flattening for maturity. One contract guard admitting he had thought privacy sounded grown-up because the station was too loud and he was too tired. One junior analyst at the annex confessing she had opened a message marked quiet handling and felt grateful, at first, that someone else might finally decide for her what level of worry was appropriate. Each time, the table held them. Each time, the route lost a little of its right to define the meaning of their own reactions.

It was not victory.

It was civilisation being taught to heal in public.

Near midnight, after the warning visits were done and the copies of the burn list sat in official legal hold, shadow archive, and Mr Idris's morally distinguished safe, Mara found Theo in the legal room on Level Two staring at the sheet again.

He did not look up when she entered. "You know what I hate most."

It was not a question.

She leaned against the doorframe. "Tell me anyway."

He tapped the column headings with one finger.

"Not the arrogance. That's constant. Not even the names. It's this." He touched witness impact. "They've learned to see what keeps people human and classify it as a systems problem."

Mara was quiet for a moment. Then she crossed the room and stood beside him.

"Yes," she said. "And now we've learned to see what keeps systems murderous and classify it as architecture."

Theo finally looked at her then.

They were both too tired for comfort to mean anything sentimental. That was one of the things the past week had sharpened properly. What passed between them here was older and more useful than softness. Recognition. Shared offence. A refusal to let the room close on one perspective if two could still stand in it.

He folded the top sheet in half.

Then, deliberately, he unfolded it again and laid it flat on the table.

"We don't burn names," he said. "We show the city what was planned for them."

Mara thought of Pell under quiet fine. Beth with her hand on the chair edge. Priya touching the bench support. Donnelly switching off the radio and using his own lungs. Nina behind the table calling the station back to itself one contradiction at a time. The clerk in Isorion writing under removal because distance was the state's preferred cruelty on both sides of the line. The room had been built inside him before it burned him. The witness asked for a room. Slow adjacency. Mercy. Order. All the bad words trying to become patient.

Then she thought of the ledgers, the ugly tables, and the astonishing brute fact that people had started choosing one another loudly enough to inconvenience the route.

"No," she said. "We don't burn names."

Outside, Melbourne carried on under rain, platform steel, sodium light, and the accumulating knowledge that not every room offering calm deserved trust. The city had not yet learned all the right lessons. Neither had they. But the burn list had done them one favour no enemy ever intended. It had made collaboration legible in the oldest possible language.

Names.

And names, once seen clearly and held under witness, were much harder to carry alone.

Chapter Eighteen: False Rescue

The call came through the table at Richmond Station at 6:12 p.m., and because the city had learned enough to be afraid of clean urgency, nobody trusted it first.

That was what saved them.

The witness table stood under the eastern concourse clock beside a shuttered coffee kiosk and a vending machine that had been out of order for so long people no longer tried to buy anything from it. The setup was ugly in all the right ways. Grey fold-out surface. Plastic kettle. Ledger open. Two station volunteers and one cleaner who had decided, after Southern Cross, that she was no longer willing to let men with radios define reality unaccompanied. Evening commuters were moving through the station in the heavy, tired current of people who had done the day already and wanted only home, shoes off, dinner, the television murmuring somewhere near sleep.

When the call arrived, it did not come over the public address.

It came to the table phone itself.

The volunteer on the seat nearest the machine, a tram inspector named Hal West who had been drafted into witness work because he had once physically removed three executives from a carriage using nothing but politeness and mass, picked up on the second ring.

"Witness table, Richmond," he said.

The voice on the line answered in the tone institutions used when trying not to sound like command while fully intending to be obeyed.

"Need immediate quiet clearance to lower maintenance access beneath the western lift shaft. One trapped witness. Partial route contamination. No broad alert. Bring Elian Cross and one legal liaison only. Others will increase closure density."

Hal listened for three seconds, no more. Then he looked at the cleaner opposite him, a woman named Aroha with a jaw like bad weather and a witness card clipped beside her name badge, and covered the mouthpiece with one hand.

"They want Cross alone with a lawyer," he said.

Aroha did not even blink. "Then they can have a chair instead."

Hal nodded once, took his hand off the phone, and said into the line, "Which legal liaison?"

A pause.

Not long. Just long enough.

The voice came back. "Markel."

Hal smiled without humour. "Lovely. Tell him that yourself."
He hung up.

At the annex, Theo Markel was already walking towards the lower lab when Hal's relay came in through Donnelly's direct line. He did not break stride. Mara, keeping pace beside him with the station incident pad under one arm, listened to the summary and said, "Lower maintenance access beneath the western lift shaft."

Theo nodded. "Lift shaft corridor."

"From the synopsis of every bad decision we've seen so far."

"Exactly."

They entered the lower lab to find Tamsin at the route board, Sera at the physiology station, Elian by Bench Three with his hands in his coat pockets as if he no longer trusted them unless watched, and Mr Idris writing the time into the evening ledger in a hand too beautiful for the content.

Theo gave the room the facts in one clean burst.

"Richmond witness table received a request for quiet extraction from beneath the western lift shaft. One trapped witness. Partial contamination. They specifically asked for Elian and me only. No broad alert. No tables. No Sera. No Tamsin. Which is why we're all going."

Tamsin looked up from the board. "How generous of them."

Elian had already gone still in that way of his that meant the route was ahead of language somewhere inside him. "Western shaft," he said. "That corridor's mostly structural steel and old service plating."

"Meaning?" Mara asked.

"Meaning if the route wants a vertical chamber without the obvious signature of a black room, a lift shaft is as close to a prayer as infrastructure gets."

Tamsin swore softly. "Of course it picked a lift. Up, down, pause, release. Binary action in a contained tube."

Sera was already pulling two medical field kits from the cabinet. "And if they really do have someone trapped, we don't send extraction into that cold."

Theo looked at her. "You think it could be real."

"I think traps often use something real because realism improves recruitment."

Mara set the station incident pad on the table. "Who is the witness?"

"Unknown," Theo said. "They refused to name them."

Mr Idris, without looking up from the ledger, said, "How reassuring."

No one laughed.

Ten minutes later, they were in the annex vehicle on the way to Richmond, rain needling the windscreen in thin diagonal threads while Melbourne slid past in sodium orange and wet black. Theo drove because he trusted himself less behind arguments than behind the wheel. Mara sat in the front with the station file open. In the back, Tamsin had the portable route reader on her knees, Sera the medical kit between her boots, and Elian by the window watching the city's lit edges with the expression of a man listening for one voice beneath many.

It was that expression that Mara kept looking back at.

Not because she doubted him. Because she knew exactly what a trap like this liked to do. The trap was never only the room. It was the person who believed they were now experienced enough to survive the room by naming it correctly on the way in.

She knew Elian knew that too.

That did not make the road kinder.

Richmond Station's western service access was behind a locked roller gate used mostly by maintenance carts, cleaning contractors, and the kind of personnel who moved through the city's underside without ever being invited onto policy panels. Donnelly met them there with Hal and Aroha and two transit supervisors who had already made the good decision of touching the handrail while they waited, one palm each kept flat against painted steel as if the gesture had become habit rather than instruction.

"Any more calls?" Theo asked.

Donnelly shook his head. "Nothing direct. But the western shaft cameras went white for twelve seconds at six-oh-nine. Then came back on with no recorded fault."

Tamsin took the route reader from its case. "And the table?"

"Held," Hal said. "One name call on the up platform, two contradictory board instructions near the stairs, all externalised. No lock signatures."

Aroha jerked her chin towards the service corridor beyond the gate. "Whatever this is, it wanted the table quiet. That tells me enough."

Theo keyed the gate, and they went in.

The passage beyond smelled of old, damp machine oil and concrete that had spent too many years carrying the river's weather through its bones. Fluorescent strips ran along the low ceiling, three of them dead, one pulsing badly. The walls were lined with conduit, lift control housings, junction boxes, and the steel service doors that made hidden city spaces feel less like tunnels and more like the back corridors of some immense, unwell institution. The sound of trains above and beyond them came not as noise but as mass translated through metal. Every arrival spoke in the shaft walls. Every door decision became a tremor underfoot.

Tamsin held up one hand.

They stopped.

The portable reader had come alive in her palm with a faint blue line across the screen, not broad enough for full false-route flare, not quiet enough for ordinary infrastructure either. She turned it so Elian could see.

"What?"

He crouched slightly, not touching the wall, not the floor, just lowering his body until the route had to meet him, honestly or not at all. "It's layered," he said. "There's a route disturbance below us, but something's masking the edges."

Theo looked down the corridor. Fifty metres ahead, around a bend where the shaft dropped to the maintenance platform, a service door stood ajar.

Donnelly said, "That was shut when we came in."

Sera's grip tightened slightly on the handle of the medical case. "Real witness or bait?"

"Yes," Tamsin muttered.

They moved carefully.

No one played hero. That was the point of everything they had learned so far. They moved in a formation witnessed by men who trusted neat plans more than people. Theo and Donnelly at the front. Tamsin and Elian a pace behind with the reader and the route map. Mara and Sera in the centre with the station pad and the medical case. Hal, Aroha, and the transit supervisors at the rear, not because they were expendable, but because this was what it looked like when a city learned not to send its thinkers into the dark without the people who actually kept trains, floors, gates, and public moods from becoming only ideas.

At the bend, the service door opened onto the shaft platform.

The space beyond was taller than the corridor had implied. A narrow maintenance deck ran along one side of the lift shaft proper, shielded by old mesh and reinforced glass, with ladder access above and below, machinery housings sunk into the wall, and emergency alcoves at intervals where a person could stand clear if the wrong kind of maintenance cart or suspended mechanism came through.

Far above, through the open shaft line, they could hear the lift cars moving and stopping in the public station world, the hidden transit of people going home while something underneath them waited with more patience than mercy.

The platform lights were on.

Halfway down the deck, a human figure sat on the floor with one shoulder against the wall and both hands over the back of the neck as if trying not to hear the building.

A woman.

Alive.

Mara felt Theo's whole body alter beside her. Real witness. Trap improved by realism. Sera had been right.

"Don't go alone," she said immediately.

Theo nodded once.

"Can you hear me?" Donnelly called down the deck.

The woman looked up.

Her face was pale in the shaft light, hair plastered damply back from her temples, station fleece zipped wrong so that one side of the collar sat higher than the other. Mara knew her from the station sheets and then the table rosters in a disjointed rush. Not close enough to claim her. Enough to matter.

"Jules," Hal said softly behind them. "That's Jules Pearson."

One of the overnight station supervisors. Mid-forties. Good under pressure. Had stood two witness shifts after Southern Cross and once talked a whole platform back from keeping clever on its own by telling a hundred strangers at once that if they were all embarrassed, at least they could be embarrassed democratically.

Now she looked at them as if some of them were in the room and some were still deciding whether to become visible.

Theo pitched his voice just above ordinary. "Jules. It's Theo Markel. Donnelly is here. Hal's here. Aroha too. You don't need to hold anything alone."

Her mouth moved before sound came. Then, raggedly, "Don't come fast."

No one did.

That was the first correct sign.

They moved in by increments. Sera crouched the moment they were close enough to judge her colour properly. Tamsin kept the reader out and angled it down the platform and into the shaft mouth. The blue line on the screen wavered twice and then split.

Elian's face changed.

Mara saw it before he spoke. "What?"

He did not look at her. "There's a branch under the platform. Not side-lane. Not studio. Something vertical. It's trying to align whoever comes in with whoever's already here."

Theo, eyes on Jules, said, "Meaning?"

"Meaning the rescue is part of the room."

That landed hard.

Jules gave a small, terrible laugh. "Yes."

Sera had reached her by then. She did not touch immediately. She let Jules see her hands, the scanner, the ordinary steel edge of the med case placed on the deck between them.

"What's happening in your body?" she asked.

Jules swallowed. "Cold. Heat. Not bad yet. Hearing keeps… layering." She shut her eyes once, then opened them too fast. "The shaft keeps telling me if I stay very still, it'll sort the room for me."

There it was. Slow chamber logic. Not burn now. Relief through stillness. Let the structure decide.

Mara knelt on Jules's other side and placed one palm flat against the wall where Jules could see it. "We don't do sorting rooms," she said.

Jules's eyes moved to her hand. Good. External anchor.

Theo stayed standing, one shoulder angled to the shaft, making himself a witness point rather than a rescuer because he had learned enough by now to know that some forms of legal power worked best as posture.

"Can you tell me how you came here?" he asked.

Jules nodded too many times and then stopped as if the room had nudged her to calm down prettily. "Name call on Platform Four. No heat. Just hearing split. Then a systems voice said west shaft had the cleaner answer. Said bring contradiction here, quieter, no crowd binding. I knew that was wrong. I knew it. But it sounded…" She grimaced with real hatred now. "It sounded like the mature version of the table."

Mara closed her eyes once.

The route had learned fast.

Sera clipped the pulse monitor to Jules's finger. "Good. Keep hating it. What happened next?"

"The corridor got longer. Then shorter. Then I was here, and the shaft said not to move because movement makes duplicate rooms."

Aroha, from three paces back, muttered, "Well, it can get stuffed."

The route reader chirped.

Tamsin looked at the display, and all the blood left her face without theatrics. "We have a deeper issue."

Theo turned his head a fraction. "How deep?"

"The branch under us isn't just watching the rescue. It's using proximity. Two bodies in contact range, and it starts aligning burden vectors."

Mara said, "In English."

Tamsin tore her eyes from the screen long enough to glare at the world. "If we grab Jules and haul, the shaft gets to decide which of us carries what, and it will use that to tighten the room."

Elian was still staring into the shaft grid. "It's trying to pair her with whoever thinks responsibility means speed."

Mara looked at him.

Then she understood.

Not because he said her name. Because he didn't.

The room had found the oldest easy lie between them. Jules needed extraction. Elian could hear the route. He would be the fastest. Mara would know that and hate it and perhaps let him do it anyway because caring and witnessing sometimes blurred under urgency.

The shaft wanted that blur.

No, Mara thought.

Absolutely not.

She said it aloud before the route could finish building the pressure properly. "No fast rescues."

The platform seemed to change around the sentence. Not physically. Morally. The shaft lost some of its assumed rightness.

Theo said at once, "Good. Then we build a line."

Jules looked from face to face with visible effort. "What line?"

"The same one we've been building all week," Mara said. "Only longer."

They did it the ugly way, which was why it had a chance.

No dragging. No lone heroic reach. No one entering the shaft pocket and becoming the whole answer. Instead, they made a witnessed extraction chain down the maintenance deck. Donnelly anchored at the doorway. One transit supervisor at the first alcove. Hal with one hand flat on the deck rail and the other on Donnelly's sleeve. Aroha behind him with her palm on the wall and language ready in her lungs. Theo and Mara are nearest Jules but not touching yet. Sera at Jules's side, pulse on one hand, steel case under the other. Tamsin and Elian were at the route edge, calling structure changes as they came. Eight breathing people. One line. One room forced to admit plurality.

The shaft hated it.

The vertical branch sharpened under the deck like a blade being drawn slowly from cloth. Lights above them pulsed. Somewhere up in the public lift bank, a carriage stopped between floors long enough to make three waiting passengers swear. The mesh screen beside the shaft developed, for one impossible second, the same pressure-depth bloom as black-room glass.

"Elian," Mara said.

"I know." His voice had gone strange, too level. "It's trying to give me a private shortcut to her."

Theo's eyes flicked over at once. "Say more."

"It's saying if I go under the chain instead of along it, the room will let me reach her before the structure fully closes."

Jules made a small sound through her teeth. "Don't."

Mara looked at Elian and saw, with the exact clarity of love stripped of its vanity, that the offer had not merely found his burden. It had found the fear beneath the burden, too. The fear that if he did not act faster than witness, then someone would die and the city would write the delay into him forever.

She wanted, for one wild and useless second, to tell him she knew all of that, that none of it needed saying between them because the work had already made their bond operationally explicit. The shaft would have loved that. Private recognition. Perfect. Adjacent and unspoken.

So instead she did the better thing.

She made it public.

"Elian thinks if he outruns us, he can spare us the sight of failing," she said to the whole line.

Silence.

Then Aroha, bless her impossible practical soul, said from the rear, "Well he can absolutely stop that nonsense."

The line laughed.

Not much. Not enough to turn this into comedy. Just enough human friction to roughen the shaft's polished logic.

The route faltered.

Tamsin seized the moment. "There. Again. Group derision disrupts the alignment."

Theo said, "That goes in the manual."

Sera didn't take her eyes off Jules. "Ready."

Mara nodded.

They extracted by witness.

Not one body carrying another. Eight bodies carrying a process too public to become neat. Jules was brought up not as a secret and not as a patient, but as a participant in her own rescue. Hand to the wall. Feet under her. One pace at a time. Each movement named before it happened. Theo saying step. Mara saying left hand to the rail. Sera reporting pulse. Donnelly and Hal holding the line behind. Aroha talking continuously, not soothing but narrating reality like a woman determined to keep the room from becoming cleverer than steel and wet boots and the fact of other people.

At the third step, the shaft tried again.

A public address voice, somehow threaded down through the lift machinery and into the maintenance deck, said in a female station register, "Jules Pearson, remain where you are."

She stopped dead.

Sera's scanner chirped.

"Don't hold that alone," Mara said at once.

Jules's face twisted. "It used my full name."

"Yes."

"It sounded official."

"Yes."

Theo said, "And now there are eight of us hearing you say that."

The pressure under the platform changed.

Jules took another step.

At the seventh, the false chamber under the shaft made its last serious move. Not speed. Not stillness. Not side-lane heroics. It offered Mara, with all the grave civility of a private state office, a small adjoining room where she could take Jules alone and interpret her gently without the others seeing how shaken either of them really was. Professional privacy. Female discretion. Adult handling.

Mara felt the shape of it and almost laughed, because now that she knew the route's accent, it was becoming, if not predictable, then at least vulgar.

"No," she said. "You don't get my tenderness by reducing its witnesses."

The shaft groaned.

The lights flared white.

Then the branch under the deck collapsed, not burned out, not broken forever, simply stripped of enough coherence that it could no longer maintain the rescue as premise. The maintenance platform became what it should have been all along. Ugly steel. Wet concrete smell. Human breath. One frightened station supervisor with a hand on the rail and a pulse too fast for elegance.

They got Jules to the door.

Not cleanly.

That was the price.

She did not come back whole in the simple way the body liked to advertise on forms. Her pulse steadied. Her heat stayed below lock. Her hearing returned to singular in patches. But as Sera got her onto the stool in the service corridor and began the field exam, tiny wrongnesses remained. Jules reached twice for instructions no one had spoken. Once, she answered Mara before Mara had finished the question, not because she anticipated the content, but because the route had left her with a half-beat eagerness to resolve open spaces. When Donnelly asked her who had sent her to the shaft, she named the systems voice first and only then seemed startled by her own answer.

Sera saw all of it.

"She's marked," she said quietly.

Theo looked up. "Define?"

"Not locked. Not closing. But the room left a behavioural resonance. Premature compliance. false resolution drift. She'll need re-entry under witness and she cannot be left alone with any authority structure for at least twenty-four hours."

Jules gave a tired, bitter little laugh. "That sounds romantic."

"It is not meant to."

Mara crouched in front of her. "Can you tell me one thing the shaft made sound reasonable?"

Jules shut her eyes, opened them, looked at Mara properly, and said, "That being quietly handled by the right room was kinder than needing other people."

There it was.

The mark.

Not a burn. Not a scar the eye could adore itself for spotting. Something subtler and, in its way, far more frightening. The room had not merely tried to kill Jules. It had tried to revise the terms under which she understood care. And some part of that revision was still in her body, a set of habits the city would have to argue back out of her with witness and time and the stubborn ugliness of public rescue.

Elian heard Sera say, " Marked, " and felt the word land where his own fear had been waiting for it.

Not because Jules was now dangerous. Because he recognised the category.

How many times, after the side-lane, after the studio of lies, after the forged packet and the false chamber, had some small wrongness lingered in him for hours after? The extra beat of compliance before refusal. The almost-gratitude at the thought of one clean authority deciding for him. The absurd shame when his own burden profile became visible under witness. How much of that had been ordinary exhaustion, and how much the route learning him by leaving a little of itself behind each time it failed to take more.

Mara saw the fear before he spoke it. Of course she did.

He turned away from Jules so the room would not make his worry about her rescue selfish, but Mara followed with her eyes and then, because she was Mara and therefore never merciful in a way that left rot intact, she said into the whole witnessed corridor, "Elian thinks he's marked too."

He looked at her sharply.

She held his gaze. No softness. No apology. Just truth, public enough to live.

Theo glanced between them and understood at once. Sera did too, though her hands stayed on Jules's pulse. Tamsin, who had been packing the route reader into its case with furious neatness, stopped.

Elian could have denied it.

The shaft would have loved that.

So he said, "I don't know if I am."

"Good," Mara replied. "Then we classify it instead of romanticising it."

Aroha made an approving noise from the wall. Donnelly, still white around the mouth from the rescue, rested one hand flat on the corridor rail as if to remind the whole corridor what was real. Mr Idris was not there, but Mara could practically hear the sentence he would have written.

Do not let fear of contamination become private mythology.

Sera looked at Elian now. "Any fast obedience drift since the shaft."

"No."

"Any desire to simplify witness after successful extraction."

He hesitated.

Mara said, "Out loud."

"Yes." The admission burned more than he liked. "A little."

Sera nodded as if he had reported a rash. "Good. That means we know where to look. We'll run the protocol."

328

Tamsin zipped the route case shut. "And I'll build you a very insulting self-report form."

That got a real laugh this time, brief and ugly and therefore useful.

Theo stood back from the corridor wall at last. "All right. We have what we came for."

"Do we?" Mara said.

He looked at Jules. Then at the shaft door. Then at Elian. "We have enough."

Enough. The most dangerous and useful word in the city.

They left the maintenance deck sealed, witnessed, and officially marked out of service for structural review, which was not a lie so much as a civic understatement. The false rescue had shown them what the next phase of the war looked like. Not only rooms that trapped and burned. Not only side-lanes that offered private heroism. But rescue architectures, chambers that let the city feel humane while trimming witness down to the point where care became governable and public contradiction looked crude by comparison.

That, Mara knew as they escorted Jules back up into the breathing station, was why the rescue mattered more than the shaft.

It had given them a survivor carrying behavioural resonance instead of a corpse carrying heat.

The city would now have to learn how to rescue not just bodies, but definitions.

Up on the concourse, Nina Fowler looked up from the table as they emerged with Jules between Mara and Sera and took in the scene in one old, quick sweep.

"Well," she said. "You all look dreadful. That's encouraging."

Jules managed a crooked half-smile. "The room was worse."

Nina patted the empty chair beside the kettle. "Sit. You can be witnessed properly now."

And because refusing private rescue had become the whole point, Jules did.

Chapter Nineteen: Weather in Steel

By dawn, the city had started answering back.

Not in language. Not at first. In nuisance, in small betrayals of material confidence, in the kind of wrongness most systems managers preferred to classify as deferred maintenance until the maintenance itself developed teeth.

The first reports came in before six. A bridge inspector on the Flinders Street viaduct logged an intermittent resonance in two support members and then crossed the note out, only to write it again three lines lower with the phrase metal singing under passing load. A night pharmacist in Docklands reported that coins in the till tray had grown strangely warm during a burst of contradictory announcements from a nearby tram stop, then cooled the moment two customers began arguing aloud about what they had both heard. A surgical nurse at St Vincent's called an old friend in station operations rather than the official fault line because three stainless instruments on a prep trolley had mistimed under her hand, not moving, not glowing, just seeming to anticipate their own use by half a beat in a way that made her skin climb her arms.

At seven-thirteen, a lift in a Collins Street office tower refused to decide between floors nineteen and twenty, doors opening, beginning to close, opening again, as if the carriage could not settle which instruction belonged to it most truly. The three people inside spent twenty seconds trying not to embarrass themselves before one of them, a cleaner from the night shift carrying a witness card in her apron pocket, slapped her palm against the wall and said, loud enough for the other two to hear, "It's doing two things. I'm not choosing alone."

The lift settled.

The cleaner reported the event to a witness table before she clocked out. By eight, Mara had the statement on her desk.

The city, she thought, was no longer improvising incidents. It was beginning to learn grammar.

In the annex, the route board had eaten an entire wall.

Tamsin Roe stood in front of it with a marker in one hand and two sleepless nights behind her eyes. The board no longer held only the ring, the black room, the studio of lies, or the side-lane with teeth. It now held Melbourne itself in rough sectors and ugly colours. Blue for lawful witness interrupts. Red for contradiction clusters. Black for known closure sites. Grey for what she called passive susceptibility, the places where steel, glass, rail, and routine formed enough of a civic skeleton that the route no longer needed to invent a room from scratch. It only had to lean on what the city already was.

Mara came in with the morning packet reports, the station ledgers, and Priya Nandakumar's second statement tucked under her arm. Theo was behind her, coat still damp at the shoulders, carrying a transport file so swollen with overnight paper it looked malignant. Sera entered last, one glove half-pulled off, having come directly from a re-entry session with Jules Pearson and three station staffers whose bodies had not locked but whose habits had learned too quickly to call private authority a relief.

Tamsin did not turn when they came in.

"We've crossed a threshold," she said.

Theo set the file on the side bench. "You say that every day now."

"Yes," she replied, still facing the wall. "That's because the threshold keeps moving."

Mara laid the station ledgers down and looked at the map properly. Overnight incidents had spread beyond transport enough that the pattern could no longer be filed under Southern Cross aftershock. Tiny red marks now sat over tram interchanges, hospital corridors, loading lifts, a jewellery store in the CBD, two tower blocks, one bridge approach, and a logistics depot near Footscray, whose foreman had described a pallet jack as "too eager to cooperate" before deciding that was not a sentence he wished to own alone and phoned the nearest table instead.

"What am I looking at?" Theo asked.

Tamsin finally turned.

Not all the way. Just enough to give him the bad side of a smile. "Weather in steel."

The phrase stayed in the room because it was right in the infuriating way her best phrases often were. Not a central event now. Not one room. Not one pane. Not one sealed station node waiting to go monstrous. Something wider and more ambient. A city whose material systems had begun taking on the route's preferences at moments of pressure, contradiction, or load.

Sera crossed to the board and read the clustering around Richmond, Southern Cross, Docklands, and the hospital corridor marks at St Vincent's and Royal Melbourne. "No heat signatures above shallow drift," she said.

"Yet," Tamsin replied.

Theo heard the word and disliked it instantly. "Give me the clean version."

Tamsin uncapped the marker and tapped three sections of the city grid in sequence. "The fast structures still need architecture, timing, and human complicity sharp enough to build closure. We know that.

Black room. side-lane. false chamber. station relay. But what's happening now is broader. Infrastructure that already carries urgency is starting to show preference behaviour under contradiction load. Lifts. rails. instrument trays. display glass. coins. bridge members under traffic stress. Not enough to close a person outright. Enough to narrow decisions and teach the environment to feel like a room before it is one."

Mara thought of Priya at Southern Cross, touching the bench support while the station tried to know her better than she knew herself. She thought of the cleaner in the office tower lift saying it's doing two things. The city was beginning to require witness not only in exceptional places, but in the ordinary movements of its own body.

"Urbanising," Elian had called it earlier. That had been bad enough. Weather in steel was worse because weather implied patience.

Theo opened the first file. "Transport wants the city statement by noon."

"Then tell them the truth," Mara said.

"They would define truth here as the most survivable sentence for ministers."

"Which is why they don't get to draft first."

Tamsin made a sound of abstract approval and began writing on the board beneath the Footscray depot mark. The city does not need a room if the room is distributed.

Theo looked up sharply. "That is not going public."

"No," Mara said. "But it is going into the internal package."

Sera had moved to the side bench and was sorting overnight re-entry notes into piles with the fastidious cruelty of someone who knew that bad categorisation killed as efficiently as bad medicine. Jules Pearson had improved. Two of the station staffers from the reassurance-room orbit had improved less. One was still overusing the word sensible whenever witness or plurality came up, as if some private chamber inside her had learned to reward minimisation with bodily ease. Another kept asking whether perhaps the station tables had become too emotionally available for a serious transport environment. Sera had written in the margin of his session notes that he had not recovered from the room so much as internalised its management style.

"Beth's stable," she said without being asked. "Jules is argumentative again, which is encouraging. One of the station guards keeps using the phrase 'quiet handling' like he thinks it's hygienic. I want him table-side until the phrase embarrasses him."

Mr Idris, already seated with the black-and-grey ribboned ledger reserved for quiet fine and slow adjacency, said, "Humiliation remains undervalued in modern therapeutic settings."

Theo almost smiled despite himself.

Mara opened Priya's second statement and read aloud the new line she had marked on the train over.

After the station, every surface seemed to have a view of me for several hours. Coins. Handrails. The lift at work. I knew that could not be literally true, but the feeling of being interpreted by objects was still there.

The room went still.

Tamsin took the page from Mara, scanned it once, and then wrote on the board under passive susceptibility: interpretation drift.

Sera said, "That's not delusion."

"No," Tamsin replied. "It's a correct perception expressed in the nearest civilian language available to it."

That was the part still catching them all, Mara thought. The city's ordinary people were not overreacting to stress. They were developing new literacy under pressure and describing it with whatever words had not yet been stolen by policy.

The intercom buzzed.

Donnelly's voice came through from Southern Cross, flattened by the speaker and bad architecture but still carrying that rough human steadiness he had earned since the district almost burned under his station.

"Table report," he said. "We've got a bridge crew asking whether singing steel counts if only two of them hear it and the third thinks they've been listening to too much witness talk."

Tamsin answered before Theo could. "Yes."

Mara pressed the button. "Where."

"Batman Avenue approach. Maintenance gantry. Traffic load event every fourth minute."

Theo took a note. Another bridge. Another rhythm. Another ordinary structure with enough pattern to become suggestible.

"And one more," Donnelly added. "Tram control got three reports of rails answering before bells. Not audio exactly. More like passengers stepping back before the warning because the track made the wrong part of them expect impact."

Weather in steel, Mara thought again.

Not because the phrase was lyrical. Because it was offensively precise.

By ten-thirty, the annex had split into three simultaneous wars.

Theo and Director Sayeed worked the visible one, fighting to keep the morning's city statement from collapsing into malfunction-and-calm nonsense while Mercer's office, now careful enough not to repeat yesterday's mistakes in person, sent beautifully engineered suggestions about "urban reassurance continuity" and "managed public interpretation corridors." The wording had improved. That made it filthier.

Mara worked the narrative front, building two packages at once, one public, with practical survival language that would neither feed panic nor harden into doctrine, and one internal, harder and narrower, for staff who still needed to understand that weather did not mean harmless. She moved between the archive room and the witness table with the notebook under one arm, collecting fresh civilian phrasing as if it were counter-intelligence. Too eager to cooperate. The room helped me stop making everything so public. It felt like the adult version. The surface had a view about me. These were not cute lines. They were route telemetry arriving in ordinary human mouths.

Tamsin worked the city map until it stopped being a map and became a systems indictment. She overlaid tram power routes, lift maintenance schedules, hospital sterilisation zones, station service corridors, bridge stress patterns, jewellery store security loops, and public-address relay trees. By noon she had the first predictive spread model. It was ugly enough that she printed it twice rather than trust a screen with the insult.

Sera moved through them all like a knife through cloth. Field sessions. Table briefings. Re-entry protocols. She rewrote the non-acute enclosure sheet for the fourth time and then a fifth. Add line for interpretation drift after shallow exposure. Add line for object authority bleed. Add line for sudden false maturity around solitude.

She did not bother asking whether the city's clinicians would resist being taught by witness tables and station clerks. She wrote as if they either would learn or their ignorance would become a matter for coroners later.

At one, Theo came down from Sayeed's office carrying the near-final city statement.

No one spoke while he read it aloud because too much depended on where it would fail.

"A coordinated infrastructure anomaly affected parts of the central transport district yesterday evening, producing contradictory system signals and one restricted fatality in a service environment currently under investigation. Public safety was preserved where people responded by seeking immediate shared verification rather than isolating under conflicting instructions. City staff and commuters are advised that if any public system delivers contradictory or personalised direction, they should touch a fixed surface, check the instruction with others nearby, and move towards staffed support points in pairs or groups."

He looked up.

The room held.

That was good.

"It's not enough," Mara said.

"No," Theo answered. "But it's publishable."

Tamsin took the sheet and scanned it with that expression she used when measuring a bridge for explosives or a sentence for cowardice. "You left out the rails."

"Yes."

"You left out the lifts."

"Yes."

"You left out the weather."

Theo almost smiled. "I did not imagine the minister would sign off on meteorology for steel."

Mr Idris, writing the noon hour in the ledger, said, "A pity. It would have improved the literature."

Mara looked at the statement again. Not enough, no. But it placed witness into the public mouth without surrendering the city to malfunction theatre. It told people to refuse isolation. It made pairs and groups sound practical rather than embarrassing. For today, that might be enough.

By two-thirty, the city answered the statement with proof.

A man in a goldsmith's apron at a Collins Street jeweller called the nearest witness line and reported that every ring on his display tray had gone warm when the lunchtime crowd outside began bunching under contradictory tram-replacement announcements. Not hot. Warm in sequence, one after another, until the tray itself seemed to be learning the logic of queuing from the street and finding it morally persuasive. He and his apprentice laid both hands flat on the counter and spoke each announcement aloud to one another until the warmth passed.

At Royal Melbourne, a registrar wrote to Sera directly that a set of laparoscopic tools had again mistimed under hand, not moving, but becoming anticipatory enough that the whole theatre team paused. A nurse who had staffed witness tables at Southern Cross the previous night said, "No one touches a thing until we all say what we heard," and the room snapped back into ordinary sequence with such humiliating speed that two consultants had gone silent for a full minute afterwards.

On the Batman Avenue bridge approach, the singing steel became measurable. Not acoustically in the ordinary sense, but as a resonance pattern appearing only when traffic load coincided with contradictory lane instructions from a faulty digital sign. One crew member heard nothing. Two heard tone. The fourth reported that the girders felt impatient under his gloves.

That word went on the board too.

Impatient.

By four, the city map no longer looked like aftershock. It looked like the first draft of a distributed chamber.

Theo stood in front of it with his hands in his pockets and read the spread pattern without vanity. "We can't keep this internal much longer."

"No," Mara said.

The statement had gone out. Call volumes to station tables had doubled. Three radio stations had adopted some version of touch something fixed if public systems conflict, one of them reluctantly and one of them with enough civic sincerity to make Mara suspicious of the host's previous life. Priya's statement had been excerpted carefully into the second public packet, not with her name, but with the line about the station no longer feeling as though it knew her better than she knew herself. The city had begun repeating it back in comments, messages, and overheard station speech with the bizarre collective speed only public language ever had when it landed at exactly the right fear-depth.

Still, the heat was broadening. Not flame. Possibility.

Tamsin pointed at the map. "This is no longer just transport."

She tapped the hospital marks. The jewellery store. The office tower lifts. The bridge girders. The freight depot. The tram power loops.

"It's wherever the city already uses metal to simplify people into movement, sequence, or compliance," she said. "You built enough ordinary obedience into a modern city and the route doesn't need to start from scratch. It just recruits the shape."

Theo rubbed one hand over his mouth. "And secrecy."

"Yes."

Mara knew why he said it like that.

The burn list. Mercer. Quiet capture. Reassurance rooms. Slow adjacency. Weather in steel did not need metal alone. It needed a city already being taught that privacy was maturity and authority was mercy.

The larger war was already hiding inside this one, Theo had said.

He had not been wrong.

The afternoon's worst report came at 5:09 from a hospital loading lift in Parkville.

Not because anyone died. No one did. Because the lift made the argument too elegantly.

A porter wheeling an oxygen cylinder trolley entered with a nurse, two supply crates, and a pathology runner who had spent the previous evening at a station table and still carried a witness card tucked inside her ID sleeve. Midway between floors, the lift stopped. Not alarm stop. Decided stop. The panel lit floor 3 and B2 at once. The nurse heard hold for clearance. The porter heard proceed now. The pathology runner heard, in a tone she later described as "helpful enough to make me ashamed of needing others," take the oxygen alone and wait quietly. She did not move. Instead, she touched the cylinder trolley and asked the others what they had heard.

The doors reopened on the correct floor seventeen seconds later.

Nothing burned.

Everything changed.

When Sera read the report she sat down for the first time in nearly three hours and looked at the wall rather than at any of them.

"What?" Theo asked.

She answered without moving. "The weather is learning triage."

No one said anything.

She turned back to the report and set it on the table. "Black-room logic in a hospital service lift attached itself to oxygen handling and clinical hierarchy. It offered the pathology runner helpful solitude. It's beginning to sort burden by domain."

Tamsin swore and then, because the sentence deserved it, swore again with more craftsmanship.

Mara looked at the report. Helpful enough to make me ashamed of needing others. The line sat beside Priya's surfaces have a view about me, Jules's adult version of the table, Beth's the room made me think I was being mature, all of it one weather now, one atmosphere of civic manipulation settling over infrastructure and the bodies that trusted it just long enough to be used by it.

"We need table doctrine beyond stations," she said.

Theo looked at her. "Hospitals."

"Yes."

"Office towers."

"Yes."

"Bridges?"

She thought of impatient steel. "Bridge crews, yes. Not tables if the structure doesn't support it. Witness points."

Tamsin nodded once. "Terms matter."

Mr Idris, writing already, said, "As always."

By six-thirty, the first expansion plan existed.

Not polished. Not remotely funded. Ugly enough to work.

Station tables remained where contradiction and crowd timing already bred friction. Hospitals got witness points at loading lifts, instrument prep corridors, and service desks. Office towers got contradiction stations at central lift banks with the instruction that no one entered a split car alone if commands conflicted. Bridge and road crews got witness partners and fixed-surface protocols written in language so practical even engineers couldn't pretend it was therapy. Jewellery stores and cash environments got printed guidance under the innocent title DISPLAY TEMPERATURE ANOMALY RESPONSE. Mercer's people would hate every page. Good.

When Mara took the first stack to Sayeed's office, she found Theo there with the city statement feedback and a face she had begun to associate with the specific pleasure of legal warfare conducted under democratic constraints.

"They hate the witness language," he said.

"Good."

"They hate the phrase personalised public instructions even more."

"Excellent."

He held up one page. "Home Affairs wants immediate authority to centralise anomalous systems messaging."

Mara looked at the request and then at him. "No."

"I know."

"They'll say the weather justifies it."

"Yes."

"It doesn't."

"No."

She put the hospital witness-point draft on his desk. "Then beat them to the noun."

He read the heading.

PUBLIC WITNESS INFRASTRUCTURE: EXPANDED CIVIC RESPONSE

A slow smile, tired and dangerous, moved at the edge of his mouth. "Yes."

That was the thing about Theo at his best. He knew when a good sentence was not just an argument, but territory.

Night came down hard over Melbourne, as it often did after days that taught too much too fast. The city's lit surfaces took on their ordinary glamour for people still fortunate enough to believe glamour and normality were cousins. Trains ran. Trams complained around curves. Hospital windows held their square yellow watch.

Office towers reflected weather and pretended to be entirely made of policy.

Inside the annex, the weather board glowed.

Tamsin had added two final lines before forcing herself, under threat from Sera, to eat a sandwich in view of other people.

FAST STRUCTURES BURN.
SLOW STRUCTURES SORT.

Elian read the lines twice.

He had spent most of the afternoon running his own self-report protocol with such honesty it bordered on violence. No new fast obedience drift. Moderate interpretation strain. One minor desire to take the Collins Street lift incident personally because he hadn't been there. Mara had read the form, circled personally, and written beneath it, in her impatient upright hand, The city is larger than your guilt. He had kept the page.

Now he stood with her in the lower lab and looked at the board while the route beneath the ring remained quiet.

"Do you think it's actually quiet," he asked, "or just pleased with itself?"

Mara considered the slow red spread over hospitals, lifts, bridges, trays, rails, coins, and glass.

"I think," she said, "that if the city were a body, we'd call this prodrome."

He let the word move through him. Warning before the full event. The body is already changing under something larger than any one symptom.

"That bad."

"Yes."

Outside, a printer in some distant office gave its little tired cough and another somewhere else answered. The city's steel kept its own counsel. A bridge under traffic load sang to no one who could yet write legislation around the sound. A lift in a tower hesitated between floor seventeen and eighteen long enough for four strangers to ask one another what they had heard and thereby deny the weather one more inch of private authority.

The city answered back, but only because the tables had taught it how.

For tonight, that still mattered more than the spread.

Tomorrow, Mara thought, it might not be enough.

But tonight Melbourne remained loud, inconvenient, improperly plural, and therefore not yet governable by the rooms that wanted to know it better than it knew itself.

She put one hand flat on the edge of Bench Three, not for symbolism, simply because the steel was there and true and ordinary.

Then she looked at the map and began planning what the city would need when weather turned into structure and structure into choice.

Chapter Twenty: The Lost Bridge

The lawful Harbour did not usually feel tired.

That was what frightened Elian first.

By the time the city lights had come on under another wet Melbourne evening and the witness tables were holding their second full day against weather in steel, the lower lab had acquired the hard-used look of a room being asked to stand between worlds with not nearly enough sleep. Cups with tea stains ringed the side bench. Two ledgers lay open under separate lamps like witnesses too old to close their eyes. Tamsin's city map covered one wall in red, black, and grey until Melbourne itself looked less like a place and more like a diagnosis. On the central monitor, the lawful route under the ring still held its basin shape, its patience, its exacting witness ladder. Yet something in it had changed. Not corrupted, not yet, but strained. Its old depth now carried a kind of grain, as if clear water had begun taking silt from somewhere upstream.

Elian stood at Bench Three and looked at it for too long.

Mara saw him before he said anything.

"What?"

He did not turn. "The Harbour feels crowded."

The room went still.

Tamsin, crouched beside the route board with a marker in one hand and a floor plan of Parkville service lifts in the other, looked up sharply. "Crowded how?"

"Not bodies." He searched for the least false sentence and hated all of them equally. "Intentions. Like the route is still lawful but being forced to carry too many arguments at once."

Theo Markel, at the side table with Director Sayeed's latest emergency briefing and a sheaf of transport directives, set the papers down. "That's new."

"Yes."

Sera Imani, who had just finished a re-entry session with the Richmond station supervisor and was stripping off gloves one finger at a time, did not waste breath on comfort. "Can you quantify it."

"No."

"Can you prove it?"

"Not yet."

Theo looked from Elian to the ring. "Then we don't say it outside this room until we can."

Mara crossed to Bench Three and stood beside Elian without touching him. The ring sat in its mount under the hooded array, innocent in the infuriating way dangerous things often were, all platinum composure and exact interior curve. But the screen above it told a truer story. The lawful line was there, yes. Beneath and around it lay weather, slow adjacency, side-lane traces, civic resonance loads, all the city's new ways of becoming suggestible under pressure. If the Harbour felt crowded, it was because the city had begun leaning against the line from too many directions at once.

She said, "Then we stabilise it."

Theo's eyes moved to her. "With what?"

Mara did not answer immediately because they all knew the obvious answer and none of them liked it. With witness. With lawful packet structure. With a bridge held long enough and cleanly enough that the lawful side could answer before the weather wrote too much of the city in its own accent.

Tamsin stood. "We should have done it hours ago."

Theo gave her a look. "And there's the benefit of hindsight arriving before the event."

"No," Tamsin said, already moving towards the console. "This is the event. If Pell's last packet was right, then the lawful side is under pressure and the older adjacencies are trying to turn order into architecture over there too. If the Harbour collapses into grain before we get clarity, the weather wins by default."

Sera glanced at the thermal monitor and then at Elian. "You're not going alone."

"That wasn't the plan," Mara said.

Theo shut the folder and stood up. "No one is improvising this. Full witness. Full room. No side work, no quiet brilliance, no one deciding mid-contact that heroism is cheaper than procedure."

Mr Idris, already seated at the ledger table with the black-and-grey ribboned volume open to a fresh page, said, "A charming aspiration."

No one smiled.

They built the room the old lawful way and the new civic way at once.

Not one witness ladder. Two. Not one ledger. Two. No hidden assumptions. No comfort layers. No elegant smoothing. Tamsin stripped the haptics to bare receive plus lawful challenge channels and brought the physical countersign matrix from Pell's heavy-method packet to the centre bench like a relic no one could afford to worship. Sera added a full physiological spread on both Mara and Elian, plus thermal traces, reflex delay markers, and one new crude but sensible column on the side monitor labelled FALSE CALM.

Theo read the terms aloud twice, once for law and once for the room. Mr Idris entered the hour and the personnel with infuriatingly graceful script. Nina Fowler, who had been brought down from the evening table rotation because this session needed someone who distrusted calm professionally, took the second witness chair and accepted the role as if she had expected nothing less from her retirement.

Above them, the city carried on. Trains. Lifts. Bridge loads. Instrument trays. Coins warming in tills. Rails learning impatience. But in the lower lab, for one necessary interval, they forced the world smaller.

Mara pulled on the right haptic glove.

Elian took the left.

Theo said, "State purpose."

Elian kept his eyes on the ring. "To assess lawful route integrity under city-scale pressure and seek direct witness from the far side regarding current strain."

Mara added, "To make no accommodation to private urgency, false calm, or order offered before witness."

Theo nodded once. "State limit."

"To withdraw on false receiving, structural narrowing, unsignalled adaptation, or any attempt to divide the room from itself."

Mr Idris wrote it down. Nina countersigned with the sort of firm, practical hand that made morality look like stationery paperwork done correctly.

Tamsin dimmed the lights.

The lawful Harbour arrived slowly, as if even it were forcing itself to breathe properly.

That was new.

Elian felt it first in his chest, not as fear, not yet, but as the awkwardness of meeting someone who had always been composed and finding them suddenly carrying visible fatigue. The basin still opened. The witness ladder was still built cleanly under the declaration. The receiving structure remained exacting, never flattering, never eager. But the old patience had roughness in it. Small eddies. Tiny delays in places that had once been clarified with the confidence of the tide.

"There," he said softly.

Mara felt it too. The lawful room was not wrong. It was crowded, exactly as he had said, burdened by pressures trying to braid themselves through it. Still lawful. Still itself. But carrying more than it should have had to carry.

Tamsin's eyes were on the graph. "I'm seeing cross-load. Not from the false chamber directly. Broader. City weather bleeding upward into route coherence."

Theo said, "Can we filter?"

"No. We can witness harder."

The Harbour deepened by degrees.

For one breath, then another, Elian thought the route might hold. The basin widened. The ladder clarified. A receiving edge formed at a distance, clean and lawful enough that his shoulders eased against his will.

Then something in the route shivered.

Not the black-room violence they knew. Not the studio's polished inwardness. This was stranger. The lawful chamber itself filled with moving grain, as though voices too far away to hear were trying to use the same architecture at once. On the side monitor the route map flickered, and Tamsin swore under her breath.

"What?" Theo said.

"Nothing I like."

Mara kept her hands steady on the timing controls. "Say it anyway."

Tamsin enlarged the interference pattern. "There are other witness ladders trying to assemble on the same lawful family. Fragmented. Some failing. Some cut short." She looked at Elian, then back to the data. "Either the far side is under concurrent load, or someone's deliberately poisoning approach conditions."

Elian heard then what he had only felt before.

Not voices. The shape of voices: attempted witness, clipped before completion, ladders almost built and then cut short. The lawful chamber was crowded with tries.

"Mira," he said.

No one needed him to explain the name.

The basin clarified by force, and for one stunning second, the lawful receiving structure opened enough for the far side to appear not as an image but as a relation. Cavara's old quiet geometry. The sense of stone and air and civic order held under strain. Then a figure within it, not body exactly, more the stable moral contour of one. Mira Sol.

Not calm. Not for the first time since they had known her.

She came to them under visible pressure, the lawful chamber around her threaded with the same grain they were reading in the Harbour. What had once felt like the confidence of a culture meeting them on equal lawful terms now felt like a council chamber trying to conduct itself while weather entered through the roof.

Her first words were clipped not by translation error but by urgency.

"The line is crowded."

Mara, relief and dread striking at once, answered before Theo could. "We know."

Mira's form sharpened. "Then listen quickly. We are under challenge from two directions. Your city teaches the older adjacencies too much. Our own frightened people teach them the rest."

Theo stepped closer to the side bench, as if law itself might lend the chamber structure. "Pell?"

The name changed her.

Not dramatically. Mira Sol was too disciplined for that. But the lawful contour around her took on a grief-edge so clean Mara felt it before she understood it.

"Gone from the central clerks," Mira said.

Silence.

No one moved.

Elian said, "Removed."

Mira looked at him directly now, and in that look he felt the answer before the words came.

"Not removed only," she said. "Taken in structure."

The room around Bench Three seemed to lose one degree of heat.

Mara's hands held to the controls through force now. "Meaning."

Mira's next sentence cost her.

"He took the cut."

Theo shut his eyes once.

Mr Idris's pen stopped.

Tamsin, who had never met Pell except through packets and curses at countersign notation, whispered, "No."

Mira did not soften it. "A lawful relay was poisoned in council transit. He held the corruption long enough for witness withdrawal. There was no body in the way you mean body. There was only route and clerk and cut. He chose himself as the break."

The lower lab did not breathe for three full heartbeats.

Then Mr Idris, from the ledger chair, lowered his head once in the oldest gesture in the world and wrote Pell Ardoc in the margin with a line beneath it so steady it nearly undid Mara altogether.

The lawful chamber shook.

Not metaphor. Not grief made architectural for convenience. The route itself took strain as Mira spoke, the grain thickening under her form. Someone or something on the far side was pressing hard enough against lawful passage that even mourning had to be abbreviated.

Theo said, very quietly, "What do you need?"

Mira's answer came at once, which meant she had already been living in it. "Not retreat. Not speed. Not order offered at the price of witness. We are losing clerks, structures teams, table equivalents, all

354

those who keep public contradiction alive long enough to remain lawful. If your side gives its city to narrow command now, you do the older adjacencies' work for both worlds."

Tamsin was writing with one hand while monitoring the route with the other. "Already knew Mercer was filth. Nice to have transdimensional confirmation."

Mira's shape almost, impossibly, flickered with comprehension of the tone if not the words.

Then the grain worsened.

Elian saw it first on the edge of the lawful basin, a darker structure trying to build itself not beneath the chamber but within its civic assumptions. Not black-room closure. Not side-lane urgency. Something slower. More dignified. A narrowing dressed in public necessity.

"Mara," he said.

"I see it."

Mira heard something in their voices and turned within the route.

That was when it happened.

The lawful chamber did not collapse. It split.

Not fully. Just enough for the poisoning to show.

One side of the route still held lawful basin, witness ladder, Mira's hard-kept civic shape. The other side briefly developed a rival geometry, a more ordered chamber, narrower, cleaner, tempting in precisely the way Pell had warned. One authority for all movement. Peace through narrowed crossings. The Adjacent Peace.

It entered the lawful passage not as an attack but as an offer to stabilise it.

The insult of that nearly made Mara scream.

Theo heard it in the room's altered pitch. "Withdraw."

Mira's voice cut over him. "No. One thing first."

Everyone went still.

She looked at Elian then, and the lawful chamber around her held just long enough to let the sentence through cleanly.

"The city is not the induction event."

The words landed and sat there like iron.

Mara's head snapped round to Tamsin.

Tamsin was already there, already seeing the inference racing ahead of them all. "Say more," she demanded at the route, not caring whether the translation etiquette approved.

Mira did not flinch from the bluntness. "Your weather in steel is preparation. Not full event. The larger act requires linked nodes brought into synchrony by contradiction, load, and managed public narrowing. It is not one station. It is a pattern. A city taught to complete the room at scale."

Theo said the thing they had all been trying not to say because saying it would force the next architecture into being.

"A machine."

Mira's answer was colder than grief. "A civic burn machine."

The room changed.

Tamsin's face went blank in the specific way it did when information exceeded outrage and became engineering obligation. She spun to the city board, overlaid route marks, station incidents, lifts, bridges, hospitals, power loops, track beds, public-address trees, all of it. On the wall the map began resolving with sickening speed, red marks no longer scattered but joining.

Sera said, "No."

Not because she doubted it. Because she didn't.

The pattern lit up anyway.

Southern Cross. Richmond. Docklands. Parkville. Collins Street. Batman Avenue. Tram power. Lift banks. Hospital steel. Station service corridors. Bridges under load. Logistics depots. Not one city, but enough of one. Enough to teach scale.

Tamsin said, voice gone very thin, "They're building a synchronisation mesh."

No one interrupted.

She pointed at the wall with the back of the marker. "Not random weather. Preparatory tuning. Contradiction events condition people and infrastructure together. Slow rooms sort witnesses out of pathways. Fast structures test closure points. Then once enough nodes are compliant…"

She did not finish because the map on the wall had finished for her.

It drew its own ugly line.

A distributed pattern through the city's metal skeleton, not everywhere, only where load, urgency, and civic obedience already lived together. A machine waiting not to be switched on, but to be agreed into.

Mira Sol's shape in the lawful chamber had begun to tear at the edges.

"Listen," she said, and now the strain in her voice was not only grief but distance becoming force. "What you call weather is induction tutoring. What you call tables is counter-memory. Hold them. Broaden them. Do not let your frightened offices turn witness into moderation rooms. If the city is taught to narrow itself in time…"

The grain surged.

Her form broke into pressure and outline and all at once she was farther away.

Elian leaned into the controls without meaning to. "Mira."

Mara caught the motion instantly, one hand hard against his wrist before the route could turn concern into private speed. "No."

Good, some last sane part of him thought. Good.

Mira's final line came through as if from a room already losing her to weather.

"The bridge is not lost if the city refuses the machine."

Then the lawful chamber went white.

Not bright. Blank.

The basin collapsed inward, not into black-room closure, not into the studio's civic lie, but into something worse for that moment. Absence. The route cut not by finality but by overload. The lawful ladder unraveled. The receiving structure dropped away. The ring on the bench gave one soft, metallic note like a fork struck under water.

Tamsin hit the receive kill.

Sera was already at Elian and Mara with the scanner.

Theo stood in the middle of the room looking at the city map and the now-blank route display and the ledgers and the names and Pell's quiet packet in its sleeve on the side table and, for the first time since Mara had known him, he looked not defeated but struck cleanly enough that the feeling showed.

Mr Idris's pen resumed.

The sound of it broke the room back into itself.

No one said Pell first because Pell was now too large for the first sentence. Instead, Mara said, "The bridge."

Tamsin understood her. "The lawful bridge just took poison."

"No." Theo's voice was rougher than usual. "It held poison. Then cut before completion. That's different."

Sera checked Mara's pulse, then Elian's, then looked at both of them and decided their bodies were still their own enough for the next truth. "Pell's gone."

There. The room took it then.

Mara sat down without deciding to. Her hands had marks in the skin where the controls had pressed against them. Across from her, Elian stood too still, not numb, not yet, but carrying the kind of grief that looked first like failure because failure was easier to inhabit than loss. Tamsin had one hand over her mouth and the other still clenched around the marker. Theo stared at the map as if law, paper, argument, and will might yet reorder what the route had just told them. Mr Idris wrote Pell Ardoc in the formal ledger this time, not the margin, not a note, but the line itself.

The city map glowed on the wall.

Civic burn machine.

The words had no right to sound that monstrous and that administrative at once. That was why they were true.

Mara looked at the red-linked mesh over Melbourne and saw, all at once, why Southern Cross had not been the event. Why the stations mattered. Why the reassurance rooms mattered. Why Mercer's offices wanted moderation nodes and central calm and witness stripped down to furniture. The city itself was being taught to complete the room. Not one catastrophic ignition in one place, but a synchronised induction across enough of its metallic skeleton that contradiction, fear, compliance, load, and infrastructure would close into something self-propagating.

Not weather.

Machine.

Tamsin finally moved. She went to the board and circled the synchronisation mesh so hard the marker squealed. "All right," she said, voice dead and precise. "There it is. The larger act. The thing under the thing."

Theo turned from the wall. "How long."

No one wanted that question.

Tamsin answered anyway. "If they keep teaching the nodes and removing witnesses from pathways, maybe days. Maybe less if Mercer gets the moderation language through and another station or hospital cluster tips the pattern."

Sera said, "And if the city starts treating all contradiction as a patient to be privately calmed."

"Yes."

Mara looked up from her chair. "Then it becomes complicit in its own ignition."

No one corrected her.

Because no one could.

Defeat did not always need a body in the middle of the floor. Sometimes it needed a clerk gone into structure, a lawful bridge cut under poison, and a city map suddenly revealing that every ugly little incident they had fought like local weather had been teaching a machine how to build itself in public.

Theo crossed to the side table and took Pell's last packet from its sleeve. He did not open it. He simply held it for one second with both hands and then laid it down beside the city map printout.

"We hold the tables," he said.

The sentence sounded too small. That was what made it right.

Tamsin nodded once. "And find the synchronisation spine."

Sera added, "And stop treating slow rooms like atmospherics."

Mara stood. Her legs felt wrong under her, not weak, just late to the fact that the floor had changed meaning.

"And we tell the city enough truth to refuse the machine before someone else tells it enough calm to complete one."

Theo met her eyes.

This time there was no almost-smile. No dry correction. No legal elegance. Just agreement and the exhaustion of a man who had reached the point in a war where naming the next work was the only available form of mourning.

"Yes," he said.

Mr Idris closed the formal ledger over Pell's name and tied the ribbon shut.

Then he opened the black-and-grey volume reserved for quiet fine and wrote the truest line in the room before anyone else had the courage to say it aloud.

The bridge was cut.
The city remains.
The city is what they mean to turn.

No one left the room for a long time after that.

Above them, Melbourne continued its evening without permission. Trains carried people home. Lifts hesitated and then obeyed. Coins cooled in tills. Bridges held their loads. Hospital instruments gleamed under lights and waited for hands. The city remained itself because cities always remain themselves for a little while after the thing that means to alter them has been named.

For a little while.

Mara looked at the map until the synchronisation mesh stopped being pattern and became intent.

Then she looked at the blank route display where Mira Sol had vanished into lawful cut and thought not of her first, not even of Pell, though his absence now occupied the room like an honest wound.

She thought of the city.

The city is not the induction event, Mira had said. Not yet.

That not yet was now the most dangerous phrase in the world.

Chapter Twenty-One: What They Feed On

The city did not so much as sleep as lower its voice.

Past midnight, Melbourne became all threshold. Wet tram lines caught sodium light like nerves under skin. Lift panels glowed in half-empty towers. Hospital corridors carried fluorescent patience through hours meant equally for healing and paperwork. The witness tables held their little islands of boiled water, cheap biscuits, ledgers, cards, and human plurality in stations, lobbies, staff corridors, and service docks. None of it looked like war. That, Mara thought, was one of war's nastiest advantages. It hid inside the ordinary so naturally that people kept waiting for terror to announce itself in a form dramatic enough to justify attention. Instead, it arrived as a room with the right chairs, a phrase like quiet handling, a bridge support singing under load, a station voice that knew your name, a clerk removed by distance, a city nearly persuaded to become the machine meant to burn it.

In the lower lab, the map stayed lit.

Tamsin had left the synchronisation mesh on the wall rather than projecting anything else over it. The red-linked lines across Melbourne's metallic skeleton now looked less like weather and more like intent. Stations. Lift banks. tram power. Hospital service corridors. Bridges under stress. Logistics depots. Display glass. Sublevel relay rooms. A city's own habits of motion and compliance turned into preparatory circuitry. The route did not need to invent everything. It only needed to teach existing structures how to prefer the wrong kind of answer.

Theo had gone upstairs briefly to brief Sayeed under witness and come back with three fresh pages of notes and the expression of a man who had stopped pretending he would be permitted grief before daylight. Sera sat at the side bench with Jules Pearson's latest response sheet and Beth Lowen's re-entry notes spread around her like cards in a patient game of anatomical insult. Mr Idris had both ledgers open now, the formal one and the black-and-grey one, and was copying selected lines between them in the slow, exact hand of a person refusing to let the categories separate too far from one another. Pell Ardoc's name sat in the margin of one and the centre line of the other, the two placements a more honest memorial than any wall plaque Mara had ever trusted. Elian had not moved far from Bench Three since the lawful bridge cut. He stood with one shoulder near the side table and both hands braced against its steel edge, not looking at the map all the time because looking only at the map would have turned the city into abstraction and he did not have the moral energy for that particular betrayal tonight.

No one spoke for a long while.

That was not weakness. They had been speaking for days. Speaking to stations, to tables, to one another, to the route, to the weather, to frightened offices, to medics, to platform staff, to the city itself. Sometimes speech needed enough silence around it to remember it was not merely performance.

The first words came from Sera, and because they came from her they did not sound like an attempt to comfort the room back into motion. They sounded like work.

"I know why Pike burned."

Everyone looked at her.

She kept her gaze on the sheets. "More precisely, I know why his body completed the process as fast as it did and why Southern Cross did not."

Theo dragged a chair round and sat. "Go on."

Sera placed three reports side by side on the bench. Daniel Voss. Hannah Quill. Alden Pike. Then she pulled another stack closer. Priya Nandakumar. Beth Lowen. Jules Pearson. Richmond shaft extraction. The pathology runner from the hospital lift. A station clerk from Platform Nine. A cleaner from Level Three who had never been in a closure room but had reported a week's worth of wrong calm every time she was told to sort a contradiction somewhere private.

The categories had been there all along. They only became obvious after the lawfully-held bridge had nearly died carrying them all at once.

"They don't feed on fear," Sera said. "Fear is noisy. Noise can save people. What they need is closure under deception, the moment a person stops holding contradiction in public and lets one false answer harden into bodily truth."

Tamsin, who had spent most of the last hour muttering at the route board like an engineer trying to embarrass mathematics into confession, turned slowly. "We said something close."

"We used contradiction as the noun," Sera said. "That was too blunt. Contradiction is only the loading phase. Southern Cross held because people kept it noisy and shared. Daniel, Hannah, Pike, they were narrowed until the body finished the lie alone."

Mr Idris wrote the sentence down before anyone could improve it into nonsense.

Mara felt the shape of it lock against everything they had seen. Daniel in the service corridor, asking which instruction was true when no table yet existed in the building to answer him with more than one human voice. Hannah behind the glass, with no route out of the room that did not first pass through the people who had built it. Pike trying to stay primary between Mercer and the radio whisper, choosing the narrowed chain because his whole professional body had been trained to mistake carrying both for competence. Priya touching the bench support and dragging the contradiction out into public just in time to stop the station finishing her. Beth entering the reassurance room and coming out flatter because privacy had made closure feel mature. Jules in the shaft beginning to let the room sort her until eight ugly breathing people refused the rescue to become neat.

Not fear. Closure.

Theo looked from Sera to the city map. "So the synchronisation mesh doesn't need terror at every node."

"It needs contradiction, load, and social narrowing," she said. "The machine doesn't just burn metal. It recruits bodies into finishing instruction chains."

Elian finally moved away from the table. He crossed to the map and stood beneath the red-linked line running from Southern Cross through Parkville and out towards the Batman Avenue bridge approach. "That's why the older adjacencies matter."

Mara looked at him. He had gone past grief's first visible edge now into that colder territory where thought sharpened because the alternative was to fall bodily into the loss and not come back in the same shape.

"Explain," she said.

He nodded once. "Fast structures make closure obvious, black room, side-lane, false rescue shaft. The older ones are worse. They teach a city that public contradiction is childish and private resolution is maturity. Once enough people learn that lesson, weather becomes infrastructure."

Tamsin swore softly under her breath because the sentence was hideous and right.

Theo rubbed one hand over his face and left it there a second longer than he meant to. "So what they feed on at scale is not only individual bodies."

"No," Mara said before Elian could. "They feed on the city agreeing to narrow itself."

The room stayed still around that.

Outside the lab, somewhere in the building, a printer gave its small exhausted cough and another answered on a different floor. The city, even now, kept doing things in pairs and echoes and accidental witness. That mattered too.

Sera stood and went to the whiteboard. She did not wipe away the old notes. She built over them. Daniel's cascade stages. Hannah's glass. Southern Cross. The studio of lies. The false rescue shaft. Slow adjacency. The civic burn machine. Under all of it she wrote, in large block capitals that made the board look almost accusatory:

THEY FEED ON CLOSED CONTRADICTION UNDER DECEPTION.

Then, beneath that, after only the briefest pause, she added:

AT SCALE: CITIES CAN BE MADE TO EAT FOR THEM.

Tamsin let out a breath. "That's the title of the inquiry report we never want to write."

Mr Idris, without looking up, said, "Then let us avoid the inquiry and keep the sentence."

Theo stood again. That was always a sign the room had moved from revelation to obligation in his mind. "All right. If that's true, then the machine is not just physical infrastructure. It is social infrastructure plus physical load plus route learning."

"Yes," Sera said.

"And if that's true, the answer is not only to shut nodes."

"No," Mara said. "Because shutting nodes through central command and private moderation is one of the things it wants."

Theo looked at her. "Then say the answer cleanly."

She could feel every eye in the room on her, not because she alone held it, but because they were all now too tired for false modesty about who did what. The city story had become one of her fronts. There was no point pretending otherwise.

"The answer," she said, "is to stop closure before it can be mistaken for maturity."

No one spoke.

So she kept going.

"We've been fighting rooms. We've been fighting routes. But what the city is learning now is a style of self-betrayal. A person hears two things, or feels the system turning on them, or feels the steel becoming impatient, and the route offers them the adult version. The calm version. The efficient version. The quiet room. The one proper authority. The cleaner answer. If they take that in alone, the machine gains a node. If they push it back into public witness, the machine loses coherence."

Theo's eyes narrowed not in disagreement but in concentration. "Meaning our next package has to say exactly that without saying any of that."

"Yes."

Tamsin made a face. "I hate that she can do this."

Sera said, "No, you don't."

"No," Tamsin admitted. "I really don't."

Elian was still at the map. "Pell said the older adjacencies would not ask for panic. They would ask for order." He traced one finger, not touching the wall, along the line from Southern Cross to Parkville. "That means every office currently saying we need calmer handling, moderated nodes, private debrief, reduced witness density, controlled messaging, all of that has to be treated as route-relevant, not merely politically annoying."

Theo smiled then, but there was no pleasure in it. "Mercer becomes epidemiology."

That got the room its first real breath of ugly humour since Mira's warning. Ugly humour mattered. It was one of the things slow rooms hated because it made meaning too communal to govern cleanly.

Mr Idris, copying the new whiteboard headings into the black-and-grey ledger, said, "One might almost enjoy that."

Theo turned to him. "Almost."

Mara moved to the table and opened the shadow notebook to a fresh page. "Then let's test the answer."

She wrote the heading without flourish.

What the city must learn now.

Under it, she began in rough, public language.

If conflicting instructions begin to feel cleaner when made private, that is not maturity.
If a room offers you relief before it offers witness, it is not helping.

If the calm version asks you to leave the table, stay at the table. If an authority asks you to stop making your uncertainty public, ask who benefits when you do.

Theo watched her write. "Too sharp for public release."

"Yes."

"Good. I wanted the truth first."

Sera went back to the table and picked up Beth's re-entry notes. "There's more. Slow-room subjects improve fastest when the relief gets reclassified publicly. Not when they're soothed. Not when they're reassured. When the room's offer is named in front of others as a narrowing trick. Beth improved after she could say it had made her think private calm was adulthood. Jules improved when she could say the shaft made stillness sound competent. The guard from Southern Cross improved when the table laughed at quiet handling. Not cruelly. Socially. They got better when the room's dignity was broken."

Mara looked up. "Humiliation."

Sera nodded. "Not of the person. Of the room."

Tamsin pointed the marker at her like a weapon. "That, Doctor Imani, is why I love you."

"I'm not discussing your thresholds."

Theo took the line seriously. "Can we build that in?"

"Yes," Mara said before anyone else could. "We stop presenting witness as comfort and start presenting false privacy as ridiculous. Not solemnly. Socially. We teach the city that some rooms are just bad manners wearing policy."

Mr Idris's pen scratched again. Good cities laugh at the rooms that want to make them obedient.

Elian turned from the map then, and Mara saw at once that whatever he was about to say had been costing him for the last several minutes.

"There's something else," he said.

They waited.

"The lawful bridge cut when Mira pushed one last warning through. That warning gave us the machine. It also told us something we haven't quite said directly enough." He looked at Theo first, then Sera, then Tamsin, and only then at Mara. "The city is not the induction event. Which means the event still requires coordination outside the city. Someone or something is trying to bring the nodes into synchrony from somewhere else. The weather teaches the steel and the bodies, but the machine still needs a conductor."

No one spoke because the map behind him suddenly looked more dangerous for lacking that one thing.

Not weather then. Not a machine alone. Orchestra. Conductor. A city taught to tune itself under contradiction while some larger intelligence waited to draw the bow.

Tamsin swore again, quieter this time. "The resonance heart."

Theo said, "The one you and Mara saw traces of in the route."

Elian nodded. "Or an urban extension of it. Something preparing to make the city's own load patterns do the final labour."

Mara felt the floor seem to shift under the idea. Not because it was wrong. Because it was now too right to avoid.

"So the machine is not only being built here," she said. "It's being synchronised from the Other Room."

Sera looked at the map, then at the ring, then at the whiteboard, then back to the map. "Then all this," she said, and her voice was very quiet now, "all the tables, the re-entry work, the warning cards, the station language, it doesn't only buy us public calm. It buys us time before they can finish tuning."

Time.

The word sat with all the weight of a temporary god.

Theo took up the marker from Tamsin's hand and went to the board himself. He drew a line down the centre and wrote two headings as if laying out a legal case the city would have to survive.

WHAT THEY FEED ON
WHAT STARVES THEM

Under the first, he wrote, in his hard, practical script:

closed contradiction
private maturity
single authority
fatigue isolation
managed calm
sorted witnesses
load without plurality

Then he stopped and handed the pen to Mara.

She took it.

Under the second heading she wrote:

shared naming
public embarrassment of false rooms

fixed surfaces
paired and group verification
re-entry under witness
ugly tables
noise that keeps meaning plural

Mr Idris let out one soft breath that might have been the closest thing he had to prayer.

Tamsin looked at the two columns and said, "Well. That's it, isn't it."

Theo glanced at her. "Not yet. But it's the argument."

"Same thing in this house."

No one corrected that because in this room, it was true enough.

The hours after the revelation moved strangely. Not faster. More exactly. The city's evening reports continued to come in. Another office tower lift. A tram depot gate. Two cash trays. A pathology trolley. A bridge crew who had started singing insults at the steel whenever it became impatient because one of them had decided ridicule counted as witness, and, alarmingly, it did. Tamsin added social derision events to the city model and discovered, with increasing disgust and delight, that the weather lost structural confidence when enough human beings treated its authority as faintly ridiculous.

By nine, Mara had the bones of the next public package.

Not a machine. Not a conductor. Not resonance heart. Not yet. But enough truth to shift the city's habits farther away from the machine's diet. Enough to name false calm as a narrowing tactic. Enough to make tables feel less like emergency furniture and more like a civic style. Enough to tell the city that if help sounded cleaner when it arrived privately, it should be suspected before obeyed.

Theo took the first draft upstairs to Sayeed. When he returned an hour later, he said nothing at first. He simply placed the signed page on the table.

Director authorisation: public witness package version three.

Mara read it and, almost, for one exhausted second, loved bureaucracy.

Not because it was beautiful. Because Sayeed had held the line where it mattered. The phrase if private relief arrives before shared verification, refuse had survived. The line about fixed surfaces remained. The instruction to move in pairs and groups remained. Even the phrase support points were public, not moderated nodes, had stayed on the page despite what must have been a very expensive fight in some office above them.

Tamsin looked over Mara's shoulder. "I'll be damned."

Mr Idris said, "Please do wait."

Sera, who had her head bent over a fresh set of re-entry charts, smiled without looking up.

At 10:17, as the package moved into the city and the witness tables began reading it aloud to station staff, clerks, cleaners, guards, and the sort of commuters who now paused at the sight of ugly laminate the way earlier citizens had paused at church doors, Beth Lowen returned to the lower lab voluntarily.

She stood in the doorway with her station fleece zipped properly this time and one of the revised public cards in her hand.

"I thought you should know," she said.

Mara looked up. "What?"

Beth lifted the card slightly. "The line about private relief arriving before shared verification."

"Yes."

"I was reading it aloud at the table and realised the room behind Staff Access B still sounds sensible to me sometimes." She said it plainly, not ashamed, not dramatising, just honest in the way re-entry had taught her to be. "Not all the time. But enough. So I thought I'd report myself before I got proud about improving."

Sera stood slowly.

No one spoke for a beat because Beth had just done something larger than she understood. She had treated her own residual resonance not as a private flaw or hidden contamination, but as a public fact that could be held and therefore starved.

Finally, Mara said, "Good."

Beth frowned. "That's what you said last time."

"Yes," Mara answered. "Because it's still good."

Beth took that in and looked at the board with its two columns and the city map and Pell's copied line and the ledgers under their lamps and Tamsin's ugly route diagrams and Elian standing by Bench Three as if still learning how not to confuse hearing too much with owing the city his blood.

"Is this what we do now?" Beth asked quietly. "Keep each other from becoming rooms."

Theo, from the doorway, answered before anyone else could.

"Yes."

It was the cleanest word in the room.

Beth nodded once and came farther in.

Outside, Melbourne continued under the weather, rails, lifts, trays, bridges, coins, glass, too old and too stubborn to understand that it was being taught to complete a machine from the inside out. But the city was learning back. That was the thing. It was learning back through station tables, through public ridicule, through hands-on bench supports and bridge rails and chair edges, through witness cards in apron pockets and by tills, through cleaners and clerks and fathers with prams and nurses with instrument trays and pathologists writing more humanly than policy allowed.

What they feed on.

What starves them.

They had the shape of both now.

Whether it was enough would belong to what came next.

Chapter Twenty-Two: Bench Doctrine

The city looked less frightened in the morning, which was how Mara knew it had become more dangerous.

Fear had edges. It made strangers compare what they had heard. It put hands on rails and bench supports. It kept mouths moving. Fear, ugly and public, had saved Melbourne more than once.

What replaced fear, if it came too early, was composure.

What replaced fear, if it arrived too early, was composure, Mercer's favourite weather. Composure in controlled messaging. Composure in moderation nodes. Composure in men telling themselves the city was stabilising when what they meant was that it was becoming quieter and easier to narrow.

At seven-ten in the morning, Melbourne looked composed.

The trains were running. The rain had washed the tram wires bright. The witness tables still stood, but the crowds around them had thinned. People were folding witness cards into wallets instead of holding them in plain view. The city was doing what cities do when it wants motion back: translating trauma into procedure.

That was exactly the moment in which a machine like this could finish itself.

Mara stood by the lower lab's interior window with a paper cup of tea cooling between both hands and watched the route board glow against the far wall. Overnight, Tamsin had refined the two columns Theo had begun until they looked less like notes and more like doctrine.

WHAT THEY FEED ON
WHAT STARVES THEM

Closed contradiction.
Private maturity.
Single authority.
Fatigue isolation.
Managed calm.
Sorted witnesses.
Load without plurality.

Shared naming.
Public embarrassment of false rooms.
Fixed surfaces.
Paired and group verification.
Re-entry under witness.
Ugly tables.
Noise that keeps meaning plural.

The city map below the words was worse this morning, not because
the red marks had spread dramatically, but because they had
thickened where the machine wanted them to thicken. Southern
Cross, Richmond, Parkville, Collins Street, Docklands, the Batman
Avenue bridge line, two office tower lift clusters, one hospital
freight corridor, and a looping tram-power spine near Flagstaff now
resolved into a more disciplined pattern than the night before. The
civic burn machine was no longer only a warning shape. It was
becoming an implementation plan.

Tamsin had not slept. No one had to ask. She stood in front of the
board in the same black trousers and grey shirt she had worn the day
before, cardigan sleeves shoved above the elbows, marker in hand,
hair tied back with the kind of practical violence that implied
scissors had briefly been considered. On the main console, half a
dozen route models sat open side by side. One showed the lawful
Harbour under grain load. One showed the side-lane family. One the
studio of lies. One the shaft branch from Richmond. And one,

largest now, displayed the synchronisation mesh with the notation
TUNING PHASE in the upper corner.

Theo came in from upstairs carrying the morning briefings and shut
the door behind him with his foot because both hands were full.
"Sayeed has the room for nine."

Tamsin did not turn. "The board's still worse."

"When is it ever not."

"Today it has data."

That got his attention.

Mara moved away from the window and set the tea down on the
side bench. Sera looked up from the medical re-entry pack she had
been revising yet again, pages now so marked in black and blue that
they resembled legal evidence more than clinical guidance. Elian,
who had been at Bench Three with the ring and the route display for
almost an hour without touching either, came to stand a little closer
to the board.

Tamsin pointed with the marker.

"Overnight reports came in from seven witness sites and four non-
table sites. Not random. Look where the improvement happened and
where it didn't." She tapped Southern Cross and Richmond.
"Stations with mature tables held under contradiction load. Hospital
witness points reduced false calm uptake by nearly half." Another
tap. "Bridge crews using partnered confirmation prevented three
interpretation drifts from becoming route-positive events." Then
Docklands. Parkville freight. Collins Street towers. "Places where
we still rely on ordinary management language or private
professional handling remained sticky. The pressure didn't need
much there. It only needed one person to decide they could be
responsible in a room by themselves."

Theo put the briefings down without sitting. "So."

"So the machine isn't merely learning the city's metal anymore," Tamsin said. "It's learning the city's governance style. The mesh strengthens where infrastructure and managerial solitude overlap."

Mr Idris, from the ledger chair, murmured, "That is one of the ruder sentences I have heard in any century."

"No," Mara said quietly. "It's one of the truest."

Theo looked at the two columns on the board and then at the map. "Meaning the tables are no longer only emergency response. They are structural opposition."

"Yes," Tamsin said. "Bench doctrine."

The phrase became real almost at once.

Not because it was elegant. It sounded like something a rail union would print on the back of a mug. That was its strength.

Bench doctrine was not the table. It was what the table had taught.

Shared verification. Public contradiction. Refusal of quiet handling. The right to embarrass a room before obeying it.

Mara felt the logic of the city shift around the words.

Theo took the marker from Tamsin's hand and added a line beneath the two columns.

IF THEY BUILD THE MACHINE THROUGH NARROWING, WE BREAK IT THROUGH PUBLIC BREADTH.

Sera nodded once. "That's almost medical."

"It offends me to hear that."

"Then heal faster."

A small, useful ripple of laughter moved through the room. Even now, that mattered. Slow rooms hated the social abrasion of ordinary humour because humour made too many angles at once to be governed neatly.

Elian had not laughed.

Mara looked at him.

He was staring at the map, but not the whole map. At one darkened cluster just west of Southern Cross where the rail-linked service corridors and utility lines converged before the city spine pushed outward into Docklands and the western depots. The resonance heart, she thought. Or one expression of it. The urban extension of the thing Mira had warned them about.

"What," she said.

He did not answer immediately, which meant the answer mattered.

Then he said, "The machine still needs a conductor."

No one moved.

He turned to the ring then, not as though it were an object, but as though it were the last clean instrument in the room and he hated needing it for that. "We can broaden witness in the city. We can starve the machine socially. We should. But the route still needs somewhere to bring the nodes into synchrony. Mira didn't say heart by accident. Pell warned us the larger act was not the weather. The weather is tutoring. The machine is civic. The synchrony is elsewhere."

Theo's face had already hardened because he could hear where the sentence was going and did not like that it was going there lawfully.

Mara said it anyway. "We need the resonance heart."

Tamsin cursed softly.

Sera put both palms flat on the bench. "No more partial descents."

"Yes," Elian said, still looking at the ring. "No more partial descents."

The room held that truth without flinching from it, which meant they had reached the point where honesty cost more than argument. The city could not simply keep broadening bench doctrine and hope the weather dispersed out of shame. Someone or something in the Other Room was teaching the mesh. The conductor would not stop because the city had become morally interesting. It would stop when the route to the heart was found, named, and severed.

Theo crossed the room slowly and stood beside Mara. "All right," he said. "Then today is not just public doctrine. It is plan day."

That was the sentence they had been moving toward all morning.

Tamsin pulled a second whiteboard from the wall cabinet with more force than elegance and wheeled it into place beside the city map. Mr Idris shifted both ledgers to the side table and opened a fresh document file for working doctrine. Sera gathered the re-entry sheets and the pathology summaries and the non-acute enclosure pages and arranged them in the order a body would hate and a city might survive. Mara opened the shadow notebook to a blank spread. Theo rolled his sleeves up once and never rolled them back down.

No one called it a war room. That would have made it sound too cinematic.

It was a room with people in it who had stopped mistaking partial success for safety.

Theo began.

"What do we need for the city."

Mara answered first because that part of the room was hers whether anyone liked the fact or not. "Expansion without dilution. Tables at all rail nodes by nightfall. Witness points at hospitals, office lift banks, bridge maintenance access, and logistics depots by staggered priority, not everywhere at once. Public package version four today, using the phrase conflicting systems under pressure, but not anomaly any more. Anomaly is too bloodless now. People need to understand that private relief and single-authority calm are not mature responses. They are risk indicators."

Theo nodded and wrote. "Good."

Sera added, "And re-entry teams attached to every high-load node. Not one medic. Pairs. One body person, one witness person. If a subject comes out of a slow room flatter, calmer, cleaner than the facts permit, they get public reclassification immediately."

Tamsin was already sketching distribution routes. "I can build the priority list from the mesh. Southern Cross, Richmond, Parkville, Docklands spine, Collins Street lift cluster, Batman Avenue bridge, then outward." She paused, then added with visible reluctance, "I'll need Transport control to stop pretending this is basically signalling."

Theo made a note without looking up. "I'll bully them."

Mr Idris said, "With tenderness, I hope."

"No."

Mara looked at the city map again. "That handles starvation. Not severance."

The room shifted one degree colder.

Sera looked at Elian. "Before we talk descent, I want something stated plainly. No one in this room is volunteering because they think grief is a strategy."

Elian met her eyes. "Understood."

"Good. Because if I hear Pell's name being used as fuel, I'll sedate everyone and let the city fend for itself."

That got a faint noise out of Tamsin that might have been approval.

Theo took up the second thread. "What do we need for the route."

No one answered immediately because pretending the route would respect lists would have been arrogant.

Then Elian spoke, slowly enough that each condition felt paid for.

"Lawful re-entry first. Not just a descent into weather. We have to rebuild a clean enough channel to the Harbour to know the heart from whatever lies in front of it. We need a full room witness on this side, not partial. We need an anchor phrase the route can't flatter. We need a way to reject city urgency once inside. And we need Mara with me."

Theo did not object to the last sentence because by now objecting would have been performance.

Mara wrote the conditions down in the notebook. "Full room witness. Clean lawful challenge. Anchor phrase. No city urgency allowed inside. Dual operator."

Tamsin, marker against her lip, said, "We also need a kill condition that isn't just heat or visible narrowing. The slow structures are too elegant for that. If the route begins making the mission itself feel more mature by becoming private, I want you both out before you can explain to yourselves why that's noble."

Mara looked at her and almost smiled. "That is a sentence only you could say."

"Yes. Respect me."

Sera said, "And physiology isn't enough either. I want moral telemetry."

Theo looked over. "That is not a phrase."

"It is now." She turned one of the re-entry pages over and began writing on the blank back. "Not heart rate. Not temperature. I want spoken markers. If either of them starts using phrases like simpler, cleaner, more efficient, not burdening the others, or we can explain later, that counts as active drift. No debate."

Mr Idris said, without irony, "Excellent."

Theo nodded once. "Good. It goes in the protocol."

Mara added a heading in her notes: FALSE CALM LANGUAGE TRIPWIRES.

Elian had gone back to the ring, but he did not touch it. He stood with both palms flat on the steel edge of the bench as if reminding himself, and perhaps the room, what counted as surface and what did not.

"There's one more thing," he said.

They waited.

"If the city is not the induction event, then the route may now be using every broadening of witness as a pressure test." He looked over at the table plans, the station lists, the witness-point rollouts. "Meaning if we do this badly, if tables become performative or thinly staffed or borrowed by reassurance language, we might actually teach the heart how to compensate."

That landed hard.

Mara thought of Mercer's moderation rooms, of trust furniture, of stations wanting support points that did not embarrass commuters with too much reality. Bench doctrine could fail not only by being shut down. It could fail by becoming pretty.

Theo said, "Then no borrowed language. No hybrids. No reassurance officers pretending to be tables."

"Exactly," Mara said.

Sera lifted her chin towards the city map. "Ugly or nothing."

That went on the board, too.

UGLY OR NOTHING.

Tamsin approved more than she meant to show. "Finally, a design principle."

By nine-forty, the room had the bones of the plan.

For the city, broaden bench doctrine faster than the machine could narrow it. Build ugly, public, low-status witness points whose very lack of glamour made them hard to centralise without revealing the theft. Embed re-entry in every high-load zone. Treat slow-room language as route-relevant. Publicly humiliate false calm where possible. Make the city noisier at exactly the places the machine needed false maturity.

For the route, rebuild lawful contact under full witness and find the resonance heart before the mesh completed. No partial descents. No single operators. No hidden burdens. No private heroism. No explanation-later language. If the route offered order at the price of breadth, they would name it aloud and withdraw. If the route offered grief as acceleration, they would name it aloud and withdraw. If the route offered a cleaner version of care, they would name it aloud and withdraw.

And at the centre of both halves of the plan sat the same unpleasant truth.

They would not beat the machine by becoming better managers than it was. They would beat it by making management too public to feed on.

Director Sayeed came down herself just after ten.

She took in the boards, the ledgers, the route maps, the half-drunk tea, Theo's rolled sleeves, Tamsin's handwriting, Sera's alarming stack of body-state protocols, Mara's notebook now three pages deep into version four of the public witness package, and Elian standing at Bench Three like a man beside a grave and a door at once.

"No one has gone home," she said.

Theo said, "No."

"Good."

That was all.

She moved to the city map and looked at it in the same way she had looked at the first heavy-method packet. Not theatrically. Not to perform leadership for the room. She simply allowed the truth to reach her without ceremony.

"The machine," she said.

"Yes," Mara answered.

Sayeed nodded once. "Then you have city authority for all witness infrastructure expansion under temporary public safety doctrine and transit-health coordination. Mercer's people have been told, in writing and in front of witnesses, that if they use the word moderation one more time in relation to a contradiction site, I will bury them in inquiry paper until their grandchildren sneeze toner."

Mr Idris made a pleased little sound.

"And for the route," Sayeed continued, turning to Elian and Mara, "you have what time I can buy you. Not much. The city is beginning to look calm enough that the wrong people will think they are winning. That is always the most fragile hour."

Mara met her gaze. "We know."

Sayeed's eyes moved to the board where Theo had written IF THEY BUILD THE MACHINE THROUGH NARROWING, WE BREAK IT THROUGH PUBLIC BREADTH. She read it once, then looked at the ring.

"Do it," she said.

No one asked her to clarify. Not because the room had become mystical. Because command, when lawful, sometimes really was that plain.

She left them with the authority papers signed and the city at their backs.

After she was gone, Theo looked at the room, at the boards, at the map, at Pell's copied line pinned beside the quiet-fine ledger, at the ugly phrase UGLY OR NOTHING, at the route display with its grain and its patience and its unseen conductor.

"All right," he said. "Bench doctrine goes citywide now. By dusk every high-load node we can reach gets witness infrastructure, and every table gets version four plus re-entry protocol. No clean rooms. No moderation. No private sorting. Not one inch."

Tamsin nodded and was already moving.

"Sera, you run re-entry lead."

Sera nodded too. No drama. Just acceptance of labour.

"Mara, public package out by noon, internal by eleven. I want the city to know enough to refuse the machine before the machine adapts to the city's new patterns."

Mara wrote the deadline down.

"Elian."

He looked up.

"We go back in at fourteen hundred. Full room witness. Full lawful challenge. We find the heart or at least the chamber nearest it. No improvised mercy. No private speed. If the route offers you any cleaner version of what you already want, you say it aloud or I pull you out by the spine."

Elian held his gaze and said, "Understood."

Mr Idris closed the formal ledger and opened the next page.

Tamsin grabbed the city witness-point kits and started assigning routes. Sera rewrote the top page of the re-entry protocol so it no longer sounded like medicine and more like civic practice. Mara stood for one second longer in front of the city map and let the size of it arrive.

Weather in steel. Slow rooms. Burn list. Synchronisation mesh. The lost bridge. Civic burn machine.

And now, bench doctrine.

Not as a metaphor. As the city's first deliberate answer.

She thought of Nina Fowler telling stations not to keep clever on their own. Of bridge crews insulting steel into honesty. Of Priya touching the bench support. Of Beth reporting herself before she got proud about improving. Of Jules letting the table reclassify her false calm before it could become personality. Of Pell writing under quiet fine while distance tried to do what flame had failed to. Of Mira holding the lawful line long enough to tell them the city was not yet the event.

Not yet.

Mara opened the shadow notebook to a fresh page and wrote across it before the room broke into motion around her.

BENCH DOCTRINE: HOW A CITY REFUSES TO COMPLETE THE ROOM.

Then she underlined city once, very hard, and went to work.

Chapter Twenty-Three: The Release

The city still lacked a settled public language for the wound.

By late morning, the danger had shifted. The trains were running again. The lift banks were behaving. The hospitals had gone from chaos to vigilance. That was exactly when silence started hardening into explanation.

From ministries, editorial rooms, and frightened offices came the same pressure. Call it a glitch. Call it a systems event. Call it crowd stress. Call it anything that lets Melbourne feel normal before it has learned why normal has nearly killed it.

Mara Vale sat in Director Sayeed's conference room with three drafts open, two dead pens, one living one, and the weight of the city's next sentence pressing against the underside of her ribs.

The room itself had become one of their more civilised battlegrounds. A long table in ugly timber veneer, no soft furnishings, a glass wall looking out over a slice of grey Melbourne determined to remain real despite every office trying to rename it. Theo stood at the far end with his jacket off and sleeves rolled, one hand braced against the table edge while he read a transport-ministry revision aloud in the voice he reserved for language that hoped to slip past his contempt by sounding reasonable.

"An isolated infrastructure irregularity," he said, then looked up. "No."

He crossed it out.

Sayeed, seated to his right with her own annotated copy and a coffee she had forgotten to drink twenty minutes earlier, did not look tired so much as narrowed into usefulness. "Too bloodless," she said. "And 'isolated' is already a lie. Next."

Mara had her shadow notebook open beside the official pages, not because she distrusted her own memory, but because trust had become a thing that needed duplication in this city. One version for publication. One for the room. One for the day when men like Julian Mercer would insist afterwards that everyone had always used softer words.

At the opposite end of the table, Donnelly sat beside Nina Fowler and looked like a station floor made human. Jacket off. Tie somewhere not worth searching for. His hair was beginning to lose the argument with the weather and work. He had become, without asking for the honour, one of the most credible men in the city, because he had switched off his radio and used his lungs when the station tried to split itself. Nina, who had refused all offers of a more senior representative on the grounds that the city did not need another man discovering his conscience at the executive level, sat with both hands folded over the witness ledger she had brought with her from Southern Cross as if the book itself had come to ensure the room remained answerable.

Sera was there because bodies still needed truth written into them. Tamsin, because systems did. Mr Idris, because records needed a spine. Elian, because there was no point pretending the city could be released into language without reference to the route, was trying to track its pattern.

The truth package sat on the table in layers.

Public statement. Public guidance. Staff briefing. Support-point map. Internal line on slow rooms and false calm. And beneath all of it, the thing Mara had built with the most care: enough truth to create witnesses faster than the machine could create obedience.

Theo put the ministry revision down and looked at her. "Your version."

She read from the page in front of her.

"Infrastructure conflict events in Melbourne are no longer being treated as isolated malfunctions. They involve contradictory system signals, personalised instructions, and environmental pressure that becomes more dangerous when handled privately. Public safety improves when people verify conflicting instructions together, move towards visible support points, and refuse private reassurance before shared witness."

No one spoke for a second.

Then Sayeed nodded once. "Again. Slower."

Mara did.

This time, as the words crossed the room, she felt the sentence settle into its proper weight. Not a perfect sentence. There were no perfect sentences left in this city. But it did not lie where it mattered. It did not call people delusional for hearing the wrong voice. It did not pretend the weather in steel was mere maintenance with bad timing. It did not give Mercer the comfort of seeing the tables reduced to temporary emotional scaffolding. It placed contradiction, privacy, and witness in the right relation.

Nina said, "That'll do."

For Nina Fowler, that was an anointing.

Theo took the page and ran his eyes over it. "We still need a line for the city not treating private calm as the adult option."

Mara had known he would say that. She turned a page in the notebook and read from the draft she had built from Beth Lowen, Jules Pearson, Priya's statement, and a dozen station-table reports.

"If help asks you to leave a public contradiction and take it somewhere private before others can hear it, refuse. If a room or authority makes your confusion feel embarrassing, that is not resolution. Stay where people can witness what you heard."

Donnelly let out a breath through his nose. "That one."

Sera nodded. "That one."

Tamsin, who hated almost all public language on principle, tapped the table once with the back of her pen. "That'll annoy the right people."

"Good," said Theo.

Sayeed looked at the packet stack, then out through the glass wall at the city beyond. "What do we show."

That was the hardest question of all. Words mattered. So did proof. Too little and the city remained vulnerable to Mercer's calm. Too much and they risked giving the machine another lesson in how public fear moved.

Mara already knew the answer.

"Not Pike," she said at once.

No one argued.

"Not the body. Not the burn. We do not teach the city to look for spectacle before it trusts itself." She turned to Donnelly. "We use the station footage of the boards blanking, the split announcements, the father with the pram, the camel-coat woman, and the table holding the concourse."

Nina's mouth twitched. "You'd better not make me sentimental."

"I'm making you operational."

"Fine."

Theo looked at her over steepled fingers. "And Priya."

Mara nodded. "A short excerpt. Her line about the station stopping feeling as if it knew her better than she knew herself."

Sayeed approved of that with a stillness that was stronger than enthusiasm. "Good. That gives people an authority test without naming the route."

Tamsin reached into the satchel by her chair and produced a printed map, smaller than the one downstairs, cleaner, but still ugly enough to tell on the city. Key nodes circled. Witness points marked. Tables indicated. Not the full synchronisation mesh. Enough structure to prove that Melbourne's response was no longer ad hoc.

"We release this with the support-point list," she said. "No exact technical language. Just where people can go if systems start conflicting. Stations, hospital service points, office lift banks, bridge maintenance supervisors, depot desks."

Theo read the list once and looked at Sayeed. "If this goes out, no one gets to tell me later they didn't understand witness infrastructure had become city-critical."

Sayeed said, "Then let them tell you that in writing."

The release plan took shape with all the dignity of a city preparing itself not to become a room.

At eleven twenty-five, the statement would go out under Director authority to the press, transport channels, hospital networks, building managers, union contacts, and every witness point now standing under the doctrine they had named ugly or nothing. At eleven thirty, station and hospital cards would update. At eleven thirty-five, a clipped public video package would go live, showing enough of Southern Cross to break malfunction theatre without feeding catastrophe hunger. At eleven forty, internal node heads would receive the expanded protocol. And at noon, Theo would stand before microphones with Sayeed and Donnelly at his shoulder and speak the city's new habit into public language before anyone else could make private calm sound like wisdom.

That was the plan.

The city, as always, had its own.

The first interruption came at eleven twelve, eight minutes before the release.

Tamsin's secure line lit and she answered it without greeting because there was no time left for manners. She listened for three seconds, then stood so abruptly her chair rolled backwards into the wall.

"Where."

The room changed.

"Who's got it?" Theo asked.

Tamsin held up one hand and listened again, face drained into precision. "No, do not move the car. Keep the doors open. Keep people talking. Touch the rail if they've got a rail. I'm patching Sera."

She handed the call over.

Sera took it, and all the oxygen in the room seemed to reroute itself around her voice.

"Yes. Tell me exactly. No summaries."

Mara was already standing. "What?"

Sera put the line on speaker.

The voice that came through belonged to a woman in a building-services jacket and the sort of controlled breathing only found in people actively refusing fear because refusal has become part of the task. "North tower, Queen Street. Car stuck between thirteen and fourteen. Four occupants. Two hearing different instructions from the panel. One says the emergency speaker keeps using her son's name. They've been in there maybe ninety seconds. No heat yet. One man wants to prise the doors."

"No one touches the doors," Sera said immediately. "Get them all touching the same fixed surface if possible. Ask them to repeat out loud exactly what they hear and what they don't."

A male voice in the background shouted something about his kid not being there and the room shrank to the size of a single frightened family, no matter what the city maps claimed.

Mara looked at Theo. He was already calculating whether the release could move, whether the city was about to force them to choose between public language and one lift car in a tower where weather had just learned to use a child's name.

Donnelly made the decision for him.

"Release it now," he said.

The room turned to him.

He did not blink. "If we wait for clean timing, the city loses the hour. The people in the lift aren't a reason to delay witness. They're the reason not to."

Theo held his gaze for one hard beat, then nodded once to Sayeed.

She reached for the marked copy. "Do it."

At eleven thirteen, seven minutes early, the release began.

Phones lit across the table and then beyond it. Assistants moved in the corridor. One of Sayeed's staff, pale and composed, took the first packet out under both hands as if carrying volatile chemistry. Tamsin sent the support-point map. Mara hit send on the public guidance language and then, because she had no intention of trusting digital channels alone, physically handed the hard-copy version to Mr Idris, who took it without a word and went out into the building at a pace that suggested nothing so much as an elderly man going to remind a city how paper moved when it mattered.

Theo stayed.

The lift incident stayed on speaker.

"Good," Sera was saying. "Again. No one decides alone. If the panel says one thing and the speaker says another, say both out loud. No private obedience."

The woman at Queen Street repeated the instruction to someone else in the background. The male voice had become a kind of frantic anger. Another voice, younger, said very clearly, "The wall is cold. I'm touching the wall. We can all touch the wall."

Mara felt, absurdly and fiercely, like crying.

Not because the room had become sentimental. Because the city was learning fast enough to be worth saving.

At eleven twenty, the first radio host read out the line about private reassurance and paused long enough on air that Mara knew the sentence had found the shape of his own life somewhere uncomfortable. At eleven twenty-two, a union organiser in Parkville forwarded the witness-point map to six other hospitals with the subject line USE THIS BEFORE THEY MODERATE YOU. At eleven twenty-three, one of Mercer's deputy offices sent an objection marked ill-timed and already failed because the city had begun speaking first.

Then the public video went live.

No burning man. No sensational cut. Just Southern Cross under station light, blank boards whitening above a crowded platform, a father with a pram shouting to strangers, Priya's hand against the bench support, Donnelly turning off his radio, Nina at the ugly table pointing not like a saviour but like a woman who had had enough of everybody's nonsense, and across the whole sequence Mara's simple overlay text.

If systems conflict, do not choose alone.
Witness first.
Stay where people can hear what you heard.

The city took the words into itself with the weird and immediate hunger public truth sometimes enjoyed when it arrived in exactly the accent fear had been waiting for.

By eleven twenty-seven, three station tables reported commuters quoting the line back at one another. At St Vincent's, a nurse taped a printout of it to the prep room fridge. In a jewellery arcade near Collins Street, a goldsmith who had already reported warm rings read the phrase aloud to his apprentice and said, "That. That's exactly what the tray wanted me not to do."

Mercer moved too.

At eleven twenty-eight, one minute after the video hit, his office released its own statement.

It was excellent.

That was the problem.

No more moderation nodes. No overt centralisation. He had learned. The language now praised "community verification points" and "layered urban calm practices" and "coordinated support environments designed to protect public confidence." He had stolen almost every noun they had fought for and sanded the blade from each of them until the thing sounded like witness while asking for deference.

Mara read the statement on her monitor and felt something in her teeth.

"He's trying to overtake the release."

Theo was already reading over her shoulder. "No. He's trying to inherit it."

Sayeed looked from one screen to the other and then to Mara. "Answer?"

Mara didn't hesitate. "We don't counter his language directly. We make his theft visible."

"How."

"We go physical."

Theo understood at once. "The tables."

"Yes."

Not more statements. Not more paragraphs. Not another round of duelling calm from offices. They would make the city witness the tables as themselves, in public, before Mercer's people could lace them with enough polish to pass.

Donnelly was on his feet before anyone asked him. "I can get camera crews into Southern Cross."

Nina, already reaching for her cardigan, said, "And they can film me telling anyone who says community verification point to buy a dictionary."

Tamsin actually laughed.

Sayeed looked at the clock, then at Theo, then at Mara. "Five minutes."

The operation that followed felt less like media and more like a coup conducted by thermoses.

At eleven thirty-three, three local crews and one national one were routed not to press rooms, not to podiums, but to the witness table at Southern Cross, the one at Richmond, and the Parkville service point outside the lift banks. No glossy B-roll. No managed backdrops. They got Nina, Donnelly, a cleaner named Aroha at Richmond, and a tired nurse at Parkville explaining what happened when a room tried to make contradiction private and why the ugly table mattered more than any statement printed above it.

Nina, when asked what the table was for, said, "It's where the city stops being stupid on its own."

Donnelly, when asked whether the public should panic, replied, "No. Panic's private. We're doing witness."

The nurse at Parkville said, "The lift doesn't need you calm. It needs you plural."

Aroha, God bless her, held up a witness card to camera and said, "Private reassurance is just a room that makes you easier to sort because you're grateful."

That one went everywhere.

By noon, the Queen Street lift occupants were out. No lock. One boy shaking hard enough that the building-services woman kept him talking about his cricket team on the footpath while Sera's field partner checked his temperature and made his mother repeat back what the panel had said versus what the speaker had implied. The route had tried to use his name. The car had not become a chamber because the building crew, hearing the public package as it went live over someone's phone, had started reading the lines through the lift doors at the same time Sera was doing it from the conference room speaker.

The city was now feeding on its own witness faster than the machine had expected.

That, Tamsin said later, was when the activation began.

Not because the release failed. Because it worked.

At 12:07, every live route reader in the annex chirped once. The lawful Harbour display went grainy for three seconds and recovered. The city map registered simultaneous load ticks at Southern Cross, Parkville, the Batman Avenue bridge, and the Docklands spine. Not contradiction events. Pressure. The kind a room feels just before everybody starts speaking at once, or just before the wrong person chooses silence and the silence starts teaching.

Tamsin saw it first and said only, "There."

No one asked what.

They all knew.

The synchronisation mesh had noticed the city choosing breadth.

And somewhere behind the route, somewhere beneath fast rooms and slow rooms and weather in steel and all the false mercy of calmer handling, the resonance heart had just turned its attention fully towards Melbourne.

Theo looked at the map.

Mara looked at the ring.

Sayeed looked at both and said, "Go."

There it was. The real command.

The release was out. The city had its doctrine in public language. The tables were no longer emergency furniture but visible civic refusal. Mercer had been forced into the open and then into theft. The machine had answered.

Now came the descent that could no longer be deferred.

Mara stood so fast her chair barely scraped.

Theo was already moving, gathering the route packet, the internal protocols, the moral telemetry sheet Sera had written in her hard practical hand, and the ugly copy of What the city must learn now. Tamsin snatched the resonance-heart overlays from the board. Sera lifted both field kits and the sedatives she kept threatening them with out of principle. Elian had not moved yet.

Not because he was uncertain.

Because he was listening.

Mara crossed the room and stopped in front of him. He looked at her and she saw at once that the route had already begun rearranging itself somewhere beyond language. Not pulling him, not yet. Aligning. Preparing a shape it believed the next descent required.

"No private speed," she said.

His mouth moved once. "I know."

"No city urgency inside."

"I know."

"If the route offers us a cleaner version of this release, we call it what it is."

He nodded. "I know."

Only then did they move.

Behind them, on screens and phones and station monitors and kitchen tables and tram depots and hospital service desks and office lobby pillars and bridge maintenance vans, the city's witness language was still spreading, fast and ugly and public enough to matter. People were repeating lines to one another. Touch something fixed. Stay where people can hear what you heard. If help arrives private before truth does, refuse. The city was not calm. It was becoming articulate.

Good, Mara thought as the lower lab doors opened before them and the ring waited under its hood with the lawful line behind it and the machine now fully engaged.

Let it hear us clearly.

The release had done its work.

Now the next answers would come in structure.

Chapter Twenty-Four: The Activation

When the machine finally moved, it did not announce itself with flame.

It announced itself with agreement.

Across Melbourne, the city's metal carried the change within seconds. Station clocks drifted by a shared second and then held. Tram wires tightened under the wet noon light. Three hospital lifts in different precincts paused between floors in the same shallow hesitation. Bridge members under load began carrying tone, not as isolated complaint, but as a pattern too coordinated to ignore. In the lower lab, every live route reader on Tamsin's consoles sang the same thin warning note and then fell silent together.

No smoke. No sparks. No spectacle yet.

Just synchrony.

That was worse.

The ring under the hooded array stopped looking like an object and became what it had been all along, a legal opening held in matter by enough law and witness to make passage possible. Behind it, the lawful Harbour did not flare. It steadied. Grain still moving through it, pressure still visible in the basin, but steadied in the way living things steadied when the hour finally asked too much and the only answer left was to become exact.

Tamsin had already killed every nonessential light in the room. The lower lab now held only task lamps, route displays, the white spill of the city map, and the pale hard shine of the ring itself. The walls had become working surfaces. The city plan and synchronisation mesh glowed on one side. On another sat the route family, Harbour, side-lane, black-room closure arcs, studio of lies, shaft branch, slow adjacency traces, all of it now subordinated to a new central model she had built in the last four hours and titled with a grimness that was almost elegant.

HEART / CITY COUPLING

Sera's moral telemetry sheet was taped to the haptic bench in full view.

If the route offers private speed, name it.
If it offers clean authority, name it.
If it offers relief from witness, refuse.
If it offers a truer self at the price of public breath, call it a lie and leave.

Mr Idris had both ledgers open and weighted with a stapler because the building's air-conditioning kept trying to lift the pages. Theo stood with one hand flat against the protocol folder, the other resting by the physical breaker Tamsin had mounted to the steel frame days earlier and which now looked less like paranoia and more like architecture finally learning humility. Sayeed remained in the room, not by impulse, but because once the city had gone public with witness there was no longer any clean fiction under which executive distance could be called prudence.

Nina Fowler had refused to leave too. She sat at the witness chair nearest the side bench with the station ledger on her lap and a thermos beside her feet, looking less like a civilian in the wrong room than a magistrate from a better republic than the one history had actually delivered.

Mara stood opposite Elian at the haptic station.

No romance. No decorative goodbye energy. Nothing the route could teach itself from. The room had gone beyond that several days earlier. What passed between them now was harder, more public, and therefore less vulnerable. They had already been named by the side-lane, by the studio of lies, by all the false architectures that wanted to turn care into a private chamber. The only usable answer left was to remain visible in the act of caring.

Theo read the limits aloud one last time.

"No independent pursuit. No private speed. No accommodation to false calm. No sacrifice language. If the city enters your mouths as urgency, you speak it. If the route offers mercy that becomes narrow once accepted, you speak it. If either of you starts sounding like a room trying to tidy the other, the line is cut."

Mara said, "Witnessed."

Elian said, "Witnessed."

Sera, without looking up from the physiology monitors, said, "Witnessed and medicated if necessary."

That got the room its final breath of ugly humour before the descent.

Tamsin's voice came from the console, low and exact. "The mesh is pushing. You'll have a clean lawful window only if the city keeps broadening. Southern Cross, Richmond, Parkville, Batman Avenue, Docklands tables are all live. If they hold, the heart won't get full synchrony. If they fold, the route below you gets much worse very quickly."

Nina tapped one finger against the ledger. "Then let's not bore the city."

Mara put on the glove.

The haptic mesh sealed against her palm. On the other side of the bench, Elian did the same. The ring's inner curve gathered light the way deep water gathered weather.

Theo said, "Proceed."

The lawful Harbour opened in pain.

There was no other honest phrase left for it. Not because the Harbour was itself wounded in any human sense, but because every route into it now carried the city's pressure on the way through. What had once been patience now felt like patience under load, like a civic structure holding while argument, fear, plural speech, and predatory narrowing all crashed against it from too many angles. The witness ladder built anyway. That was the miracle of it and the obscenity both.

Mara felt the first rung settle, then the second, then the lawful basin's old exact receiving shape taking hold not as welcome but as permission earned against strain.

Elian said, very softly, "It's still there."

The Harbour deepened.

For a fraction of a second the lower lab ceased to feel like a room and became what it was pretending not to be, a bridgehead built from ledgers, tea, physiology sheets, ugly doctrine, public language, and the stubborn belief that breath in company mattered more than any clean authority. Then the Harbour accepted them and the city vanished not in sensation but in moral distance, enough that the work below and the work above had to be held together deliberately if they were to remain part of one fight.

Mara felt Cavara only in fragments now. Not the old composed civic broadness of first lawful contact. That had been changed forever by what both worlds had learned of one another. Instead, she felt the lawful side as pressure lines and structures held against fracture. Council chambers answering weather with procedure. Table-equivalents carrying noise like a civic duty. Mira Sol somewhere beyond sight but still within the logic of the basin, holding too many obligations and too little time.

The heart did not appear.

That, too, was a kind of lesson. The route no longer had any reason to let them walk neatly to the centre of it as if truth rewarded those who had already understood enough.

Instead, the Harbour held and around it the city spoke.

Not voices at first. Conditions. Southern Cross becoming noisy in the good way. Richmond broadening a contradiction cluster before it could settle. Parkville medics pulling a registrar back into public language. Batman Avenue bridge crews insulting the steel into honesty. Office tower lifts opening their doors and refusing private stillness. The city, in other words, enacting bench doctrine as though it had always belonged to it, and every enactment kept the lawful basin from losing shape outright.

Tamsin's voice came thinly through the witness link. "Good. Keep them where they are. Mesh not fully closed. You have a path."

The path was not a corridor.

It was an ethical gradient through pressure.

Beneath the lawful chamber, not under it exactly but in the lower logic through which the city's synchronisation was being urged, Mara felt the first clue of the heart. Not a room. Not a machine. A convergence of route choices arranged so that all the city's narrowed answers would eventually agree. The resonance heart, she realised with a kind of cold admiration, was not built as a place things entered. It was built as a place everything else leaned toward until it forgot that leaning had once been optional.

Elian felt it at the same time.

"The city is being taught to prefer one answer," he said.

Mara answered, "Yes."

The false architectures noticed them then.

Not with speed. That phase of the struggle was gone. They noticed them by clarifying alternatives. To the left of the lawful gradient, a side-lane of practical rescue, all the old burden profiles sharpened and repackaged. To the right, a slower chamber where the city above had already been stabilised, all tables absorbed, all witness made official, all contradictions sorted into managed calm. Ahead, farther down the pressure slope, a widening dark where the heart wanted them to call inevitability by some kinder name before entering it.

Tamsin saw the split on the board. "Triptych."

Theo said, "Translate."

She did not bother. "Speed. Order. Fate."

Mara almost laughed because the route was finally becoming vulgar with familiarity. It could not invent new hungers quickly enough, so it had arranged the old ones more neatly and hoped they would look like destiny.

Elian said, "It's offering three ways to stop carrying the city."

Sera cut in at once. "Name which one tempts you?"

He answered so quickly Mara knew he had already begun fighting himself. "Speed. The left path says the city won't hold long enough and the heart can be cut faster if I go in alone and let witness become aftermath."

Theo's voice, rough and immediate. "No."

"I know."

"Not enough. Say why."

Elian's mouth tightened. "Because if I do that, the route gets to decide whether the city's plurality matters only until the real work begins."

Good, Mara thought, and held to the line.

Then the slow chamber on the right opened its hand to her.

Not dramatically. That was the obscenity of it. The rightward structure offered no triumph and no intimacy. It simply arranged the city in her mind under a calmer grammar. Southern Cross already steadied. Mercer marginalised by superior competence rather than public humiliation. Tables kept but cleaned, standardised, made enduring by becoming less embarrassing to institutions. A chamber in which she could carry the release, the city, the doctrine, all of it, without having to keep needing a room full of breathing people to hold the contradictions with her. Not secrecy. Governance. The adult form of care.

She felt the appeal like a bruise being pressed.

"Mara," Sera said sharply.

Mara heard her own voice before she had chosen the sentence fully. "Order. The right chamber says I can save the city by making witness legible enough for the state to adopt without the state having to endure what witness actually is."

The rightward chamber recoiled, not violently, but with the same injured decorum all false civility adopted when called by its real name.

Nina spoke then, from the witness chair in the lower lab, and because she was Nina her interruption landed with the full force of an older civic sanity.

"Bullshit," she said.

The room fell silent.

Mr Idris wrote that down.

The central dark widened.

Fate, Tamsin had called it. But that was too poetic. What lay ahead was not fate. It was the route's attempt to make the city's own distributed choices feel as though they had always meant to arrive here. The heart wanted them to accept the machine as the natural maturation of weather. To believe that because enough nodes had been taught to narrow, the narrowing itself had earned the right to become structure.

Mara felt the city at her back then, not as image but as noise carried lawfully through the basin. Table staff. train crews. clerks. cleaners. nurses. fathers with prams. bridge workers insulting girders. Priya Nandakumar touching a bench support. Beth reporting herself before she got proud about improving. Jules sitting at the station table and relearning what care sounded like in public. Donnelly using his own lungs. Nina's ledger. Pell's pressure marks under quiet fine. Mira Sol holding the lawful line long enough to be heard.

Fate did not survive contact with that many witnesses.

"No," Mara said to the widening dark.

Elian said it too. "No."

And because everyone in the room had learned from everything that came before, Theo, Sera, Tamsin, Sayeed, Nina, and Mr Idris all answered from the lower lab in one strange, grounded chord of human refusal.

The heart revealed itself.

Not by opening.

By losing the ability to pretend it was only a direction.

On the route board, in the haptics, in Mara's bones, the central convergence resolved into structure. Not a room, not in any human sense. More like a civic loom made from closure arcs and harmonised pressures, a place where fast rooms, slow rooms, side-lanes, shafts, reassurance nodes, weather in steel, all of it fed inward until contradiction could be finished at scale through the city's own metal spine. The machine was not simply planned there. It was being rehearsed there, every public hesitation translated into timing, every private calm translated into alignment.

Tamsin's voice broke with genuine awe and disgust. "Oh, you bastard."

Theo said, "Can it be cut?"

The lawful basin shuddered.

Mira appeared then, not fully, not in the old calm civic contour, but enough. Enough for the room to know it was not imagining her. Enough for the route to make the next seconds expensive.

"Not cut," she said. "Broken by refusal where it expects completion."

Mara's hands steadied on the controls. "Where?"

Mira turned within the lawful chamber and the answer came not as coordinates but as relation. The heart had no single switch. It had a confidence point, the place where the city's narrowed answers were being fed in most fully under the assumption that public breadth had already failed. Not a physical machine exactly. A route confidence. A hinge. If that hinge could be forced to take enough witnessed contradiction at once, the synchrony would miss itself.

Elian felt it. "The node under Southern Cross."

Tamsin confirmed before the sentence had fully left him. "And Docklands spine. They're coupled."

Mira's voice tightened. "Then two fronts. The city must remain noisy where the machine expects calming. Here, you must make the heart take plurality."

Theo did not hesitate. "City side is ours."

He turned instantly to Sayeed and Donnelly. "You push every table, every witness point, every transport and hospital channel. If any node starts asking for private handling, you flood it with bodies and language. No beautiful messages. No calming. Breadth."

Sayeed was already moving for the upstairs comms room. Donnelly was on the station line before his body had fully left the witness chair.

Nina took the second phone and, as if she had been waiting her whole life to scold a metropolis into survival, began calling tables by name.

"Richmond, listen carefully. If anything asks for quiet handling, fill the space with people. Southern Cross, no one gets taken to any room not visible from the concourse. Parkville, if the lifts start acting grown-up, make them ridiculous. Batman Avenue, keep insulting the bridge. I'm serious."

Tamsin split the board into dual-front monitors. Southern Cross load. Docklands spine load. Bench doctrine saturation. The mesh brightened. The city above them began answering before the machine could finish asking.

Mara and Elian had no more time for caution that wasn't already embodied.

The confidence hinge opened before them as a narrowing arc where the heart assumed they would accept the machine's own logic long enough to enter. Its confidence, Mara realised, lay in something almost embarrassingly human. It believed that when pressure reached this scale, everyone would eventually prefer one answer to the humiliation of plurality.

She felt Elian arrive at the same understanding beside her.

"It thinks everyone will choose one voice in the end," he said.

Mira's contour thinned further. "Prove it provincial."

Mara would remember that sentence for the rest of her life because it was so strange and so exact. Provincial. Not universal. Not inevitable. Just one ugly, local arrogance pretending to be law.

She looked at Elian.

This was the moment the route had been building toward all along. Not the kiss. Not the confession. Not the private sacrificial gallantry some worse instinct would have mistaken for triumph. The visible choice not to become cleaner than the city they meant to save.

"Out loud," she said.

He understood at once.

Not a declaration of love. The route had already tried to turn that into private elegance. Something rougher. More public. The kind of truth that could survive witnesses.

"I do not get to carry the city for them," Elian said.

The heart trembled.

Mara answered with her own burden split open to the room. "And I do not get to organise the city into safety by making witness less embarrassing."

The hinge shook.

Theo, from behind them, added the sentence the law had come to say at last. "And no office gets to finish a contradiction by moving it somewhere quieter."

Sera's voice cut through next. "And no body in this room completes the machine by calling false calm maturity."

Tamsin: "And no infrastructure gets promoted to destiny."

Nina, impossible, magnificent Nina: "And no room gets to think it's cleverer than a city with a table."

Mr Idris's pen scratched once and then, to Mara's amazement, he too spoke into the room.

"History remains public."

That did it.

Not because the sentence was magic. Because it was ridiculous and true and human and too many voices had now occupied the same moral space for the hinge to go on pretending one answer was waiting patiently to be chosen. The heart convulsed.

Above them, Melbourne roared.

Not in fear. In refusal.

At Southern Cross, tables had been turned sideways to widen the support points and commuters were being made to repeat contradictory announcements back in groups loud enough to drown the station's more intimate lies. In Parkville, nurses and porters lined both sides of the service corridor and read the witness card aloud to the lift doors as though conducting a secular liturgy for a future that had not yet been stolen. On the Batman Avenue bridge, crews pounded gloved hands against the rail and cursed the steel by name every time it sang. In office towers, cleaners held lobby stations while lift cars were emptied into public foyers and made to wait there with managers, junior staff, and all the little hierarchies slow rooms liked best. Docklands, the spine itself, filled with workers on phones and radios and lungs, calling contradictions out before any one signal could earn the dignity of finishing.

The city refused the machine in its own accent.

The heart had not planned for that.

Its confidence point broke.

On the board the mesh lit white-hot and then misfired itself. Southern Cross and Docklands lost synchrony by nineteen seconds. The Batman Avenue line lagged. Parkville overcompensated into breadth. Collins Street lifts opened every door at once instead of narrowing into one clean chain. The city's own ugliness, its overlapping authorities, its shared embarrassment, its citizen mess, all the things Mercer and his cousins had spent careers resenting, became structural sabotage.

In the route, the civic loom tore.

Not the whole machine. Not all at once. But the resonance heart's confidence failed and with it the hidden assumption that Melbourne would eventually decide to become governable rather than plural. The closure arcs around the hinge opened under strain. The central pressure dark lost depth. For one instant Mara saw it clearly, not as enemy or god, but as a design built on contempt for breath.

Then Elian did the last necessary thing.

He did not rush forward. He did not sacrifice himself. He did not outrun witness or choose private speed. He simply held the lawful line steady and said, into the broken hinge, the truest sentence he had.

"You don't get to finish us for us."

The heart collapsed.

Above them, the city shuddered.

At Southern Cross, every board on the western span blanked white and then returned with ordinary lateness. At Parkville, the service lifts settled. On Batman Avenue the bridge gave one last offended note and then became only a bridge again. Docklands power loops spat a harmless sheet of static down one wet wall and died into silence. Coins cooled. rails stopped anticipating. instrument trays returned to being tools rather than impatient advisers. Office towers gave people back to themselves one floor at a time.

In the lower lab, the route cut not by poison this time but by successful refusal. The lawful basin closed like a hand around a final, hard-kept truth. Mira Sol's contour broke apart into distance and then, at the very last edge of the link, reappeared long enough to let one line through.

"The city held."

Then she was gone.

The room remained.

Just the lower lab again. Task lamps. Sweating tea cups. Ledgers. The city map glowing with dying white traces. The ring inert in its mount. Theo bent over the breaker but not needing to pull it. Sera already at Mara's wrist and then Elian's, counting, scanning, searching for the aftertaste of false calm or heroic contamination. Tamsin at the board, disbelieving and furious and alive in the same exact measure. Nina with one hand over her mouth and the other still on the phone, station noise roaring through the open line from Southern Cross because no one up there yet knew whether they had survived or only been reprieved.

Mara sat down because her body had reached the oldest of all negotiations with truth and decided it would prefer a chair for the next phase.

Theo looked at the board.

Then at the city.

Then at Pell's last packet, still in its sleeve on the side bench.

"We stopped the event," he said.

No one answered immediately because they all knew what kind of sentence that was. Necessary. Incomplete. Heavy with all the things it did not and could not mean.

Tamsin was the one who finally said it. "We stopped this event."

Yes.

Sera took her hand off Elian's pulse and looked around the room one by one. "No lock. No thermal rise. Moral telemetry ugly but survivable."

"That," Theo said, "is the closest thing to praise I've heard from you all week."

"Don't get used to it."

Upstairs, then, and only then, did the city begin sending in what it had become during the last nine minutes.

Station tables were full but holding. No new lock signatures. Dozens of contradictory instruction reports were broken by group verification. Two lift incidents were resolved by public flooding of the lobby. One bridge crew requested a replacement ledger because their current one had become too wet to insulate steel properly. Hospital service points were overloaded with bodies and, by Sera's lights, therefore functioning perfectly. Priya Nandakumar texted the station line to ask if it was normal to cry over a bench support and was told by Nina Fowler that, in this city, it certainly was.

The immediate catastrophe had been stopped.

The city had not burned.

Melbourne, not yet knowing how close it had come to becoming its own civic torch, staggered back into itself with all the dignity of a person caught halfway through making a terrible choice and deciding, with witnesses present, to remain complicated instead.

Mara felt the room returning by degrees from structure to flesh. Sera's hands were still moving from wrist to wrist. Theo had finally sat because standing any longer would have turned vigilance into theatre. Tamsin kept one hand on the board as if she did not yet trust the city to remain ordinary without supervision. Nina was still on the line to Southern Cross, voice blunt, alive, making sure relief did not become private anywhere before dawn. They had given Melbourne back its right to remain noisy. For the moment, that was enough.

Chapter Twenty-Five: What Comes Through

And beneath that relief, beneath the station noise and the released lifts and the ordinary profanity of public survival, the day kept one last obscenity in reserve.

No one in the lower lab mistook relief for safety now. The ledgers were still open. The phones were still live. Upstairs, staff were still talking to commuters, nurses, clerks, and bridge crews through the ordinary aftershocks of not becoming a machine. The room had only just remembered how to breathe when the board decided it had one more lesson to teach.

Tamsin's board chimed.

No one moved for one second because no one wanted the room to turn one more time after all that it had already cost. Then Tamsin swore, not loudly, but with the full exhausted conviction of a person for whom swearing had become both science and prayer.

"What?"

It was Mara who asked, though she already knew from Tamsin's face that the answer would not fit in the room kindly.

Tamsin enlarged the final route dump captured in the moment of collapse.

There, nested not in the mesh or the hinge or the city nodes, but in the heart's own dying confidence trace, lay a structure none of them had seen before. Not black-room family. Not a studio of lies. Not side-lane. Not a shaft branch. Larger. Stranger. Less room-like by an order of magnitude. The thing did not resemble an architecture waiting to receive bodies or cities. It resembled a transit of architectures themselves, a convergence field in which rooms were only local expressions of something broader and far less intimate.

The route dump had included one last pressure line beneath it.

Not translated. Not even really words. More like the idea of a warning impressed in material so hard the machine had failed to finish hiding it.

Elian stared at the shape and felt all the surviving air leave him.

"It's not another room," he said.

Theo looked from the board to him. "What is it?"

He answered without certainty and with all the certainty he had.

"What comes through."

Silence.

Mr Idris's pen had stopped again. The ledgers lay open under their lamps. Pell's name. Mira's last line. The city held. And now this.

Mara went to the board on tired legs and stood looking at the new structure until it stopped behaving like a symbol and became a threat. It was bigger than the Cauterists. Bigger than the black rooms and the studios and the city machine. Those had all been ways of teaching a species to become narrow enough to host something else.

Mercer had called it an order. Pell had called them older adjacencies. Mira had called it, in effect, the point beyond the city.

Now the route had left them its own final obscenity.

Not a room. Not a machine. An arrival condition.

The city had been preparation.

Melbourne, tables, witness, ledgers, rails, glass, black rooms, false chambers, all of it, had been this struggle because the city had needed not to become the event in order for the next thing to remain possible.

Theo sat down very slowly.

For the first time in days, he truly sat down, as if his body had reached the point where legal posture and civic fury no longer counted as structure enough by themselves.

Mara turned from the board and looked at the room that had held through it all. Theo. Sera. Tamsin. Elian. Nina. Mr Idris. The ledgers. The city map. The ring. The thermoses and the biscuit crumbs and the protocol sheets and the ugly doctrine by which a city had refused to finish itself.

The truth arrived in Mara not as triumph but as scale.

Daniel Voss had died asking which instruction was true. Hannah Quill had died trying to obey. Alden Pike had died holding two chains too long. Melbourne had looked at all three deaths and, for one night at least, refused to learn the lesson intended for it.

They had not killed a monster. They had stopped the city becoming its first mouth.

Outside, Melbourne remained loud and alive and stubbornly, gloriously untidy.

Inside, the board glowed with the shape of what had not yet come through.

Nina Fowler, still on the live line to Southern Cross, looked at the room and then at the board and said, in the tone of a woman who had run out of patience for the universe some time in 1989, "Well. That looks worse."

No one contradicted her.

Theo took a breath.

Then another.

Then he looked at Mara, and for the first time since this began, there was no law in his face, only the blunt honesty of a man who could hear the next war already finding its feet.

"What comes through," he said, "we do not open for."

For a beat, no one moved. The sentence settled over the room with the blunt weight of a vow made too late to be ceremonial. Mara crossed to the board and stood beside Elian, not touching him yet, close enough that the nearness itself became witness. Across the room, Theo lowered his head once over the ledger, and Sera, seeing the tremor fatigue had left in all of them, set the re-entry file down without fully closing it, as though even now the city needed a human hand kept in the page. They had survived one war and inherited the outline of the next in the same breath.

Mara looked at the ring.

Elian looked at the board.

Sera closed the re-entry file over the city that had held.

Tamsin saved the route dump in four places and one ugly safe.

Mr Idris wrote the last line in the ledger with the same calm hand he had used all along, because someone had to remain civil enough to make history readable.

The city was still human.

The line held.

What came through was not a room.

And beyond the annex, beyond the rails and the lift banks and the bridges and the station tables under fluorescent light, Melbourne carried on breathing under a sky that had no idea yet what shape the next war would require of it, only that it would need the city not to become quiet before the thing arrived.

Continue the journey in Book Three of The Lines We Do Not Cross

What Comes Through

The door was never the danger.
What mattered was what answered.

After the discoveries of *Do Not Open* and the deepening revelations of *The Other Room*, the final novel in *The Lines We Do Not Cross* trilogy brings the hidden architecture of contact to its most dangerous threshold yet. Warnings have been ignored. Boundaries have been tested. Human ambition has pressed too hard against forces it does not fully understand. Now the last question remains: when the barrier no longer holds, what comes through—and who will survive the answer?

The final stage of contact is not arrival. It is consequence.

Author Bio

Robert G. Pranic was born in Melbourne, Australia, in the 1960s and loved books from an early age. After a long and successful career in information technology, where he became known for creative problem solving and complex documentation, he turned his focus to the work he had always been drawn to: writing fiction. Over the past decade, he has developed a growing body of novels across multiple genres and now writes full-time, building an ambitious catalogue of original fiction through his independent publishing venture.

Other books by the author

<u>Detective Barzani Mysteries (Crime/Noir):</u>
Barzani Episode One: "Call Me Sam."
Barzani Episode Two: A Gentleman's Murder
Barzani Episode Three: Death at Ravenwood Manor
Barzani Episode Four: The House on Briar Lane
Barzani Episode Five: The Hush Order
Barzani Episode Six: The Velvet Noose
Barzani Episode Seven: The Art Gallery Murders

<u>Cosmic Reckoning (Superhero/Sci-Fi):</u>
Cosmic Reckoning: The Rise of Aeloryn (Book 1)
Cosmic Reckoning: Aeloryn, Guardian of Earth (Book 2)
Cosmic Reckoning: Consent Engine (Book 3)

<u>The Lines We Do Not Cross Science Fiction Series:</u>
Do Not Open (Book One)

<u>Science Fiction:</u>
Ashes of the Final Dawn
The Robots' Slaves
Chronosight
Crowned in Ash and Sorrow
Armstrong's War and Hope's Destiny
Specimen Zero One Zero: The Abduction Trials
Terminal Lucidity: Death is Just the Beginning
The Mars Deception

<u>The RIFTBORNE Series (Superhero/Sci-Fi):</u>
The RIFTBORNE Origins (Book One)
The RIFTBORNE Shadows of the Quantum Veil (Book Two)
The RIFTBORNE Shadow Veil Siren (Book Three)

<u>*Thrillers, Crime and Horror:*</u>
Amongst the Southern Lights
Code of Vengeance
Our Spore Fathers: Black Rain

<u>*Historical, Romance and Western:*</u>
Falling Walls
Stagecoach Mary (aka Mary Fields): A Biographical Western Dramatisation
The Last Outlaw Volume One: Smoke & Iron
The Last Outlaw Volume Two: The County as Theatre
The Last Outlaw Volume Three: River of Reckoning

REVIEW REQUEST

If you enjoyed this second novel in *The Lines We Do Not Cross* series, please consider leaving a review. Your support helps independent authors reach new readers.

www.ingramcontent.com/pod-product-compliance
Lightning Source LLC
Chambersburg PA
CBHW012011050726
47590CB00009B/3140